Yes, Miss Thompson

Yes, Miss Thompson

Based on a true story

Amy Boyes

N₁O₂N₁

CANADA

Publisher's note: This story is a dramatization based on a true story and real events
and was drawn from a variety of sources, including previously published materials
and interviews. While it reflects the author's recollections and research over time,
some names and characteristics have been changed, some events have been compressed, and some dialogue has been recreated.

Library and Archives Canada Cataloguing in Publication

Title: Yes, Miss Thompson / Amy Boyes.

Names: Boyes, Amy, 1985- author.

Description: "Based on a true story".

Identifiers: Canadiana (print) 20230446671 | Canadiana (ebook) 2023044671X |
ISBN 9781989689530 (softcover) | ISBN 9781989689578 (EPUB)

Classification: LCC PS8603.O99585 Y47 2023 | DDC C813/.6—dc23

Printed and bound in Canada on 100% recycled paper.

Now Or Never Publishing
901, 163 Street
Surrey, British Columbia
Canada V4A 9T8

nonpublishing.com
Fighting Words.

We gratefully acknowledge the support of the Canada Council for the Arts
and the British Columbia Arts Council for our publishing program.

*To Marjory, the great-grandmother
whose time was over before mine began.*

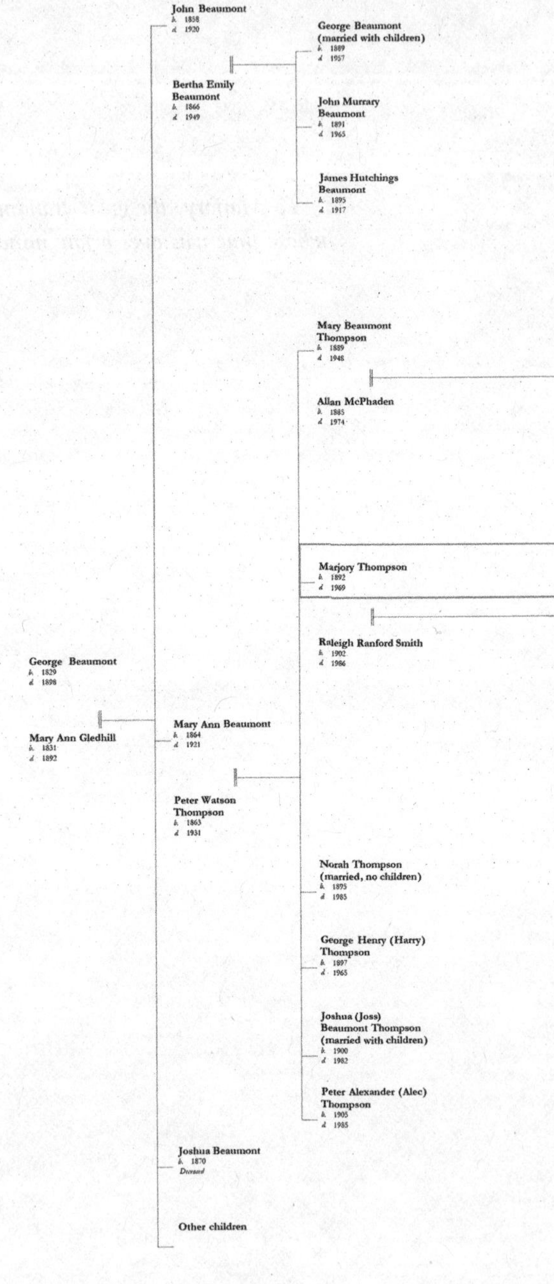

George Beaumont
b. 1829
d. 1898

Mary Ann Gledhill
b. 1831
d. 1892

John Beaumont
b. 1858
d. 1920

Bertha Emily
Beaumont
b. 1866
d. 1949

George Beaumont
(married with children)
b. 1889
d. 1957

John Murrary
Beaumont
b. 1891
d. 1965

James Hutchings
Beaumont
b. 1895
d. 1917

Mary Beaumont
Thompson
b. 1889
d. 1948

Allan McPhaden
b. 1885
d. 1974

Marjory Thompson
b. 1892
d. 1969

Raleigh Ranford Smith
b. 1902
d. 1986

Mary Ann Beaumont
b. 1864
d. 1921

Peter Watson
Thompson
b. 1863
d. 1931

Norah Thompson
(married, no children)
b. 1895
d. 1985

George Henry (Harry)
Thompson
b. 1897
d. 1965

Joshua (Joss)
Beaumont Thompson
(married with children)
b. 1900
d. 1982

Peter Alexander (Alec)
Thompson
b. 1905
d. 1985

Joshua Beaumont
b. 1870
Deceased

Other children

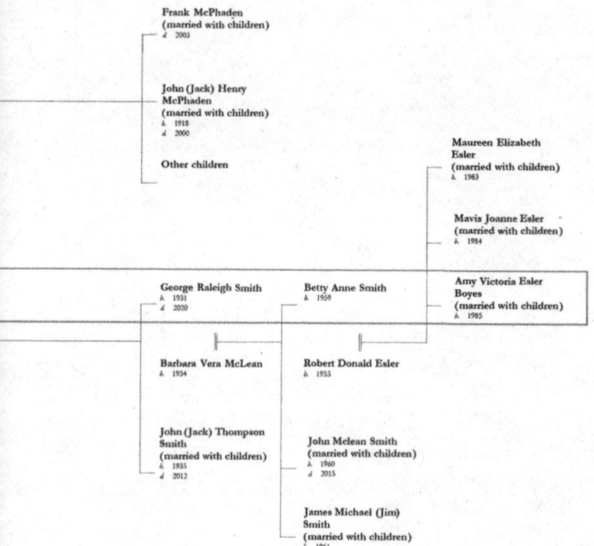

Frank McPhaden
(married with children)
d 2003

John (Jack) Henry
McPhaden
(married with children)
b 1918
d 2000

Other children

Maureen Elizabeth
Esler
(married with children)
b 1983

Mavis Joanne Esler
(married with children)
b 1984

George Raleigh Smith
b 1931
d 2020

Betty Anne Smith
b 1959

Amy Victoria Esler
Boyes
(married with children)
b 1985

Barbara Vera McLean
b 1934

Robert Donald Esler
b 1953

John (Jack) Thompson
Smith
(married with children)
b 1935
d 2012

John Mclean Smith
(married with children)
b 1960
d 2015

James Michael (Jim)
Smith
(married with children)
b 1961

Part I

When as a child I laughed and wept,
Time crept.

Amy's Story
December 26, 2018
Near Pilot Mound, Manitoba
Amy is 33.

A ground drift rolls over the farmland, blurring the fields under waves of snow. Unlike endless ocean currents, these waves keep their shape—cold and crusty ridges rising through canola stubble as far as the eye can see, which isn't very far today. The horizon is obscured, half by blowing snow, half by low clouds resembling gray smears from a painter's thumb across a canvas.

I drive slowly, unsure where the gravel ends and the ditch begins. I may be driving my father's Ford-150, but I have no desire to test its off-road capabilities.

Winter visits to Manitoba are never my favourite. Blizzards. Extreme cold. Crowded airports. Cranky toddler. Manitoba is much more enjoyable in summer when prairie skies are clear, and fields are lush with crops. We're not cooped up then, sustained by Scrabble and drugstore Christmas chocolates, the best ones gone, second layer and all.

As I drive, I note small changes since my last visit. My cousin has constructed grain bins, 50,000 bushels, metal monstrosities lined up in a row. A neighbour has bulldozed a row of ageing trees into a twisted mass. He'll likely burn them come spring. Another neighbour has built a house outside a shelterbelt; the newly planted trees surrounding it are mere saplings.

These changes reflect progress, financial health, even. But mostly everything is the same as it was during my childhood. Flat fields, surveyed into grids, lie buried under the snow. Farmyards, or the remnants of homesteads, dot the horizon. Pine trees planted a lifetime ago peek cautiously above the ground drift as if to check conditions. Still blowing? They seem to ask.

Some farmyards are deserted but have equipment left behind by previous generations. Manure spreaders, hay bines, swathers and augers—these implements are too narrow, rusty or obsolete to be of any practical use. Grain production has transformed since my grandparents' day. Farms are bigger now. Equipment is larger. The rural population is smaller. But these graveyards of equipment that rise out of snowdrifts and catch the wind in icy swirls remind passers-by that many farmers came before the ones that currently wait for the snow to melt and fields to dry.

My grandma's ancestors homesteaded in the 1870s when Canada was just a staggering toddler. They sailed from Northern Ireland then took the train as far as the rail line was built. Past bison skulls, sod shanties and newly broke fields, they trudged the last 90 miles to the land that would be theirs.

The community is filled with their descendants—cousins, second cousins, or cousins so faintly related that even my mom shuts her eyes and scrunches her face when forced to explain the family connection. Grandma's story is so well-known, oft-repeated with pride, that I have come to realize I know little of my grandpa's tale. His story usually begins in 1958, the year he married my grandmother. It's as if he has no beginning, no place of his own. I remember none of his ancestors. They all died young on his side of the family, it seems, not like my grandma's elders whose lives stretched on and on until it seemed impossible they too would die.

As a child, I remember shards of Grandpa's past filtering through the family lore. Little hints would emerge, sometimes at Saturday night dinner when a special platter was used to serve the roast—"That's Mother's china"—or when discussing politics—"Mother always voted Liberal, you know."

I found a scrapbook tucked in my grandparents' hall closet when I was ten. The scrapbook was old, not as in the garish colours of '70s interiors or the questionable eyewear of the '80s, but properly old with black and white pictures of young women in flapper dresses and perky cloche hats, arms linked and smiles bright. The album bulged with hotel receipts, menu cards, train tickets stubs, postcards of glamourous cruise ships, a piece of cedar greenery and even a hotel shoeshine cloth jauntily described as "stolen property." Scribbled in white chalk on thick black pages, a commentary described a long-ago holiday on the Great Lakes.

I turned the pages gently, lingering on the styles from the past. It seemed men wore suits no matter the occasion or the temperature. Women teetered in high heels for all outings, their legs wrapped in baggy stockings, nylons still a thing of the future. Trains and boats were the preferred methods of transportation. Hotels were very grand.

"Who is this?" I asked, pointing to a lady posing beside roaring Niagara Falls. Her face was angular. Her eyes were sharp. "She looks like Mary Pickford. You know—the actress from the talkies."

"That's grandpa's mom, Marjory," Grandma answered. "She was on a Great Lakes cruise in 1929, just before the Crash. People did that back then. They'd take the train to Thunder Bay, or Port Arthur as it was called, and bob around for weeks. It was popular. Very glamourous."

"My great-grandmother," I murmured, stroking the picture. Even then, I knew I didn't resemble her and never would. My face was round and my arms were pudgy. I was bouncy. She was elegant.

"Be careful, Amy!" My mom cautioned, peering over my shoulder. I was only a kid, and the scrapbook was old, fragile. It wasn't meant to be touched somehow. It was meant to be put back into the shadows, high on the shelf to be rediscovered by someone older and less likely to tear pages than me.

So now, two decades later, I crunch to a stop in my grandparents' snow-covered yard, much older and still curious. What became of the woman who turned her face to the sunlight bouncing off Niagara Falls and listened for the Brownie camera to click? Who was she? And why do we never talk about her?

—

"Hush up, Sasha!" Grandma Barb yells at the overweight collie-husky that barks from under the kitchen table. "Don't mind the dog, Amy. Just come in!"

I never mind the dog. She's too old and tired to present arms, as it were. She just barks as if to say, "Yes, I can see you're a visitor, but don't think you belong here. Not like me. I am the DOG. DOG! I tell you. The queen of this house."

I weave around a chair left in the middle of the porch, dab smack between the back door that bangs closed and the kitchen. Grandma needs the chair when she tugs on winter boots so it remains in the way of all other traffic.

"Hey!" I say, my coat still on. "How are you today?"

"Fine," Grandma says but makes a face. The face counterbalances her claim of fineness. After all, she was too unwell to join us yesterday for the Christmas gathering, so she can't be that great.

"You're not feeling well today either?" I press. Grandma is rarely truthful when it comes to her health. She's deteriorated a lot in the past few years but won't admit it.

"I'm fine," she says again but doesn't look it. Grandma Barb was never a tall woman, but now she's much shorter than my five foot four, leaning as she is against the kitchen counter. Her short hair has been refreshed recently with a dose of platinum blonde, spruced up for the holidays. Her baby blue sweater hangs off her shoulders, though the folds of the fabric still remember the shape her body used to be.

"You've lost weight," I say, pulling her into a hug. I kiss the top of her head, not her cheek as I used to when I was a child. Her head is closest to my lips now.

"A bit," she says, attempting to straighten up. Her legs, twisted and bent from various ailments, don't allow her. "You've got thin. Are you eating? Not dieting, are you?"

I ignore the inquiry, repeated at every visit. To my grandmother, a healthy diet is akin to an eating disorder. "What can I do to help?" I ask, shrugging off my coat and laying it over the back of a kitchen chair. "Are we having coffee?"

"It's on," she says, gesturing to a pot filled with a dark substance best defined as "tar stripper."

"I'll grab some cream," I say, heading to the fridge, which yields a litre of half and half. "How's Grandpa?"

Grandma makes the face again. "I don't think he has the flu or anything, just his normal."

Grandpa's been unwell. Prostate cancer and dementia have caused his recent problems, but Macular Degeneration robbed him of most of his vision before that. It has been a long winter for him already, and it's only Christmas. He copes better in summer when he can putter around the farm, mowing grass and keeping track of my cousins' activities.

"Go find him, will you?" Grandma asks.

Grandpa is not hard to find. He spends his days in front of the living room television, watching as much as he can see or perhaps just listening to Fox News on nearly maximum volume. I would lose my mind but this is routine for him.

"Hey, Grandpa!" I call over the din of American news coverage.

He turns to face me and says hello politely though he doesn't seem to recognize me.

"Amy from Ottawa!" I say with a laugh as if to joke about giving him unnecessary information.

Grandpa nods, then shocks me. "Josh with you?"

He might not remember his own wife's name, but a split second's clarity gives him my husband's.

"He and Madeline are at Mom's," I say, "but they'll both come by this week. Want some coffee?"

"No, thank you." Grandpa shakes his head, then returns to his television.

"George!" Grandma calls from the kitchen doorway where she's been watching our exchange. "Come here and visit with Amy. She's come all the way from Ottawa to see you."

Grandpa gets up with a sigh as if the inconvenience is great, the sacrifice substantial.

"Don't worry," I say. "They won't have impeached Trump by the time you return."

Grandpa laughs. "They might try."

They sit in their customary places at the kitchen table, Grandma by the radio that blares country music, Grandpa by the cordless phone that only recently replaced the dial phone, Sasha underfoot. I sit between my grandparents, doctoring my coffee with as much cream as the Corelle mug will hold.

"Like a little coffee with your cream?" Grandpa jokes and I laugh. It's impressive what he sees, what he catches. Little actions bring back jokes, old lines, never worn out.

Grandma asks about life in Ottawa and I answer, reassuring them about the steadiness of our employment, the continual increase of house values, the safety of our suburban neighbourhood. They are happy with what I tell them and make no further inquiries. They just want to know all is well, that our lives are continuing in a logical trajectory: mortgage, kid, camping at Algonquin, swimming lessons. Further details are not required. Besides, details exhaust octogenarians.

I ask about their health and receive vague answers, cushioned in qualifiers. They are "pretty" good, never plain good. They sleep well "most" nights. They have "some" appointments coming up. Pain is downgraded to discomfort. Confusion to forgetfulness. Falling to stumble or even the circus-inspired tumble, which makes it sound downright fun to wipe out on the kitchen floor.

I let them think they are informing me, but I know the details of their conditions from Mom. As their primary caregiver, she manages their appointments, prescriptions, and mobility devices. The three of them exist in a complicated struggle. My grandparents need help but won't ask for it, so my mother gets frustrated with their independence. It's not easy for any of them.

I suppose our conversation is typical for most family members who rarely see each other. We hit the high points of current events, not getting to the heart of any issue. What I want to know would be strange to ask: Are you surprised every day you got old? Is this how you pictured the end of life? Are you happy with your kids? With your life accomplishments? Do you think of your parents, even now, in your eighties? Do you feel lost without them?

But they wouldn't answer any of those questions. They'd just laugh and say some platitude like, "Everybody gets old, you know."

And so we drift through small talk. After an hour, we're caught up, the circle of easy topics exhausted. Grandma looks worn, so I stand to go. I don't want to wear them out.

"Random question, Grandpa…" I say, not knowing how to broach the topic but still curious. "You know that scrapbook of your mother's? The one she made of her trip to the Great Lakes in '29?"

Grandpa squints. I don't know if he remembers the book, so I hurry on.

"I was wondering if I might borrow it while I'm here. I'd like to look through it."

Grandpa looks blankly at Grandma, perhaps to judge the situation by her reaction.

"You can keep it," Grandma says. "We've got so much stuff. It's good to get rid of things."

"If you've got an interest," Grandpa agrees, "you should have it." Then he taps the table and points as if he's just thought of something for the first time in a long while. "Mother made that trip before she married Father."

"When she taught at La Riviere?" I ask, referring to a nearby tiny village. I have a vague memory she taught there in the 1920s.

"You've got that right." He nods. "She went on the cruise with a teacher-friend. Mother wasn't from here, you know. She didn't have family around."

"Where was she from?" I ask, expecting this. No relatives of Grandpa live in nearby farmhouses, so I always knew his people were from away.

"England," Grandpa says.

"England?" I look at Grandma. Is Grandpa confused? Wasn't his mother born in Canada?

"She came as a child," Grandpa clarifies. "Eleven years old. Immigrated with her family to a farm north of Brandon. The farm was primitive, even for the time. Wasn't very prosperous. They lived in a log cabin for years and years. Six kids too."

I'm surprised by this rush of information. It's as if Grandpa recites his mother's facts to remind himself of what he knows. He can't be prodded on further though. He just says his mother taught school in different places before eventually settling in Pilot Mound. "She was a good teacher," he says as an *adieu*, the closing argument in his brief account. Then he abruptly stands up and shuffles into the living room, back to his television without saying goodbye.

—

"It's not here!" I stretch on my tiptoes to see the top of the hallway closet.

"You need more light," Grandma says, hovering in the doorway from the sunroom. She flicks a switch, but the single bulb just creates a shadow with the closet door.

"No, really." I shake my head. "I can tell. It's not here."

The closet is shallow. As I shove each album against the back wall, they all thud true. There's nothing behind them.

"Your mom must have it," Grandma says.

"She would have told me. She knew I was looking for it."

"She's forgotten then. I'm sure I gave it to her."

"I'll look at her house," I say, but I don't feel hopeful. I had imagined the scrapbook in the closet as it was when I was a child. I hadn't even considered it might not be there. I'm surprised by how upset I am. This is how history gets lost, one misplaced album at a time. Stored, forgotten, then donated to a charity shop, items from the past lose their meaning when they lose their families.

I follow Grandma back to the kitchen, a slow journey of grabbing onto walls and bookcases, her feet tangling and twisting as she maneuvers her body over them. I feel bad for her, but she won't take help.

"Would you try a cane, Grandma?" I ask, but she ignores me, or maybe she doesn't hear me.

I grab my coat off the kitchen chair. "I'll let you get on with things," I say.

"Oh, sit." Grandma rolls her eyes. "For a minute. You're never here for very long, and then you hurry off. Besides,"—she retrieves a cigarette pack and a lighter—"I'm going to have a smoke."

She assumes the smoking pose I remember from childhood: one arm across her stomach, the other elbow resting on its fist. I smother the urge to cough and mentally give my winter coat up to the cleaners.

"Marjory was a strange one, you know." Grandma talks over my shoulder to a spot on the wall.

"How so?" I ask, leaning forward.

"She was a good teacher. Everyone said that. She taught me. Taught my mom. Mom's siblings too. But you had to work hard for Marjory. She once told me I didn't have half the brains of my uncle."

"That wasn't very nice," I tut.

"No, it wasn't," Grandma agrees. "I was nervous of her when I started going out with your grandpa, but it was Grandpa's father who bothered me. Raleigh. He was a nasty piece of work, that one. Was hard on Grandpa and his brother Jack. Very cutting. Not a nice father at all. That's why your grandpa never talks about his parents. He didn't have a happy childhood. No birthdays. No Christmas. It wasn't poverty or anything. It was something else." Grandma picks some residue from the cigarette off her tongue and then resumes her pose. "It was a kind of sadness, you could say. Later, your grandpa would have got his mother away, but that's not how they did things back then."

"Domestic abuse was rather hidden, wasn't it?"

"Well, everyone knew but no one talked about it. People pretended it wasn't going on for the sake of Marjory's pride. It wasn't fair to your grandpa or anyone else but that's how it was."

Grandma is silent now. The ashes on her cigarette have grown long and curvaceous. Somehow, I've never thought to notify her she's about to lose ashes everywhere. The family disapproves of her smoking habit for her health's sake, if not everyone else's, but we just ignore it and all its downsides in a silent protest.

"And Marjory was well-respected?" I prompt. "Professionally, I mean."

"Quite." Grandma flicks ashes into the drags of her coffee. "She taught until she had to quit because she was going blind. Same ailment your grandpa has, Macular Degeneration.

"And his brother, Jack, too."

Grandma nods. "It's hereditary. That's why your mother takes a thousand supplements. Not that they'll save her. Either your genes are going to get you, or they aren't."

"And Mom knew Grandma Marjory?"

"Oh, yes. Your mother was Marjory's little pet. She would eat her lunch on Fridays at Marjory's house. They lived near the school, you see. You ask your mother. She'll remember all sorts of things. Or she won't. Goodness, if she doesn't remember she has that scrapbook, then I'd say she's losing it."

I snort. "Mom losing it? Impossible."

Grandma smiles blandly. "We all fall apart eventually. Every one of us wakes up one morning and can't believe the old legs don't work, the eyes don't see, and the fool ears don't hear. It's a shock, yet it happens."

"On that depressing note, I'm going to leave you," I joke, "get out of your hair so you can get on with the morning."

Grandma nods. Undoubtedly, she has a to-do list for her day, all planned out. But really, I just wish she would go back to bed. She looks so rough, the poor thing.

———

"Grandma says you have the album," I say almost accusingly as I stride into my mother's kitchen.

My mom, Betty, rolls her eyes and shrugs. "Maybe I do. Who knows? You're always saying I'm a hoarding packrat, so anything is possible." She shoves a tray of open-face sandwiches into the oven, reincarnations of yesterday's Christmas turkey and dinner rolls.

"I've never said that," I retort, "just that you have hoarding tendencies."

My parents have lived for thirty years in the same farmhouse. It was built spaciously as prairie dwellings often are. Cheap real estate invites sprawl. A full basement stretches under the house, giving ample space for a "canning room" filled with jams and preserves, a freezer room for copious amounts of garden vegetables, a large recreation room lined with overstuffed bookshelves, and two or three storage rooms filled with everything from an old accordion to novelty cake pans to the collected works of Charles Dickens.

"Where should I even look?" I ask, slightly fatigued by the prospect. "The cedar chest in the front hallway? The bookshelves in the playroom? One of our old bedrooms?"

"Try the playroom. But don't run off. Tell me how they were."

"Seemed okay. Grandpa came and talked a bit. But it's getting hard to engage him. He used to tell stories from the past or repeat things from television programs, but it seemed difficult for him to collect his thoughts today."

Mom nods. My report likely matches her observations. Grandpa's descent has not been swift or even cataclysmic. It's been gradual, some days better or worse than others which gives family members contrasting viewpoints. It's easy for those of us who live far away to have a reasonable conversation with him and assume he's fairly well, perhaps more subdued than usual. But those who see him often notice the decline, despite Grandma downplaying his symptoms into "forgetfulness." She's the one that suffers from the denial. The caregiving spouse always does.

"Grandma Barb said you used to have Friday lunches at Great-Grandma Marjory's. Do you remember that?"

Mom stops chopping carrot sticks and squints at a poinsettia on the kitchen table, her mouth set in a line. "That's right. I did. When I was nine or so. They lived across the street from the school, so I'd walk over. She was old by then, nearly blind and a bit crippled too."

"And Grandpa George's dad, Raleigh—was he ever around?"

"Not much. He kept to himself. Wasn't pleasant."

"So I gather. How old were you when Marjory died?"

"Ten at the most. She had a stroke and didn't last long." Mom returns to chopping carrots. "Go look for that scrapbook then help me with lunch."

"I'll be quick!" I say, calling over my shoulder, feeling guilty for leaving her with lunch preparations yet relieved she hasn't corralled me into tedious tasks like folding napkins or peeling cucumbers. It's funny how one reverts to juvenile behaviour in one's childhood home.

I find my husband and young daughter in the playroom, putting together the same puzzles I played with as a child. "How were they?" my husband asks.

"Oh, you know," I vaguely reply.

I dismantle an ironing board by a bookshelf and move Christmas wrapping paper out of my way. The bookshelf is filled with photo albums—my sisters' and my wedding pictures, baby books of nieces and nephews, vacation pictures from Mount Rushmore in the '90s. There's nothing old about any of these books. Certainly, nothing predates my parents' padded wedding album from '81.

But then I see it. Tucked into the far end of the shelf, my great-grandmother's scrapbook hangs over the edge, its black spine standing out further than the rest of the books. I tug it gently from its resting place and ease open the cover.

Like stepping into a time machine, the years fall away. Jazz music plays. Pearls swing. It's the summer of 1929, and the world is young and careless, perhaps for the last time.

Betty's Story
November 29, 1968
Pilot Mound, Manitoba
Betty is nine years old.

It isn't big, my Grandpa Raleigh and Grandma Marjory's house. It sits at the far end of the schoolyard, across the soccer field. The house is simple, like a childish drawing: a two-storey box with a peak, windows on either side of the front door, one window under the eaves. I imagine it drawn in blue crayon; H-O-U-S-E sketched underneath in red. My grandpa built it, and maybe he got tired before a porch or an awning could be added because the house is plain, just a flat front without so much as a door knocker. The house is painted white, and it looks like all the other houses on the street. Plain and simple. No fuss nor colour. Flashy is not the prairie way.

I walk to this plain house with my head down, a toque pulled low on my ears against the north breeze that sweeps across the soccer field. I go to my grandparents' house every Friday for lunch. It's a tradition.

My mom, Barbara Smith, is a school teacher, just like Grandma Marjory used to be. Mom found me in the hallway as I ran out of math class—"Put on your toque, coat and mittens, Betty. Don't forget."

I grumped at her because I didn't want to put on my toque, as ugly as it is, but I'm glad I have it now that I'm walking. It's only November, but the wind is cold. Manitoba is like that. Cold and windy for at least six months of the year, sometimes longer. Our house isn't great for heat either. Mom says she doesn't know what I'm complaining about, but Mom likes the house cold. She wouldn't have even put her coat on to run over to her in-laws. She'd have lit a cigarette, said "Hurry up," and taken off across the frozen soccer field in her high heels. That's my mom—take charge, take no lip.

Mom is a school teacher with a reputation. She doesn't teach little kids, probably for the best, but rather the big high school kids. "Don't mess with Mrs. Smith"—is the adage she likes to hear. She might even say it herself, just to strike fear in hearts. I dread going to her class, but that won't happen for a while. I'm only nine.

I look both ways before crossing the street out of habit, but there aren't any cars. The town grinds to a halt over lunch. The banks, grocery, hardware store—everything shuts down. It's inconvenient to Mom, who might like to run a quick errand on her lunch break, but that's the way it is in a small town. Besides, Mom probably would rather have a laugh and a cigarette in the teacher's lounge than pop by the bank. She might complain about inconveniences, but I know my mom. Funny and honest, she's popular with the other teachers and likes to chat over sandwiches.

Grandma Marjory opens the door to the plain house even as I walk up the chipped concrete slabs that straggle up to the steps in a slightly crooked line.

"Hi, Grandma," I call, wanting her to know it's me. She's mostly blind, so I don't know how she knew I was coming. Maybe Grandpa Raleigh was watching at a window.

My grandma is tall and thin. Thin as in really, really thin. She's not like Mom, who is soft when you hug her or like my other grandma, who has strong arms that hold you tightly. Grandma Marjory's face is gaunt. Her cheekbones protrude from under her eyes. Her skin is paperwhite and oddly translucent. She is pale and tired-out, what adults call "frail." Funny that even saying the word "frail" makes you feel sad. You have to work up energy to get the f and the r perched at the front of your mouth, and then your mouth slumps for the ail. Frail. That's my grandma. And blind too.

Grandma wears a beige sweater with pearl buttons over a collared blouse. Her thin legs appear from under a shapeless skirt in baggy stockings. Her white hair is pulled high behind her ears in a modified beehive, not nearly as thick and full as Audrey Hepburn's. She reaches for my coat and stabs at the armholes with a hanger. I help by directing my coat sleeves to the ends of the hanger.

"Thanks," I say easily, not wanting her to feel bad she's blind. It isn't her fault. It's Macular Degeneration, a couple of complicated words that have made her life difficult. "It started as a black spot in the middle," I've heard her say. Imagine that— staring straight at two black spots all day, knowing they're going to get bigger and nothing you can do will stop them from taking over every view. The sink full of dishes. The school across the street. The sun setting through the trees on the west side of Pilot Mound. It's all going down a black hole.

As I suspected, Grandpa Raleigh sits by the living room window, close to an ugly, brown enamel stove. He's stout and seems more so, sunk low in the chair. His pants don't entirely cover the white socks on his ankles, pulled up as they are against his legs. His jowls are blotchy red, and his bright white hair stands up on end. He looks nothing like the pictures of him as a young man. He was handsome then with kind eyes. But now, thick eyebrows shade his eyes. His face is covered with a thousand lines. A beer rests between his feet on the linoleum floor.

"Hi, Grandpa," I say, mustering up cheerfulness.

"Hi, Betty," he murmurs back.

Grandpa is tricky so I leave him be and follow Grandma into the kitchen. Mom says I've nothing to worry about—Grandpa is just grumpy—but I don't chance it. He's certainly not like my other grandpa who spoils me and my brothers rotten, tells funny stories, and gardens all summer. This grandpa is better left to himself and his beer.

Grandma Marjory moves slowly, one hand out to guide her along the wall. She has a limp from a car accident the day I was born, August 4th, 1959. The doctors said she would die for sure, but she didn't die. And then they told her she'd never walk again, but she proved them wrong about that too, just like me. I proved doctors wrong. I was born two months early, and I wasn't supposed to live because I was tiny, and the Pilot Mound hospital is a long way from anywhere. But both of us lived, though Grandma isn't walking so well.

Grandma's kitchen is barebones, to use an expression of my mom's. Bare. Bones. Like a bone the dog has chewed down to the shiny whiteness, no meat or fat on it. The counters are clean, which is funny because I don't know how Grandma can see dirt. My mom has perfect eyesight, and our kitchen always looks like a tornado blew through—dry macaroni noodles hiding under the edge of the cupboard, coffee rings on the counter, a potted azalea drying out on the drainboard, cigarette ashes careening over the side of the ashtray. But Grandma's kitchen is spotless. Absolutely spotless. I have no idea how.

"Would you like to sit?" Grandma points to a little stool by the kitchen window. I always sit there, so I hop up and wait as Grandpa Raleigh shuffles in from the living room. This relocation takes a while because he moves very slowly and doesn't speed up when Grandma says, "Come along, Raleigh. Betty's got to have her lunch." He just scowls and sinks into a creaking kitchen chair opposite my stool.

Grandma sits beside me and folds her hands. "Would you say grace, Betty?"

Nodding, I launch in with the speed of an auctioneer at a calf sale: "For that which we are about to receive, may the Lord make us truly grateful. Amen." Maybe I pray too quickly because my grandparents smile as I open my eyes.

"I taught your father that prayer," Grandma says wistfully.

"And he taught it to me!" I say. "It's a good short one, eh?"

"It is a good prayer," Grandma says. "Gratitude comes from God. It's easy not to be thankful, but gratitude is helpful in life." She pulls a small plate of sandwiches out of a bread bag, repurposed as a cover, with a shaky hand. Her hand is covered in dark purple veins like a map in my geography book, the rivers marked with firm black lines over the flat nothing of the prairie. "I hope you like tuna sandwiches."

"Sure, tuna's swell," I say easily, using a word I've heard the bigger kids in my school use. If I were more truthful, I'd say tinned tuna isn't my favourite, and God is going to have to bestow buckets of gratitude upon me if I'm going to eat it cheerfully, but I know better than that. If I said any of that to my mom, she'd tell me off, and I don't want Grandma to feel bad about the food she serves. At home, on the farm we share with my other grandparents, there's lots of good meat. One or two steers a year usually find their way into our freezer rather than the auction barn. We regularly have sliced roast beef, short ribs, and juicy steaks, not tinned tuna nonsense, but these grandparents don't have much money.

Grandpa Raleigh was a carpenter, so "no pension there"—as my dad says. I get the feeling that even in his prime working days, money was not especially plentiful. Now, my grandparents live off of Grandma Marjory's teaching pension. She used to be the principal of my school so I tell her what's going on.

"We are practicing for our Christmas program," I announce around a mouthful of tuna sandwich. I tried not to breathe through my nose as I took the bite of tinned tuna. It smelled fishy, but not in a good way like the fresh catch the fish man peddles from northern Manitoba lakes. That fish is laid out neatly on trays of ice, not crammed into a tin, sloshed in some mysterious fluid.

"That's nice," Grandma says. "Who is directing?"

"Mom."

"English teacher. That makes sense."

"She gets annoyed when kids don't listen in the practices."

"I can see that. I found inattentive students distressing as well."

"I'm going to get a new dress for it. Granny is making me one."

"That's nice." Grandma suddenly looks sad.

I realize I shouldn't have said anything about my other grandma sewing for me. Grandma Marjory's eyes are too poor for things like sewing. Mom volunteers to sew little things for her like buttons. Grandma Marjory thanks her, but I know my other grandma does the mending. I can't think of a time when my mom sewed. Well, once. Dad was late for work and he split his pants. Mom grabbed a needle and thread and went at his seat, giggling the whole time. As Dad tells it, she sewed his pants to his underpants. I suspect the entire mess went into the garbage at the end of the day.

"What colour is your dress?" Grandma asks, but I don't want to talk about it anymore, not if it's going to make her sad.

"I dunno," I shrug my shoulders. "It's just a dress."

She changes the topic. "Have you made a list of what you'd like for Christmas?"

"I have!" I say, setting down the sandwich to explain with both hands free. "I want a Raggedy Anne doll, a toy telephone, and a Spirograph!"

"What on earth is a Spirograph?"

"It's a set of flat plastic pieces that have holes in them. They're like stencils. You put them on paper and draw around them to make pretty designs."

"That sounds lovely. What about your brothers? What do they want?"

"I dunno," I say carelessly, picking up my sandwich again. John and Jim are my younger brothers. John is eight and Jim is seven. We fight a lot. They say I'm bossy, which isn't true, but they do so many dumb things. This past summer, our other grandpa convinced them that "Every man eats a peck of dirt before he dies." They sat right down in the garden and made a start. I mean, honestly. Who is that dumb?

"Have you heard them talking about what they'd like for Christmas?" Grandma prods a little more.

I hear them talking, endlessly talking, but I don't listen to what they say. I decide to make something up so Grandma doesn't think I'm stupid. "John wants a pop gun and Jim wants a toy cash register." I jam the last bit of the sandwich in my mouth. It wasn't too bad.

"Such different Christmas treats than when we were children," Grandma says, almost to herself. "Figs. Oranges. Apples. Sometimes a little doll."

"Did you even have Christmas in the olden days?" I ask, which makes Grandpa laugh.

"Oh yes," Grandma says. "A tree. Big dinner with family. When I was your age, we still lived in England. It was all very civilized, though our holiday was different. Shorter. Less time off from school. Less glitz."

I think about that for a second. "You lived in England?" I ask, surprised.

Grandma looks equally surprised. "We didn't come to Canada until I was nearly twelve."

"But England is on the other side of the Atlantic Ocean. I learned that in school. How did you get across?"

"On a ship. It took a long time."

"Were you afraid? I can't swim, you know."

"A little bit afraid. Our lives were comfortable in England, and there were many unknowns about moving to Canada. But we took our traditions with us, and we had each other. We had little treats on Christmas morning, even in the new world. Maybe we didn't have Spirographs and pop guns, but we had oranges and nuts and concerts at school, just like you."

I squint a bit at Grandma. Olden-day Christmases don't sound at all like our Christmas celebrations with a tinsel-loaded tree and piles of presents. Grandma looks happy though, as she talks about them, so maybe I'm missing something.

"Did you have snow for Christmas in England?"

"Sometimes. I remember we had snow the Christmas before Father left for Canada."

"Your dad left without you?" It's a big deal in our house when anyone makes a day trip to Winnipeg, never mind crossing the Atlantic on a ship.

Grandma looks at me, again surprised at what I don't know about her. "That was quite common at the time. A father would leave before his family to start a homestead. Things were very rough back then. We didn't understand how difficult farming would be, but Father knew it would be better if he went first. Mother wasn't very strong, you see, and we children were all young."

"How long before the rest of you went?"

"About two years. Father worked for several farmers before he bought our farm. He had much to learn about planting and harvesting crops, caring for animals, preserving food and surviving winters."

Grandma reaches for a tin of shortbread off the cupboard. She holds it against her ribcage to pry the lid off with her long, thin fingers. "Would you like a biscuit before you go back to school?" she asks me.

I love shortbread so I gobble two in the time my grandparents both eat one. When I reach for a third, Grandma suggests I eat it on the way. "You don't want to be late."

I hop off my stool but turn back to ask Grandma what she wants for Christmas. She smiles serenely and says she has everything she needs, which is a typical adult answer, the maddening things they say when they don't want to bother giving a more complicated answer. It can't be true though. Her faded living room furniture must have left the factory before the Depression. The settee's olive-green upholstery is permanently rubbed in one direction. The armchairs have dark stains. Grandma even wears the same three dresses all winter, threadbare, faded things. And, as I pull on my winter boots, I notice her boots have worn toes. But oddly enough, Grandma seems satisfied, as if the poverty around her is completely acceptable, or at least unavoidable. Old people can be strange that way.

"See you next week," Grandma calls from the kitchen, unable to move as quickly as me. She rarely sees me to the door.

"Okay!" I yell, throwing on my coat, mitts and the ugly toque. I accidentally slam the door, which I feel bad about. Mom would tell me to be more careful. Grandma Marjory's blindness makes loud noises hard for her to deal with. She jumps nervously when things fall or clatter, so I need to be more careful. I don't want to be an annoying little kid.

I munch the last shortbread as I run back to school over the frozen grass, thinking about what Grandma said. Nuts and oranges for Christmas? The olden days sound awful to me.

"You can't be serious, Peter." Uncle John glares down the table at Father. He points his fork in the air, his elbows on the table, his white shirt sleeves bright under the gas chandelier.

I'm not supposed to be in the dining room. I just wandered in to see if there was any gravy left. I'm supposed to be in Aunt Bertha's kitchen with the rest of the children, finishing up our Christmas dinner.

We hardly spoke as we devoured roast goose, boiled potatoes, green peas in cream. Steaming in weighty china dishes, our Christmas dinner released fragrances that mingled pleasantly with wood smoke from the kitchen stove. Leah, Aunt Bertha's maid, left the stove door open, and the fire flickered and crackled as we ate, all the cousins together. The boys eyed the desserts on the kitchen sideboard: mince pie, plum pudding, and something called ladyfingers laid alongside cedar branches and bits of holly.

"Eat up, my loves," Leah called to us, and we complied. Christmas dinner is always wonderful at Uncle John and Aunt Bertha's house.

But I wanted one more slice of goose and a bit of gravy, so now I stand behind my parents' chairs in the dining room, holding my plate, waiting for a good moment to interrupt. No one pays me any mind though. Father has made his big announcement, the secret we've meant to keep quiet, and the aunts and uncles look upset. Forks are down. Lips are bitten. Everyone has stopped eating. Well, everyone except Father. Father calmly forks another bite of Christmas dinner into his mouth, ignoring

Mother's pursed lips and folded hands. Her face is drawn up in tight lines, like when my older sister Mary pulls Mother's corset stays—"Breathe out, Mother! I can't get them any tighter unless you breathe out!" Mother sits still, but her calm veneer isn't play-acted like Father's. Hers will crumble. I don't know how or when, and that worries me.

I feel queasy, watching the grown-ups being upset with each other. Heat rushes over me. My face flushes from the fire in the dining room fireplace. Encased by a massive, red and grey mottled marble hearth, the fire flickers on the red, wallpapered walls. Over and over, the wallpaper's damask pattern repeats, blood-red on brick-red, straining the eyes. Oil paintings break up the mesmerizing design. Framed in gold, hung high and angled downwards on long wires, Herefords graze in pasture, a bonneted milkmaid peers through a garden gate, and snow-capped mountains tower over a fishing pond. I focus on the art, trying to ignore the wallpaper patterns that bounce so dizzyingly.

"Immigrate to Canada? You cannot be serious, Peter," Uncle John repeats. His brow is furrowed; his mouth, full of half-forgotten food.

Uncle John is tall, over six feet even without his work boots in which he tramps through his woollen mill. His hair is a little long on the top, combed off to one side in dramatic waves. He has a thick brown beard from which cream sauce drips. He leans forward on his elbows, his eyebrows high as if he can't calculate the depths of the stupidity in my father's outlandish announcement.

Father doesn't respond, except to say, "Delicious goose, Bertha. What a triumph," which makes Mother fold her arms and sigh. Father is eating goose as a protest, and she's aggravated he doesn't answer her brother. I know what Father is doing though. He is resisting the temptation to argue with Uncle John over Christmas dinner. It can take some resisting. Uncle John loves to argue.

"You just returned to Yorkshire. You have employment in the mill," Uncle John presses. "And now you want to go farming in Canada? Gracious, Peter. What do you know about farming?"

Father leisurely scrapes his plate, a lovely piece of transfer-ware from France. Red vines and flowers languish under the remains of sauces. After an uneasy pause, Father takes his last bite and sets down his fork and knife.

"John, I'm grateful for the work you've given me," he says, "but Canada has opportunities that don't exist here. Jobs! Land! I don't have the capital to start my own business. My father, being a minister, bless him, didn't have anything to pass on. I have to make my own way, but I haven't got a trade or any real skills I can put to use here, and I can't keep taking from my wife's family—"

"You're not taking anything," Uncle John interrupts. "I give you employment and you give your labour. Hiring you was not an act of charity. You put in a good day's work. And you know, Peter, Beaumonts aren't farm labourers. We're in Burkes' and Debretts' Peerage, for goodness' sake."

"Oh really, John!" young Uncle Joshua protests now. Thin and jovial, Uncle Joshua balances out Uncle John's severity as manager of George Beaumont and Sons, Woolen Merchants. The joke is that Uncle John may keep the woollen mill running, but Uncle Joshua keeps the workers coming. He certainly doesn't mind pulling Uncle John up short on nonsense.

"You exaggerate profoundly," Uncle Joshua says. "Our Beaumont roots may stretch back to the Norman invasion, and there may be an impoverished Baron Beaumont or two about, but really now. Our family branch has been firmly in the trades for generations. So don't argue we're gentry, John. It won't stick. Farming is hardly beneath us."

"And there's nothing wrong being a farmer, or a labourer, for that matter," Father argues. "Most of Canada is made up of labourers. I want to build a future for my family. It isn't a crime to want to earn money!"

Mother lays a hand on Father's arm. She doesn't like this kind of conversation at the family Christmas dinner. "It's all very common, this money talk"—I can hear her saying. Grandfather George would have retorted that's what you get with common people like us. Woollen weavers. Cloth dyers. Labourers.

Common people talk common talk. But Grandfather is gone now. Dead. And perhaps it's just as well. Grandfather didn't get on with Father. He would have demanded to know what Mother thought of this emigration idea, and then he would have accused Father of dragging her off to the wilderness.

Mother hasn't offered an opinion since Father started talking about Canada, or at least she hasn't said anything in front of us children. I now wonder if Father asked her about any of our moves. Maybe he just announced one day we were moving back to Yorkshire. "Your brother will give me work," I can hear him say.

We moved back to Mother's people a couple of years ago. We older children hauled sacks and boxes of this and that—a cast iron frying pan, a mother-of-pearl hairbrush, a copy of "Jane Eyre"—on a third-class rail carriage, while Mother carried the baby and Father man-handled trunks himself to avoid paying the porter. We took a rented house close to the Beaumont mill where Father took a job. But Father had bigger plans. I see that now. Perhaps he only moved us back to Yorkshire so he wouldn't have to worry about us when he leaves for Canada— Mother, Mary, myself, Norah, Harry and baby brother Joshua. We will stay with family. We will be looked after.

But perhaps he assumed too much. I'm only a child, but I can see Uncle John is not pleased with Father's announcement. Even Aunt Bertha has left her chair to calm Uncle John at the other end of the table. Her taffeta skirt flows to the floor as she leans against his chair and wraps an arm around his thick shoulders, perhaps to cool his temper.

"Tell us more, Peter," she says soothingly, her pearl-drop earrings swaying prettily below her swept-up chignon. "Where in Canada do you plan to go? Ontario?"

Father shakes his head. "All the good farmland in Ontario was gone forty years ago. Even most of Manitoba, along the border with the United States, was settled in the '70s. No, I'm looking north of Brandon. Farmland is still cheap and plentiful there."

"Cheap," Uncle John speaks the word with an air of disgust. "That is fortuitous, is it not?

Aunt Bertha gives him a sharp look. It's no secret we are the poor relations. Father worked as a mail manager when he caught Mother's eye years ago. Mother sang in the Wesleyan Church choir and he played the violin. Making eyes over the anthems, they were soon in love. Grandfather George wasn't happy though. Mother had been sent to the Belvedere Ladies' School. Knowing the value of a shilling, Grandfather resented the expense of private school, but Grandmother convinced him a well-educated young lady would attract a prosperous husband. As it turned out, Father may have been well-educated, but he certainly wasn't prosperous.

"And what do you plan to grow, Peter?" Aunt Bertha sensibly asks.

Father describes cattle pastures, hog pens, and wheat and barley fields stretching as far as the eye can see. Manitoba is flat, apparently, and the grain grows in windy ripples like the ocean's gentle waves. The soil is fertile and the rains are regular. Supplies are available by trains and towns are springing up all over.

The aunts and uncles listen carefully. Threshing machines, granaries, ploughs, and pitchforks—these are not the tools and devices of cloth manufacturers. These things are new to our family. This landscape is as foreign as the darkest jungles of Africa, described to us by the fervent missionaries that visit our Sunday School.

"And are they still fighting the natives, Peter?" asks Uncle Joshua who likes to stir things up with a bit of ill-timed humour. "It would be a shame to have your pretty head of hair decorate a chief's loincloth, wouldn't it?"

"Don't be disgusting." Mother glares at her youngest brother.

"You've no cause for concern, Joshua." Father folds his napkin carefully. "The North-West Rebellion was over fifteen years ago. Louis Riel was hung and the natives were placed on reservations. The prairies are safe for homesteading though I shouldn't blame those poor souls if they did resent us, pushed off their lands as they are."

"Are you sure you're not just looking for excitement, Peter?" Uncle Joshua pressed. "Making up for missed adventures from your youth? You could join the army and spare the bother of immigration. They are using armoured trains to fight the Boers now. Doesn't that sound exciting?"

"I'm not looking for excitement." Father sounds slightly offended. "I'm looking for opportunity.

"Opportunity to work harder and lose more money than you ever thought possible," mutters Uncle John under his breath.

"Opportunity to make a new society," Father continues. "Schools for all the children of the district. Farms for anyone who wants work. A society based on equality. You must admit the concept is appealing. No bowing and scraping. Just wide-open spaces and opportunity!"

None of the aunts or uncles responds to his impassioned speech. They just look at their folded hands, their mouths drawn tightly, their eyes red. Unlike Uncle John, they are too polite to say what a terrible idea immigration is, but I know they think it. I've heard them talk about people who have left Yorkshire. They think people who immigrate to the New World couldn't find work in England due to their own faults. I don't think that's always true. There must have been many faulty people in Huddersfield because many have left. Hundreds. Thousands. Year after year, generation after generation, ever since the factories sprang up and wool weaving moved from the cottages to the big brick mills, people have left. Up and down the streets of Huddersfield, relatives write letters to faraway places like Hamilton, Ontario, or Queensland, Australia, knowing they are being forgotten and the next generation will not bother writing back. Why would they? They've never seen the smoky valleys of Yorkshire, the lions on the top of the Huddersfield train station, the castle on the hill. But immigration is like that. Families get broken.

I feel sick to my stomach now. Maybe I ate too much or perhaps it's the thought of moving to Canada where you can see for miles and no one lives close to you. Across the ocean. So far away. The new world is filled with danger—sicknesses and diseases, droughts and floods, poverty and misery.

I close my eyes, but Leah rushes in from the kitchen carrying a tray. "Excuse me, Miss Marjory," she says, dashing past. She moves so quickly that the faded peacock feathers on the mantel-piece dip and sway over silver candlesticks.

Aunt Bertha rises. "Shall we retire to the drawing room?" she asks while Leah starts clearing the table—platters scraped bare, silverware by the handful, an empty gravy boat. I guess sometime between the discussion of the price of wheat per bushel and the expected yield of an acre, Aunt Bertha gave the signal to Leah: this meal is over. It was time to clean up, time for everyone to stretch their legs and absorb the news without being trapped together at the dining room table.

I relinquish all thoughts of gravy and wander back to the kitchen to eat my goose dry, holding back the tears that burn my eyes. I don't care that Leah has served dessert to us children. I don't care about anything. I just want Father to stay here with all of us, where it's safe.

—

Before Christmas dinner, we had walked to the Wesleyan Chapel high up on the hill, a little way from Uncle John and Aunt Bertha's house. Our whole family is Wesleyan or Methodist. There's not a Church of England parishioner among us. Our family history shows we were early converts to the teachings of Wesley. Baptism notices, marriage banns, death records—generations of events were written in thick books titled "Non-Conformist," a descriptor that appeals to our sense of independence. Uncle John says Methodism suits the tempera-ment of industrious, no-nonsense people like us. Uncle Joshua just says the King Henry's church is filled with Papist claptrap, whatever that might be.

The Chapel was cold at first but warm by the end, so warm I slept through the sermon. The carol singing finished—"Hark the Herald Angels Sing" and "Come, Thou Long Expected Jesus"—and Father's arm was strong to lean against. He pretend-ed he didn't notice me drift off with St. Luke's "And there were shepherds in the field abiding" drifting across my ear like snowflakes in the wind. Then the resounding organ woke me, and we shuffled back down the hill to the rowhouses on Somerset Road, careful not to slip on the way. It was time to eat and we were hungry.

But now the announcement has been made, the calmness of the church service feels a world away. Aunt Bertha sends us children outdoors to play, but only the boys pelt each other with snowballs. They form sides along the garden walls, the trunk of a leafless black alder their only protection again the volley of snowballs they fling at each other. We girls stand by the kitchen door, out of the trajectory of the snowballs. We watch, half-interested, woollen scarves and tams pulled close around our faces. We've seen our brothers fight before. They yell and call names and pretend to be soldiers. It's all rather childish for me as I'm a big girl and know the grown-ups are quarrelling. It's hard to play anything when you know your aunts and uncles think your father's ideas are foolish. I just want everyone to be happy, as happy as the boys pretending to kill each other.

"A penny for your thoughts, Marjory," Father suddenly says. I hadn't noticed him come outside, but he stands beside me, his hands in his trouser pockets, his grey overcoat flung on but not buttoned.

"Nothing." I cross my arms.

"Come now. There's never 'nothing' going on in that little head of yours."

I squint into the bright winter sun as I look up at Father. His blonde moustache has a hint of frost. His cheeks are red from the wind. Father is a young-looking father, not bearded and hulking like Uncle John. He looks thin in his Sunday-best trousers, his suspenders doing their best to keep his pants from sliding off his narrow hips. His face is pale from working in the mill, though the smoky air from the dozens of mills in Huddersfield is hardly healthy, indoors or outdoors.

"Are winters cold in Canada?" I ask.

"Not too bad, I don't think," Father says, but I can tell he's lying. Everyone knows winters in Canada are cold. I learned that in school. Snow falls for six months. Lakes freeze over. The wind blows snow so fiercely you can't see the horse pulling the sleigh. People lose fingers and toes. Sometimes they die if they get caught outside in a storm.

"That's not what my teacher says," I retort, but Father watches the snowball fight and ignores me. "My teacher says immigration to Canada is a brave undertaking," I press. "Brave, Father. Are we brave?" I pull his coat to get his attention.

"Of course, we're brave, Marjory!" He laughs. "We're the bravest people I know."

"Now you're teasing me. We're not the least bit brave. Mother won't read the police report in the newspaper because it frightens her, and Harry thinks there's a gremlin in the wardrobe, but only at nights with full moons."

Father chuckles and bends down to kiss me. "Mother is terribly, terribly brave. She married me no matter what anyone thought. And, as for Harry, it's only his imagination that scares him. There's nothing real he won't fight. Look at him!"

I do look at Harry. He's pinned Cousin James to the ground and is pummelling him for some infraction of the rules. "Take that, you nasty dog!" he shouts.

James, older and bigger, easily pushes him off, but Harry keeps swinging until Father intervenes. "Crackerjack time!" Father calls. "Back inside, you hearty soldiers!"

I pull on his coat again. "You won't freeze to death in Canada, will you?"

"Unlikely." Father wraps an arm around me. "Don't tell your mother, but I'll bring my little brandy flask to keep me warm."

—

Crackerjacks, stockings and presents—we go at them with relish, shrieking with delight, jumping around the Christmas tree as we open our treats. The tree fills the sitting room window. It is odd-shaped, far from symmetrical, as Uncle Joshua points out—"Gracious, Bertha, where did you find this mangled bit of vegetation?"

But Aunt Bertha is unperturbed. "John cut it," she answers. "Perhaps in the grove behind the mill warehouse. I don't know. He doesn't like spending money on luxuries, only assets."

"I've noticed that," Uncle Joshua says dryly.

Although there are thin candles in the tree branches, Aunt Bertha won't light them. "It's daytime; how silly to light them," she says when pressed by the cousins to do so. Most likely, she's afraid for the thick drapes that swath the front window behind the tree. Harry would be sure to knock a candle over and set the curtains on fire. He has a talent for catastrophes.

Aunt Bertha's front room is only a little less red than her dining room. The plush settee and chairs are rust-red with fringes along the legs which are fun to run your fingers through, but the wallpaper is gold leaf instead of red damask. The room is cluttered with things that build up over thirty years of one family living in a house—bits of furniture, the kind that scarcely have a purpose, like the plant-less plant-stand on which Uncle Josh rests his coffee mug, or the bulky tête-a-tête settee in the middle of the room on which no one ever sits. Why would you? Two people can't look at each other without straining, as the seats point to opposite corners of the room.

Faded peacock feathers grace the mantel in this room too. It seems every nice home in our village has a vase of peacock feathers on the mantel. Perhaps the peacocks up at Whitley Hall, the ancestral home of some distant Beaumont relatives, scamper more quickly when they see a village woman heading their way. They must fear being plucked like a Christmas goose.

Saving the plush seats for the adults, we older cousins sit nicely on the floor and open our presents of adventure books and children's stories, while the younger cousins immediately begin playing with the dolls and wooden horses they receive. Amid the chaos, I notice Father and Uncle John step across the front hall, back into the dining room, carrying their coffee with them.

When no one is looking, I slip through the kitchen into the butler's pantry to find a shadow in which to hide. From behind a thick curtain, I can hear what Father says, though I don't understand much of it. Ship passage. Outlaying costs. Line of credit. Estimated costs, only estimates, mind you. Projected income. Unforeseen expenditures. Father leans across the table, talking rapidly, emphasizing his points with hand gestures. I had no idea the cost of suckling pigs and the price per bushel of feed corn in Manitoba could be a source for such an energetic monologue.

Uncle John leans back in his creaking chair, tipping it slightly with his black booted toe, and lights a cigar. He rarely smokes and certainly never does inside the house, but it's Christmas, so perhaps he feels the luxury is warranted. He lets Father talk without showing much emotion. I don't understand why Father tells him how much farming in Canada will cost. Uncle John thinks the idea of immigration is absurd. Why go on about it?

But then Father gets to the crux of the matter. "So, I need capital," he says, "The outlying costs are too much for me to cover, even with the help of the bank."

"What amount are we talking about?" Uncle John unbuttons his vest, which pulls tightly over his stomach. He seems more relaxed now the shock of Father's announcement has subsided. Perhaps Father has dropped a little brandy into their coffee just to smooth the edges from the conversation.

I strain to hear Father's answer. How much money do we need to immigrate? Is it a large amount? Are we even close with our own savings?

But then, Leah strides into the butler's pantry, carrying an armload of clean dishes to put away in the cupboards. "Miss Marjory!" she startles. "I didn't see you there. Come away and play with the others. No good comes of eavesdroppers."

I leave my post reluctantly, embarrassed by being caught and ashamed by what I heard. Are we so poor that Father must ask for money? Uncle John already thinks Father's idea is terrible. Why is Father making things worse by begging like a common peasant? It feels so helpless. Childish even.

I wander back into the front hall but don't rejoin the others in the sitting room. It's too loud in there, too crowded. Instead, I climb the stairs and settle on the top step, out of sight. I hug my knees to my chest and let the tears come. I cry because we're poor and have to ask for money. I cry because I'll never see this house again once we leave. And I cry because I don't want to go to a place where winters are cold and people live in sod shanties. This is the worst thing that could happen to us. We'll be dirty and cold and poor forever. We won't know anyone in Canada and everyone here will forget us.

I hear a water flush from the water closet behind me, then footsteps echoing on the wooden floor. I try to sniff up my tears, but it's too late. Uncle Joshua sits on the step beside me and pulls his knees up to his chest.

"Why are you crying, Marj?" he asks softly.

"I don't like that name, Marj," I snap.

"That's why I call you that."

I roll my eyes at my uncle. He really can be infuriating.

"Why are you crying?" he insists.

I shrug my shoulders.

"I saw you in the dining room earlier. Did you know about your father's big plan before today?"

I nod, still sniffling.

"And what do you think?"

"It makes me sad." My chin quivers.

"It makes me sad too. I don't like you living where polar bears hunt children."

"Stop!" I hit him as he laughs. "Polar bears live in the arctic. Not on the prairies. Everyone knows that."

"Oh, Marjory. I can't get anything past you. But moving to Canada may be the best thing that ever happens to your family. Your father might get absurdly rich farming wheat or barley or whatever it is he's going to grow. As the smartest little girl in the district, you might even go to university. Your brothers will work hard and have big families, and the Thompson name will be spoken with awe and reverence. 'There be the Thompsons,' people will say as they pass your grand estate."

"You're teasing me." I pull a handkerchief from my uncle's breast pocket, wipe my nose on it, and then hand it back.

"Many thanks," he mutters, stuffing the used handkerchief back into his pocket. "You never know what's going to happen,

Darling. I might be teasing, or my words might come true. That is the wonderful thing about life. My dear wife might inherit a fortune from a long-lost relative, and I'll live in luxury for the rest of my life, or I go on working the mill with Brother John 'til I drop dead one day on the carding machine."

I giggle, picturing him crashing like a silly character in a children's pantomime. "Be careful around the carding machine."

"I will. But you should be excited about this. Your Father is planning carefully, and he'll go first to make sure everything is all right, that you have a nice house and a healthy crop of sorghum."

"What's sorghum?"

"Don't ask me. Your father droned on and on and I stopped listening. Agricultural factoids are not the most interesting things about emigration." Uncle Joshua looks thoughtful now.

"Would you like to emigrate?" I ask, wrapping an arm around my uncle's shoulder. "To Canada or someplace else, I mean?"

Uncle Joshua thumps my knee. "I can't, Love. That's the double-edged sword of privilege. Father left John and me the mill and we must think of the employees. Brother John is a bit of a bear some days, so if I left and something went wrong, well, all the employees be out of work, wouldn't they be? I have to stay. And that's the trick of life, Marjory. Once you have something, you have to stay and mind it."

"We don't have anything to mind," I say.

"That is why your father is considering this move. He's getting you something to mind. And land is something, Marjory. Land is what roots you to a place. If you don't own any, you're always worried things could change, and you'll be out on your ear."

"But here we have Mother's family to take care of us. What will happen if we get in trouble in Canada?"

"I wouldn't worry too much." Uncle Joshua teases. "You can always skin a buffalo. Eat the meat and wear the coat."

I roll my eyes. Some people refuse to be serious.

Just then, Aunt Bertha sweeps up the stairs, her skirts rustling on the baseboards. She looks surprised to see us. "Dear

Marjory—the children are looking for you. What are you doing up here?"

My tears well up again, so Uncle Josh replies, "She's sad to leave us, bless the child."

Aunt Bertha crouches down to my eye level, pursing her lips as if she is searching for the perfect words. "I have found, Marjory, that life passes quickly, and the things I worried over turned out to be nothing. My distress was wasted. Do you understand?"

"So, I shouldn't worry about emigration?" I ask, confused. How can I not worry about that?

Aunt Bertha and Uncle Joshua exchange glances as adults often do when a child misses the point.

"Maybe… don't worry yet," Uncle Josh offers. "You're not leaving for a long time."

"And today is a good day." Aunt Bertha pulls me to my feet. "God doesn't promise us endless supplies of Christmases. So go now. Have fun with your cousins."

She shoos me away, down the stairs to be with the others. But as I go, clomping sulkily in my church shoes, I hear Uncle Joshua hiss under his breath, "Honestly, Bertha. What is Peter thinking?"

Mother holds Uncle John's hand tightly. "I can't do this," she sobs, covering her face with her handkerchief.

We're on the train, Huddersfield to Liverpool.

Mother presses her face against Uncle John's shoulder, her hat careening precariously. Mother was going to wear her newest hat, a *chapeaux de la maison amicy*, straight from Paris, a farewell present from Aunt Bertha. Mother calls it a triumph. Its wide brim sweeps down from her left ear to nearly her right shoulder. Artificial orchids and ostrich feathers billow out the top. It matches her travelling dress perfectly, but when it was time for us to leave, Aunt Bertha urged Mother towards practicality—"Pack the triumph and wear something sturdier." And so, Mother wears a plain hat, a cap really, lined with the same brown wool tweed of her travelling dress. The soft velvet trimming on her sleeves and bodice repeats along the hat's brim. A few folds, a bit of trim, a short ostrich feather—this hat will hold its shape, which is good as it is being crushed into Uncle John's shoulder at the moment.

Uncle John pats Mother's hand. "Don't be afraid. The children need you to be strong."

"I don't want to be strong. I want to be home!" Mother sobs. "And I'm afraid of going on the ship. What if the children fall ill or we hit an iceberg?"

"There are doctors on the boat," Uncle John soothes. "And once you get to the icefield, the captain will go slowly. These modern ships don't sink like they used to. They're unsinkable now."

I look at my gloved hands, my bony ankles popping out from under my petticoat, the countryside speeding past—anywhere but at Mother. Although she'd be the first to tell us children to pull ourselves together, she's beyond the reach of ordinary, dignified behaviour. She is heartbroken to travel to Canada where only Father will recognize her. Everyone else will rush past. On the boat, on the train, across Canada, she'll just be another English lady heading west to a homestead, a thousand miles from anywhere, five wide-eyed children in tow.

I wish my uncle were going all the way to Canada, not just to Liverpool. Mother is so distraught that my fifteen-year-old sister, Mary and I will have to figure out what to do next. What if we get on the wrong train in Montreal? What if we head east not west? What if we can't find Father? But Uncle John can't travel the whole way with us. Even going to Liverpool costs him a full day at the mill. He has to return to the relatives to whom we said goodbye at the train station in Huddersfield.

Mother said silly things like "We'll come back to visit!" but I knew, as I walked up the steps of the station, between the tall columns soaring upwards to the thick cornice and pediment, that I would never walk back down those steps again. No one comes back after immigrating. At least I've never heard of it.

On the platform, we hugged and kissed our family—aunts, uncles, cousins—wishing each other well, those who remain in the old country, those who travel to the new. We were parting ways, probably forever. Bystanders looked on curiously but with no shock or amazement. People leave for Canada all the time. Everyone has relatives who have gone abroad, always to make a livelihood, always with hopes for something better.

I cried as porters loaded our trunks and mother's hat boxes onto the train. They handled our things so carelessly as if they didn't realize these were the only things we had, the only belongings we'd carry with us to the new world.

Once we settled in our compartment and the whistle blew one last time, we stretched our hands out the window. We clung to our family as they called, "Good luck to you! God speed!" Then, as the train rolled forward, the aunts and uncles stepped back to let the cousins run the length of the platform, still grasping our fingers. But even they stopped at the platform's edge, patent toe boots skidding to a sudden halt, their hands releasing ours into thin air. Then, as the train picked up speed, their faces faded into their bodies and their bodies into strange shapes that returned to rock houses, woollen mills, cobblestone streets, and gentle hills shrouded in smoke from the mills. They had homes, but we were immigrants now. On the move. Homeless.

I look at my older sister, Mary. She is much calmer than Mother, more resigned. She sits upright, alert. When a gaunt man with a long nose and sharp eyes pulls the door open to our compartment, she shoos him away firmly. "This compartment is fully occupied," she snips.

The man looks at her, surprised, his wrinkled face shadowed under a grey top hat decorated with a lemon-yellow ribbon. He doesn't question her even though we could have squeezed together to accommodate him and his large case, emblazoned with "Omega Oil. It's Green!" on its side. Perhaps he had no desire to spend the journey to Liverpool with a weeping woman and five children.

Mary takes our travel documents out of Mother's handbag. "Review these with me, Uncle," she says. "I want to be sure I understand what we must do." Mary separates six tickets from the rest of the papers. "We board the Canadian Pacific steamship Lake Manitoba this afternoon out of Liverpool, so we'll need these first."

"I'll help you get on the boat," Uncle John promises. "I might even be able to get you into your stateroom if there's time."

Mary nods. "After nine days on the ship, we'll land in Montreal where we'll board the Canadian Pacific Railway at Windsor Station. Father says we're to ask someone about a rooming house, but if we're too tired to look around we'll get a room at the Windsor Hotel instead."

Uncle John reaches inside his overcoat and pulls out his wallet. "Here." He counts out banknotes. "I don't want you wandering around Montreal in search of rooming houses." He presses the money into Mother's hand.

"John, you've helped us so much already," Mother protests.

"I insist." He does the buttons back up on his waistcoat. "A good hotel in Montreal and another in Winnipeg too. Once you've been on the train for a week, you'll be exhausted. Take a day in Winnipeg to see the sights. You might not be back for some time."

"Peter wrote not to waste time as winter may strike early; one never knows, apparently." Mother sniffs, folding the banknotes into her handbag carefully.

"Winter?" Uncle John snorts. "My dear sister, it's only September 27th. You'll be in Montreal by October 9th and in Manitoba by the middle of the month, surely."

Mother shrugs. "I don't know. It's just what Peter wrote."

We sit in silence now, watching Yorkshire speed past our windows. It's hard to imagine that by day's end we'll be on a ship, sailing into the Atlantic. I wonder if I'll be ill on the ship. I'm always ill on trains unless I face forward. I'm still worried about this an hour later when we pull into Riverside Station in Liverpool, under high arches.

"Follow your uncle and stay close together," Mother cautions as we clamour off the train, joining the crowd on the platform.

We follow my uncle's broad back and bowler hat as a rush of bodies carries us under signs marked Telegraph Office, Tickets, Cloak Room, and Refreshments. Coal smoke is heavy on the platform, though the smell of bacon grease and coffee wafts from the door marked Dining Room. We weave around porters pushing carts of trunks and crates, then step onto the street where a long line of cabs wait. The stench of saltwater and rotten fish hang heavy in the air. We're still for a moment, dazzled by the peddlers, sailors, gentlemen and fishwives who rush, brushing shoulders with each other as they step around horse droppings.

"Where are our trunks?" I yell, but my uncle doesn't hear over the din of the street. Instead, he helps Mother and the little children into a waiting cab, then turns around for Mary and me.

"Where are our trunks?" I yell again. "Where is the sewing machine?

"They're to be sent through to the dock. The railway takes care of it." Uncle John turns to the cab driver. "The Canadian Pacific Steamship waiting rooms, if you please."

"The CP waiting rooms?" The cab driver laughs, his cap pushed up high on his forehead.

My uncle squints at the man, suspicious of his mirth.

"I can take you, but it will be faster to walk." The cab driver points over our heads to the train station we just left.

Uncle John looks around, confused. He obviously doesn't understand the cab driver. How can the train station lead us to the docks? We just came from there.

"Look!" My brother, Harry shouts, pointing over the top of the train station toward the water. "It's the S. S. Lake Manitoba!"

We turn to see a ship rising high over the train station's roofline. Its four masts and shiny gold smokestack soar far above the squat buildings on the dock. The words "Lake Manitoba"—emblazoned on the side of the black hull—are as big as a train car.

"Gracious Providence," Mother whispers, holding her hat as she cranes her neck to see the ship that will take us to the new world. Towering and ponderous, the great vessel lies in the dock. Black smoke curls from her funnel to hang over the sunlit waterfront.

"If that's your ship," the cab driver says, "cross back through the station and go out the other side. The train station is in the middle of the dock. You've come out the city side, but you need the wharf side. You'll see the CP offices, waiting rooms, refreshment halls, all that. Don't waste time as she pulls anchor tonight and, whatever you do, get your luggage before your train leaves. The porters miss bags all the time."

We set off at a dead run at that, panicked and unruly as peasants, shouting our thanks to the cab driver over our shoulders. Uncle John scoops up my little brother Joss while the rest of us hold hands and run back through the station lobby to the train platform we just left. To our relief, our luggage is heaped on the platform. The sewing machine case leans precariously against the trucks. Some of Mother's hatboxes are on their side. The one with the triumph has split open, its feathered content flop onto the ground where passengers step gingerly around it. But at least our things are off the train, which is now pulling out of the station.

"My new hat!" Mother cries while Uncle John yells for a porter. One hurries over with a cart and helps us load our things, beginning with the sewing machine. Harry gapes at the porter. He's never seen a black man before.

"I'm so sorry, Mary Ann" Uncle apologizes to our mother, beads of sweat forming on his forehead. "I was certain the ticket said all luggage would be transported from the train to the ship."

Mary picks up Mother's hatboxes. "I read luggage would be moved from the ship to the train," she says in a superior voice whilst whacking Harry who still stares. "Canadian Pacific doesn't run the rail line from Huddersfield, obviously. Why would they be responsible for moving luggage off of it? What you read must refer to our transfer from the ship to rail in Montreal."

"Yes, yes, Mary," Mother shushes. "Follow your uncle now."

The porter leads over the train tracks beneath a sign marked "To Ships," which seems much more obvious than it did ten minutes ago. Brutally obvious. And there we wait, behind all our train's passengers who did not walk in the wrong direction.

"Well, this is an auspicious beginning," Mary mutters under her breath.

—

"There he is! There he is!" Harry points over the ship's railing into the crowd at the bottom of gangplanks. Uncle John stands tall between a coil of rope and a stack of crates, all marked "London." He waits calmly for the ship to move away from the Prince's Pier. He must be glad the ordeal is over, all the sorting, organizing, and confusion.

Mother's anxiety only increased in the overheated Canadian Pacific waiting room when a stout gentleman (his moustache the most profound I'd ever seen) stood on an overturned Webster's and Sons beer crate and droned over the din, "Trunks or packages for staterooms should not exceed fifteen inches in height, two feet in width, or three feet six inches in length. Heavy baggage such as large trunks, bags, etc., not wanted on the voyage should have been dispatched one week ago for placement in the ship's hold."

"Our trunks are far bigger than that!" Mother wailed. "Whatever shall we do?"

Uncle John eyed them up. "That old one might be a bit large," he said, pointing to a rounded top trunk of my grandparents', its wooden body and metal strips deemed sturdy enough for a transatlantic voyage. "But I'd bet a fiver they don't want to load more bags into the hold of the ship. We'll push through."

The bag boat came next. It was a sturdy little vessel that pulled alongside the landing pier, its propellers beating against the water. There was a great press as everyone tried to get to the bag boat at the same time, but Uncle John pushed through, shoving our cart of bags and trunks. He was head and shoulders taller than most who scurried towards the pier, but we kept our eyes fixed upon him, lest we lose him in the crush.

Then, the gangplanks were lowered, and the passengers shifted to those bridges, the links between land and boat. We crept forward with the rest, one small step ahead of the other. Shuffling up the gangplank, I tried not to breathe the pungent air from off the docks. I didn't look down at the water either, dark and slimy. After all, it was only the River Mersey, not even the Atlantic, but it still left me with a cold feeling of dread. When I stepped onto the ship's deck, I realized I had left England. I might have tapped my foot on the pier or touched the ground one more time if I had thought of it. But it was too late by then. We were on board, and the chaos was even worse than in the Waiting Room.

Mother repeated our stateroom number under her breath as if she was worried she might forget it. We shuffled along crowded corridors, pushing past passengers heading in the opposite direction to the one we chose at random. Crocodile-skinned hatboxes were stacked on piles of leather portmanteaus with gold letters emblazoned on their sides. Who were F. G. S. and H. W.

P., I wondered, and would we ever meet them on this massive vessel? And would we ever find our stateroom in this tangle?

Harry stepped on Mother's skirts in the crush. "Take care, Harry!" she cried, but she would have cried more if she had seen the boot mark he left.

My uncle stopped a harassed-looking steward, the first we found once aboard the ship. "The second-class staterooms, if you please?"

"If you would, Sir." The white-coated steward stretched a stiff arm in the direction from which we came. We followed him closely as sheep follow a shepherd, our necks craning, brows furrowed. He trotted briskly down a richly carpeted staircase, through a gaslit hallway, past other passengers discovering their cabins.

"This isn't too bad," I heard someone say.

"I doubt the wash water will be hot," another quipped.

The steward halted in front of two identical doors. "Adjoining staterooms," he said. "The doors are unlocked. You'll find your keys on the wash tables. Do enjoy the journey." He spun on his heels and headed for the staircase to help other lost souls find their way.

"Thank goodness he left so quickly," Mother murmured. "I thought I'd have to tip him."

The staterooms were simple. Bunk beds and a plush couch on opposite walls faced a washing-up cupboard in the middle. Complete with a mirror and water basin, the cabinet was built of sturdy wood and matched a small wardrobe at the foot of the bunk beds.

"The other room is the same," Harry announced after going through a little door to the adjoining stateroom. "I'll take the top bunk."

"You'll be sharing with Joss," Mary said with a sly smile.

"I can't share with Joss!" Harry complained. "He kicks! I'll be booted off."

Mother ignored Harry and Mary. Our trunks had already been delivered, which pleased her. "How fast! How efficient!" she cried. "We can all change our clothes before tea."

"Why would we do that?" Mary demanded. "We aren't that dirty and laundry will cost money now."

Uncle John cast her a dark look and patted Mother's shoulder. "If you want to dress for dinner, you should, Mary Ann. Think of this like a luxury hotel, a floating vacation."

"Too true!" Mother clapped her hands as Mary rolled her eyes.

Just then, we heard the ominous, long-drawn peeling of the visitor's bell. Visitors ashore! At last, it was all over and Uncle John would have to leave us.

We trudged back up the stairs to an empty space on the deck where Uncle John pressed each of us children to his chest. "Be good and don't fight with each other. Listen to your mother," he whispered in our ears. Then he straightened up and held Mother tightly with tears in his eyes. "My dear sister. I am so proud of you. Father and Mother would have been heartbroken to see you go, but they would have known you are making great sacrifices for your children, that you are a wonderful mother. Remember that when you can't go on. Remember that everything you're doing is for the children."

And then Mother sobbed again. Despite all the clamour of winches raising and lowering, children shouting, and dock hands calling, I could still hear her sobs. But she was not alone. There were many sorrowful partings, up and down the decks. Grandmothers with furs wrapped tightly around their necks, tears streaming down their faces, tightly held squirming children. Fathers shook hands with grown sons, their faces drawn and eyes sad. The deck was a vista of unhappiness. The only ones seemingly unmoved by the scene were a group of boys and girls my age. They stood in a tight circle, grinning. "Glad to be away," one said. "Canada can only be an improvement from the orphanage, I expect," another said.

Uncle John gave us all one last pat on the head. "I promise, Bertha and I will visit you once you are settled."

"Don't make such promises." Mother sniffed. "It's too far to go for a visit."

"But what an adventure it will be! I'm looking forward to it already. I'll get to see your beautiful farm, bountiful produce, and fat, healthy children." We giggled at this, despite our tear-streaked faces. "You will be prosperous and popular in the district. Peter will play violin at every event and you'll sing. And back home, back here in old Yorkshire, we'll speak with pride and admiration of those brave Thompsons, the ones who weren't afraid of crossing the Atlantic."

Mother kissed him one more time, held him in an embrace, and then patted his shoulders, almost to push him away. We pressed the railing, straining to see our uncle descend the gangplank into the smaller crowd, the crowd of "those we left behind."

We're there now. The crowd is more subdued than before as there's no need to rush. The goal of all efforts has been achieved: travellers are onboard the correct ship with their belongings stowed in the correct staterooms. Tears have been shed; emotions spent. But still, the crowd waits through an unendurable tension as the last sundry boxes are hoisted aboard. Then comes a silence, emotional and suspenseful, broken suddenly by the boom of the ship's siren.

I don't feel the ship move at first, but I notice the shore, almost imperceptibly, slide to the right. "We're off!" comes the cry, and my uncle waves his bowler hat above his head. His grey woollen overcoat flaps in the breeze coming off the water, waving at us as if to say, "Farewell! Farewell! And God be with you!"

—

"This looks tasty!" Harry tucks a white linen napkin into his collar, reading from the menu card, "Pea soup, corned beef, hotpot, potatoes, apple tart, biscuits and cheese."

"How can you even think of eating!" I exclaim. My stomach has not been right since we left port.

"Things aren't as bad as that, Marjory. I'm starved and I'm going to enjoy my dinner whether or not you women–folk are weeping."

"Harry, don't be crass." Mother smooths her napkin over her lap. She looks over the dining room, rapidly filling with hungry passengers, and sighs. "The stewards seem to know their business, at least."

Mother asked the steward for coffee the moment she sat down rather than waiting until the end of the meal like everyone else. He obliged her with a gallant smile, and now she's acting as if he slew a dragon in her honour. "What a delightful man he is. Such wonderful service," she murmurs, sipping her coffee appreciatively.

Mother is a handsome woman, I suppose. Not a stunning beauty but one who knows how to make the best of her appearance. Uncle Joshua has told us stories about Mother as a young lady. It seems she knew how to turn heads with smiles and witty conversation. It's a skill she carried through her adult life and she uses it to her advantage. We never have to wait in line at shops or tea houses because she's made friends with the proprietors and their young assistants. When they see Mrs. Thompson, they beckon her to one side and we're instantly served. This attention pleases her to no end, but I wonder how happy she will be on the farm in Manitoba if she doesn't have daily interaction with admirers. What will she be like if she's no longer fashionably dressed and beautiful? Now, at forty years old, if Mother wants to be charming, she can still acquire coffee before everyone else and secure a table away from the drafty dining room doors.

We fill a table for six on our own, so we don't make acquaintances as others do. Instead, we watch our fellow passengers with curiosity. Introductions are made, inquiries to the places of origin—"Liverpool, thanks. And you?"—and final destinations—"I've a cousin in Toronto. We'll start there." I look for the orphans but can't find them. They are probably in the third-class dining room. We're in second class, though there isn't a first-class on the S. S. Lake Manitoba, which is confusing. Mother says we're in the "best class," which settles it.

The chatter of the diners echoes off the tinplated ceiling. White Grecian columns, wood-panelled walls, and crystal glassware elevate the room from a necessary station to feed the hungry to an elegant banquet hall. It's strange to think we'll dine in luxury from Liverpool to Montreal. Somehow, I expect the wood panelling to disappear and the crystal glassware to shatter by the time we reach Canada. We're going to the wilderness, aren't we? Is it possible there are nice things in Canada too?

I try a few bites of food, but I can't stop my stomach from lurching with each roll of the ship. The dining room smells of pea soup, which makes me ill. I want to lie down on my bunk or even on the floor under the table.

"Mother," I whisper, "I feel awful."

"Eat up, Darling," she says. "Food will revive you."

"It's doing me wonders," Harry says, tucking into a plate of corned beef. He eats quickly, energetically. All my family eat like this is the first meal they've had in a week. I don't understand their enthusiasm. The smells. The look of the food. It's all so ghastly.

"Mother! I'm going to be sick!" I cry.

My grim face must convince her of the genuine possibility of me being sick, right over my new travelling dress, the Canadian Pacific dinnerware, and the white linen tablecloth, for Mother shoves her chair back and takes me by the hand. We weave between tables towards the heavy doors that lead to the deck.

Once I breathe the sharp night air, I'm in no danger of vomiting, but Mother leads me to the railing regardless. "If you need to be sick, over the side of the ship will do."

I take deep breaths. "I just needed the fresh air."

"Well, breathe then. And look at the shore on the horizon, not down at the water."

I look out across the grey waters, but darkness smothers the coastline. Twinkling lights disappear into mist as England fades before our eyes. It's as if a mighty painter swishes black paint over the view. Little by little, the land disappears until all that's left is the water rushing past.

"Will we ever be back?" I ask softly, but Mother doesn't answer. Instead, she presses a hand against her high collar and shakes her head. She knows. She must know. People don't return from the New World. At least not many. And if they do, there's an air of failure about them. Even if you're starving to death in Canada, you can write jolly letters. You don't need to tell the relatives how rough things are. But if you return to England, everyone knows. Everyone knows you couldn't make it. That's the real tragedy of emigration, not that it might be a miserable failure but that you must always pretend it isn't.

We watch until the last light fades, then Mother rallies herself, almost as if she's been dreaming. "Father waits over there." She points west into the darkness. "Think of how happy we will be to see him. We'll be so proud of ourselves—a lone woman crossing the Atlantic with five children. We've never even so much as gone to London altogether! Manchester even! Just think of that."

We leave the railings though I'd rather stay out in the fresh air. Our journey feels more palpable outside. In the dining room, the comforts of home are recreated, but on the decks, the ocean rushes past, and it's obvious how quickly our surroundings are changing.

Back inside, enterprising passengers canvas each table in search of talent for an impromptu evening concert—"What is your forte, Ma'am? A gift for the monologue, perhaps?" Mother assures them no depths of talent lie undiscovered at our table, and they hurry on in search of ballads, airs and recitations.

"You could sing, Mother," Mary urges, to which Mother rolls her eyes.

"What would I sing? 'Safe in the Arms of Jesus?'"

"That would be an excellent choice if the ship goes down," Harry offers.

"Harry! Don't even speak those words," Mother snaps.

It's not that we don't consider shipwreck, despite our confidence in the vessel's indestructibility, but the skippers we've seen, clad in dripping oilcloth, seem to know their way around so easily that we feel in good hands. The depths of our ignorance are so profound that we assume their wisdom flourishes in direct proportion. Besides, what else can we do but trust the captain and his men? Surely, they'll see us through. Passenger ships don't go down anymore anyway.

The evening entertainment begins shortly after dessert. In the glittering drawing room comes the tinkling of a surprisingly well-tuned piano. A crowd gathers, warm and comfortable from the delicious food. The talent is more or less entertaining and begins with a stout Scotswoman singing, "Sailing O'er the Ocean," her ample chins vibrating as she trills, "Staunch and true the vessel that bears us o'er the tide! Soon we'll cast the anchor upon the other side!"

"Isn't this a hymn about dying, for goodness' sake?" Mary whispers down our row as we sit listening, somewhat like in church.

An energetic American saves the day by plunking out a rag at the piano. "It's the rage in New Orleans!" he says, by way of introduction or perhaps even apology. "It's a little number called 'The Entertainer' by Scott Joplin, one of America's finest coloured composers."

"What's a coloured composer?" My little sister Norah whispers to no one in particular.

"The Entertainer" is the strangest piece I've ever heard, without expression or beauty, but Joss bounces in his chair and Mother taps her high-heeled boot toe to the beat. I'm mesmerized by the American's left hand, which dashes up and down the keys without him watching. I imagine it guided by an extra eye than the two God gave.

"Extraordinary what Americans come up with," says a man behind me, not entirely complementing the effort though applauding its finish all the same.

"Best raise the tone," says a little man with an Irish accent. He hops up and weaves through the crowd to the front, his shoes clicking the wooden dance floor.

"In case anyone be missing the Emerald Isle," he says, holding his bowler hat in his hands, "we'd better have a song to warm our hearts."

With that, he launches into "The Minstrel Boy" in a dark, thick baritone that seems to emanate from a bigger body than his own. By the time he finishes, his hands clasped, his voice tremulous, not many eyes are dry, not even English eyes that might usually roll at a lament for an Irish boy fighting against the Crown. But these were not normal circumstances. English, Irish,

Scottish, Canadian, American and even, it is rumoured, a few Scandinavians in third class are together in this great steel vessel, steaming across the cold, black waters of the Atlantic. Desperate in our belief that the benefits of the new world will outweigh the risks of the ocean crossing, we stepped on a floating beast, settled in her belly, and then made merry to distract ourselves. Race and nationality don't matter. Given a chance, the Atlantic would swallow us all democratically, without prejudice. And for this reason, we kneel before our bunks at night, clothed in our warmest nightclothes, and pray for safety and good health, hoping to see our earthly father before our heavenly one.

—

We reach the Canadian Pacific Railway Station in Winnipeg after nine days on the ship and two days on the train. For most of the train journey, we watched trees slip past our windows, one after another, until we concluded that Father must have got the wide-open spaces wrong. Canada was obviously covered in trees. But, by the time breakfast was served one last morning—$1 for Mother, fifty cents for the rest of us—the train broke free of the trees, and flat farmland stretched as far as the eye could see.

"Why is nothing growing?" Mother asked the porter.

"The crops are all in, Ma'am," he replied. "Harvest is through. It was warm last week, but the paper calls for frost every night this week."

"Frost?" Mother squinted at the man. "Already?"

The porter nodded slowly then backed away from us with a bemused look on his face. Perhaps he was horrified by Mother's ignorance, or maybe he couldn't stand the smell of us.

We had side-by-side compartments in the sleeping car—simply furnished, upholstered, with rough linens for purchase. The washstand could hardly keep up with our cleaning needs, though Mother made us scrub ourselves each night. We were out of clean clothes and couldn't get to our trunks to fetch more. Harry and Joss smelled especially bad because of their morning excursions to the horsecar. Accompanied by an affable porter, the boys assisted with the morning feeding of the horses. They always returned in good spirits, but Mary complained about their smell—"What did you step in?"

"Don't fuss," Mother would say. "It gives them something to do for twenty minutes. We'll acquire a hotel room and sort ourselves out."

Now we're in Winnipeg, standing with our fellow passengers on the busy platform, trying to accept the ground as a stable thing, not a rolling vessel or swaying train car. We are a motley crowd, dazed and serious—men with soiled linens and lacklustre boots, women with straggled hair and hats awry, hungry children with sticky hands and dishevelled collars. Our exuberance at landing in Montreal has been spent, and we are now dispirited, filthy and exhausted. We don't disembark the train inside a station, rather on street level. We had to climb down the train steps then jump into mud. This uncivilized way of arriving in Winnipeg feels like a relic of the past, and indeed it is, for just up the street, a monstrous, red brick building with columns rises through scaffolding.

"New CPR station still under construction"—a porter quips as he unloads our bags into a cart. "Running behind schedule, so it's the old station for now."

We don't enter a train station though, old or other. Instead, an officious-looking chap strides down the length of the train, roaring and pointing, "All passengers from the Pacific Express report in the Immigration Hall further down Higgins!"

"Surely we don't have to do that," Mother says dismissively. "We're English."

"I think we'd better," Mary says. "Everyone else is."

We follow the train passengers squeezing their luggage carts down the street. A porter pushes our cart, but it wouldn't be difficult to find our way. Everyone shuffles towards the Immigration Hall.

Squat log shacks tumble together along the muddy street in no particular order. Some look to be builders' huts; others, storage sheds and shops of dubious quality. The scent of coal smoke from the trains mingles with the stench of unwashed bodies and horse manure. A woman with a painted mouth, frizzy hair, and garish dress calls, "Come on, boys! Just north of the tracks."

As we get closer to the Immigration Hall, passengers from other trains join us. We're no longer the northern European crowd that we were on the train. There are other people now, women with blankets over their heads, children crying while mothers calm them in strange languages. Workers scurry around us. A Chinese man pushes a wheelbarrow of sheets. Harry points to a black railway porter.

"Where did all these people come from?" Harry shouts at Mother over the din of humans advancing towards a darkly lit hall, each traveller determined to be the first in line.

Mother ignores him, listening carefully to our porter.

"You're English, so you won't have any problems," he says, nodding to another large building also under construction. "Immigration Hall No. 1. Intended for first-class passengers as yourselves, but not open yet." He leads us to a building with several doors open to the street. "In you go," he says to Mother, who looks confused by the chaos around her. "I'll stay with your children and the baggage. Walk in and tell them you are English and your husband already has a homestead. If they know you have a place, they won't make you stay in the Immigration Halls for weeks on end. You don't want that."

Mother casts us a worried look then gets in line. We can see her through an open doorway, standing with other passengers from our train. They must all have places to go, for everyone leaves the line with a quick step, back towards the train station, not flopping down on the ground like the foreigners around us who await instructions from harried immigration workers.

Young boys add to the din by yelling out the newspaper headlines. The cries of "Borden to leave Conservatives in November 3rd Election! Read all about it in the Telegram!" compete with "Vice-Admiral Beresford to teach the Czar a lesson! Read all about it in the Tribune!"

English passengers purchase newspapers, some tucking the paper under their arms, others quickly flip through the paper, searching for some information. When one gentleman in a straw hat says to his wife, "Ah! There's one at 2:30," and then strides back up the street to the train station, I realize train departures must be printed in the newspaper. We hadn't considered that. We could have made a plan earlier if we had known.

Mother reappears on the street, looking relieved and possibly proud of herself. "We're free to go," she says, turning to the porter as if he is our personal tour guide. "What do we do next? We need to get to Brandon."

The porter looks at her blankly. "Then why didn't you stay on the Pacific Express, Ma'am?"

"I thought Winnipeg was the end of the line," she says.

The porter smirked slightly, pushing his hat up onto his forehead. "No, Ma'am. The Pacific Express heads right to the Pacific Ocean, by way of Brandon."

"Whatever shall we do?" Mother is dismayed by this turn of events.

"It's too late to get back on the Pacific Express, or the CPR 97 as it's called. It doesn't stay long. But you can transfer to the CNR for Hartney Brandon Branch. You'll have time."

"What is CNR?"

The porter stares at her again as if she's the most ill-informed passenger he's ever encountered. I highly doubt that. The hoards of passengers from Warsaw, Dubrovnik or Athens don't look better informed than us.

"You said 'CNR.'" Mother says impatiently. "You said we need to get on a CNR train. What is a CNR train?"

"The Canadian National Railway, Ma'am."

"What? There are two railways in Canada?"

"There are several, Ma'am."

Mother looks shocked. All we know is the Canadian Pacific. It operated the S. S. Lake Manitoba and the Pacific Express train from Montreal. It is a familiar name to us. We didn't realize there were more options.

"Is that the only way to get to Oak River?" Mother asks.

"No, Ma'am. You can wait until tomorrow for the CPR's next Pacific Express. But if you leave today on the CNR, you'll arrive in Brandon by tea time. You can spend the night and catch a train to Oak River first thing tomorrow, back on CPR's Miniota line."

Mother hesitates, looking over each of us with a wince. We all need to be bathed and fed, but she looks at her pocketbook, perhaps subconsciously.

"Hotels are cheaper in Brandon than here," the porter says, correctly surmising the state of our finances. "It may be wise to press on."

We spent the equivalent of nearly 200 Canadian dollars for ship passage. Father wrote Mother that the sailing could be accomplished for less than a hundred if we'd only sail third-class, but Mother said it wasn't safe. People in third-class have diseases, she said. But we're nearly out of money now, though Mother smooths out a Dominion of Canada banknote into the porter's hand.

"Would you get a cab to take us to the CNR station? And a telegraph office too?" she asks.

I suspect she paid him too well, for the porter pockets the banknote with a smile. "Right this way!" he calls, lifting Joss and Harry on the luggage cart. "You'll be there in no time!"

—

The telegraph office can be heard from the street, even over the shrieking newspaper boys who have switched to more sensational headlines such as—"Winnipeg man murders wife with axe." The clatter from the telegraph machines deafens as we press ourselves into the office and wait alongside other travellers desperate to make contact with family across the prairies. Young operators in dark jackets and funny hats sit at clattering devices. Long strips of paper trail from the machines, some pieces floating over the shoulders of operators, others drifting to the floor.

When our turn arrives, Mother calls, "I'd like to send a telegram to Oak River," with a note of despair in her voice as if she'd rather have tea, but this is the necessary thing to do.

The teller wears a green shade that shadows his face right down to his handlebar moustache. His sleeves are pushed up with black bands. "At your leisure, Madam," he says, his quill-tipped pen poised over a sheet of paper.

Mother hesitates as if she's surprised by the speed of this transaction. She must now send a message to Father and she doesn't know what to say. "The telegram is to Peter Thompson of Oak River, Manitoba. Is that address enough? That's all I ever put on an envelope."

"That will suffice," the operator says. "Small town station masters are generally acquainted with all the district residences. Is Mr. Thompson a farmer?"

"How did you guess?" Mother exclaims.

"Oak River is not a large town, Madam. I expect most everyone in the district farms."

"Oh, I see." Mother seems disconcerted by this information as if she expected Oak River to be a bustling metropolis with numerous professions unlinked to agriculture.

The operator smiles. "And your message?"

"'We have arrived in Winnipeg. We will be on tomorrow's train. With love, Mary Ann.' How does that sound?"

"Well put, Madam. Very well put. However, as you will be charged per word, might I suggest the following: 'In Winnipeg. Stop. Arrive tomorrow. Stop.'"

"Not even my name?" Mother asks.

The operator angles his head. "Does your husband expect you?"

"He has a general sense of our arrival date."

"Then I propose that this message, howbeit economical in length, will achieve the desired effect. There's only one passenger train to Oak River. He'll know when to meet it."

Mother pays the man out of our dwindling funds with a worried look on her face.

"For future reference, Ma'am, a telegram can be left at the train station upon your arrival in Winnipeg. There is no need to visit the telegraph office."

Mother doesn't even respond to this. She just says, "Come, children!" then shoves our way onto the street. Our cab still waits and we clamour back in. "To the CNR Station!" she calls, then sinks back into the seat cushion with her eyes closed. "I guess that's it. We're not going to a hotel after all. This chaos is absurd and I don't want to make another mistake. We're leaving for Brandon as soon as possible."

Mary slumps against the seat and Joss starts to cry. I'm disappointed too not to have a hot bath, but the sights and sounds distract me. I press my nose to the cab window. All around, signs advertise cotton goods, crockery, abattoirs, and undertakers. Streetcars clang between tall buildings that all seem to be banks—Bank of Ottawa, Montreal, Hamilton, British North America, and Commerce; Dominion, Union, Merchant, and Imperial too. Wagons clatter, loaded with goods—barrels marked "Ogilvie's Flour," boards split for roofing, chickens squawking in crates. Delivery boys whirl past on bicycles, shouting to pedestrians who dodge in front of them. The commotion is constant. But despite the panic that seems to motivate the drivers, civilization still reigns. There is a sense of purpose in the activity, a different atmosphere than that of the shanties close to the CPR station. There, small children played in the mud alongside horses' hooves, their faces dirty, their clothes ragged, while drifts of smoke lingered over the low roof lines. "That is a breeding ground for the plague," Mother had said.

—

"Surely you are jesting me!" Mother sputters. "I sent a telegram from Winnipeg. It cost a fortune and now you're telling me it was never delivered?"

We stand on the dusty platform of the Oak River train station. Wind whips dirt off the flat farmland that lies beyond the train tracks, stinging our cold faces. From the platform, we can see clapboard buildings on one side of a dirt road. The squat buildings face the railway tracks as if their builders were afraid of missing something exciting at the train station should their backs be turned. Some stores have large, roughly painted signs on their front porches—Hardware, Blacksmith, Grocer—while others lack signage. The only buildings that break up the horizon are a two-storey brick building marked "HOTEL," a church with peeling paint, and the grain elevators. Not one tree shades the bedsheets that flap on clotheslines behind single-storey houses. Chickens and pigs wander the insides of crude backyard pens. Smoke drifts from chimneys. Horse manure litters the streets. Wagon wheels turn slowly.

We should have known the train station at Oak River would not be an improvement over the one at Brandon, but we held out hope there might be a waiting room or refreshment hall, not just a blank platform attached to a freight room and ticket counter at the edge of a grubby little town.

The train station at Brandon wasn't elegant and columned like the station in Montreal, nor as promising as the new CPR station in Winnipeg. Brandon's station was wooden and dirty. Ploughs and sacks of seed wheat were piled up on the platform, not tidy stacks of transatlantic luggage. Signage was absent. Food was served from a counter, not even at tables. Porters were scarce and dressed in peasant clothes, not in pressed uniforms.

And now we quickly surmise Father is not here to meet us because the station master did not deliver our telegram. This is one blow too many. Mother is furious.

"What is the point of a telegraph office if no one delivers telegrams?" Mother stands with her hands on her hips, staring down the station master. She's just travelled across an ocean and half a continent with five children, several of whom fought like cats on the train from Brandon. She spilled coffee on her travelling coat when the train ground to a halt for a passing cow. Her hair refuses to stay pinned in the prairie gales. She's not at her best.

The station master smiles sheepishly behind a bushy beard. "We do things a little differently here. We're the wild west, ya know."

I'm sure he wouldn't have spoken so flippantly if he knew how close she was to bursting into tears. And perhaps he notices the redness in her eyes, for he changes tacks. "The name is Elwood Glasgow," he says, offering his hand to Mother. "We've sure enjoyed Peter's musical talents down at the Methodist."

Mother shakes Mr. Glasgow's hand with a quizzical look, perhaps realizing this man is not another anonymous railway worker like all the others we've encountered on our journey. He is someone she may meet again, perhaps at church on Sunday.

"Mary Ann Thompson," she says stiffly, "Peter's wife, though you've probably concluded that."

"And Peter's children!" Mr. Glasgow smiles at each of us.

"Mary, Marjory, Norah, Harry, Joss." Mother stabs a finger at each of us as she calls our names.

Mr. Glasgow nods at us. "What fine children! Won't Peter be pleased to see you? My goodness, what a brood! All right, my team is hitched up. I'll take you out there. It seems I have a telegram to deliver to Peter anyway." Mr. Glasgow chuckles at his joke as he picks up one of our trunks and carries it through the station, out the door to a waiting wagon.

Mother rolls her eyes then rallies. "There we are, Children. A solution has presented itself. Pick up your bags. Mr. Glasgow doesn't need to do all the work. Hurry. We'll get cold standing here."

We follow Mr. Glasgow through the small station onto the dusty street on the other side. His wagon is hitched behind a plough horse. Like the rough Yorkshire wagons filled with vegetables in bushel baskets for market, the wooden wagon has a narrow bench up at the front and two long benches in the back. There's a rickety step at the back of the wagon, but Mr. Glasgow lifts each of us children as if we weigh nothing at all. When it's Mother's turn, he politely offers a hand which she accepts. One high-booted foot on the step, Mother tries to lift her other leg onto the wagon bed but can't make it and totters backward. Mr. Glasgow catches her from behind and gracelessly shoves her up the rest of the way.

"Whoops-e-daisy!" he exclaims.

Mother is embarrassed but covers it by clucking at us like we've caused all the fuss. "Mary, move over. Don't just sit there, Norah. Make room." There's barely enough space to squeeze our feet in beside our trunks that lie between the benches, so we sit almost sideways, crowded together.

"Not a fine carriage, but it will get us there!" Mr. Glasgow says, climbing up on the front bench. He slaps the reins but there's no lurch forward, just a slow roll. It's then I notice the horse hadn't been tied. It had been completely satisfied to stand untethered in front of the train station, biding its time.

The horse does not move very quickly, even with Mr. Glasgow prompting it with cajoling words—"Come on, girl. That's it. Pick up those feet." We creep down the street barely faster than a walk. At this nominal pace, we are well able to take in the sights of Oak River.

Straggling alongside the train tracks on muddy streets unimaginatively named North Railway and South Railway, a dozen buildings offer the town's best in provisions and services. Three grain elevators cast shadows over us. Tall with peaked roofs, the wooden structures have names painted on the sides— Manitoba Grain Co; Ogilvie Milling Co; and Bready, Love & Tryon. The elevators are the most exciting features of the town. Visible from miles away, their whitewashed structures catch the sunlight, providing some deviation to the otherwise flat horizon.

"How extraordinary," Mother murmurs, craning her neck to see the tops of the elevators. "Are they full of grain?" she asks Mr. Glasgow.

"They were," he calls over his shoulder. "By the end of harvest, they were filled up. But they've started to move grain out in rail cars. Best to get some out before winter comes. There are nearly a hundred thousand bushels stored in there. Some grain from your farm too."

We don't have much pride in that thought, mainly because Father bought the farm at the end of summer and had nothing to do with this year's grain production. Nevertheless, he wrote about it—long, rambling letters filled with calculations as if he's working out his plans for the farm. Our $1000 capital must stretch for input costs for at least four years, maybe five. We must purchase seed and fencing right away and upgrade farm equipment as soon as possible. Father has his eye on a drill, but the costs are alarming.

Open prairie lies beyond the grain elevators and the horse seems content to amble down the dirt road, with flat, open fields on all sides. After a few minutes, Mother sighs and elbows the boys. "Off you get. You can walk. We're too heavy for this poor horse."

Harry sputters. "Walk? Six miles to the farm?"

"You can take turns with the girls," Mother says, shoving him off the end of the barely moving wagon.

After heading west for a mile, Mr. Glasgow turns the horse north, off the dirt track that leads from town, onto a far worse track with numerous ruts. "Up this way!" he says.

Now a piece from town, we find ourselves surrounded by nothingness. We can see where crops grew—short stumble remains from the summer—but otherwise, the view from one side of the wagon to the other is indistinguishable. A few trees dot the horizon but they are short and grow at odd angles, whipped by the north breeze. Even though it is mid-day, low clouds block much of the sun, leaving us in a melancholy shadow. Our ride is utterly silent except for the swish of dried grass against the wheel spokes and the jingle of the harness, keeping time with the shuffle of the horse's hooves. The sky is big though. I don't remember being so impressed with the sky in England, the horizon filled with houses, trees and hills. But here—I crane my neck to watch birds fly overhead, their names and destinations not yet known to me.

We bump together, Mother, Mary, Norah and I in the back of the wagon, our knees smashing into the trunks every time the wagon bumps over a rut. After a mile or two of jostling, Mary says, "I've had enough," and jumps off the back of the wagon to join the boys. I follow her in a flapping, awkward leap, trying to free my legs without hooking my petticoat on the rough wood. I hit the ground hard and have to use my hands to stop my fall, but Mother doesn't show concern or even reprimand us, which shows how distressed she is. In England, she would have told us to climb down like ladies. But what does it matter here? No one sees us. No one cares.

We tramp behind the wagon, happy to stretch our legs after many days of sitting on a train. Harry and Joshua run ahead, then fall behind the wagon again. Something about all the wide-open space seems to intrigue them, for they smile broadly and point out wild turkeys across the field with excited shouts.

Mary scowls though. "What is this place?" she mutters under her breath.

"I thought it would be more, you know—civilized," I whisper so Mother won't hear.

"There are a few homesteads." Mary points to whiffs of chimney smoke rising from short bluffs of trees that sporadically dot the landscape.

"But the farms are far apart," I say, thinking of Huddersfield with all the townhouses crammed tightly onto streets meandering up the valleys.

"Exactly," Mary says. "There aren't many people. I knew it wouldn't be like England, but this is very lonely, isn't it?"

We walk slowly, and as the miles fall behind us, we come upon a little building, nearly a shed, in the middle of a field. A stove pipe emerges through a puncture in the roof. A tiny privy in the yard leans slightly to the south.

"Bankburn School." Mr. Glasgow calls over his shoulder. "That will be the closest school for your children, Ma'am. All the grades. One teacher—Ethel Sparling."

"How does one teacher manage all the grades?" Mother asks. She pulls her coat collar around her neck and holds onto her hat in the wind, its feathers badly mangled.

Mr. Glasgow shrugs. "I don't think anyone leaves speaking Latin, but she takes them through their paces."

"Extraordinary." Mother sighs. Perhaps she calculates the number of books she brought from England and wonders if they will suffice in educating us. She squints at the little school until we've passed it, then stares north again for a glimpse of our farm.

Ahead, a rock house comes into view, about a mile to the west. It looks sturdy and warm, with a bit of smoke drifting up through the chimney.

"Is that our house, Mr. Glasgow?" I cry.

He turns around and smiles. "No. McPhaden is the name. Seven children they have in that house."

As if on cue, three men appear over a rise in the road. They walk alongside two fine horses, pulling a sledge of logs. Seeing us, they lead the horses toward one side of the track and raise arms in greeting, seemingly ready to make our acquaintance.

"Hullo!" Mr. Glasgow calls, pulling on the reins of his plough horse, which is only too happy to stop.

Clearly father and sons, the men wear heavy coats over dirty pants. The father looks wrinkled though not old. The sons are fair with cheeks red from the wind.

"Hugh McPhaden and sons Allan and John," Mr. Glasgow says, clearly delighted to be an instrument of introduction. "This is Peter Thompson's family."

"How do you do?" Mother offers a hand over the wagon's side to the older man who removes his hat. "Forgive me for not descending. How very rude of me."

The McPhaden men stare at Mother curiously as if her polite English accent was more than they were expecting. Mother practised her elocution at school so she wouldn't sound like a mill worker. It set her apart as an educated woman in Huddersfield, but in the middle of nowhere in Manitoba, it sounds strange, even to my ears.

"Not at all," Mr. McPhaden says in a Scottish brogue, pressing Mother's hand in his. "If there's anything we can do to help ye, let us know. It can be unsettling, crossing the Atlantic."

"We are splendid, thank you, and have enjoyed our journey very much. It has been relaxing for me and educational for the children," Mother says, pulling back her hand, which the earnest Mr. McPhaden still holds. Our appearance must defy Mother's speech. All of us have wrinkled clothes, dishevelled hair, and dirty faces. We've been sullen and testy with one another for days and are weary of hunger and filth.

Mr. McPhaden overlooks our deficiencies to politely inquire after our names. It's then I notice Mary blushes right down to the roots of her hair, which she only just started wearing up in a bun like a proper lady. She looks at her feet and pushes a pebble with her toe. Mary is never shy, but she clasps her hands tightly behind her back. She doesn't say anything, not even when Mr.

McPhaden says, "Hello, dear children, and welcome to Manitoba." She smiles at the son, Allan and Allan smiles back. I realize he's rather good-looking. Both boys are. He's probably older than Mary, but he has a friendly smile and bright blue eyes. He looks strong, likely from hauling logs.

"Hugh, here," Mr. Glasgow says, "is a hero."

"Come now." Mr. McPhaden looks embarrassed.

"It's true! Hugh ran supplies for the Royal Canadian Mounted Police during the Rebellion with Riel, bumping along in an ox cart from Winnipeg to the forts in Saskatchewan. Weren't any roads then, were there, Hugh? Just an old Hudson Bay Company trail."

Mr. McPhaden doesn't reply. Instead, he just looks away, across the fields.

"We'd still be fighting Riel if it weren't for good lads like Hugh supplying the Mounties."

"Well, we're hauling logs today," Mr. McPhaden says, rather obviously considering his load.

"What for?" Mr. Glasgow asks.

"A house," Allan says simply.

"For you then?"

"For Father," Allan replies.

"What's this, Hugh?" Mr. Glasgow turns to Mr. McPhaden. "Where are you building?"

"On the west half. We've bought it, and Allan can keep the old house."

"He'll be needing a wife next, he will," Mr. Glasgow jokes. "Thank your lucky stars, Allan, I'm delivering such pretty girls to the district."

"You're nearly home now," Mr. McPhaden says to us, breaking off Mr. Glasgow who giggles like a schoolgirl. "A mile more and your journey's through. We won't detain ye further, though Mrs. McPhaden will be after us for not bringing you in for tea."

"How kind!" Mother gushes. "But we're anxious to see Mr. Thompson. We've not laid eyes on him for two years."

"How glad he'll be to see ye."

Mr. McPhaden raises a hand of farewell and steps back. Mr. Glasgow flicks the plough horse on the back with the reins and we set off again, us older children still walking behind. Mary turns around for a glance, and I feel the men still watching us.

"Really, Mary," I snip. "It's like you've never seen a man before."

"Don't be ridiculous," she snips back, but there's a smile on her face, or at least there is until Mr. Glasgow pulls back on the reins one last time and says with a note of apology in his voice, "Well, here we are."

—

At first, I don't know what he means. Surely this can't be Father's farm. Barren and untidy, it bears no resemblance to the vibrant CPR posters that advertise bountiful plantations in the new world. Those houses are always white with porches. Barns are bright red, not crudely constructed out of weather-worn boards. The place seems deserted as if God made it, despaired, then moved on.

There is only a squat log cabin with a single window. A stove pipe jams roughly through the roof, and tall weeds grow close to the foundation. At the back of the cabin, a clapboard lean-to shelters a wagon once painted green. A slightly larger shack must be the barn for I hear a low moo from within. Chickens wander around firewood heaped in a pile. Two muddy pigs wallow in a square pen that employs the north wall of the barn as a segment of fencing. They lazily gaze at us through the rough wood slats without interest, gnawing on cobs of corn. Dried stocks decay in a garden plot cut out of the prairie grassland. A tiny outhouse lies close to a bluff of squat poplar trees. A stiff north breeze frenzies their branches but isn't strong enough to clear the stench of manure.

As Mr. Glasgow climbs down and unloads our trunks, I quickly surmise this motley homestead is the prosperous farm Father wrote of in his letters. I realize he exaggerated its beauty and financial potential. As I stand with my siblings, our eyes wide and mouths gaping, I can only see work to be done.

Mother clamours off the wagon, tearing her dress on a nail head. She hastily flicks the cloth loose and covers her mouth with her hands, her eyes wide, her shoulders shaking. "Peter?" she calls tremulously, pacing the yard in a tight circle. We hear nothing, no response to Mother's greeting, just wind whistling through the trees, dry grass rustling in the breeze, a door rattling on its hinges.

"Peter?" Mother calls again, more frantically. I can see she is about to cry. Her chin is wobbling. She wipes her nose with the back of her gloved hand, an unpardonable sin in her books.

Mary grabs her arm. "Stay calm, Mother. I'm sure Father is close by."

"Peter!" Mr. Glasgow yells much more loudly, startling us all. His cry is effective though. We hear a dog yelp on the far side of the trees. We rush towards the sound, past the poplars, through the tall dried grass, right to the edge of a cultivated field. Beyond a pond, a man pushes through bulrushes with a gun in his hand. A small deer is slung over his shoulders. His pants are covered in blood. He has a thick, bushy beard. Filthy. Unrecognizable. He looks like the sketches of prehistoric cavemen in our school books. At the sight of us, he raises his gun and waves it wildly above his head. He whoops with joy and starts to run, the dead deer bouncing against his neck.

Mother sucks in her breath and drops to her knees on the dry grass, brand new travelling suit and all. "Mary—what is this?" she cries, holding herself as she gasps for air against her corset stays. "Why is he carrying that?"

But Mary has no answers. None of us does. Instead, Harry runs through the bulrushes towards the hunter, his arms flailing. "Father!" he shrieks. "We're here! We're here! We're finally here!"

I realize the worst is happening.

"If Farmer Smith bought three fields at \$10 per acre, and the three fields are 14 acres, 21 acres, and 25 acres, what is the average price per field that Farmer Smith paid?"

Miss Sparling writes the details of the question on the blackboard with her back to us. The white chalk's scraping sound only partially muffles the incessant sniffing of Barclay McPhaden behind me. Barclay sniffs to annoy me. He doesn't do it very loudly, just loudly enough for me to hear. I've complained to Miss Sparling but it didn't do any good. Barclay said it was dust from the harvest bothering his nose. Miss Sparling sighed and suggested a handkerchief to which Barclay said he'd bring up the subject with his mother. But that was two weeks ago and still, Barclay sniffs.

I don't bother writing down the math equations. 10 is an easy number by which to multiply. 140, 210, 250. I can do the arithmetic in my head. 140 and 210 are 350, plus 250 is 600. Divide by three for an average of \$200 per field.

"Miss Sparling!" chimes the whiny voice of Barclay McPhaden behind me. "Marjory isn't doing the question. She might be daydreaming."

Miss Sparling turns to face the class. Fifteen of us cram into shared desks. My sister Norah shares a desk with me and she turns to scowl at Barclay. "Don't be so senseless," Norah hisses.

"Now Norah called me senseless," Barclay says.

Miss Sparling pushes her spectacles up her nose, leaving a trail of chalk dust on her cheek. Her hair is parted down the middle and pulled up in a bun in two sections, suggesting horns high up the sides of her head. She's pretty though. A tiny woman, shorter than most of us girls, she was the first teacher at Bankburn School back in 1901 when there wasn't any school building, just a granary with a stove. The children sat on plain benches, not even desks. When Miss Sparling left to obtain her second-class teaching certificate, the teachers that replaced her each gave up after a few months. Ours isn't an easy school. The stove doesn't heat well, and the schoolteacher is responsible for hauling and chopping wood. She has to board with families in the district who have children in the school. The pay is terrible. Boys only attend school intermittently, especially in busy seasons on the farm. No one attends when the weather is inclement. So, when Miss Sparling came back last year, the district parents rejoiced. Miss Sparling could maintain order. Miss Sparling was a local girl. Her family farm was just up the road. No one would have to board her and she was already used to hard work. She didn't mind hauling wood or breaking the ice in the water pail each winter morning. Miss Sparling was precisely what was needed.

There was talk she only came back to marry Walter Delamater, a bachelor farmer from the other side of town. But Father heard a rumour in the hardware store that Walter is hard-up, so perhaps the departure of Miss Sparling is less than imminent. She may wish to take her chances as the wife of a hardworking farmer though. She'd certainly be no worse off considering the pittance the school board pays her.

Miss Sparling drops the chalk on her desk and brushes dust off her long brown skirt with quick, sharp strokes. "Marjory Thompson, the answer, please."

"$200 is the average price per field," I say.

"Barclay McPhaden, no good comes to those who meddle. Have you completed your equation?"

"No, Ma'am," Barclay says, "but I know the answer is $200."

Snickers ripple throughout the classroom. Miss Sparling shakes her head and turns to write the next question. The farm theme continues. Farmer Smith is now buying wheat seed.

"Know-it-all," I hear Barclay whisper behind me.

I might have accepted that taunt without retaliation, perhaps even accepting it as a confirmation of my superior math skills, but then Barclay sniffs and something explodes inside me.

I whip around, grab Barclay's nose, and give it a good twist. "Blow your snout, you sniffly little swine!" I snap to everyone's shock and amazement, my own included. The schoolroom, quiet to start with, is now deadly silent. A dropped piece of chalk would cause us all to jump.

"Marjory Thompson!" Miss Sparling calls from the front of the room. Her eyes are wide and her face is red. Strangely enough, she looks like she could cry. "Marjory Thompson!" she says again. "That sort of behaviour is not tolerated in my classroom. Apologize immediately!"

I slide into the aisle and face Barclay who smiles from ear to ear. I sigh loudly. "I would like to apologize for my display of temper. It was uncalled for and did not reflect the virtues of temperance and patience."

"Well put," Miss Sparling says, folding her arms. "Now shake hands."

I am just warming to my theme, however. "I was rash, shockingly so," I say, carrying on with my apology. "It was unwarranted and unforgivable. How very distressing this must be for you."

"That will do, Marjory," Miss Sparling says. "Shake hands and return to your seat."

I take Barclay's outstretched hand but it is wet. I don't know from what, so I quickly drop it and wipe my hand on my skirt. Miss Sparling shoots me a warning look.

"Children, this is only the 20th of September. We have a long winter ahead of us. I will not tolerate disruptive behaviour. Marjory and Barclay, you will both stay after school and clean the blackboards and the floor." Miss Sparling turns her back and resumes scratching the next equation on the board.

I plunk down beside Norah on our narrow bench. "You're going to catch it at home," she whispers.

—

Barclay and I finish cleaning at the same time; me, the chalkboards, he, the floor. There isn't much to clean in our school. Occasionally, someone straightens the faded Union Jack in its stand, closes the coat cupboard door, dusts a frightfully outdated map of the world (Alaska still Russian) or tidies the lone bookshelf's contents—"The Rational Speller," "Leading Facts of British History," "Fifth Eclectic Primer," or the rather daring "Tragedy of Pudd'nhead Wilson And the Comedy of Those Extraordinary Twins."

Barclay and I don't speak as we leave school. Instead, we tramp down the dirt road with our heads down. Miss Sparling walks in the opposite direction to her family's farm. She probably has hours of chores waiting for her, as we do.

It's a long way to school for all of us, but the McPhaden children have a pony to pull a Red River ox cart in summer and a sleigh in winter. Apparently, John McPhaden even had his own horse when he was in school. He'd ride to town after classes and work at Glinz's grocery. He's out of school now, working on the farm every day, but that story stuck with me. We certainly don't have horses or labour to spare. Our Clydesdales—Wellington and Napoleon—are needed every day on our farm and we hurry home to help with chores after school, not to cash jobs in town. I'd love to have a little cash to call my own.

Although I can see my siblings, Norah and Harry, trudging home on the dirt track far ahead of me, I can't see Barclay's siblings at all. They must already be home in their little cart, repeating all that happened at school to their parents. Barclay must think of this too, for he breaks into a run, perhaps to minimize his delay in hopes of lessening the punishment he'll receive for being kept by the teacher. Barclay's father, Mr. McPhaden is on the school board. He'll have to find a new teacher if Miss Sparling quits, so he won't be happy to hear Barclay made trouble.

My father won't be happy either, though Norah will defend me. Barclay irritates her too, though she is more patient. Not like me. I have no patience. Miss Sparling said as much as she watched me clean the chalkboard.

"You have so much potential, Marjory," she said, "but you've got to control your temper. I see you as a school teacher someday, but if you teach, you will have your temper vexed if not by students seeking to raise your ire, then by students creating disturbances for their own pleasure. Your academics are excellent, so you need to think about your future, what you want out of life. If you want to leave Oak River—ever—you need to adjust your behaviour. Consider my words carefully, Marjory."

Miss Sparling didn't give Barclay a lecture, I noticed. She just dismissed him with the suggestion he ought to do better. Perhaps she was afraid of being too harsh since Mr. McPhaden is on the school board or maybe she didn't see the point. Barclay isn't going to continue with high school. He will leave school at the first possible moment, so why lecture him about his future?

But her words sunk into my mind like rocks dropping into a muddy slough. I know she is right and I cry a little as I walk home. I need to be more patient. But it's hard to be patient. Even at home, it's difficult. Tempers are short. Living conditions are cramped. Our log cabin is small and drafty. Last winter, I was never warm. On the coldest mornings, our blankets were covered in frost even though Father had stoked the fire multiple times throughout the night.

"Wait to get out of bed, girls, until the fire warms a little," Father would unnecessarily say.

Mary, Norah and I share a straw-filled mattress behind a sheet. Harry and Josh share one in the attic. Mother and Father have a bed in the bedroom. That leaves just enough space beyond our sheet for the stove, a table, seven chairs and a washstand. If a visitor comes at mealtime, one of us children perch on a steamer trunk, still filled with Mother's good china. A few plain planks nailed to the walls store our kitchen supplies—sugar, salt and baking soda. Simple tin and cast-iron baking pans hang from nails on the wall. A washtub hangs from another nail and the bathtub is stored in the barn between Saturday evenings. Lines hang from one side of the kitchen to the other, more effective as something on which to catch your head than to hang clothes.

Father spends his evenings making furniture, a venture at which he's not particularly talented but is attempting due to financial necessity. After harvest finished, he made a mysterious item. He wouldn't say what it was, but as Mother's waistline grew it became apparent Father was making a cradle.

Mother doesn't speak of her condition, but she spends more time resting. Father tells us girls to pick up the slack—"You simply must do more to help your mother." But we've always done lots of chores, since the first day we arrived. Milking cows, running the herd in and out of the pasture, feeding the horses and pigs, hauling wood, tending the garden in summer, mending clothes, cooking the copious amounts of food the boys eat, boiling water for washing clothes—chores are endless. Some tasks, like rendering pork fat into lard or butchering chickens, were unimaginable to Mother. The smell of burning fat and the feeling of a still-warm chicken under the fingers made her ill. She tried to help but ended up vomiting instead. Father urged her to rest, then read passages of "The Frugal Housewife" from one hand while wielding the butcher knife with the other. "When legs of meat are put in pickle," he'd read in a commanding tone, "the thickest part of the leg should be placed uppermost, that is, standing upright, the same as the creature stood when living. The same rule should be observed when they are hung up to dry; it is essential in order to keep in the juices of the meat."

Mary caught the worst of it. She didn't go back to school when we arrived in Manitoba. Instead, she stayed home and helped Mother. Occasionally, she goes on supply runs to Oak River, one pace behind Father in the grocer's and hardware store. But it's a long, bumpy ride to town and the shops' wares are basic at best. Glinz's Grocery is the most exciting store because it sells candy, but we can't afford it anyway. Mary enjoys services at the Methodist Church, but our attendance was rare last winter. Storms and cold kept us at home and Mother didn't like to venture out when the north sky looked like snow. So Mary was at home all winter with Mother. Mother was listless too, mostly from melancholy but also from nausea that plagued her.

She helped feed us breakfast then disappeared back to her room until it was nearly time to start the evening meal. Mary was left with endless chores and she might have slipped into melancholy too, had there not been so much work to distract her.

Summer improved Mother's spirits, but then she found it difficult to move, her middle growing larger and larger. So, even then, as the days grew longer and the temperature climbed, Mary still did most of the work.

For all of us, summer was spent trying to grow things—crops, garden, a few sunflowers by the cabin. We hoed, watered, and swatted mosquitos all summer long. I had no idea a creature as small as the mosquito could inflict such agony. Father and Harry's necks were bright red with bites after cutting hay down by the slough. Even though they covered every inch of themselves, the mosquitoes still bit through their clothing. Little Joss scratched his bites until they bled. Mother huddled behind netting, but Mary swatted and carried on. Perhaps more than Mother, she realized the mosquitoes were only a distraction. Tending the garden was essential if we would eat well this winter.

I was delighted to return to school just to get away from the farm. But Mary had no escape unless you count Allan McPhaden.

Mary is smitten with Allan. His farm is tantalizingly close to ours, a mile to the south. He doesn't come calling though, much to Mary's chagrin. He just speaks to her, a few minutes after church or a social event at the school, until a sibling runs a message—"Father says we're leaving." Other people, town people, step out to McDonald's, Oak River's only ice cream parlour, but we're not like town people with time on our hands, money in our pockets, and easy access to shops. We're farm people who intermittently come into town on Saturdays, sometimes at the same time as our neighbours, sometimes not. The odds of Allan and Mary ever sampling vanilla ice cream with other young people are slim. Instead, they talk for a few minutes when they can, mostly pleasantries about the weather and crops. Harry jokes they sound like old men on front porches—"How are the oats looking on your north quarter?"—but what else can they do? Allan is busy clearing farmland to increase his arable acres—backbreaking, exhausting work—and Mary is constantly working on our farm. Besides, Mary is still young. Only sixteen.

As I walk up the dirt road towards our farm, I see Norah and Harry stopped ahead, waving their arms and yelling frantically. Our cows have escaped the pasture and are headed across the road towards McPhaden's oats cut in swaths, recently for harvest. Cows escaping from our poorly constructed, half-rotten fences is not an infrequent event, but they must be stopped before they trample the oats.

I hurry to help Harry and Norah in their efforts. "Don't get dirty!" I yell. Mary will be cross if they come home with mud all over their school clothes. They can't hear me though, not with the north wind drowning out my words.

Norah gathers her skirts and climbs over the broken section of the fence to retrieve the missing board. Harry drops his school books and runs out ahead of Good Queen Bess, the most aggressive of our milk cows, waving his arms and hollering, "Away, Bess! Back to the pasture!"

Bess stomps a hoof, but stops her advance towards the oat field. Norah clamours out of the gap and screams, waving her arms as Harry does. Forming a triangle between themselves and the gap, Harry and Norah succeed in herding Bess back into our pasture. The other cows follow, their adventure at an end. I reach Harry and Norah as they stand heaving, doubled over and short of breath.

"Go get Father," Harry says. "Tell him to bring his tools. I can't fix this fence by piling the boards back together. We need nails. I'll stay here until he comes so the cows don't get out again."

Norah and I gather his school things along with our own and set off at a run. Ours is an awkward gallop. It's not easy to run with petticoats wrapping around your legs. I gather my skirts as a sack and run madly, my pantalettes showing to my waist. Norah looks shocked, but there's no one about for miles, so she follows my lead, gathering her skirts immodestly. Together, we race like cows thrilled by the sight of cut oats. By the time we reach the farm, my lungs burn and my dress is soaked with sweat. My hair has come loose from its braid and blisters form on my ankles.

Norah and I shout for Father, hoping to bring a quick end to the current crisis, even though our existence in Manitoba has been a continual crisis.

—

"Where have you been?" Mary yanks open the cabin door.

"The cows were out. The fence is down," Norah gasps. "Where's Father?"

"He's gone to get the doctor." Mary brushes her palms over her forehead. Her hair is wet along her collar; her face is shining. "Marjory, go get Mrs. McPhaden."

"Mrs. McPhaden? Why?" I sputter, not anxious to pay a call on the McPhadens at this particular moment.

"Because Mother is having the baby and I don't know what to do!" Mary is crying now and Mary never cries.

"The doctor will come. Father will bring him." Norah tries to comfort Mary, but Mary is beyond comforting.

"Father left ages ago. Dr. Kirk probably wasn't in his surgery, so who knows where Father had to go to fetch him. Maybe he is helping some other woman have a baby. I don't know what to do, so run, Marjory! Run! We need help."

I see panic in her eyes. Mary is usually capable but childbirth appears to be beyond her. Then, I hear Mother and I understand why Mary needs reinforcement. A low moan through the cabin wall grows into a wail and then a shriek. It's a terrible sound and the hairs on the back of my neck stand on end as Joss runs out of the cabin, covering his ears.

"Has she made that horrible sound all day?" I whisper, shocked by my mother's agony.

"Yes, you ninny!" Mary snaps. "Now go!"

"Norah, take Joshua to the barn to play with the cats," I order. "I'll ride Wellington bareback."

"You can't ride Wellington," Mary argues. "Father took him to pull the wagon."

"I can't ride Napoleon!"

Wellington is a gentle horse, used to children and well-behaved, but Napoleon is a dark horse, barely broken, cheaply bought this past summer from a homesteader who was selling out and returning to Ontario.

"Then run to the McPhadens!" Mary cries. "I can't leave Mother."

Mary slams the cabin door in our faces as I drop my school things into dirt. I hoist up my skirts again, and set off running, ignoring the squish of blood in my boots.

—

The McPhaden farm lies to the southwest. I shorten the distance by running across a field. After harvest, the wheat stubble was cultivated into deep furrows. Sinking into the soft dirt, I stumble and scrape my hand on a rock. Blood quickly rises to the surface, but I get up and keep running, my lungs burning, chest heaving.

McPhadens' bull is in pasture on the north side of their yard. Mr. McPhaden says the bull is mostly a gentle soul, but the children stay clear. I follow suit and skirt around the fence line, having no desire to encounter any more bovine today. I couldn't outrun the bull on fresh legs and my legs are far from fresh. They're jiggly and painful.

I run across the farmyard and bang the kitchen door as uproariously as a bailiff collecting debts. "Mrs. McPhaden!" I cry. "Mrs. McPhaden!"

I hear a chair scraping and a slow footfall. Mr. McPhaden opens the door and, beyond him, I see the family at dinner, steam rising off serving dishes. The children crane their necks to see who has arrived in such an uncivilized fashion, banging their door over the supper hour. I even see Allan dining at his mother's house.

"Are you all right, dear girl?" Mr. McPhaden stands on the threshold, his shirtsleeves rolled up, his brow furrowed.

"Yes, thank you. I am well. And yourself?" I ramble, then launch into my plea without stopping for breath. "Mother's time has come and Father went for Dr. Kirk ages ago but he hasn't returned so Mary is asking for Mrs. McPhaden to come."

"Your mother's time has come?" Mr. McPhaden squints as if he hadn't noticed Mary Ann Thompson in the family way. Perhaps Mother has been so reclusive that even our closest neighbours are unaware of her condition. It's certainly not something we talk about at church or school.

Emily McPhaden comes to the door, pushing Mr. McPhaden gently off the stoop. "Marjory!" She looks me over from head to toe. "Did you run over the field?"

Mrs. McPhaden is a stout woman, not five feet even with the assistance of tall boots. She has dark brown hair piled on her head in a tight bun. Her apron tucks into a mysterious crevice under her bosom, above her ample stomach. She fills the doorway, widthways, at least.

"Yes, Ma'am," I answer. "Father has the only horse that doesn't buck and I can't even get a bridle over Napoleon without him biting me."

She smiles at that, but only for a moment, then calls over her shoulder, "Myra! Run and get some clean towels and a big sheet to tie them together. Percy! A loaf of fresh bread. Barclay—now here's a good job for you—go hitch a horse to the cart as fast as you can."

Barclay pulls on boots and dashes past me. To his credit, he doesn't smirk at my dirty clothes. He just runs to the barn to do his mother's bidding.

"You're all right?" Mr. McPhaden still has a quizzical look as preparations are made around him.

"Yes, Sir," I say, looking down.

"What about your hand?"

I forgot about my hand in my haste, but I see now blood has mixed with dirt, forming a mucky paste.

Mr. McPhaden leads me to the washstand beside the magnificent woodstove, an Othello Range with an extra-large oven, a six-hole top and a towel rack. It cost $18. We looked it up in the Sears Roebuck catalogue out of curiosity.

Mr. McPhaden pours water out of a beautiful china pitcher I instantly recognize. "That's the same pattern as the one my aunt Bertha has!" I blurt.

"Back in England?"

"Yes, Yorkshire. She has a beautiful home. Lots of nice things. Not like our cabin, you know?"

It's strange that McPhadens have beautiful things and we don't. Yes, they homesteaded long before us, but they are Scottish. In the old country, Scots were deprived and unable to rule themselves. Not as bad as the Irish—they fought with the Boers against England, just to be ignorant—but Scots resent the English. We all know that. But here, in the New World, the McPhadens, Sinclairs, McTavishes, and Campbells are friendly to us. They loan tools, offer advice, lend a hand, and do favours. Even the Reids from Ireland are treated as equals by English people too. It's extraordinary.

Mr. McPhaden smiles as I wash my hands. "Your cabin is all right," he murmurs. "It's serving its purpose. And you're good girls, you are. Not complaining. Looking after your mother."

"Mary does most of it," I say. Later, I will tell Mary I spoke well of her to Allan's father. That ought to be good for some favour, perhaps some assistance getting my school clothes clean before tomorrow morning. I don't know if I'm going to school tomorrow though. Everything seems upended today.

"Are you ready, Marjory?" Mrs. McPhaden appears in the kitchen doorway carrying a bundle of things tied up in a sheet. She pulls a shawl tightly over her wide shoulders. A plain straw-hat perches miraculously on top of her hair bun, perhaps by the assistance of a fearsome hat pin as long as a ruler.

Mrs. McPhaden is a capable woman. Her house is always tidy. Her kitchen is always clean, even now, in the middle of a meal. Her vegetables grow taller than ours and her children make it to school on time, a feat we scarcely ever manage. She sells surplus butter, cream and eggs to the town people, funding luxuries like store-bought dresses for the girls, family portraits at the photography studio, and home furnishings of which we can only dream.

We wait by the kitchen door as Barclay leads the pony and cart from the barn. He holds the reins as we climb up onto the bench. "Drive 'er easy, Ma," he says.

Mrs. McPhaden flicks the lines hard onto the horse's back and the pony breaks into a canter. She shouts more orders over her shoulder as we jolt over the ruts, bouncing against each other, "Begin bread for the morning, Myra! Cream into the icebox please, Lillian. You could start the ironing tonight and tell John to cover the tomatoes. I feel frost!"

"Yes, Mother!" the girls call as we rush down the farm lane, out of earshot.

Mrs. McPhaden seems fearless in comparison to my mother. Mother doesn't drive horses at all, not even Wellington. She's afraid of them, having no acquaintance with them in England. There, she'd either walk to the shops or hire a livery. I suppose our unsightly farm wagon isn't very agile either and the thought of maneuvering it over rough, muddy tracks doesn't appeal. Perhaps one day we'll have an elegant buggy or even a handy cart, but until then, Mother relies on Father for transportation.

"When did your mother start having pains?" Mrs. McPhaden shouts over the clatter of the cart.

"This morning, I think."

"Morning? Oh, dear. How old is your mother?"

"I don't know."

"Think, Marjory. How old was she when she was married, and how old Mary is now?"

I bite my lip and do the sums. "She's probably 41."

"Aye." Mrs. McPhaden nods. "Not so young then."

As we turn north towards our farm, I scan the horizon for any sign of Father, but I only spot Harry, alone on the far side of the pasture, still waiting by the gap in the fence.

—

Father arrived with Dr. Kirk as darkness fell. The doctor strode into the cabin, but Father lingered in the yard. He brushed down McPhadens' pony, helped Harry herd the cows for evening milking and then patched the fence so the cows could be let out for the night. Norah and I did our chores—feeding, forking and sweeping as usual—all the while minding Joss so he didn't get kicked by a cow. After a while, Mary wandered out to the barn but she didn't help. She just lay in a mound of fresh straw and shut her eyes. Her hair had come loose from its bun.

"It's horrible in there," she whispered to Father.

"You're a good girl, Mary," Father whispered back.

"I didn't get the butter churned today."

"It's all right. We'll have cream on our porridge tomorrow."

We finish our chores and huddle together on the straw, eating our suppers with bare hands, like gypsies camping in the woods. We dine simply—the loaf of bread from the McPhadens, a few strips of pork fried much earlier in the day, and some apples still left on the ground under the tree. We are a far cry from the family we were a few years ago in England. Father isn't pale and thin from working in the mill. His face is red and leathery from the summer sun. His arms are muscular and he never seems to tire, no matter how many miles he walks behind a plough. Harry looks like he's always lived outdoors. His hair, nearly always in need of a trim, lightened over the summer. Blonde and stringy, it flops over his eyes as he munches an apple. Norah eats more primly, pulling pieces of pork apart with her fingers, her hair bows still miraculously intact since school.

Immigration seems to have affected Norah the least of all of us. She isn't a stoic martyr like Mary, nor does she run through the pasture whooping for joy as Harry does. She just sings under her breath, as she always has, watching sparrows swoop low over the farmyard. She doesn't panic like Joss every time a new calamity arises. Of course, Joss was only four when we immigrated, so the move upset him—he didn't understand what was happening—but he still whines incessantly and clings to Mary. Father says it's off to school soon for Joss which may upset him further. But Father wishes to relieve Mary and Mother from one small charge, now that another is taking Joss's place.

It is nearly dark when we hear faint cries from the house, from a baby this time, not Mother. We all sigh with relief except for Joss, who has gone to sleep, and Harry, who looks confused. "What in heaven's name is that?" he asks, his eyes wide.

Mary stares at him. "The baby of course. What do you think?"

"What baby?"

Father chortles. "Harry, lad. Did you not notice your mother was getting rather stout 'round the middle?"

"Not really." Harry scratches his head.

Mary rolls her eyes. "What did you think was happening, doctor and all?"

"I thought Mother was dying," Harry whispers, his chin quivering.

"Oh, Harry." Father tousles Harry's hair as he climbs off the ground and brushes straw from his clothes. "I'll go check on your mother."

He strides across the yard with the pride of a new father, but Mrs. McPhaden meets him halfway. "You have a bonny son!" she calls, smiling.

"God be thanked. And how is Mary Ann?"

Mrs. McPhaden turns serious, motioning Father to follow her further down the lane, so we can't hear their conversation. From the light of a lantern hanging on the outside of the barn, I see concern on her face. When Father returns, his face is drawn, sad even. "Mrs. McPhaden will spend the night," he says. "Harry, you'll sleep here in the barn with Joss so the girls can sleep in the attic and Mrs. McPhaden can have their bed. I'll return the doctor to town but I might not be back till after midnight. Be very quiet inside the house. Your mother is feeding Alec, so you'll have to wait to see him in the morning."

"Alec? Is that the baby's name, Father?" I ask.

"Peter Alexander. Alec for short. Not a bad name."

"Not bad at all," Mary says, pushing loose pieces of hair back into her bun.

—

The men leave, Father in the creaky wagon with Dr. Kirk on the bench beside him. I had never seen the doctor up close.

He is Presbyterian and we are Methodist, so we never meet at church. I'm shocked to see how young he is. I thought all doctors were old with whiskers, but he is clean shaved and youthful. I am suddenly embarrassed that he attended to Mother. I wouldn't want him to attend to anything beyond a wart on my hand and even that would embarrass me.

Mary fetches warm nightclothes and blankets for the boys. "What a treat!" she says to crestfallen Harry, who doesn't fancy a cold night in the barn. "You'll get to camp out like real men. Father never lets you sleep in the barn! This is a first." Her pluckiness cheers Harry as he makes a bed beside Joss in the hay. They lie down like two young calves in spring and Mary covers them in our warmest wool blanket.

Norah hesitates to go into the cabin. "Is the mess cleaned up?" she whispers.

"Not at all," Mary says, bluntly. "There's a pile of bloody sheets on the table."

"Maybe we ought to get a pail of water," Norah suggests. "Blood doesn't come out unless you soak it in cold water."

Mary disappears into the cabin again, easing the door shut to keep it from banging. She returns with two washtubs and the soiled sheets. She wears one of Father's clean shirts off the clothesline over a petticoat. "Marjory, get out of your muddy clothes," she says. "My dress is filthy too, so we'll soak them both overnight along with the sheets."

"What will I wear to school tomorrow?" I ask.

"You can wear something of mine. I don't care."

I squint at my sister in the near darkness with astonishment. Suddenly, Mary seems quite grown up. Maybe she's exhausted or perhaps she is mature enough not to bother about clothes and who wears what. Usually, she has fits if I borrow a simple shirtwaist without asking.

I creep into the cabin, ducking behind the curtain that hides us girls' bed and clothes cupboard from the kitchen. I pull off my filthy school clothes and tug on a simple work dress handed down from Mary. I pull the ribbon out of my braid and let my thin, brown hair fall over my shoulders.

Beyond the curtain, the door to Mother's room opens, rubbing the floorboards. "I'll fetch another towel," I hear Mrs. McPhaden say as she retrieves the last of our clean linen hanging over the stove. She mustn't have heard me tiptoe into the cabin, for she keeps talking as if there are no children about: "Mary Ann, you ought to be done. Six children is a grand family. Peter can't complain."

"Don't tell me," Mother says. "But you know what men are like." Her voice sounds weak, strained. "Emily, what I wouldn't give for a cup of tea."

"Kettle's on. Bread and butter too?"

"Thank you. I'm suddenly hungry."

"Aye. After I birthed Percival, my mother fed me mashed potatoes and roast beef."

Mother laughs softly. "I don't remember having such a hard time with the other children."

"You were younger then." Mrs. McPhaden pours boiling water into the teapot.

"It wasn't just that," Mother says, her voice drifting away.

Mrs. McPhaden crosses back to the bedroom. The door frame creaks as she leans against it. "You were scared today, aye?"

"I was," Mother whispers, sniffing.

"'Tis natural. A log cabin six miles out of Oak River, Manitoba. Giving birth with only poor Mary to run for help." Mrs. McPhaden is laughing now. "God knows how any of us have survived out here."

"Poor Mary," Mother chuckles. "She works so hard. I feel guilty. I really do but, Emily, I don't want to be here. Not just today. Any day. I don't want to be so far from a doctor, or a hospital, or a decent school, not that one-room establishment with poor Ethel Sparling doing her best."

"I know, Mary Ann," Mrs. McPhaden soothes.

"I want to be home in England, but Peter..." Mother breaks off. "He's so determined to make this work. And for whom? We'll be cripples before this farm prospers."

"Think of the children. Everything we do is for them—that they can have land. There was never any chance of us owning land in Scotland, nor in England for you, I suppose."

"But we did own land. My family did, at least. And here! The children don't even want this life. Take Mary! She's miserable. She doesn't see young people or take music lessons. She's read all of my books three times. I grew up with balls, tennis courts, museums, castles, libraries, but Mary doesn't know any of that. And Marjory... I don't know what to do about Marjory."

My breath stops.

"What do you mean?" Mrs. McPhaden asks. "Marjory is all right."

"She's a clever girl, yes. But she'll need to go to high school. Maybe even teachers' college. She won't be happy here churning butter and growing green beans."

"I must tell you a funny one about Marjory," Mrs. McPhaden snickers, "and then we'll stop talking and you'll rest. I heard this straight from my Myra and Percy."

"Oh! What did Marjory say now?" Mother asks and I shut my eyes.

Mrs. McPhaden laughs outright. "It seems Barclay, my bonny rascal, gets under her skin by sniffing in her ear. Apparently, she turned around today, grabbed his nose and told him to 'blow your snout, ya snuffly little swine!'"

"I'm so sorry." Mother sounds exasperated. I picture her shaking her head.

"Don't be. I can't tell you how Hugh and I howled with laughter when we heard that. 'The little miss is a mistress of alliteration,' my Hugh said."

Just then, Mary sweeps into the cabin for the last of the laundry and I manage to escape as they help Mother into a fresh nightgown. Red-faced, I slip out to the front yard where Norah bends over a washtub. We're still there, scrubbing laundry, when we hear horse hooves in the darkness. To our surprise, Allan McPhaden trots his mare up the lane.

———

Mary stands in her ragtag outfit, her proper blouse and skirt soaking in the washtub at her feet. Her hair is half in a bun, half tumbled down around her shoulders. She looks exhausted. Yet, as Allan climbs down off his horse, he stares at her as if she's the most beautiful girl in Blanshard Municipality. Neither of them speaks and for a moment, Norah and I don't exist. It's just the two of them, in a dark prairie farmyard, a hundred miles from anywhere.

"Your father stopped on the way back with the doctor," Allan finally says. "Mother needs a few things." He offers a bundle of fresh towels and blankets. Mrs. McPhaden likely ascertained that our supply of clean linens was depleted.

"Of course." Mary stammers, snatching the bundle as if she thought he had some other purpose in visiting at this late hour. "We're very grateful to your mother."

It's odd that Allan has come. Typically, one of the McPhaden girls might run an evening errand because the men are occupied with milking. And on a day with childbirth, it's unusual for a man to call. Childbirth scatters men a considerable distance, I'm told.

"Are you girls laundering? Now?" Allan finally notices Norah and me on our knees at the washbasins.

"Just soaking things." Mary waves a hand over the proceedings as if to dismiss them as perfunctory. "The day's events took a toll on our linens and Marjory landed in mud."

"I did note Miss Marjory's clothes earlier," Allan says with a twinkle in his eye.

I giggle. "I must have been a sight."

"You were a sight, but you were in haste for your mother and that is commendable." Allan grins at me. I can see why Mary's crazy for him. He's as agreeable as his father and handsome as can be. But Allan didn't come tonight to call on Mary. He came to deliver a parcel, and now that he's done so, he seems at a loss.

"I'll bid you goodnight then," he eventually says, mounting his horse. He turns the mare around, walks her two steps towards home, then pulls a rein to face us. "Mary!" Allan calls through the darkness. "Once things quiet down here, would you like to go to a dance at the Hall? There may not be many nice Saturday evenings left."

Norah and I gasp in unison and look up at Mary. She looks like a dishevelled fish wife, but her hair glows in the lantern's light, making her shimmer like a Madonna in a painting. She doesn't smile though, nor even blush. She just stands there.

Allan goes on, as if to convince Mary of the wisdom of the scheme. "I spoke to your father a while ago and he said it would be all right. You know, some night when your mother can spare you."

Mary closes her eyes for a second. Silence stands heavy. Then she blinks hard and says, "That would be nice, thank you," in a level voice.

Allan nods, hiding a grin, then rides off as Norah and I squeal with delight. "Mary! He asked! He asked! He finally asked!"

But to our amazement, Mary doesn't giggle. She doesn't clasp her hands over her mouth and jump as we do. Instead, she bursts into tears. Shoulders shaking, still clenching the bundle Allan delivered, Mary weeps. And I can't understand why.

Part II

When as a youth I waxed more bold,
Time strolled.

Marjory's Story
November 8, 1909
Pinkerton School, Outside of Treherne, Manitoba
Three years later. Marjory is sixteen years old.

I'm nervous. I imagined this moment over and over—on the train, in a cold attic bedroom last night. I had my gestures, my introductions planned beautifully. But now that I'm standing in front of my eight pupils, I suddenly lose confidence. I'm just sixteen. I've completed grade 10 and four weeks of teacher training. That's all. I have a third-class teaching certificate but no experience whatsoever. I only got this post because the teacher was dismissed in the middle of the term. I've been handed an opportunity, as young and inexperienced as I am. This is my chance to make something of myself, to prove myself as a teacher.

Pinkerton School is a decent school at least. It has clapboard siding, a proper foundation, and a cellar, an anomaly for most one-room schools. Light filters into the cellar through tiny windows, illuminating a woodpile. I am responsible for tending the schoolroom stove and the task is simple enough, or so Mr. Carter, the school board trustee, explained very early this morning. "Run enough wood to last a day from the woodpile in the cellar, back up the narrow steps to the wood box by the stove. Make a fire and stoke it well first thing and again at lunch. That will keep everyone warm."

I put on an act of bewilderment, so he carried enough wood to last a few days and lit the fire for me. I'll have to figure out the process eventually, or we'll freeze in our desks.

Three windows, trimmed in emerald green, run up both sides of the schoolhouse. From these windows, I see a swing for the children, a flagpole with the Union Jack, and the outhouse roof. The outhouse was built just over the hill, exasperatingly out-of-sight of the schoolroom windows. I'll never know if a student is using the privy or just stretching their legs.

The schoolroom is small but adequate. Eight children sit at their desks, facing mine, though twelve could be accommodated. They look at me evenly—freshly scrubbed faces peeking out of cotton and gingham. The little ones sit in the front, the bigger ones in the back. There may only be eight pupils, but many grades are represented. The district inspector warned me that children attend school sporadically and their ages and grades won't correspond to educational norms. This is the reality of country schools, he said. Farm work comes first. And then there's foul weather. Few children go to school when the weather is poor. And then there's the extreme cold. One can hardly expect a six-year-old to walk two miles to school when the thermometer rests at minus 35. That wouldn't be safe. And then illness can take hold, to both children and parents. He droned on and on. Immigration, pestilence, poverty, and acts of God—it seemed miraculous that any of the children attend, never mind leave Pinkerton with a proper education.

I promised to keep a watchful eye on potential gaps in their development and the inspector was mollified. He promised to visit shortly but warned the hundred schools under his supervision took him a great many months to inspect, and I shouldn't hope to see him for quite some time. I took comfort in that.

I may only be sixteen, but I have my family's confidence and the Province of Manitoba's, more or less. I don't think there are high expectations for third-class teachers in rural schools, but I've been certified and sent regardless. I have John McPhaden's confidence too, though no one knows about that.

John has always been present. The McPhadens are our closest neighbours and our extended family after Allan and Mary married last summer. But the night before I left for Pinkerton, John stepped over to our farm, asking if he might write me while I was gone. I was surprised. He's five years older than me and there are rumours he is sweet on Maud Glinz, a town girl. But there he was, literally with hat in hand, asking if he might write. I said he could, but I didn't feel excited. I want to leave farm life, go to university one day, see the world. Spending a lifetime churning butter next door to my sister and my mother does not appeal to me. Still, it's just letter writing. No harm in that.

I take a deep breath. "My name is Miss Thompson," I say, writing my name on the chalkboard. I note that chalk is in short supply so I write in small letters. I don't want to supply chalk out of my monthly wage. I have plans for those $50. Perhaps I write my name in too small a letter for I notice a red-headed boy squinting at the board. The boy probably needs glasses and I wonder if an optometrist is anywhere near.

"Now, each of you will introduce yourself." I turn to face the children with what I hope is a welcoming smile. "Names and ages, please. Starting here." I point to a little girl in the front row. She shares the desk with an equally freckled lass with pigtails and a case of the giggles.

"Ena," she whispers, blushing red then giggling as if Ena was the funniest name in the world.

"And how old are you, Ena?" I ask, bending down to her level with my fountain pen poised over my register. The inspector told me to keep a strict attendance record. A little stroke this way, another stroke the other way, tiny circles, black ink, red ink—his elaborate system documents the pupils' attendance at Pinkerton.

Ena cannot answer this question, from shyness or ignorance, I cannot say. Instead, she giggles and blushes until a gangly boy stops scraping his teeth with a toothpick long enough to say, "She's six, Miss."

"And you are?" I ask, straightening up.

"Leonard Stanford. Twelve. Ena's brother," he says easily, resuming his dental exploits, some residue from breakfast no doubt troubling him. He slouches on his bench. His farm boots protrude into the aisle, their tops grazed by pants far too short.

"From now on, Leonard," I say, as sternly as I can, "Ena must answer for herself. Furthermore, your toothpick is out of place in the schoolroom. Kindly place it in your desk until the lunch hour when you will dispose of it."

Leonard looks embarrassed, but he ducks his head and stashes the toothpick in his desk. "Yes, Miss Thompson."

My correction may seem severe, but I will begin as I mean to go on. Shyness, like any impediment, must be overcome and cannot be used as a crutch. Ena will answer for herself, especially to questions as simple as what her age might be. And regarding the toothpick, there is no call for that.

I raise my eyebrows at the next giggly girl in the front row. "Name?"

"Beatrice Chambers. Seven years old," she says proudly. "I'm a year older than Ena."

"So you are." I nod, then move on to a girl with flaming red hair, the kind I've only seen as a wee child on vacation in Scotland with my aunt and uncle. Freckles dot her high cheekbones like stars on a clear night. Her face is thin. Painfully so.

"Mary McLachlan," she says, unsurprisingly with a Scottish brogue. "Gone ten."

I mark her down. Mary sits alone and as there are no other girls similar in age, I let her enjoy the extra space. I'm not sure she'd be amenable to sharing a desk. Scots are a forthright, perhaps even defensive people, or at least they always seem ready to prove themselves and guard their property. I like that in people and I like Mary already.

Twelve-year-old, red-headed Gordon McLachlan, obviously a sibling to Mary, sits in the row behind her, still squinting. I walk to him on the premise of him checking my spelling of "McLachlan," but I actually intend to check his close vision.

Gordon takes the attendance record from me and holds it near his face. I realize the poor boy is nearly blind, for goodness' sake.

"You've got the spelling right," he whispers shyly.

Sharing a bench with Gordon is Archie Carter. He introduces himself with a cheeky grin, his teeth protruding at odd angles. His roughly cut hair flops across his forehead. I pretend not to have already made his acquaintance at the breakfast table as he's the youngest son of the family who boards me. It's an absurd charade. All the students know I'm boarding with the Carters. But I don't want anyone to think I'll treat Archie differently because I board with his family. In fact, I'm less likely to favour Archie based on our domestic proximity.

When I received notice of the family with whom I was to board, I hoped their children would be lively and amusing. But alas, Archie and his siblings are not lively and amusing. They are dull and loud. Mr. and Mrs. Carter are as harried as one might expect from those who have not discovered how to best harness their children's energy. Instead, they plead for their offspring to "Get a move on," and "Hurry along," without much success, as far as I could see. There was an unruly crowd around the breakfast table with Archie crammed between older, thicker farmhands. Archie whined about something—I never determined what—and his pleas were met with a dismissive, "Eat yer por'dge," from his father.

The farmhands stared with frank, open gazes. I am in no danger of unwanted attention, plain and sharp as I am, though pretty Norah would have been another thing. As it is, the boys disappeared for morning milking without even replying to my curt, "How do you do? Fine weather, wouldn't you say?"

I was placed with the Carters, not for the benefit of their farmhands, but because their two older daughters were deemed "good company" for me. So far, I've found them indistinguishable. They set off in gales of giggles by the slightest provocations, and I predict a very long winter, keeping company with them all.

The last student to introduce herself is Eva English, thirteen years old, with curly hair and a beautiful lace shirtwaist. Eva cuts a stylish figure and she speaks well. Something tells me she'll give me trouble. I'm not old enough to be taken seriously.

"Well then," I say, my attendance record concluded, "we'll start with mathematics."

Eva's hand darts up and without waiting for me to call on her she chirps, "Excuse me, Miss, our previous teacher never began with mathematics. She began with grammar, then mathematics and then literature. It broke up our mornings to have mathematics between those more similar topics."

I stare at her as if shocked by her statement. I'm not the least bit shocked. I knew she'd give me trouble. But I'm not going to tolerate it.

"Eva," I say, kindly and firmly. "You will not raise your hand unless you have a question or an answer or the school-house is on fire. You will keep your hand raised until I call on you. You will not speak unless I ask you to. Do you under-stand?"

Eva's eyes quickly fill with tears and I realize she's never had her opinions thus disregarded, her advice cast so roughly aside. But she nods her head so vigorously her curls bounce. A few smirks break out across the classroom and I suspect that Eva has been a teacher's pet. Pretty girls often are, especially if a young man is teaching. It's not a preferment I ever experienced, but my mother jokes about how little French her besotted tutor taught her. Well, I will have no pets. Everyone will have to work equal-ly hard. No favourites. No exceptions.

I begin again, calling out three different page numbers in three different mathematics textbooks only to have every hand in the classroom raised. They all have protests. It seems that even within the same grade, none of the children is in the same place in their textbook. Some grades are only off by a page or two. Others are finishing while a classmate is just beginning. None can jump ahead without me first teaching the material to them. None can lag as they've already worked all the problems and I don't have time to create new ones.

All I can do is have them turn to the next page in their text-books and attempt those problems. I'll have to teach each student individually as there are no universal subjects they all might learn, no overriding themes to discuss. It's as if they are all on their own educational journeys, and I'm trotting alongside to keep their company.

I realize with a heavy heart that this job will be much more complicated than I anticipated in my meagre four weeks of teacher training.

—

"Where are you going?" Archie demands, turning west on the mile road which leads to his family farm.

It's the end of the school day. All the children are anxious to get home and finish chores before supper, so they quickly scatter from the schoolhouse, walking through the sharp north wind that sweeps over brown fields, whistling through patches of bare trees.

I had been pleasantly surprised to see that Pinkerton School was situated in rolling farmland. The countryside was not mountainous, nor even hilly, but rises and falls on the horizon provide some relief to the endless "flat-as-a-pancake" view that characterizes most prairies.

"I'm going to visit Mary and Gordon's parents," I answer, scowling at Archie's quizzical expression. I don't need to report my activities to Archie. It's none of his business where I go or what I do. My only duties to the Carter family are to keep my room in the attic tidy and clean up dishes with the girls after supper. It's a simple bargain and I feel lucky not to be milking cows.

"But, Miss Thompson…" Archie shakes his head.

"Good afternoon, Archie!" I snip. I'm fed up of his nosiness, and he takes the hint, heading home over an open field.

I put Archie out of my mind as I walk with Gordon and Mary. Their farm isn't far away, they assure me. Just a mile to the east. As we walk, the children tell me about their recent immigration, their father's plans to grow wheat, and the productivity of the laying hens. They ask about my family, and I tell them about Oak River, my little brother Alec starting school and Allan and Mary's pretty wedding summer before last.

As we walk up their farm lane, I feel sure the children are mistaken, or are perhaps playing some joke on their new teacher. It looks like they've brought me to a woodlot or a deserted yard. I expect a snug clapboard house, much like the Carter's with its peaked roof and tiny bedrooms over at least three rooms on the main floor. Carter's yard holds an impressive barn, granaries, a smokehouse, summer kitchen and various other sheds and pens. Their garden is large and tidily cleaned up for the long winter.

But the McLachlan farm has none of this. A small shack of timber, nay sticks, covered in mud now dried and roughly painted appears to be the house. Thick piles of sod support the walls like the rock foundation of a medieval castle. The roof is made of wood poles and is covered by thatch, which blows about in the wind. Chunks of sods, here and there, hold the whole thing down.

My childhood farm could not hold a candle to the poverty and squalor before me. I've heard of such dwellings, but I've never seen one. Sod shanties were common twenty years ago, but the house is the last of its kind, sinking and heaving back into the earth from which it came. They say the Ukrainians up north build house like this, but they are poor and unlikely to live like English people. You wouldn't expect it. But the McLachlans are Scottish. They speak our language, more or less. The children dress decently. They are probably Presbyterian and surely toast the King. How can they live like this?

"Father!" Duncan yells, startling me.

"He'll be about," Mary says simply, heading towards the shanty. "Likely in the cowshed."

"Ah! Mary," I say, suddenly quite nervous about what seemed like a good idea only a few minutes ago. "I'm happy to speak to your mother instead."

Mary and Duncan slowly turn to me. Their faces are pinched. They look forlorn.

"Our mother's dead," Duncan says with a quiver in his voice.

"Last winter with a fever," Mary adds, then looks away.

"I'm so sorry." I now regret making this visit, especially without knowing more about the family. But an idea has hatched in my mind and I'm determined to see it through. "I'll speak to your father then," I say, gathering courage.

Duncan nods towards what must be the cowshed. It's as derelict as the shanty and of similar construction. Boards lean against the walls, possibly structural supports, possibly forgotten pieces of firewood. Frayed rope, sooty lanterns, and bits of worn harness hang from hooks. Beyond low double doors, a man milks a cow in the gloom.

I rush forward, glad to find the object of my search. "Mr. McLachlan!" I exclaim, stupidly extending my hand to a man who is busy milking a cow.

Mr. McLachlan winces in my direction. Weathered by the wind and sun, his face is nearly as red as his beard. Deep lines etch away from his eyes, though I speculate he's not even thirty-five years old. He's a handsome man but not with the smoothness of a Sears Roebuck sketch—gentlemen dressed in their finest waistcoats—but with the roughness that comes from hard labour.

He finishes milking the cow in silence, then straightens up. I see he's a huge man, far larger than I realized when I first saw him squatting on a milk stool. He flicks the cow's rump with the back of his hand and she wanders into a pen where several other cows stare at us with large, tired eyes.

"Duncan!" he calls. "Get your clothes changed. Cows to milk."

Duncan runs in the direction of the shanty, leaving me quite alone on the threshold of the cowshed.

Mr. McLachlan wipes his hands on filthy pants and reaches out to shake my hand. "You the new marm?" he asks, without smiling.

"Aye," I answer. "Miss Thompson."

"So, it's your first day, and here you are. What trouble has Duncan made?"

"None whatsoever!" I shake my head. "Both of your children are excellent scholars. They're well-mannered and studious."

"Good." Mr. McLachlan strides to the middle of the cowshed and leans an arm against a pole. I'm not sure the pole is sturdy enough to hold both his weight and the roof, so I hurry to my point.

"I'm very sorry to intrude on milking. I was raised on a farm so I know how important it is to get chores done. But I wanted to speak to you about Duncan's eyesight." Mr. McLachlan squints and I realize with a rush of insight that Duncan's vision problems are probably hereditary.

"Duncan's vision is quite poor," I rattle on. "He has difficulty seeing what I write on the board. He has to hold books very close to his face to make out the letters."

Mr. McLachlan continues staring me down. I wonder if he's noticed how blind his son is.

"I was wondering," I say, gaining courage, "if he might be fitted for spectacles in town. I don't know if there are any spectacles ready-made at the drugstore, but someone might be able to point you in the right direction. Improved vision would make such a difference in his education."

"Is he failing?" Mr. McLachlan demands.

I shake my head. "It's only my first day, but I don't think so." Then, seized by some boldness, I press on with my proposition: "I would like to pay for Duncan's spectacles," I say briskly, "as I care very much that he receives the best possible education and I don't believe he's able to now."

"You've come to tell me Duncan is blind as a bat and you're going to pay to make it right?" Mr. McLachlan demands.

"I wouldn't put it that way." I don't understand his remark. Why isn't he thankful for my help? Doesn't he see Duncan needs help?

"What kind of a father do you think I am? You offering to pay for spectacles like we were living on the street, Salvation Army and the like?"

I don't know what to say. I've never seen such an irrational response. Such ingratitude.

"I'm only trying to help. I wouldn't want you to think of it as a charity. It's just that"—I gesture to the squalor around me with a half-hearted wave—"you might wish for some help."

Mr. McLachlan's face turns very red and I realize I've pushed matters too far. He isn't going to take me up on my offer. He's offended and I've only made things worse. Duncan will wander through childhood with a permanent squint, all because of me.

"I'm sure you mean well, Miss Thompson, but we're fine here," Mr. McLachlan says, gesturing to Duncan who approaches the cowshed wearing work clothes. "Duncan," he calls, "walk the miss out to the road. She's on her way."

Mr. McLachlan turns his back then strides into the pen to pull the next cow into position for milking. Our interview, such as it was, is over.

—

I awake the following day to the sound of voices in the yard. It's still early so I pull the pillow over my head and hope for a rapid diminution of noise.

Last evening wasn't easy. Tidying up after supper turned into a complete scouring of the kitchen. Mrs. Carter hadn't asked me to clean as thoroughly as I did, but her kitchen was filthy and the stove needed blackening. Dishrags hung from nails, dried stiff with whatever fluids they had mopped up. Bread pans hung from nails, bits of baked-on dough still clinging to their sides. I went at the mess from just after six to nearly nine. Soaking, sweeping, and scrubbing, I resurrected the kitchen from a haven for spiders into a hygienic place for cooking. I still had marking and lesson planning, so it was quite late when I fell into my little bed in the attic. And now, I'm woken before the sun is even up.

I pull a blanket around my shoulders and tiptoe across the icy floorboards towards the window, careful not to rouse the Carter girls with whom I share a room. I pull back the lace curtain and rub a spot on the window pane with my elbow. Between condensation, soot from the stove, and Mr. Carter's tobacco smoke, the windows are far from clean in this house.

To my horror, I see Mr. Carter standing with Mr. McLachlan in the garden. I can't understand their conversation, not with the Carter lasses snoring as they are, but I make out the words, "school," "Duncan," and "cheek." My heart sinks.

When I returned last evening, Mrs. Carter stirred a pot of gray stew on the stove with a disapproving scowl set into her jaw. "Archie tells me you were off to McLachlans," she said, her legs firmly planted into bulky work boots. It was then I noticed how badly the stove needed blackening.

"I needed to speak to Mr. McLachlan about getting Duncan spectacles," I replied irritably. Why must I make an account of myself to the Carters? How vexing it is to answer their queries.

Mrs. Carter wiped her nose with her apron (the whole family seems struck with continual sniffles without a single handkerchief between them). "Successful, was it?"

I couldn't tell if she was being sarcastic or not. It's difficult to know with people who don't smile. I wouldn't be beaten though.

"Tolerable," I replied. "He didn't say no, which is halfway to yes."

Mrs. Carter patted her apron back down, then snorted. "We're waiting on you for our supper."

Supper was that grim stew—scarcely any meat, though what bobbed up was grisly and didn't taste like beef. It wasn't thickened properly either—lumps of flour floated—and the chunks of carrots were still wooden in the middle. But I was hungry, so I ate it. Nothing more was said about my visit to McLachlans, and I thought that was the end of it. But now I realize I was mistaken.

I dress quietly, not wishing to wake the Carter girls. I don't want them pressing their noses to the bedroom window, speculating my fate. Besides, if Mr. Carter thinks I ought to be dismissed, the other school board members will have to be consulted. That will take time and that delay will buy me today at least. I'll make a wonderful impression in the classroom so the children will go home singing my praises. I'll be engaging. Colourful. I'll make up stories in history class if I have to. The children will love me. I will not fail. Not on the first day of my first post. Not with Mother counting on my wages so she can buy Christmas presents for my younger siblings, fabric for my dresses, and sugar for baking. Not with John McPhaden writing to me—the latest girl to go away as a school teacher.

I decide to take my lumps early. As soon as Mr. McLachlan leaves and Mr. Carter tramps into the kitchen, I sit and watch the clock for ten minutes. That will be long enough for Mr. and Mrs. Carter to have a conversation. Any longer, and the rest of the family will be up.

After ten minutes, I tiptoe down the stairs and into the kitchen where Mr. Carter sits, coffee and porridge before him. I take a chair and thank Mrs. Carter as she places the same fare in front of me. There's a chip in the coffee cup. The porridge is lumpy, the consistency of wallpaper paste.

"Are you off to school?" Mr. Carter asks after much throat clearing.

"Aye," I answer. "It's early but I have to light the fire and write some equations on the board."

I decide against asking for more chalk. That can wait until tomorrow if I'm still employed.

Mr. Carter nods and swirls the last bit of coffee in his cup. He clears his throat again and I notice the Carters exchange a meaningful glance. The suspense hangs heavy in the air, so I jump in, wishing to conclude this interview as quickly as possible.

"Did Mr. McLachlan call to discuss my visit?" I ask.

Mr. Carter hums and haws but then nods. "There were a few agenda items, but yes, that certainly came up. He said you offered to pay for spectacles for Duncan. I'm sure your heart was in the right place, but he felt the interference uncalled for."

"I did make the offer," I say, remorseful though privately indignant that anyone would take a well-meaning offer so poorly. "I didn't mean to meddle. I wanted to help."

"The McLachlans have had a rather bad time of it," Mr. Carter says. "They came here from who knows where in Scotland, poor as church mice, having bought the farm sight unseen. God knows the house is hardly inhabitable, but some people are unscrupulous. Land agents return to the Old Country with big stories and beautiful brochures. People don't know better. Anyway, when they arrived, they discovered the farm much as you saw it yesterday—falling down. They did their best, but it's hard if you have no capital." Mr. Carter's voice trails away.

"And are too proud to ask for help," Mrs. Carter chimes in.

Mr. Carter shrugs. "They're Scottish," he says as if being Scottish explains all peculiarities of temper or behaviour. "And then Mrs. McLachlan took sick, the poor little thing. It was dreadful. She was laid low on the Atlantic crossing but a fever took hold. By the time the doctor was called, it was too late." Mr. Carter takes the last of his coffee in a swig—head back in a quick jerk—then stares out the dirty kitchen window to the golden light of sunrise. "Poor man," he murmurs.

"And then there was the last schoolteacher," Mrs. Carter says. "The one you've replaced."

Mr. Carter cuts her off with a little wave. "I'm not sure that's relevant."

"I think it is," Mrs. Carter argues. "Had Marjory known yesterday, I doubt we'd be having this conversation today."

Mr. Carter mutters, "I suppose not," then nods at Mrs. Carter. It's now her story to tell though she turns back to the stove to shift around pots.

"Did the previous schoolteacher meddle too?" I ask impatiently, trying to hurry her along.

Mrs. Carter sits down heavily at the end of the table and sighs. "Not meddle. No. It wasn't like that. It was quite different with her." She bites one side of her lip. "You'll recall from your teacher training that teachers aren't to fraternize with gentlemen, not while under contract to the school. I suppose it happens everywhere. Teachers are young and many don't consider teaching a vocation, just an opportunity to meet new people. Many are on the lookout for a young man."

"Mr. McLachlan isn't so young," I say indignantly, to which Mrs. Carter draws herself up.

"He isn't thirty-five! And he's a nice-looking chap, especially when he shaves that mulberry bush of a beard and gets a haircut."

"Anyway," Mr. Carter interrupts, "the schoolmarm felt sorry for them—motherless children and all that—so she'd do a kindness, like teaching Mary how to mend clothes on her lunch break or helping Duncan with his mathematics. After a few months, the children grew quite fond of her."

"Suddenly, we started to see Mr. McLachlan at community things," Mrs. Carter explains. "Hatbox socials. Church dinners. It was good for him and the children to get out and about. He even came to a dance at the schoolhouse once and, to our amazement, he danced a highland fling. Everyone clapped to keep time and the fiddler played like mad. Each round went a wee bit faster and that huge man danced like a fiend! You wouldn't think it by looking at him, but my lands! He can dance. And then he took the schoolteacher's hand and she joined in. Well, all could see they were smitten. So we turned a blind eye. Yes, there were rules, but it was harmless, and everyone felt so badly for McLachlans."

Mrs. Carter stops there and the two of them look pained as if the story would be best remembered from this vantage point. A highland fling. A long look. Many knowing glances.

"But it never stays that way," Mrs. Carter finally says. "That's why there are rules."

"It was my fault, really," Mr. Carter interjects. "Mine and the rest of the school board. We should have warned her not to jeopardize her contract. Should have told her."

"Told her what?" I ask. "Did he propose marriage?"

"Heavens, no," Mr. Carter says. "That would have been easy. Of course, she would have been dismissed, but only pending term end when they would have been married. We would have been very civilized about it."

"What then?" I press, not understanding what they are so hesitant to say.

"You see, he was in no position to take a bride, not with the farm the way it is, a house falling down, chickens on the roof. A year or two and things might improve. Perhaps he could build a house. Get a little more capital in the bank."

I can hear the Carter children rising now, stomps and scrapes on the ceiling above us. The noise seems to prompt Mrs. Carter to finish the tale in a rush of words.

"They were discovered. The two of them," she blurts. "At the schoolhouse on a Saturday evening when they thought no one else would be around."

The truth begins to dawn on me. "In a compromising position?" I whisper.

"Yes," Mrs. Carter says with a disapproving look. "In a compromising position. It was quickly surmised they were well-acquainted with the schoolhouse on a Saturday evening. It may have been their intention to marry in the long run, once they could save some money, but she was packed off the next morning, Sunday and all. There was no choice. The school board couldn't turn a blind eye to those goings-on."

"And Mr. McLachlan?" I ask. "What happened to him?"

"Nothing happened to him," Mr. McLachlan replied. "He wasn't the one employed. He hadn't broken any contracts, though God knows he acted foolishly. He said he intended to marry her, the very next day if it could be arranged, but a telegram had already been sent to her father. She was in disgrace and her father wanted her home. She left and that was that. The whole thing was McLachlan's fault, but I'll not take any criticism for the dismissal either. She should have known better. However…" His voice trails off again. "I think they were both terribly lonely."

"So leave McLachlans be, Marjory," Mrs. Carter says. "You're young and you mean well, but not every problem can be fixed. Not everyone will cheerfully welcome you onto their farm and it's good to remember that."

"I'm sorry," I whisper and the Carters purse their lips. They must feel they've accomplished their mission. I'm warned. Contrite. Shocked by what I've heard. But really, I have so many questions: do Mr. McLachlan and the schoolteacher write each other? Surely someone at the post office would know. Will they get married eventually? Do the children miss her horribly? But these are romantic questions. I might have blundered in my meddling but I'll not be foolish with my inquiring. Real-life doesn't have the resolutions, the pretty conclusions, of an Elinor Glyn novel. Life keeps stumbling forward, people crashing into each other then fading out of each other's lives forever. People stop pining after each other eventually, no matter how sincere their affection was at some point.

"Lest said, soonest mended," Mr. Carter says, slapping the tabletop as he gets up. "The school board need not know about yesterday. It was your first day and you know better now."

"Thank you, Mr. Carter," I say meekly. "You are very kind."

And I might even believe that, perhaps now that I know his sympathies for a poverty-stricken farmer and a lonely, young school teacher.

—

"You'll never get it going like that, Miss," Leonard Stanford says over my shoulder.

I'm trying to light a fire in the schoolhouse stove with little success. As soon as the flame catches the kindling, the stove fills with smoke and the fire burns out. I'm not used to lighting small, potbelly stoves. I can light the big cookstove at home without any problems but the fire never really goes out in that stove. This tiny stove, not big enough to even heat a kettle, must be completely dampened before we leave for the day. The school board is concerned about a chimney fire in the night.

"It needs more air, Miss Thompson. Ventilation."

"Yes, I know," I say, none too patiently. "I've tried fiddling with the dampers but it's still not burning. Where did this stove come from? It must be a hundred years old!"

Leonard doesn't answer. He's too busy coughing from the smoke filling the room.

I slam the stove door and start opening windows. Most of them stick, but I shove them up with all my might. It's well below freezing so the air blowing into the school is bitingly cold. It feels refreshing though. I worked up a sweat fighting with the stove.

"The stove was a donation from the railway," Leonard finally answers.

"A donation!" I sputter.

"Yes. It was the dickens to light every morning at the train station so they gave it to the school and bought a new one."

I shake my head. So typical. Schoolhouses always get the second-hand good, the stuff no one in their right minds would keep in their house or, in this case, their train station.

"Would you like to try, Leonard? You probably have done this before."

"Ma sent me over early this morning to show you how. I'm quite good with this stove," he says proudly.

As Leonard completes an elaborate choreography of adjusting the damper, blowing into the flame, and feeding tiny pieces of kindling, the rest of the students arrive. One at a time, they bang the schoolroom door, hang up their coats and scarves in the small cloakroom, and set their tin lunch pails on a shelf. Mary McLachlan carries her lunch in an old Dixie Queen Plug Cut Smoking Tobacco metal box, its pretty turquoise and crimson design with a beautiful southern belle a bright spot on the shelf of otherwise plain tin pails.

As the students find their seats, they politely say, "Good morning, Miss Thompson," then wait on the cold benches for lessons to begin. Some heat radiates from the stove but it isn't much. I realize that although children hung up their coats, I still wear mine.

"How would we like to keep our coats on for a while?" I ask. "Just until it warms up?"

Grins break across faces. Heads nod wildly.

"Off you go then!" I say, setting off a stampede to the cloak-room.

I catch Mary McLachlan by the arm. "Where's Duncan today?" I ask.

"Father says to apologize for his absence," Mary answers, "but they're off to town. Duncan is to be fitted with spectacles after he broke his old pair last week."

My jaws drops. "So he's always wore glasses?"

"Oh yes, Duncan is blind as a bat, as we all know. Father just had to finish cutting firewood to sell before he had cash for spectacles."

"Even yesterday, you knew Duncan was to get spectacles?"

"We both knew, but you never asked us. You just told Father it needed to happen. And I'm afraid Father doesn't like to be told what to do." Mary looks glum at this, then goes to fetch her well-worn overcoat. It's rust-red wool with frayed elbows. The hem dangles down by her ankles. I wonder if it was her mother's. It doesn't look like her size. But Mary pulls it tightly around her neck and slides in behind her desk, still smiling at me.

I'm suspicious of her speech. Perhaps her father is trying to save face, keep his pride but put me in my place. However,

Duncan is undoubtedly blind, and his father is low on cash. He may well have been saving for the purchase.

The circumstances don't matter though. Duncan will be able to see and that is the most important thing. No harm has been done in the long run. I shake my head at the whole affair and face the classroom.

The schoolroom may be drab with unpainted walls and creaky floorboards. Another layer of soot may coat the windows, thanks to my misadventures with the stove. The school may be cold, isolated, and unimportant in the whole scheme of Canadian education. But a fire is roaring now and Leonard looks as proud as a peacock. My students face me with cheerful expectancy. Their eyes are bright. Their smiles are broad. They want to learn and I am one of the few people standing between them and the monotony of rural life. I can open the doors to worlds I don't even know, to a past and a future I can only imagine. I may be young and don't know much, but I can point them in the right direction. And if I learn as much every day of my teaching career as I did the first day, I'll be all right.

"Good morning," I say. "We have so much work to do. Between now and Christmas, I want you all to complete your current readers, finish three chapters in your mathematics texts and be able to recite every capital city of Europe and the Kings and Queens of England. Everyone will learn ten spelling words a week on a subject of your choice. Fairies! Farming! Frogs! Whatever you want. We have a Christmas pageant to plan with songs and recitations and we need to think about costumes, decorations, music and dancing. There is so much to do; we haven't a minute to lose. My—what a wonderful day we're going to have!"

"Yes, Miss Thompson!"

Marjory's Story
May 10, 1912
Oak River Train Station, Manitoba
Three years later. Marjory is nineteen years old.

"I see the train! I see the train!" Alec shrieks, pointing to puffs of smoke dotting the skyline. Against the horizon, the puffs vary in length and height, some long, some short, all originating from a locomotive that pulls passenger cars across the prairies. The train slows as it approaches town, its brakes squealing in the cold, crisp air.

A recent, late-in-the-season blizzard dumped a fresh layer of snow over the fields. In the morning sun, the glare dazzles us, and we shelter our eyes with gloved hands as we face east, towards the oncoming train.

Alec doesn't know who he cheers for, just that he didn't need to go to school today. None of us went—not me, as I'm between teaching contracts, nor Norah who would love to go to college but works at the drugstore instead, nor Harry who should be studying for his grade 10 exams rather than chasing a grouse along the train tracks. Harry is delighted to be away from school, not like Joss who mourns the loss of a day in class.

Regardless, Father and Mother declared we would all meet the train. Even Mary, Allan and baby Frank attend though, by the look of her, Mary ought to stay at home and put her feet up until her second baby arrives. She leans on Allan's arm and yells at Harry who still chases the grouse. "Leave it, Harry! What are you doing? You'll get your shoes dirty!"

Harry pays no mind until the grouse flies off, leaving him no occupation. He returns to the platform and waits with the rest of us. As I wait, I tidy my handbag and find a postcard sent from

Eva English earlier in the winter. It's a pretty card with gold foil flowers growing out of a basket.

Dear friend, Eva wrote.
Just a few lines to let you know I am living yet. I guess you thought I would not write to you again. We had the threshers for five weeks. What do you think of that? That's pretty good. Mother and I did all the work. We are skating now on the lake. Now you should be here. There is snow on the ground. We are having a fine time.
 My teacher arranges Leonard and I together in everything. I didn't like it. Well, I will have to say goodbye.
Eva English

I smile, picturing Eva and Leonard working together on every subject. Yes, I expect Miss Eva does not enjoy that as Leonard probably works more slowly than her. Their new teacher is likely pairing students to eliminate separate lesson plans. I immediately feel sorry for my replacement. Pinkerton is probably her first post as it was mine. After a couple of years, it was time for me to leave. I learned much, but third-class teachers are treated precisely as they are: third-class. I returned to Teachers' College in Brandon for my second-class teaching certificate this past year. I received the second-highest results in the province for my examinations and have a stack of congratulatory postcards on the top of my wardrobe. Friends from Normal school, former students—everyone reads the Winnipeg Tribune the day the marks are printed. Even John McPhaden wrote me.

I'm staying on the farm for now but I will start teaching in Norquay, Saskatchewan this fall, a location John protested. "You might stay closer to home. Your folks would like that."

"You must be expecting guests," Mr. Glasgow says, appearing from the station as the train conductor blows its warning whistle to any stray animals or farmers crossing the tracks with wagons.

It can be slow going for trains chugging over farmland. Cows wander across the tracks, confused by the rails, dumbstruck by the big, black beast churning out smoke. Most trains have cowcatchers attached to their fronts, long sloping pieces that deflect obstructions, but today's train is still outfitted with a snowplough. It's too early for cows to be in pasture. Snowdrifts are still the prime concern.

"Indeed, we do, Mr. Glasgow," Mother says mysteriously, without any explanation of the contingent of Thompsons currently crowding the train station platform.

"It is our Uncle John and Aunt Bertha from England," Norah says impatiently, ending the suspense for Mr. Glasgow. "They will stay for a week and will sleep at the hotel."

The hotel is a sore point in our household. Father thinks it would be perfectly reasonable to send most of us children to Mary's small house, or Allan's parents' overcrowded house or even the barn to make room for our guests. But Mother is horrified by the thought of guests sleeping on straw mattresses on the floor or even in the bedroom with its rough log walls. And perhaps she's right. Uncle John and Aunt Bertha have a fine house. They're used to staying in beautiful hotels by the sea. They might find our cabin with its bugs and smells primitive. And it is primitive, for goodness' sake. Mother and Father haven't made definite plans to bring Uncle John and Aunt Bertha out to the farm either, instead they'll wait for them to rest. Perhaps after a night or two in the hotel, Father will fetch them in our wagon and Mother will feed them a farm meal.

I suspect Mother has never written home about the log cabin. I can imagine her describing it as a farmhouse whereas shanty might be the more accurate descriptor. We can't hide the secret now and I know Mother feels the shame of it.

The train squeals to a halt and we scan the faces pressed to the windows. Oak River is nearly the end of the line so the train is mostly empty. Every time I came home in the past three years, from the Pinkerton School or Normal School in Brandon, I always had the feeling Oak River was the last stop anyone would wish to make, and whatever lies beyond was probably not worth the effort of seeing. Civilization has spread slowly across the prairies and Oak River sits along the fringes, still a frontier settlement. I imagine my uncle and aunt will feel the same as we did, that windy October day eight years ago when we arrived, Mother with her hatboxes, us children, filthy and exhausted.

"I can't see them!" Mother sighs as a few locals step off the train. Mostly they hurry past, though Mr. Glinz, the local grocer, stops to tip his hat.

"I've had the pleasure of meeting your brother and his wife," he says, presumably returning from a buying trip to Brandon. "They'll be off in a minute. They're gathering their things."

"Oh, thank you!" Mother gushes in relief, turning again to scan the train cars.

At last, the most elegantly dressed passengers ever to grace Oak River step off the train. Aunt Bertha wears a trim grey travelling suit that doesn't drag on the ground nor flow behind her like Mother's dress. The skirt hangs straight down from her hips in a column. The matching jacket is sharply tailored with a wide white collar. Luxurious crimson feathers and a thick black ribbon adorn her wide swooping hat.

"Hello, dear family!" Aunt Bertha cries, waving her tiny beaded handbag in the air, running towards us in high-heeled boots with pointed toes. She is a vision of loveliness and, by comparison, we look like we've lived in a log cabin at the end of the earth for the past decade, which of course, we have.

Mother kisses her and tells her how beautiful she is while we stand dumbfounded. It's been a long time since we've seen our aunt. We're suddenly shy.

"My! How you've all grown," Aunt Bertha exclaims. "Ten years since you left. I can't believe it. John! Look at these children."

Uncle John is more circumspect than Aunt Bertha as he embraces us and shakes Allan's hand. "I'm sure you've heard the news about the Titanic," he sighs, buttoning his overcoat against the cool spring breeze. He looks much older than the day we left England. His hair is almost entirely grey. His shoulders are stooped.

"We have," Father says. "We prayed for your safety on the Virginian."

Uncle John nods. "The Virginian, eastbound to England for our sailing, picked up the Titanic's distress signal. It turned around, but by the time it arrived, the Carpathian had already picked up the lifeboats, and there wasn't a single soul nor bit of wreckage to be seen."

"Dear John," Mother says. "Were you anxious about sailing?"

"Not really. It was an iceberg that took the Titanic. It's probably safer to sail today than it was a month ago. The captains have a mortal fear of icebergs now."

"Our crew were affected. You could tell," Aunt Bertha adds. "Their apprehension was obvious. Lots of scanning the horizon when we sailed through the icebergs."

"But you're here now!" Mother says, lifting the gloom that so quickly settled.

"And look at this town!" Aunt Bertha laughs, glancing over our shoulders at the hodgepodge of buildings that compile Main Street. Other than the hotel, all the buildings are squat and need paint—Youngston's Barber Shop, Hume's Hardware, Glinz's Grocery, Delamater's Massey-Harris dealership. Parker's Bakery loses the battle of aromas to Storey's Livery. Throw in two blacksmiths, a bank, a church, and the grain elevators, and that's all Oak River has to offer. The sidewalks are fashioned of boards, flung haphazardly over the wettest spots. Weathered hitching posts lean in front of shops. A few telephone poles dot the horizon, leading out of town, though not many farms have the telephone installed. Busy at the moment, Oak River will be completely dark and quiet at night, not like Brandon or Winnipeg, which have power-generated lamps and constant streams of traffic.

Mother waves a hand. "It isn't much, is it?"

"Look! I see an automobile!" Aunt Bertha points to Clarence Cleland rattling down North Railway in his horseless carriage. He swerves around potholes much more slowly than the twelve miles-per-hour speed limit set by the Municipal Council. When Clarence's automobile arrived by train from the Winner Auto Company in Cleveland a few years ago, it was accompanied by an instruction book. A chap in town said he had once steered an automobile so he was deemed the local expert. The two of them got right to work and the car was shortly in motion, providing rides to nearly every villager who would dare. The maiden run was not successful though as Clarence forgot how to stop. He rammed a gate and came to rest halfway through a garden shed.

"But the town is exactly as we pictured it!" Aunt Bertha exclaims. "Isn't it, John?"

Uncle John stands firmly on the station platform, taking in the view. "It is picturesque."

"Picturesque?" Mother protests. "In what way?"

"You know—those CPR posters with a few cows, a red barn and tiny village," Aunt Bertha says. "Those villages are so charming."

"Charming?" Now it's Norah's turn to protest. "Do those posters ever show mud? As in swamps of mud marauding as roads?"

"Or women wearing rags, chopping wood beside log cabins?" Mary adds.

"Girls!" Aunt Bertha laughs. "You must show us everything! The farm. The town. The school. Everything!"

Mother and Father exchange glances.

"We'll put you up in the hotel," Father says slowly. "Perhaps tomorrow you might like to come out to the farm."

"The hotel!" Uncle John laughs. "No need for that. We'll sleep anywhere. Don't worry about hotels."

Mother and Father exchange another glance.

"The problem is," Mother says, "that we haven't any place for you to stay."

"Anything will do," Aunt Bertha presses.

"No. Really. We don't have space for you to even lie down on the floor."

Uncle John and Aunt Bertha stop short at this. They look at Mother closely, perhaps to ascertain the truthfulness of her words. Is it possible, I imagine them thinking, the house is so small that one can't lie on the floor? What is this place, this farm where the Thompsons live?

"The hotel it is then!" Aunt Bertha says, perhaps sorry to press a point that causes my parents such obvious discomfort. "But we must go to the farm today. I am beside myself with anticipation!"

"I would lower my expectations significantly," Harry mutters, taking one end of their steamer trunk with Joss at the other. As the boys lug the trunk across the street to the hotel, Aunt Bertha starts divvying out parcels—"Gloves and lace collars for you girls. Suspenders for you Peter. That hatbox is for you, Mary Ann."

Aunt Bertha has always been the most wonderful aunt, but I don't think she'll be able to maintain her enthusiasm for a week. It's going to flag at some point, probably at first sight of our farm.

—

"It's so absolutely wonderful!" Aunt Bertha pronounces.

She was jostled and bumped over six miles of rough country roads. Her hat blew off twice, shedding its colourful feathers. Alec, who suffers from motion sickness, nearly vomited on her. Yet Aunt Bertha is still enthused, circling the farmyard in her tiny boots.

"Look at this barn!" she calls to my uncle who stands in the yard with his arms folded across his chest. He smiles and nods with his lips pursed. "And the pigs!" she cries, hovering over the pen.

Alec gets into the spirit, climbing over the rails to introduce the swine. "This one's the mom and the dad is over there in that pen." He points to a second, rickety pen alongside the barn. "They mated in the winter so she'll have babies soon!"

"Oh!" Aunt Bertha seems startled by this intelligence.

Alec is only seven but he has a clear-headed view of farm life. Details of animal husbandry were mysteries to me at his age, but his upbringing is different than mine. He's seen calves being born. He knows the difference between a boar and a sow. He knows too what purpose pigs have on the farm. They are not playthings like cats or sources of milk like cows. They are meat. Delicious, fatty clumps of meat.

Alec climbs back over the fence. "Would you like to see inside the barn?"

"Of course!" Aunt Bertha says, though her bravery fails her. She holds out an arm to my uncle and together they follow Alec into the gloom. More like a shack than a barn, our barn is low, two short storeys, with a plain, peeked roof, not a fancy hip or arch roof like the ones on the big, red barns in the area. Inside, there's hardly any light, just whatever sunshine floods in once the heavy wooden door has been pushed open on its creaking rollers. Whoever built the barn, way back when the land was first homesteaded, must have assumed prosperity was around the corner and a larger, more elegant structure would be built shortly. Attention to detail was not paid. Gaps between boards admit the winter wind. The foundation is far from level. The door hangs at an odd angle.

Inside, three horse pens line one side of the broad aisle while a larger pen for calving and an area to tie milk cows line the other. The pens are empty as the animals are in small pastures during the day. During the winter, Harry and Father feed the animals from the haystack though the spring grasses will soon be tall enough for the animals to graze in the meadow.

Bits, collars, blinders and reins vie with kerosene lanterns and hammers for rusty nails on which to hang. Nippers and cinchers, hoes and forks, washtub and cream separator—the items piled up on rough shelves and leaning against walls tell the story of our farm. Horses, garden, milk cows and children must all be maintained for the farm to function, the future to be bright.

Aunt Bertha draws a handkerchief to her nose. The ceiling is low. The air is close. Straw and dried manure cake the floor, but she gingerly steps around the piles.

"It's a barn, isn't it?" she laughs then ducks back into the sunshine where we all stand, amused at the tour Alec is leading.

Our sheltie jumps around our guests, despite Mother's admonitions for someone to "calm that animal down." Our aunt is humoured by his antics though.

"Tell me your dog's name," she says, bending down to pet the dog who has rolled onto his back, exposing his underside for a belly scratch, his chin pointed into the sunshine with delight.

Alec happily complies. "He's called King!"

"After our good King George?" Aunt Bertha asks.

"Maybe," Alec says. "Or maybe King Solomon with all the wives. Are those kings related? I forget."

Aunt Bertha thinks this is very funny, though I am less impressed. Who has been teaching Alec his English history or his Bible stories? The depth of his ignorance astounds me, but I suppose he's no worse off than most children in the Bankburn school.

Uncle John stays in the barn a minute longer than Aunt Bertha. "Well, Peter…" I hear him say, though Mother calls me before I hear more.

"Marjory," Mother says with some urgency in her voice. "I don't know if I can manage the dinner. I'm feeling a little drained." Pale as a sheet, she looks worn from all the excitement. She has prepared for this visit for days. A fresh apple pie sits on the shelf in the kitchen. Bread cools on the back of the stove. A roast from last fall's butchering simmers in the oven along with root vegetables from our garden. Perhaps we haven't noticed her fatigue.

"Go rest," I whisper. "Aunt Bertha will be fine. We'll entertain her."

"Bertha," Mother calls. "Why don't we ladies retire to the cabin while the gentlemen inspect the animals? Norah's made us tea."

Aunt Bertha comes along spritely, perhaps relieved to leave the animals and mud. She takes Mother's arm and allows herself to be led to the cabin as if she couldn't find it on her own. At the low doorway, she dips her head to fit her feathered hat under the rough, log frame. Inside, she blinks twice, overwhelmed by darkness as one always is when entering our cabin during the day. As eyes adjust though, one considers that perhaps the cabin isn't so dark after all. Maybe it was the sunshine that was bright.

Aunt Bertha removes her hat, gloves and overcoat and hands them to Norah who lays them gently on Mother's bed. She glances around the cabin, taking in the sheets separating the space into rooms, the cookstove dominating the kitchen, the open shelves holding the last of our winter supplies, the roughhewn table on which Mother's delicate china oddly contrasts, and the sewing machine placed under the lone window for light. Nothing is hidden. The plain bottle of Joy's Improved Extract Rennet for Cheese Making sits alongside the crimson can of Marquis "Good as the Wheat" Spices. Celluloid starch. Watkins cloves. A chipped crock of flour. A small jar of apple sauce, quite brown on the top, possibly rotten.

Aunt Bertha's shoulders drop. Her smile fades. I notice a few flecks of grey in her hair. "Well, Mary Ann," she manages. "You must run a very efficient household to manage in these rustic surroundings."

"Primitive, you mean." Mother gestures to a chair. "Marjory will fetch some slippers so you can get your feet out of those boots."

"Yes, please!" Aunt Bertha laughs, immediately sitting down to free her feet from their pointy-toed boots, the laces unmercifully tight.

"What are those made of?"

"Calf with kangaroo tops. Waterproof, apparently."

"What were they sold as?"

"Bicycle boots. Fit for any kind of weather!"

"I'll never. I'm afraid we're terribly out of fashion here. Though we do receive the Sears Roebuck catalogue, don't we girls?"

"Indeed, we do," Norah chimes, reaching for the catalogue which rests alongside the family Bible. She lays it proudly on the table, perhaps intending to establish our authority on matters of fashion.

"Do they ship to Oak River?" Aunt Bertha leafs through pages of everything from cambric corset covers, to embroidered tablecloths, to the same style of suit she wears but we never buy. Homestead dresses. Dressy frocks. Smart things for women in taffeta, messaline and voile. The 1200-page Sears Roebuck catalogue is a God-send for us. When the catalogue arrives, we take turns, turning the pages gently, worshipping each picture, poring over each item.

"Mostly," Mother says. "I suppose we use it more as an idea book for our sewing. Farm supplies are available in town anyway."

Aunt Bertha flips past the shirtwaists and corsets, jumps over the men's wear, opens the following pages randomly, and jokes, "That's what I should get Norah for Christmas," pointing to the poultry keeper's supplies section. "Or would you prefer the bull ring piercer?"

Norah giggles. "Harry would love any of those things."

Aunt Bertha accepts a cup of tea from Mother, then sips it slowly, looking pensively at us. "What do you girls do for fun?"

We're silent and Mother looks down.

"We don't have the same opportunities here as in England," I finally say. "So, we make our own fun. We skate in winter. We put on plays. We even had a newspaper printed when we were in school. I was the editor and Norah the foreign affairs reporter." Aunt Bertha smiles at that. "There are no concerts of any significance, and even if there were, we probably wouldn't be able to get to Hamiota or even Oak River to attend them. It's a long trek to town, so most of our entertainment happens at the district school."

Aunt Bertha looks into her teacup for a moment. "No libraries either?" We shake our heads. "Dances?"

"Some." We look pointedly at Mother who rolls her eyes.

"I don't like the girls out late at night," she says.

"That's understandable, but could Harry take them?" Aunt Bertha asks.

Mother changes the subject. "Marjory has been in Brandon this past winter, studying for her third-class teaching certificate. She's going up north to teach in Norquay, Saskatchewan this fall, so she'll have lots of opportunities to socialize."

"Second-class," I correct.

"What?"

"I completed my second-class teaching certificate this year."

"Really?" Mother looks astounded.

"Yes, Mother. I did my third-class certificate exam in 1909. How else could I have taught at Pinkerton?"

Mother waves a hand dismissively. "And Norah takes in many events now that she works at the Glinz's Grocery."

"Some events." Norah corrects. "Mother has me come home every Saturday and Sunday so I miss most things. However, Marjory and I are desperate to get to Brandon for Nellie McClung's Mock Parliament."

"Mock Parliament?" Aunt Bertha's brow furrows. "Is McClung a suffragette?"

Norah nods enthusiastically. "She performs the Manitoba Premier in the play and she's against male suffrage as men might wish to leave their rightful place on the farm and gad about, casting votes willy-nilly. The play has rave reviews in Winnipeg and it's coming to Brandon. We're desperate to attend, aren't we, Marjory?"

"Aren't we?" I echo pointedly at Mother. But she is silent now. She looks at the floor again. Perhaps we've gone too far, Norah and I. Maybe we have been a little too honest about our lives. But there's no reason why Norah couldn't stay in town on the weekends and enjoy concerts and church services. She comes home because Mother wants her help. It's unfair to Norah but we don't fight it. We only have one mother, after all.

Aunt Bertha sets her teacup down and smiles at each of us. "What adventures you've had!"

"Adventures?" I sputter. "How so?"

"None of the young ladies I know in England have half your gumption. Even the ones who work in the mills are not as brave. In the few days I've been in Canada, I've noted that young people are very confident. I think that comes from immigration. You've had everything familiar ripped from you, and now that you're in the new world, you realize the endless possibilities ahead of you. Yes, they will take work, but you can do anything. There isn't a strict social order that glares down—'You're kitchen staff. Don't pretend otherwise.' You can study at university. You marry anyone you fancy and no one asks about your family—'Are they an old family? Do they own land?' Everyone owns land here! My—this must be so liberating."

Mother looks proudly at us, but we don't say anything. Norah gets up to pull the roast out of the oven and I stare into my teacup, surveying the last few drops of tea. We are all stupid, provincial, and uneducated. Alec doesn't know Rembrandt from Dickens. I've never played tennis. Norah forks manure.

I'm not sure Aunt Bertha understands.

———

Aunt Bertha is silent as we jostle in the wagon through the twilight. Father drives the team while Norah and I sit with our uncle and aunt in the back. We're bringing our guests to the hotel and Norah to her boarding house. The wind has died down, but the air is getting chilly. Aunt Bertha carries her hat on her lap and wears one of Mother's heavy wool shawls over her head like the Ukrainian women on the trains heading north. She holds the shawl closed with her smooth grey-gloved hands, a half an inch of bare wrist showing between the glove and her sleeve. The fading light shadows her face and she leans towards my uncle who gazes over the farmland with a furrowed brow.

"Extraordinary place," Uncle John says to no one in particular.

"Is it what you expected?" Norah asks.

"I thought it would be more fertile."

"You've come the first week of May," Norah points out, rather obviously.

"True." Uncle John shrugs. "But all those CPR posters..."

"Sheaves of wheat seemed ubiquitous," Aunt Bertha murmurs.

"Harvest is beautiful," I say.

"I'm sure it is." My aunt smiles. "How our boys would enjoy it—adventurous James especially. The equipment. The animals. The wide-open spaces!"

"Harry seems to have taken to farming," Uncle John calls to Father. "I've never seen such energy—milking, shovelling, mucking, chopping. And with zeal! No wonder he tucks away such quantities of food."

Father leans back from the front bench. "Harry will make a good farmer, aye?"

Uncle John nods. "I won't lie, Peter. I'd rather send my boys to you than worry about this talk of war."

"Pssh," Father scoffs. "What talk of war? Only newspapermen talk of war."

"Aye, but politicians do too. We are in a great race with Germany for the largest navy, and trouble in the Balkans fill the newspapers."

"We've always competed for the biggest navy! Do you remember the Spanish Armada from your school books?"

"I do. But we've never cared so much about the trouble in the Balkans or Africa or other places. The world's grown small with all these fast ships and telegraphs, and now the telephone. We can't seem to help sticking our noses into everyone's business."

Father is silent as a flock of geese flies above our heads in a lopsided V formation. Every year, they return from the south, a marvel of migration and memory.

"How beautiful!" Aunt Bertha cries. "Where are they going?"

"Towards a slough with open water, I should think," Father says. "Someplace to spend the night."

"Slough?" Aunt Bertha raises an eyebrow. "What is a slough?"

"Sometimes dug by man," Father explains, "sometimes by God—they're small ponds of runoff on prairie land, usually found in low areas without much drainage."

"Slough," Aunt Bertha tries the word again. "Rhymes with flew?"

"Yes, but illogically spelt o–u–g–h," I say, the schoolteacher rising in me.

"What about you, Marjory?" Aunt Bertha says. "Teaching in Saskatchewan next year. Then what?"

I hesitate. My whole family knows I want to attend university, but money is tight, and I'm not sure if Father has paid off the loan to Uncle John. The last thing we need is Uncle offering more loans we can't pay back.

"I'm not sure. I need to teach for a few years to save money. Norquay is a small town, so I imagine the temptation to spend money will be limited. It will be a good chance for me to improve my education through reading as well."

"All work and no play makes Jack a dull boy," Uncle John teases. "You might get a husband."

"John!" Aunt Bertha flicks a hand at his shoulder.

"A nice boy like Mary's Allan," he presses.

Norah giggles. "On that topic…" I shoot Norah a warning look which is no deterrent whatsoever. "Marjory does entertain a young gentleman and he's certainly like Mary's Allan. Can you guess who?"

I cut Norah off. "Allan's brother John occasionally accompanies me to social events and is kind enough to write me while I'm away. But that's all there is to it. I can't see myself marrying a McPhaden, next door and all that."

I think of the postcard John sent, congratulating me on the results of my examinations. He was charming and his postcards are lovely to receive when far from home.

"Are you the girl that thought you wouldn't pass?" he wrote. *"Did you get very thin worrying before the results came out? You certainly did well. What would you have done had you taken the whole year?*

Norah giggles even more. "Can you imagine Marjory as a farm wife? Stirring a vat of soap with one hand whilst holding a book in the other?"

Aunt Bertha laughs but then turns to Norah. "And for you? A farm boy for you?"

"Indeed not!" Norah tossed her pretty head. "I don't want to work that hard. I'm going to be a famous singer."

Father sighs and I roll my eyes.

"Why not?" Aunt Bertha protests, but she's laughing too.

"Mostly because Norah hasn't any training, connections, or money," I sensibly offer.

Norah giggles. "I can dream, can't I?"

"Of course, you can!" Aunt Bertha says. "Why don't you sing something for us? We'd love to hear you!"

"Unless the night air is injurious to your vocal cords," I say rather sassily.

Norah ignores me and points her face to the last glowing rays of the sunset. "There's a land that is fairer than day," she sings, softly and sweetly, accompanied by bird song. "And by faith we can see it afar. For the Father waits over the way. To prepare us a dwelling place there."

And then we all sing with her. With various ranges and senses of tonality, we sing in the twilight, "In the sweet by and by, we shall meet on that beautiful shore. In the sweet by and by, we shall meet on that beautiful shore."

And so we creep along a dirt road, my English uncle and aunt, tired and dishevelled, we Thompsons, resigned, yet hopeful there might be fairer things in store for us.

—

"Your mother, Marjory. Is she all right?" Uncle John catches me by the arm in the hall.

We've seen my aunt and uncle to their hotel room—a small accommodation with narrow beds, a rough wooden wardrobe, washstand, and threadbare rug. Father waits in the wagon for me. We need to get back to the farm before darkness falls. Days are long in May, but I must not keep him waiting.

I shrug my shoulders.

"Because she's aged twenty years in the past ten," Uncle John presses.

"I don't think it's as bad as that." I pull my shawl tightly around my shoulders, suddenly embarrassed. "She had a hard time when Alec came—you know," I say, unwilling to discuss any more details with an uncle I haven't seen in a decade.

Uncle John strokes his beard and squints, his eyes receding into deep wrinkles. He too looks significantly older than the day we left him on the docks of Liverpool, but I don't mention it.

"But the house," he scoffs. "It's a hovel."

I'm suddenly annoyed at my uncle. "It's not a hovel! It's a well-cared-for log cabin. And maybe if we still weren't paying back debts to you we'd have money to build a better one."

Uncle John looks blankly, and I have a sinking feeling I've missed the mark tremendously. I have a knack for that, as I learned with the disastrous McLachlan affair at Pinkerton.

"Is that what your father told you? That he's repaying loans to me?" Uncle John asks.

I'm ashamed. "Forgive me, Uncle. It's not my place. You were very kind to loan us money."

"Is that what your father has told you?" he demands again, folding his arms over his dusty brown suit.

"No," I say slowly. "I guess I assumed. I heard you talking the Christmas before Father left. He asked for money, and I assumed you gave it to him, and that's why we never seem to have money. We're repaying loans."

"Marjory—dear girl—even if I had loaned your father money, it would be fair of me to expect repayment. But no, I didn't lend him money. In my experience, if a bank won't loan a fellow money, then neither should anyone else. Your father is perpetually out of cash because he began that way—with no serious education or employment prospects. He married your mother without our father's blessing and then jumped from job to job, city to city, continent to continent, always searching for something better. I am not the cause of your poverty. Your father is. And you'd be wise, Marjory, to heed my words: Get a good education and get your siblings through their paces. If they don't attain something, there will be nothing but dusty log cabins in any of your futures."

I stare at him with tears rising in my eyes. I don't cry easily, but I'm shocked by the fervour of his words.

Aunt Bertha opens the hotel room door. "John," she whispers, glancing up and down the deserted corridor, "why have you raised your voice at Marjory?"

We're both silent for a moment, looking at our feet. We've been arguing in the hallway of a public place. This is not the behaviour of civilized people, never mind loving family.

"It's nothing," I say quickly. "I got him started on Whigs."

"Don't do that," Aunt Bertha laughs. "Forgive him, Marjory. It's been a very long day. Your father is waiting, dear. You'd best run along."

Uncle John stands stonily as I bid them a good night. And I wish, for once, I could bite my tongue.

—

"We'll not take no for an answer," Aunt Bertha says.

I'm embarrassed, but I don't know what else to do. I take the envelope of money. I have no idea how much there is, but the envelope is thick and I can't say no.

Aunt Bertha smiles. "It's all right, Marjory. We all need a little help now and again. You. Norah. Joss. You will all need help if you're going to get an education. There's no shame in that. And it's not much money, just enough for your first term of rent or something like that."

As she releases me from her embrace, I walk to my uncle. He stands off to one side of the train station platform, staring over the wide-open fields to the south. He frowns into the sunshine, his bowler hat firmly planted on his head.

"Immigrating soon?" I quip and he laughs.

He shakes his head. "Not many sheep 'round here for wool."

"You could farm!" I joke.

"No, I couldn't. That's the biggest lie the chaps who immigrated believed. They thought farming would be easy, and you have to blame the gentry for that. The English think to own land is to be wealthy. But it isn't true. To own land is to be burdened—to the government who gave the land to settlers to homestead, to your neighbours who are itching to buy your farmland should you sell up, and to your children for whom you homesteaded in the first place." He shakes his head again. "What the chaps back home forgot was England has been homesteaded for a thousand years. The Romans had a go at it long before we Normans washed up. Our family doesn't remember breaking sod or building houses from whatever can be found within a day's walk. We live in a system, a flawed but stable system in England. Civilization has been around long enough that everyone's needs are anticipated. Need a bow tie? There's a shop. Take your pick. Want an education? There's a school in your village. That hasn't happened here. Everything is still in its first draft. Time hasn't sanded off the rough spots."

"Yet," I say simply.

Uncle John smiles. "It never will. Yes, there are cities, big cities even, but this country is so vast. We sailed past the Maritime provinces for two days until we reached Montreal, then we took a train for two more days through Ontario, and they tell me there are three more provinces over there"—he gestures dramatically to the west—"yet to be settled. I can't imagine how Canada can be governed, organized into a common purpose. God help them that try."

"Some find the expanse exhilarating," I suggest.

"Ah!" My uncle nods. "The young. The young find it exhilarating. Us old ones grow tired."

He looks tired too. Tired of the squalor. The mud. The cool breeze. I haven't heard them say anything was picturesque for days. The novelty has passed.

"Thank you for the money," I say simply.

Uncle John looks down and smiles. "I'm sorry for speaking harshly the night we arrived. Perhaps I should have loaned your father money all those years ago. I don't know. I didn't want to make it easy for him. I wanted him to work for what he wanted. He has, but your poor mother suffered instead."

We're silent for a minute and watch Aunt Bertha blow kisses to my family. Neighbours stare curiously at her magnificent hat and elegant suit. Her spirits seem to have rallied now that the visit is at an end. She can return home to her beautiful house, pleasant garden, servants, and children.

"Mother isn't well," I finally say, turning to Uncle John again.

He nods. "She hates it here, doesn't she?"

"Yes. This country brings her none of the joy it brings Father, none of the 'exhilaration.' She's depressed by the mud.

The weeds growing in the middle of the street. The constant battle with insects, disease, and drought. You have to love nature to be a farmer and Mother loves civilization."

"But there are things in town—little things, amateur of course, but things she might enjoy. Maybe some plays or concerts."

I shrug. "It's not an easy drive, six miles on bad roads. And it's hard when one's spirits are low to make the trek in poor weather. It can be dangerous in winter, and then folks are too busy for gatherings and social events in summer. We grew up only knowing the children from school. And Mother, of course, didn't attend school. Barely church."

We glance at Mother. She cries as Aunt Bertha presses an envelope into her hand. Poverty has diminished her resolve to refuse charity. When you're the poorest dressed woman in church, after arriving from England as the most fashionable, you can't say no to money.

"Some people adapt to change, Marjory," Uncle John says. "Your father has. He doesn't try to recreate the old world because what he has here is better. His parents had very little, you know—rented houses, a small salary based on the donations—so this is an improvement. Your mother, however, grew up with much more. I remember the day she left for finishing school. Most young ladies were either not educated or had governesses back then. But your mother insisted on the school and our parents were convinced. Off she went! As grown-up as can be. Long skirts. Hair pinned up. And she excelled—all the ladylike pursuits of sewing, music and art. Poor dear. I bet she's only used her sewing skills since arriving."

"I don't think she ever learned mathematics," I mutter, "never mind the sciences. I haven't heard a word of French ever."

Uncle John chuckles. "It was a fashionable school, meant to prepare young ladies for matrimony to prosperous young gentlemen." He shakes his head. "What a turn-up your father was."

We look down the platform where Father is negotiating a bargain with Mr. Glasgow: when the spring wheat seed arrives on the freight train, will Mr. Glasgow send word immediately

so Father can get a bag before Delamaters and McPhadens snag
it all?

A train whistle interrupts the scene on the platform. It's the
return train to Brandon, rolling in from the northwest, barreling
southward towards civilization, one grimy mile at a time. The
crowd on the platform instinctively turns to the sound. Farmers
with wide hats and nicely trimmed moustaches, housewives with
faded flowers bobbing on their bonnets, a few tradespeople on
supply runs to Brandon—everyone readies themselves to board
the train.

"Hasn't this been wonderful?"

"My, time went by quickly!"

"We sure did enjoy ourselves."

Correct things are said with enthusiasm, but we mostly talk
to fill the time, the minutes that slip by while the train is unloaded and then loaded again. Those that came to bid farewells hang
back along the edges. The others press forward, anxious to climb
into the dark interior of the passenger cars, even though the tiny
windows are covered in soot and the benches are hard and filthy.

At last, the train whistle blows. "All aboard!" comes the cry.
We indulge in one final round of embraces, kisses and loving
words. But really—my uncle and aunt look as if they can't wait
to be gone.

I know we'll never see them again.

I spot Mr. Glasgow driving his plough horse and wagon out of our farmyard. The horse is different than the plough horse that pulled us on our first day in Oak River. Likely bought from some farmer who declared it too old to work, the horse is perfect for Mr. Glasgow's purposes. Pulling slowly, head low, the horse nips at the grass growing along the side of the road. Mr. Glasgow doesn't seem to mind. He lets the horse graze and dawdle along.

Old habits remain with Mr. Glasgow even though times have changed. The telegraph office didn't use to be busy. Not until the recruiting, enlisting, and fighting started in earnest did the telegraph machine clatter regularly. Now, boys leave every week, Harry and John McPhaden among them, and news arrives at the telegraph office every few days. Mr. Glasgow receives these short, fateful messages, then hitches his horse to the wagon and sets off across the prairie to find the farmer whose son will never return. He's lost his jolliness, poor Mr. Glasgow. He rarely smiles. His face is set in a permanent look of sympathy, like an undertaker who dares not be himself, not even on a sunny day when wheat breaks through the fields in a rush of vibrant chartreuse.

"Come, Alec!" I say, pulling his hand.

Alec is eleven, too big to hold his sister's hand, never mind his school teacher's. But hearing my urgency, he doesn't protest. I've been his school teacher for a couple of years. I'm back to help on the farm, my adventures at Pinkerton and Norquay far behind me.

"What is it?" Alec asks as we charge up the road.

"Probably nothing," I say, not wishing to alarm him.

Alec adores his oldest brother Harry. So when Harry announced last summer that he'd enlist after harvest, Alec disappeared to the barn, hiding in the hayloft where he cried out his broken heart.

"Harry, my boy," Mother wept, still homesick in her soul. "You're going back to England!"

Joss rolled his eyes. "Goodness' sake, Mother! He's going to war, not a tea party. He'll likely be shot the first day!" he unhelpfully added.

Father never said anything. He just pulled Harry into an embrace and that was the end of it.

The day Harry boarded the train for Winnipeg was the last day Joss went to school. Harry's farm work had to be done and Joss, at sixteen, found his education complete, his dreams of high school and university quickly fading.

And now, months later, Father grows more worried with each newspaper. Names are listed in long columns—Jacks and Johns, Alfreds and Andrews, Herberts and Henrys. Sons of folks we know. Some are listed in active service, others as missing in action, still others as killed. Father mourns for the parents who have lost sons. They'll never see their boys again, not even their bodies, buried as they are in far-away France. Gas, bullets, shrapnel or some other hideous means have taken those blue-eyed boys, lads who ran through pastures, swatting mosquitoes and chasing cattle beneath the vast Manitoba sky. It could happen to any of us—a telegram delivered, then the mourning without a body, just a piece of paper announcing that a death has occurred. A life has ended.

As schoolteacher, I sympathize with each family who has someone overseas. I worry when siblings miss school for several days, only to return nonchalantly—"Apologies Miss, but we had to help butcher the hogs." Each family has someone. Any of us could get news. Suddenly, the fights we thought we were fighting—farming, educating, civilizing—are irrelevant. The focus of all efforts is a conflict in Europe. Our Manitoba farms are not that important. Our education plans are roughly cast aside. It's as if everything we've worked towards as a community, even as a family, is of little consequence. All that matters is winning a war that has no personal effect. Not really. We can still plant wheat and feed pigs regardless of the size of the Austro-Hungarian Empire, the unification of Prussia, or the division of the Balkans. But the fight has been thrust upon us and we must rise to the call, for England's sake, we say.

"Is that Mr. Glasgow?" Alec asks, shielding his eyes from the late afternoon sun.

"I think so."

"Why would he have been at our farm?"

"I don't know. That's why we're hurrying." I tug his hand.

"A couple of chaps at school said Harry might get killed in the war. Is that true?"

"I wouldn't listen to the chaps at school about anything," I reply sharply. "I correct their history papers and, trust me, their understanding of world events is tentative at best."

"But isn't that what Mr. Glasgow does? Deliver bad news?" Alec presses.

"We shouldn't speculate," I say, my left arm growing tired from carrying my books and lunch pail. I let Alec's hand go and spread my load over both arms. I have much correcting to do tonight. My grade ten class lacks algebra and geometry books, so I must create lessons for them. I try to distract myself by thinking up a word problem as we walk. *If a farmer built a hog pen with four unequal sides*—"Why would he do that?" I can hear one of them ask—*ten feet by twelve feet by six feet, what would be the length of the fourth side? The pen's square footage? The angle of the widest corner?*

"Marjory!" Alec shouts, breaking through my plans for my geometry class. "Look! There's Father by the woodpile."

Beside the barn, Father leans his axe against a stump and stares south across the open farmland. He seems lost to us, a statue—"Man with Ax Considering Fate."

We run to him, calling out, "Father! What's the news? What's happened?"

Father turns slowly. His brow is furrowed. His mouth is pulled. He looks old as if he has seen many things and would like to rest. But he can't. He has to keep working.

"Harry's been gassed," he says simply. "While driving a team with supplies to the front, he was gassed."

"Is he dead?" I blurt.

Father shakes his head. "He's the lucky one."

"What do you mean? Is it John McPhaden?"

Father hands me a telegram. At the top, an image of the globe lies beside the Canadian Pacific logo, "Cable Connections to All Parts of the World." In Mr. Glasgow's shaky script, I read, "James wounded in action. Stop. Died in hospital in Boulogne. Stop. John Beaumont, Huddersfield. Stop."

"Oh, Father!" I cry. "Cousin James is dead?"

Father nods, tears flooding his eyes. He doesn't speak; he just stares over the flat farmland, now vibrant with the new crop.

"He was so young," I whisper. "Oh, poor James. What a horrible war this is!"

Alec tugs my arm. "Who is James?"

I ignore him. "How was he wounded, do you think?"

Father shrugs his shoulders. "It's impossible to tell. The telegram doesn't say and perhaps his parents may never know."

"Was he shot?" Alec asks, unmoved by the death of a cousin he's never met.

"Wounded in action can mean many things," Father says. "Run inside, Alec, and change out of your school clothes. I'll need wood stacked in a minute."

Alec takes my books and lunch pail and hobbles under his load towards the log cabin.

"He only thinks of Harry," I say. "He doesn't know James or the old country."

Father nods. "Maybe that's better. No memories. Nothing to mourn." He continues to lean on his axe handle, looking forlorn. "The papers tell a terrible tale. The losses. Every day so many men are dying and not just Englishmen. Canadians too. By the thousand. It makes me want to go myself. Sort out the high command, if nothing else." Father kicks at a splinter of wood left behind from chopping. "And today, I read the Internment Camp in Brandon is not filled with suspected war criminals or enemy aliens as we were led to believe, but poor Ukrainians. They can't speak English. They've lost their farms and have no possible means to return to fight with the Huns, even if they should wish to. So why intern them when we're so desperate for farm help? Why is this government so intent on misleading?"

I steer Father away from this topic. The unfairness of the internment camp is a favourite frustration, and I'm more worried about Harry than the Ukrainians at the moment.

"How do you know Harry was gassed? Did he write?"

"Aye. Mr. Glasgow brought our mail out with him. Here— read for yourself."

Father pulls a letter from his shirt pocket and I recognize Harry's scrawl. I should. I struggled to decipher it as I helped him study for his grade 10 exams years ago. I take the letter but I don't go inside the cabin. Norah will be cooking supper and she hates cooking. Norah was much happier when she lived in town, working in a shop, but times have changed with the war. It's hard to get farm help, and twenty-three-year-old Norah returned to our tiny log cabin, though she's anything but pleased about it. Last fall, Harry taught her how to drive the grain binder, just in case he'll still be gone by this year's harvest. At the time, it seemed unbelievable that the war would stretch on that long, but now it seems inevitable. Harry wrote to me at Norquay with glee about Norah perched high on the binder, her floppy hat bouncing in the breeze. According to Harry, even the horses could tell she was tense and behaved accordingly.

Joss has also been cross since Harry left. Not being able to finish school upset him badly. He tries to read at night, but there's not enough light in the winter and squinting at the pages just adds to his frustration. The only one unaffected by the war is Alec. He crosses the yard, back to the woodpile, wearing farm clothes and whistling. "Norah says for you to hurry up," he reports.

I ignore him and duck into the lean-to beside the cabin to read Harry's letter.

Dear family, he writes.
I have just a moment. I'm also short of ink which is ironic since my supply wagon likely has a few ink wells tucked somewhere.

Snagging one of those ink wells would be a crime against his Majesty, as they are earmarked for delivery to some beleaguered battalion up the line. Finding lads who need the ink will present problems. Troops get spread out, decimated, and absorbed into other battalions.

We travel in a caravan from headquarters to the trenches. I drive a team that pulls two wagons linked together like railway cars. Despite their big wheels, the wagons are scarcely larger than Red River carts. Sometimes I ride one of the horses. Sometimes I'm behind, shoving with all my might to liberate the wagons from the sea of mud which seems to have overtaken France this spring. I hear the mud can get so bad that shells have to be tied to the backs of mules and walked in on foot.

Once we get close to the trenches, we pack the supplies on our backs and go in at night. The concept is that jerries can't see us, but they light up the night and blow our cover. Boy, do we hit the dirt when the firing starts.

We often can't find the lads we're supposed to supply, at least not on our first attempt. Some helpful sarge will notify us of our error—"We're fine for Bully Beef but could use some ammo pretty quick. And no, the 17th is further up the line. God knows where. Any mail for the 22nd, by the way?"

On one of these close encounters, I experienced Jerry's medicine—gas. I had only heard of it before, and I wasn't wearing my mask. Not sure what kind of gas it was. Jerry likes combinations. I'm all right though. Didn't get it as bad as some of the lads.

Must close. Darkness is falling. We're moving out.

Your loving son and brother,

Harry

P. S. John McPhaden and I have been separated. He's driving teams too, but he's pulling gun wagons into place. Will be at the front lines, I should think.

———

Supper is a solemn affair. Only Alec talks. He chatters about geese returning from the south, whole flocks flying overhead. He doesn't need much encouragement. An absent-minded "Is that right?" or "What do you know?" keeps him going. Alec is a lovely boy, not a smart mouth like Harry or a thinker like Joss. He sees beauty in the farm that perhaps the rest of us struggle to see. Oak River is all he knows. He never saw the pretty, civilized houses in Yorkshire, or the wild coastline, or the S. S. Lake Manitoba. The grand train station in Montreal is just a story to him. He once asked if Heaven was a train station, as our glowing reports of high columns and beautiful windows blended with streets made of gold.

Father tousles Alec's hair occasionally and tells him how clever he is but otherwise eats his meal in silence. It is a glum meal, not helped by the lack of variety that is typical of our diet just before the summer produce comes in. Our supplies are low; the meat from last fall's butchering is nearly gone. We haven't eaten fresh fruit since the oranges at Christmas. But Norah did her best with the evening meal, and we eat biscuits with gravy, beans soaked then boiled, and a pie made with dried apples. The food is bland and unappetizing, but we can't complain. There's plenty of it, and we're not sitting in wet trenches like the soldiers Harry supplies.

"I wonder what they'll do about a funeral," Mother says softly, picking at her plate of food.

"I've read they've started cemeteries in France," Father says. "I expect James will be buried there. And without a body..." his voice trails off.

"What will be the point in having a service in Huddersfield?" Mother finishes his thought.

"I read a fascinating article in the 'Free Press Prairie Farmer,'" Norah says, out of the blue. I expect she's trying to distract us from the gloom which has settled on the supper table. No one inquiries further, but she presses on undaunted. "It was a letter to the Home Loving Hearts column."

"Not another woman, deserted and impoverished because her drunken husband took off to the Klondike," Joss mutters.

"No, indeed." Norah sniffs. "Besides, one wonders how those deserted, impoverished women have the time or where-with-all to write newspaper columns when they are destitute, nibbling crumbs on a dust-heap. Anyway, what I read today was a solid argument for prohibition."

Father's head jerks up. "Let's hope the Premier doesn't read it then."

"If the government is urging 'breadless' days to save wheat, then the use of thousands and thousands of bushels of grain in breweries must cease. It's only logical and inevitable. The federal government will come to its senses at some point, and the country will be better for it."

"How was school today, Marjory?" Mother asks, perhaps trying to deter Norah from the subject of temperance. Norah has many opinions on the matter and even more on women's rights and child labour. None of us feels like listening to her tonight, not even if we agree with her, which I certainly do.

"Tolerable, thank you. The stove gave me trouble," I say pointedly at Father. "It may be late May, but the mornings are quite cool, so it's nice to light a little fire, at least for a cup of tea."

Father is a school board trustee for the Marland School. He pushed to have it built so Alec and the children living close to us wouldn't have to trudge the two and a half miles to Bankburn School. A mere mile and a half from our farm, Marland is a simple, one-room school built in six weeks one summer. The teaching position is far from glamourous, and the pay is minimal. But I can board at home and save money. And Norah and I had plans for that money—big plans. She was going to go to Brandon College and take secretarial studies and maybe even take singing lessons. I was going to go to the University of Manitoba and take my arts degree. But the war has squashed all those plans, at least for now. It costs so much to study and live away from the farm. And now Joss is out of school, and he dreamt of university too. As it is, he'll be lucky ever to finish high school with all the farm work. And if Harry never comes home, Joss can say goodbye to getting off the farm.

"The stove must be treated gently, Marjory," Father says. "You can't be in a hurry with the larger logs, or you'll never get a proper flame. Just a little kindling at a time."

I sigh and Joss smirks. "What do you need a fire for anyway, Marjory?" he pesters. "It's warm by midday. Have the children stamp their feet through their morning lessons, forgo your customary pot of tea, and you can avoid a fire altogether."

Father doesn't look up from his biscuits. "Joss, you might haul a small supply of firewood to the school this evening. I chopped some expressly for that purpose."

It's my turn to smirk at Joss, but he ignores me.

"Were the children attentive today?" Mother asks.

"They were excellent," I say.

"No, they weren't!" Alec protests. "What about the ones you had to thrash?"

"Despite some unruly moments which were quickly contained, the classroom was productive." I glare at Alec. I try to create an image as a calm, sophisticated schoolmistress, even to my parents. Although the school board appreciates that I use the strap without hesitation, they prefer I keep order by inspiring competitiveness and industriousness. Occupied children are far less likely to cause problems than bored, sullen children. But I have found that nothing settles the mind and motivates the scholar like the threat of corporal punishment. And so, I walk the line—creating a sophisticated persona while threatening thrashings.

Mother loses interest in the conversation. She wanders over to the cookstove and adds another log to the fire.

"Is another log necessary?" Father protests. "I'm all but sweating."

"I can't get warm," Mother says simply, moving closer to the stove. Mother is increasingly frail. After Alec's birth, she never regained her health. Her hair is thin and grey. She was always a slim woman, but now her eyes sink into her face. Her skin is paper white though all of us lack colour by spring. Somehow, I've given up hope she'll return to the feisty woman of my childhood. She's become too dependent. Too childlike. And she doesn't have Mary at home to lean on anymore.

"Mary!" I say, suddenly slapping the table. "Has anyone gone over to tell her the news?"

"I did," Joss says. "Before supper."

"How did she take it?"

"Fine. The stove was finicky, so Mary couldn't get the heat up to boil the potatoes. Little Frank and Jack were crying because they were hungry and Baby Roy had a temperature. Allan was milking cows so he was no help. Mary took a little break from the chaos to vomit in the slop bucket. Apparently, she's not feeling so well these days." Joss raises his eyebrows. "So, all things considered, she took the news quite well, though I'm not sure she was listening."

"Did you help her with the stove?" Father asks.

"I tried but you know how Mary is. I wasn't doing it properly, so I left her to her plight and walked home."

Norah bursts out laughing, which Mother reproves. "Norah, you shouldn't laugh at your sister's misfortunes."

"I'm not laughing at her, *per se*," Norah says. "I'm laughing because she thought life with Allan McPhaden would be so much better than life with us."

"I expect it is better," Father says. "There is satisfaction in building your household, even in its trials and difficulties."

"I wouldn't know," Norah says. "I'll be washing dirty laundry for my brothers forever, won't I?"

"And Marjory!" Alec counters. "You wash Marjory's dirty laundry too."

"But Marjory's doesn't stink like yours does," Norah jokes, to which Mother puts a stop to their banter.

"Hush children. That isn't proper. No more foolish talk on a night like this. We must remember our loved ones, far away, suffering so much. After milking tonight, we will pray for a quick end to the war and the safe return of Harry. Then everyone can get on with their lives."

"Absolutely," mutter Joss and Norah in unison.

—

Norah and I lie beside each other in the darkness. I can hear Father snoring through the wall, Mother tossing and turning.

"Are you asleep?" Norah whispers.

"Yes," I answer.

"Mother isn't well. She doesn't eat and she's in pain."

"Pain where?"

"Her stomach. It's why she doesn't eat."

"Does Father know?"

"I expect so, though I couldn't say for sure."

We're silent now, grown sisters still sleeping on a straw mattress as we did as children. I may be twenty-five, but I feel precisely the same age as I felt the night Alec was born, not because I feel like a child now, but because I felt like an adult then. We've had to be responsible, grown-up, to counterbalance Mother's despair.

"Mary knew, didn't she?" Norah whispers.

"Knew what?"

"That Mother was going to get harder and harder to live with."

"Mary loved Allan. She wanted to marry him."

"Yes, but she also knew Allan was her only way out. She was lucky he was good-looking and crazy about her. She jumped at marriage with arms wide open. Of course, her life is more complicated now. Frank. Jack. Baby Roy. And your way out is teaching, Marjory. But what is mine? Will I have to keep house forever?"

I pat Norah's shoulder. "We'll find a way. This war won't last forever. The soldiers will come home, and Harry will start working the farm again. You won't get stuck here. I promise. Once the war is over, I'll look for a better post. One with more money so I can help you go to college."

"Father's drinking too much," Norah whispers. "Mother's never minded a glass of sherry here or there, but it's not that. It's the bottles stashed away. The one behind the stove pipe. The one in the barn rafter."

"There's a bottle in the barn rafter?" I sputter.

"Rye. Alec found it while hunting for kittens."

"I thought we were a temperance family."

"I think that's still the goal," Norah mutters. "But after that incident at the hotel..." Norah's voice trails off.

I know to what she refers. A few years ago, the Oak River hotel caught fire. The wooden buildings that line the main streets of prairie towns have tendencies towards going up in smoke. It's the dry wood coupled with stoves and men smoking pipes and cigars. Father was enjoying a drink on a Saturday evening when the cry went up that the hotel was on fire. A careless guest perhaps had let sparks fly out their stove onto the bedsheets. The men scattered onto the street but realized at the last second that Peter Thompson still snoozed at the long bar in the dining hall. They went back to retrieve him, but his reputation for enjoying a drink was established that day.

"Do you notice Father occasionally plays his violin, but Mother never sings anymore? She used to be known for her singing back in Huddersfield."

I think about that for a second. I hadn't noticed, but I've been gone on and off for the past eight years. Pinkerton, then Brandon for Normal School, then Norquay—one classroom after another has had my attention. I haven't thought much about life at home other than knowing I didn't want to experience it.

We're silent again. The fire crackles in the stove. Wind whistles up on the roof. Joss turns a page at the kitchen table. He's trying to read even though it's late and he should be sleeping. Seeding will start soon, and he and Father will need to put in long hours on the land.

"What was Brandon like?" Norah whispers, referring to the year I spent at Normal School.

I chuckle. "You know what it was like. Living in a boarding house with a dozen other girls, attending classes all day and washing out clothes in the ice-cold water the landlady spared us. That was Brandon."

"You make it sound so glamourous."

"If that sounds glamourous, you need to get out of Oak River. What was life in town like?" I ask, trying to lift her spirits with happy memories from the past.

"Unfortunately, much the same as your life in Brandon, except I didn't sit in a class. I stood behind a counter and measured out pounds of canning sugar."

"You went to dances," I counter.

"Not many. And all the boys are gone to war now. Even if there were dances, Mother wouldn't let me go, not even with Joss. 'Too far, too cold.' You know her lines. She doesn't want us to have any fun. We have to stay at home and milk cows and start tomorrow's bread. Not a great way of meeting men. Do you wish to be married, Marjory?" Norah asks softly. "To John or someone else?"

I'm silent. I don't know the answer to the question.

"Come on," Norah prods. "You must think about it."

"It's like anything. A teaching post. A new school. A marriage. The appeal depends on the details. I would love to take a post with decent wages and a teacherage. I don't want to teach somewhere for next to nothing and have to board in a farmer's kitchen attic. So, yes, if the terms were good, I want to teach. It's the same way with marriage. The terms have to be good."

Norah giggles in the darkness. "You're a sentimental fool, Marjory."

"I'm a realist," I counter. "I'm not a pretty girl. You have no trouble attracting boys like bees to honey, but I'm skinny with a sallow face and flat hair."

"You should try curlers at night."

I sniff.

"But John McPhaden likes you. He always writes to you. You know he's thinking about you from France."

"But I'm not sure I want to marry John. My life will be exactly like Mary's. Lots of babies. Lots of work. I want to go to university and teach in big schools. John might not come home either. I have to remind myself of that. Or he might come home missing a leg or an arm."

Norah is silent now. I roll over, my face mere inches from the thick log wall. I stare at the long splinters in the near darkness.

We Thompsons always seem to be waiting. Waiting for Harry to come home. Waiting for summer. Waiting for prosperity.

Waiting for opportunities. Are we fools or optimists? I don't know. All I know for sure is that I have to be responsible for my siblings' futures. There will never be money to spare from the farm. Every dollar is earmarked for next year's seed, or a new mare, or a new binder. Or for a bottle of rye. If I don't work for my siblings, they won't have the chance to succeed. We'll all be stuck on the farm.

I don't know what our parents thought would happen to us. The farm can't support us all indefinitely, nor can it fund our futures. We're caught in limbo, and the war has only made things worse. Harry is occupied in a foreign struggle. Joss and Norah's educations are on hold. And I just want to sleep in my own bed in my own house, somewhere where the wind doesn't blow between the chinks in the log cabin.

Maybe Mary was the smartest one after all—marry into stability. The McPhadens have warm houses and plenty of farmland. But by Joss's description, she's not having the easiest time of it either. And that's the catch: even an escape can be a challenge. Mary thought marriage was going to be more exciting than it was. I know that, even if she won't admit it. Of course, with her luck, she was expecting baby Frank right after the wedding and was sick as a dog too. Poor Mary.

I shut my eyes and try to fall asleep, but I can't help but think of Harry, running over mud in the dark, trying to find the lads who want ink to write home to their mothers.

—

"Goodness' sake, Allan! Mother will be of no help to you."

I hear Norah snap from the other side of the sheet that separates our sleeping area from the kitchen. It's morning, still early. I wrap a blanket around my shoulders and flick back the curtain to see Norah staring down Allan. He wears his coat collar high around his neck and a cap pulled low. It's a cool morning for May.

"What is it?" I tug the blanket around my neck. The stove died down through the night so the cabin is cold.

"It's Baby Roy," Allan says. "He's been sick, fevered, but he took a turn in the night. He's much worse now. I have to go for the doc."

"Allan wants Mother to go help," Norah says, her hands on her hips.

"Why not?" I ask, confused.

"Do neither of you realize how sick Mother is? She spends her mornings in bed. She'd be hopeless with small children."

Joss stamps into the cabin, banging the door. "Milk to separate," he calls to no one in particular, setting two pails of frothing milk on the kitchen table, then ducking out again.

"I'll go with you, Allan." Norah slams more pots around the stove. "Mother can manage here. Just let me get dressed. Marjory—finish cooking porridge, eh?"

Norah disappears behind the curtain, leaving me standing in my nightclothes with a blanket around my shoulders. I'm embarrassed, but Allan is family, so I suppose it doesn't matter. I shuffle to the stove to stir the pot of porridge Norah started. "What happened?" I ask.

"Mary couldn't get Roy's temperature down. It might be influenza. I don't know." Allan pulls off his cap and runs his hand through his hair. "My mother's helping her, but I need to get the doc, and I've got no one with Frank and Jack."

"Is Mary all right?"

Allan shrugs. "I haven't seen her since I went to get Mother in the night. She's expecting, of course, and I'm worried for her too."

Allan looks exhausted. He probably didn't sleep much, if any, last night. Lines streak back from his darkly shadowed eyes. The stubble on his cheeks is mostly gray. His haggard look is not just the result of a single night's lost sleep; the last ten years have been hard on him too. Small children, endless farm work, many responsibilities and financial strain—the effect is noticeable.

"Mary will be all right," I say, more confidently than I feel. "She's a tough one, that girl." To be fair, I haven't seen Mary much since I returned home to teach at Marland or even since her marriage. She's only a half-mile away, but I was away teaching soon after she was married. And even when I'm home, Mary is always working, always trying to accomplish the next task with a child on her hip and another pulling dishes from a cupboard. She doesn't have any help either. Everyone on both sides of the family is occupied with their own work. Besides, our mothers never had any help when they had young children. Somehow, they managed on their own.

"Father had a letter from John," Allan says.

"Yes?" I ignore the porridge for a moment.

"John's been gassed too. Seems all right, but time will tell."

"I'm so sorry, Allan," I murmur, tears coming to my years.

Allan nods, looking at the floor. "'Tis a dreadful thing, this war. I wish I could be there to help him, you know? He's my brother." He bites his lip.

"But who would see to the milking and the seeding?" I joke, trying to lighten Allan's mood. He's under enough pressure with the sick baby without blaming himself for John's wartime experience.

Norah flicks back the curtain. "I'm ready," she says, grabbing her overcoat from a rough nail peg by the door. "Don't burn the porridge, Marjory. That pot is terrible. And before you leave for school, butter the pans, form the bread, and set it to rise. Mother can cook it. I usually separate the milk in the mornings, but Joss will have to do it. Have him fetch some more wood for the stove. The box is nearly empty. I haven't made your lunches yet, so you'll need to do that too."

"I have to leave in twenty minutes!" I protest.

"You'll have to hustle, won't you?" Norah says unsympathetically as she pulls on boots. "I also forgot to darn dear brother Alec's last pair of decent socks last night, so expect a big scramble about two minutes before you're to leave when Alec discovers he has no socks to wear."

I glare at Norah, and she smiles broadly before following Allan, banging the door. The cabin door doesn't hang well on its hinges. If you push it shut as you might a well-hung door, a narrow shaft of light, a chilly draft and an amateur botanist's collection of bugs appear. The only way to seal the door is to give it a proper slam.

Mother wafts into the kitchen, still dressed in nightclothes. "What is all the commotion? Did I hear Allan?" Mother's frailty is most apparent in the morning. Her hair isn't in a chignon yet. Instead, it droops over her shoulders, giving her a drawn-out appearance. Mostly gray, her hair lacks the lustre of years ago when she'd brush it until it shone like the mane of a thoroughbred on racing day.

"Baby Roy is quite sick."

"I must go help Mary."

"Norah's gone."

Mother nods. "Perhaps that's better. I'm exhausted."

"You need to see a doctor, Mother," I say.

She waves a hand. "Doctors cost so much and those Squibb tablets are doing me good. You know—the ones I take with the fish liver oil."

I nod encouragingly but roll my eyes as soon as Mother drifts back into the bedroom. Mother's fish liver oil isn't doing her one bit of good. She's still weak and pale. Any improvement is just in her head.

I scramble through making sandwiches and getting dressed. I can't be late. It sets a poor example for the children to have their teacher late. I've run the first mile to school many times, walking the last mile to calm my breath before arriving at the schoolhouse.

As I slap butter and pork slices onto bread for sandwiches, tears roll down my cheeks. We seem to flit from one disaster to the next in our household. Mother's health is fading. Something plagues her, and we might as well acknowledge it. Baby Roy is ill, and Mary needs more help than she's getting. Harry and John McPhaden are being gassed, and we've had a cousin killed.

I look up at the ceiling and exhale all the pent-up breath in my lungs. I feel helpless. If this is adult life, I want none of it. I want the simplicity of childhood, the naïve optimism we felt on the ship—on the way to Canada to make our fortune! This isn't a fortune. This is a series of crises, one unfolding right after another. Meanwhile, Father drinks and Mother fades away. Everything depends on us children getting educated and finding good jobs. But we're stuck. Stuck on this miserable farm that was supposed to be the answer to our wildest imaginations.

I think of Uncle Joshua, on the stairs in Uncle John's house at Christmas, all those years ago. "The Thompson name will be spoken with awe and reverence," he had said. "'There be the Thompsons,' people will say as they pass your grand estate."

No one passes our estate except the neighbours, and they only say "There be the Thompsons" with sympathy. There's not much reverence for a dingy log cabin crammed full of Thompsons though there may be a little awe. Uncle Joshua was only talking to make me feel better. I know that now.

My feelings of despair continue throughout the day, only made worse when I arrive home to the news that Baby Roy didn't live to see the doctor. Despite everyone's efforts—the broth, the hot vapour, the poultices—he's with the angels now.

"Your mother isn't going to make it through the night." Dr. Kirk stands by the kitchen table, leaning one hand on the rough surface. His voice takes the same note of personal despair as if he was announcing the impending passing of his own mother. He looks exhausted too. His eyes are deeply shadowed, and his once-straight back is now stooped. Indeed, he is not as young as when he brought Alec into the world. Nearly fifteen, Alec stands alongside the rest of us as we hear the doctor out.

"She suffers from a severe case of influenza. I don't know if this strain is the Spanish Flu which has inflicted such horrors on the world. However, she was weak to begin with, and she has been unable to overcome the fever. Her lungs are infected, and they no longer produce sufficient oxygen. I will be frank—she is quite frail. She has no strength to fight this final battle."

"Is she in any pain?" Mary whispers, her hand against her throat, her face pale.

"No. She'll sleep."

"Should we move her to hospital?" Harry asks. "It seems a shame she should die in this log cabin that she hated so much."

Norah casts him a sharp look. "It couldn't be helped, Harry," she whispers.

Dr. Kirk shakes his head. "No. Moving her would only disrupt her. The roads are rough. It's better to leave her as she is." He goes on, explaining the procedure of dying. It seems simple: keep the patient comfortable. Say anything you wish to say. Read Scripture. Brace yourself for the end.

We listen, nodding our heads, murmuring words of agreement: "Yes. We shall." We have complete confidence in the doctor's ability to predict Mother's passing. Our respect for authority has been so disciplined over the years that we don't question his prognosis. Besides, his words are supported by our observations. Mother hasn't been well for years. We didn't take it seriously until we saw her disappear before our eyes, first her spirit, then her energy, then at last her body, one pound slipping off her until there was nothing left but the fragile frame—skin and bones. Her spirits slumped further when we received word that Uncle John died at Christmas. It wasn't clear in the letter what had taken him. He had been weakened from the Spanish Flu, but I wonder if James' death affected him more than anything. That dreadful war.

"Your father will stay with her through the night," the doctor continues, "but he'll need to be spelled off. Mary," he says, turning to the oldest of us, the leader of the forlorn group of adult children gathered before him, "you might fetch your father a drink. He could use something stout."

Mary rolls her eyes and sighs, clearly repulsed by the suggestion.

"I'll do it," Harry says, fetching a glass off the shelf. "What does it matter, Mary? Father is having a bad time."

"Yes, he is," the doctor says. "And it's going to get worse. Have you employed an undertaker before?"

We collectively shake our heads.

"Just for a baby," Mary answers.

"What's an undertaker?" I hear Alec whisper.

"I will provide the death certificate, and they will prepare the body for burial. I assume there is no family plot in the cemetery?"

Again, we shake our heads then collectively glare at Joss who squishes a spider crawling across the table with his thumb. To be fair, the cabin is infested with bugs.

"We didn't think it would be this soon," Norah whispers.

"I sit on the cemetery committee. I'll arrange it." The doctor nods, pulling on his cap, then taking his leave. Alec enthusiastically hand cranks the Model T Ford for the doctor, then watches it disappear into the night, fascinated by the new-fangled motorcar.

In the cabin, Mary cries. She and Norah both. But I don't have the urge to cry. Instead, I start to feel relief, as if the sun is just beginning to rise after a long night.

Every morning this past winter, as I hurried across frozen ground to school, I would watch the sunrise. Still dark as I left the house, the snow-covered fields would brighten with soft light. As I gathered enough wood for the fire, a pink glow would illuminate the horizon. As the fire warmed the schoolhouse, I would stand on the front step and watch the glow turn into a sliver of orange, then a ball of warmth. The sun was up. The darkness was over. A new day had begun. Peace and strength filled me each morning, and now I have that same feeling. I must get through this trial, this bit of darkness, before the sun can shine again.

Mary fills the kettle from the water pail and adds wood to the stove. "I'll stay the night," she says. "Mother needs her daughters near." Mary looks pointedly at me, but I ignore her. I haven't been home much this summer, and Mary resents this. I'm taking a summer course in Physics at Brandon. If I don't pass, I won't be able to teach all the courses required at my new post in the fall. I must pass, so I waited until today to return home, books under my arm, homework wrapped up in a satchel. Mary can look as pointedly as she likes, but it doesn't change that I have to pass the course to work this fall.

"Why stay, Mary? There's no point," Norah argues. "And there are no beds with Marjory and I at home. You might as well go and come back in the morning."

Mary hesitates, looking over her shoulder at the bedroom door. "I'll go in for a minute," she says, "just to say goodbye." Her voice quivers, and her shoulders shake. But she doesn't walk to the bedroom. She just stands in the middle of the cabin and cries.

Mary has changed since Baby Roy's passing. More children have come to take his place, but Mary's sadness is still present. She was so tough when we were children, but now she seems fragile, as if she, like Mother, has discovered the endlessness of sorrow.

Farm life is hard for everyone, but it's particularly hard for women. Mary might like to get off the farm and visit neighbours occasionally, but she's buried under mountains of laundry, endless cooking for hungry children, sewing and mending the entire household's clothing, and scrubbing dirt and horse manure off of everything. And that's just a normal day. Other days demand much more. If anyone is ill, it's up to the farmwife to figure out a remedy. Sometimes, as in Baby Roy's case, illness progresses too quickly. Other cases, like Mother's, stretch on and on until it's hardly taken seriously.

Harry takes Mary in his arms. His whispers are muffled against her hair: "It isn't your fault, Mary. She was ill. It couldn't be helped."

Harry has changed too; the war transformed his character. He used to be a wise-crack, and though his wit hasn't abated, he's kinder now. It was noticeable from the first moment he set foot on the Oak River train station platform. He didn't run to us, though we ran to him. He just clung to Father. "I thought I'd never see you again," he wept. He was years older, more than the two years he had been away. He had seen boys killed, lads who never saw the guns that fired at them or smelled the gas until it was upon them. He had seen towns pulverized, and he looked at Oak River with new respect. "Golly! What a nice, sleepy little town!" he said, raising his tear-streaked face from Father's shoulder. "Am I glad to be home. I'm fine never to leave the farm again."

He holds Mary now and lets her cry. "It's going to be all right. Mother is going to a far better place."

"I should have known!" Mary sobs. "She was unwell for years, but I didn't make her go to the doctor when something might have been done."

We're quiet at this. Why didn't Mother see a doctor when her health started to fail? Did we think she was only pretending to be ill to get out of work or keep us all at home? She wasn't happy on the farm, that much we knew. But she didn't try to improve her health or make new friends. She just sunk into her mattress, day after day. But influenza… that was hardly her fault.

The kettle whistles. I make tea and then look at the clock. It shows midnight.

"Did anyone milk cows?" I ask.

"I did," Joss says. "Hours ago."

Joss sits quietly in a corner. He hasn't said much. Perhaps he calculates the effect of Mother's impending death on his own prospects. He's twenty now and hasn't finished high school. He'll never return to the Marland Schoolhouse. That much is obvious. The war disrupted his education, and now he is too old to return. I don't think the current teacher, a little slip of a gal from one of the neighbouring farms, would garner much of his respect. He has probably out-read her anyway. No, he plans to attend high school classes in Brandon at the college preparatory program for adults. It will cost more, but Norah is looking for work in Brandon, and they plan to board together to economize. Another year and they might be able to put their plan into action.

He swirls the tea in his cup but doesn't drink it. His long, handsome face is mired with a frown.

"What is it?" I whisper, coming close enough that no one else can hear.

"Mother is dying, for goodness' sake, Marjory," he answers impatiently.

"But it's more than that, isn't it?"

Joss is silent. He rubs a hand over his face and blinks away exhaustion. "I'm drowning here, Marjory. I don't love the farm as Harry and Alec do."

"Yes, but you can go to Brandon and finish school there, Joss. This doesn't need to be the end of the road for you."

"I haven't got the money. Maybe Father can chip something in after harvest, but it will be too late. And now there'll be a funeral to pay for. Father has no cash reserves, and the war threw everything off. Norah didn't work. She was here. Even your teaching was spotty during the war. It was all about saving the farm. And Harry? His war pay was abysmal. So it's not like any of us have money." He casts a guilty look around the room. "But we shouldn't be talking about this, not tonight."

I nod and lean against the sewing machine case. I don't like the despair in his voice. I've noted it, time and again, one schoolhouse after another. Some boys want to farm, and that's fine. Wonderful even. But others want to get off the farm as quickly as they can. The dirt, manure, and monotony offend them. They want to learn more than their fathers know. They want to push themselves and accomplish things, things they only read about in the few well-worn books that topple over on slanted schoolhouse shelves. After delays and stumbling blocks, they work harder than anyone else. They're thrilled to prove themselves. Those that don't make it off the farm, remaining behind despite their dearest wishes to depart, often grow bitter. Dreams crushed—cows to milk.

"Joss," I say slowly. "I've got a good contract for teaching this fall, that is, if I can pass this Physics course. The pay is much better than at my last post. I can save thirty to forty percent of my paycheck if I live frugally. That should be enough for your first-year tuition. And then we can keep going like that. You work for your room and board, and I'll pay the tuition. It will take me a year to get the money saved, but we should be up and running after that."

Joss takes my hand. "That's hardly fair to you."

"You can pay me back when you're through and making good money."

"I have no idea how long that will be."

"I know. But we have to help each other."

Joss nods as Mary slips out of our parents' bedroom. She bites her lip, then simply says, "Our mother is gone."

The cabin becomes still as we absorb her words. There are tears—downcast eyes. My siblings mourn and I hear Father sobbing. But all I feel is relief and then guilt—the two mix in a thick sorrow in the pit of my stomach.

—

"For we brought nothing into this world, and it is certain we can carry nothing out."

The familiar words sweep over us as we stand around the gravesite in the middle of an otherwise green meadow. The headstones of the early settlers line up in long rows around us. Some family names are familiar to me; I can picture their descendants. Other folks seem to have immigrated only to die on the prairies with no kin to remember them.

We stand tall, the men in their Sunday suits, Norah and I in borrowed black dresses. Mother's passing came as such a surprise we didn't have time to order something suitable. Mary had her own black dress, but the McPhaden girls loaned Norah and me their funeral dresses—simple frocks with plain hats to match. These dresses are shorter than what Norah and I typically wear, but styles are changing. Plain black silk, with a drop waist and a bit of lace embellishment, my dress scarcely grazes my knee. I was offered the veil that matches, but that seemed a bit much in the July heat. Besides, Mary is the only one who needs a veil's privacy. She sobs while Norah and I stand with dry eyes.

Neighbours surround Mother's casket, farmers who set aside a morning's work, put on their best clothes, hitched a team or cranked a Model T, and then drove miles to be with us. It's a good morning for cutting hay too, not a cloud in the sky and a slight breeze. Alfalfa would dry in a hurry. And harvest plans must soon be made. Workers from the east will arrive by train, and the Henry Brothers will hire a crew to work the steam-powered equipment.

John McPhaden stands across the grave, holding his hat. He wears the same brown suit he wore before the war, but it hangs off his frame, mocking the shape he used to be. I can tell he's looking at me, but I ignore his gaze. He's not so young anymore, 32, and he's not the same as before the war. He's still sweet, thoughtful. But he was gassed many times and shot at Passchendaele.

It's a strange story, unbelievable even. John was driving a four-horse team, pulling a gun wagon into position. He must have got too close to German lines because he saw a Jerry aim at him. John got down between the horses for protection, but the bullet went through the horses and lodged behind his right ear. He was shuttled from field hospital to field hospital after that. Amazingly, he survived. And when he stepped off the train at Oak River, he blinked into the sunshine as if he'd never seen the bright, prairie sky before.

Everything changed between us after that. John came home subdued, glad to farm the land on which he grew up. But I was still wild to get away. Perhaps if I had fought in France, I would feel the same as Harry and John. They never want to leave. They just want peace and quiet. They were good, sheltered boys, and they saw so much carnage. They have been to the other side, a place where bodies were ripped open, and men were sent over the top, again and again, with very little progress to show for it. John came home wounded, but I am still whole. Nothing more is ever going to grow up between us now. I ignore the pointed words, the hints, from our connected clan, that perhaps I've let John down, that he sacrificed so much, and I don't think he's good enough for me. I ignore it all because it's not true. I don't think I'm too good for him, just ill-suited. Ignoring the relatives is the only way to break free from their opinions.

Beyond John, our neighbours crowd in meandering rows, skirting around headstones and gopher holes. These farmers paused their labours to remember their neighbour—the first glamourous and then reclusive Mrs. Thompson.

"I remember when your mother first arrived," Mrs. McPhaden said at the start, pressing my hands in hers. "She was such a slight thing, and she could see how much work was ahead of her. But she still took the good china out to serve me tea, bless her." Another neighbour told me she envied Mother's beautiful hats in church and her lovely English accent. "I didn't realize how ill she was by the end," yet another said.

Perhaps none of us knew what little time she had, a mere 16 years after immigration. Besides, it never took—immigration. Mother never rallied beyond the initial disappointment. Her heart was always a long way away. I wonder if she would have wished to be buried in England, beside her parents in the

Yorkshire hills. It isn't possible, but I still wonder if she would have wished it.

"Ashes to ashes. Dust to dust." The minister's final words are our signal.

We take turns, starting with Mary, down to Alec, placing flowers on mother's plain pine casket, the one marked in the undertaker's display window as "Solid Value for Money." The flowers are from Mary's garden or Mrs. McPhaden's; I don't know which. Allan cut them this morning as we were getting dressed. Our flower garden is in shambles. We've always kept a vegetable garden, but the flower garden got away from Mother years ago, and Norah and I haven't had time this summer to weed it. So we use flowers from other gardens. Like the funeral dresses, the flowers symbolize our family's collective failure to plan for the inevitable, to see what was so clearly under our noses.

Neighbours line up now, one after another, to press Father's hand and tell him how sorry they are. They promise to stop by some evening once the haying is through for a wee chat. They say they'll never forget Mother. They are kind people, our neighbours, and Father accepts their wishes with gratitude.

I don't want to hear them though. They don't understand. They think the farm was a comfort to Mother. They assume Mother loved her home as much as they love theirs, for they are proud of their farms with the red barns whose roofs peak over the tops of orderly shelterbelts. They rest on their front porches with satisfaction at nightfall—a hard day's work done. They don't realize Mother was mad with loneliness and pain. They don't realize she wasn't at community events because she was busy pickling beets, but because she was curled up in bed, staring at the wall. Or if they realize this, they spare us our blushes.

But Father smiles and agrees with everything. He seems happy to accept the alternative view of the facts, for perhaps this is the view he wishes were true. He doesn't mind pretending here at Mother's grave that she was his rock, and he'll be lost without her. It is a fantasy in which he's pleased to indulge.

Harry and Joss walk away, weaving between the headstones of the early settlers. Perhaps they too wish to avoid the neighbours and their misunderstood impressions. They turn their backs to the gathering and pull the odd weed missed by the careful hand of the cemetery caretaker. I walk with them, running my fingers over the tops of headstones.

"Do you remember the ship?" I ask, out of the blue.

"From England?" Harry squints into the sunshine.

"Yes. When we came with Mother as children."

"I was too young," Joss says. "I don't remember anything except how long the bell tolled when we pulled into the harbour. Why?"

"I wonder if Mother ever was excited about the journey. Was there ever a moment when she thought moving to Canada was a good idea?"

My brothers are silent. Joss pulls a sow thistle and then a red root pigweed. Harry stares out across a wheat field starting to head out. "I dunno," he finally says. "I remember her telling another woman on the boat that Father had a large herd of cattle, and she dreading the bother of hiring household help."

We snicker at this.

"I don't think Father embellished the truth that much in letters," Joss says.

"No. I don't think so either," Harry says. "That was all Mother. She wanted to be gentry, to own land and be a mistress. That's why she agreed to emigrate. She just didn't anticipate being a servant to the land, a labourer, howbeit a landowning one. Creating an image of wealth and prosperity had always been necessary for her happiness, her pride. You know the Beaumonts, always mindful of their history. Mother started to collapse when she realized she couldn't hide in Manitoba, couldn't pretend. The neighbours knew we lived in a log cabin. They knew how many arable acres we had. And they certainly knew how many cows we owned because they helped herd them back into pasture innumerable times. Mother couldn't have any pride, not here. Everyone knew too much."

"And since she couldn't compete with the McPhadens, Sinclairs, and Sparlings, she didn't bother leaving the house?" I offer. "She was beaten and she didn't like it. Do you think that's what it was?"

Harry shrugs. "That and being ill."

"True," I whisper. "It's hard to remember she really was ill. I feel awful it took her death for me to believe that."

The neighbours are leaving now. The minister too. It's just us Thompsons lingering. Joss, Harry and I walk back to the gravesite, still open, the flowers wilting in the mid-morning sun.

"What happens now?" Alec asks, gesturing to the dirt pile beside Mother's casket.

"The undertaker's boy comes at noon," Father answers.

"Would we save a little if we shovel ourselves?" Harry asks, practically.

"Harry!" Mary snaps. "Don't be so tight with money." She signals to Allan and the children who lay flowers at Baby Roy's grave. It's time to leave.

"It's all right, Mary," Father says wistfully. "Harry will make a good farmer. Frugal. It's that Yorkshire blood in him." Father laughs a little then smooths down his elaborate moustache as he always does when he's about to make a speech. "I remember the first time I laid eyes on your mother. My father was a circuit preacher for the Methodists so we travelled a lot. All over England. We had a meeting in Huddersfield, that great town of mills and merchants. Father preached on the evils of loving money, gathering to oneself treasures on earth, and amassing fortunes that don't benefit those less fortunate in faraway lands. He was earnest, fiery even. And all those long-faced Yorkshire mill owners never batted an eye. The louder my father railed, the less interested they were. Then, at the end of the service, your grandfather, George Beaumont, shook my father's hand and said, 'You did us all a great service by warning us of the temptation of money. We had gathered quite an offering for you at the start of the service, but we've heeded your words and we're sending it off to the foreign mission instead. We'd hate to tempt you.' Well, you should have seen my father's face. He still got his offering, but your grandfather Beaumont wasn't letting him off lightly. Those Yorkshiremen had a hard time parting with their money in the first place."

"And Mother? Was she at the meeting?" Norah asks.

"Aye. She was. She was a beauty, that girl. She stood in the back row of the sopranos, being tall, and she sang like an angel. I decided, right then and there, I was staying in Huddersfield. And I did. I got a job at the post office and I did everything I could to impress your mother."

"What did you do, Father?" I ask.

"Oh, foolish things, I suppose. Huddersfield was known for its 'Sings,' grand choral affairs where hundreds of people would gather to sing. Your mother always had a beautiful voice. That's where Norah gets hers. I would play my violin and try and catch her eye. Picture your mother. Up on stage, blending beautifully with all the others. Not giving us musicians the time of day. I would seek her out after the singing, over the tea-table. I'd try to be funny and she'd laugh at all my jokes. After a bit, her family got wise to me, and her brothers would wander by and stand guard."

We laugh a little at this, picturing a young Uncle John with a frown on his face.

"But we were quicker than them. We worked out a system, places to meet, locations they wouldn't think of, like the choir robe cupboard or the music stand closet. Then, after we talked for a while, Mary Ann would run home and pretend she'd been there for ages when the boys finally came home, distressed they'd lost track of their sister."

"You were devious." Norah laughs.

Father nods. "But I loved her. And my poor Mary Ann. She gave up so much for me."

Father stares across the headstones then taps his leg as if he's remembered something. "I must write Bertha. Poor dear, I must tell her about your mother." He shakes his head sadly. "I hope your uncle John did not judge me too harshly after they visited and saw how ill your mother was."

"Come, Father," Mary says, taking his arm and leading him towards the waiting horse and wagon. "Don't think about the past or Uncle John. He's gone too. What does it matter? Your family is here. So let's go home."

Father doesn't resist. He wants to leave, I can tell. He probably needs a drink and none of us wants to be here when the undertaker's boy comes 'round to cover our mother in the Manitoba dirt she so loathed.

——

Lunch is a simple affair, provided by the ever-helpful Emily McPhaden. We pick away at the roast beef slices and fresh bread. There are crisp, sweet carrots pulled from the garden and an apple pie waiting on the stovetop.

We eat in silence. Much was said this morning, and we are all content to enjoy the meal quietly. We eat enthusiastically, perhaps surprised at our appetites, though breakfast was ages ago and no one felt like eating then. But now the worst is behind us. The service is done. Mother's body is buried. We can get on with things.

When Norah slices the pie, Father pushes back his chair and disappears into the bedroom. He returns with a handful of things, some of which I've never seen before.

"Mary," he says, "you must have Mother's sewing machine. You hauled it across the ocean, and it's yours now. Harry, the chest of silverware is yours though please don't sell it as it's the only set we have."

Harry laughs. "I won't, Father."

"Norah, Mother's china will go to you. Joss, you can have Mother's wedding ring, perhaps to give to some young lady in the future. Alec, this Bible was given to your mother and me when we were married. You'll keep it for us." Father pushes the large family Bible across the table to him. On the top lies a small blue book, Mother's birthday book where all the family birthdates were recorded. "Also, you're the youngest, Alec. You'll live the longest so you'll be the keeper of this family's history."

Alec nods, tears in his eyes, the responsibility weighty on his mind.

"And Marjory," Father turns to me. "My smart, witty girl. I have a special treasure for you."

He opens a purple velvet case which I've never seen before. Inside lies a necklace of interlinking, carved silver in a bed of purple silk.

"Father!" I gasp. "Where did it come from?"

"Beaumonts," Father says simply. "Your mother's parents gave it to her, and now I give it to you. This is my thanks, Marjory. I know your plans to help Joss and Norah with their tuition. You are taking on what your mother and I should have done but couldn't. I owe you a debt. This won't cover what I owe, but it shows my heart is in the right place."

"And what about the silver tea set?" Mary asks, referring to an outrageously ornate wedding present of my parents.

"I don't know." Father waves a hand. "We still use it, so let's not get carried away."

Joss snickers at this, and Mary casts him a dark look.

"Do as you wish with her clothing," Father says. "Take what can be used and then donate the rest to missions. Someone will make use of her things."

I think of Mother's collection of marvellous hats. Twenty years out of date, those hats belong in a museum. No one will wear them now, but perhaps Mary's girls will enjoy playing dress-up with them.

"Children," Father says, using a word we no longer feel applies, though perhaps comforts him to use. "It's not been easy for us, these sixteen years. Cows to milk. Pigs to butcher. Crops to plant and harvest. I thought homesteading would be easier. But I believe we're at the brink of something better. Joss and Norah will continue their education; Norah in business, Joss in science. Mary and Allan will raise their healthy brood, building on the prosperity and success of the McPhadens that came before them. Harry and Alec will work this farm and perhaps have families of their own. And Marjory—heaven help the scholar that doesn't mind his Ps and Qs because Marjory will be the best schoolteacher they've ever had. I'm so proud of you all. I ought to tell you more often."

Father has always had the gift of the gab, sometimes more readily with a drink in his hand. But he speaks from the heart, on the most trying day—the day of his wife's funeral.

—

"It's John." Joss pulls back the curtain at the sound of a door knock. "He'll have come for you, Marjory."

I glance at Norah, but she shrugs her shoulders. "Go," she says. "Mary and I will tidy up the dishes."

I get up slowly, not entirely ready to face John, but he stands in the yard, still in his suit from the funeral. I can't avoid him, so I walk out into the yard to meet him.

"I'm sorry to interrupt your lunch," John says, "but I wanted to see how you are."

"Very kind of you," I murmur, walking past him to the woodpile, under the shade of a poplar tree. "Your family has done so much. We're so grateful."

John sits beside me in full view of the kitchen window. I imagine Norah and Mary casting glances. They might be curious, but they're not gleeful or even hopeful. We are not the three giddy girls we were fifteen years ago when Allan came calling on Mary. We're not idealistic anymore. The tragedies of life have chipped away on our optimism, our naïve belief that marriage to the neighbour boy will make all our dreams come true.

John takes off his hat and runs his hands through his hair. As he squints into the sunshine, little streaks of untanned skin disappear into wrinkles. Then he leans his elbows on his knees and sighs.

"What is it, John?" I say, willing him to begin whatever he's come to say.

"I dunno," he whispers, flinging his hands open in frustration. "You're determined to leave again, aren't you?"

"Do you mean my teaching position at La Riviere?" I ask, slightly aggrieved.

John nods glumly.

"Of course. I have to work. There's nothing for me here on the farm."

"Nothing for you at all?" John asks, touching the scar on his neck, perhaps subconsciously.

I let silence hang in the air before I whisper, "John, this has nothing to do with you or the War. Yes, you left for years. And yes, you were injured. But all of that is irrelevant. Can't you see that? You were always going to farm a half-mile to the south, alongside my father and brothers. And I never wanted to be Mary! I want to go to university and help Norah and Joss go too. And I can't do that if I stay here."

John turns to face me. "But that's why I'm so fond of you, Marjory. You are the bravest girl around. You were such a little thing when you got your first teaching job—just sixteen—and I thought you'd get teaching out of your system. All the boarding and cold, drafty schoolhouses. I figured you'd be happy to chuck it all after a year or two. But then you just kept going. More studies. More contracts...one after another. Pinkerton. Norquay. Now La Riviere. No matter where you were called, you packed your bags and hitched a ride to the train station. And that was it. We wouldn't see you for another year. You were fearless. And I kept hoping each time that would be it. That you'd come home."

I stare at him. This could be the longest speech he's ever made.

He takes my hand. "Would it help if I asked you to stay?"

I freeze. I shouldn't be surprised, but I am. "No, John. No, it wouldn't help," I say, pulling back my hand. I feel panic now, something I felt every day during the war. It became a reflex whenever I'm trapped, whenever someone makes decisions for me. "I don't want to be here," I say. "That's always been the problem. I don't want a second-class teaching certificate to be the pinnacle of my achievements. I don't want to 'chuck it all,' as you say. It's been too much work, too much fight, to quit now. I don't want to stay in Oak River."

"And I don't want to leave," John says sadly. "Before the War, maybe I might have considered trailing behind you. But not now. Every night, in the middle of the mud and death and all the mangled bodies—men and horses both—I prayed that if

God would let me survive, I'd be happy with the simplest things. Just to grow grain. Raise animals. Nothing more. I'd be happy. And I wanted to do it with you, Marjory. I pictured it all. The vision kept me alive, you see, all those wretched months I lay in the hospital."

I feel his frustration, but I also see he imagined a fantasy. If he truly knew me, he would know I would go mad on this little patch of farmland. I would be stuck as my mother was, deposited at the far end of the earth on a wild whim of my Father. She had no means or even will to leave, and I would be precisely the same. Always working. Never enjoying a moment's reprieve with a book or even a weekend trip to Brandon. The sheer desperation would slowly drive me mad. John is grateful to be home, but I am not, and we shall always be at cross purposes. We'll never get beyond this.

"I'm so sorry, John," I whisper. "I'm so terribly, terribly sorry. But it would never work between us. One of us will always be unhappy!"

I'm crying now. It's all too much. Mother's gone—dead, along with her unfulfilled dreams. The finality of her passing unsettles me as much as the uncertainty of my future. And I've disappointed John, who is such a good man, patient, and understanding. For better or worse, I'm breaking ties with home. I can't come back now with John just a half-mile up the road. I'll always be avoiding him. Everyone will be disappointed in me, and I'm angry at myself too. I should have told John years ago to marry some sweet young thing, someone who could have loved him for who he was. But I was too weak. Too cowardly. I liked his attention. The thrill of getting a postcard in the mail. The respect from walking into a dance on the arm of a prosperous farmer. I should have been stronger. I can see that now.

John stands now and runs his hands over the sides of his head as if to calm himself. "No, Marjory, I'm the one who should apologize. I shouldn't have come today. I guess I wanted to know where we stood, that's all. If there was any chance."

"Oh, John!" I whisper. "Please don't leave like this."

He turns for a second, perhaps to comfort me or tell me one last thing. But he must think better of it, for he shakes his head and walks away. And for the briefest moment, I wonder if I've made the worst blunder of my life.

Part III

When I became a full grown man,
Time ran.

The first week of July catches Manitoba at its best. The grass hasn't turned to brown crunch, though it will. Rains have been plentiful so the canola is tall, crazy tall. Dad shakes his head. "All stock, no pod." But he always complains. That's what farmers do.

Gardens are bountiful. My mother's dark loam has rows of beans, peas, carrots, early potatoes, cucumbers, strawberries, raspberries, and saskatoon berries. The colours are bright. The crunch of freshly picked produce is unmistakable. Metal pails are stacked up by the back door, each filled with the wealth of the garden. Every day is a picking day; something always needs attention. We complete the same rituals our mothers, grandmothers, and great-grandmothers did before us: pick produce, wash it in ice-cold well water, contemplate what can be eaten fresh, what should be preserved. These rituals fill the days.

The summers skies have been kind this year, not like some years when visits home to Manitoba require continual hauling of pots and patio furniture into the garage, covering of delicate plants, or numerous refreshes of the Environment Canada website to monitor the latest storm. Tornadoes. Hail storms. Wind sheers. The prairies can be violent, cruel even. Trees that took decades to grow big enough to block wind and snow are obliterated in a single storm, their backs broken, their trunks destined for the woodstove.

But this summer has been gentle, peaceful, and I feel the ease of it as I drive to my grandparents' for a visit after lunch.

During my childhood summers, my sisters and I would spend many afternoons on Grandma and Grandpa's farm, helping them in their garden. It was always a beautiful yard. My great-grandparents won awards for it. They cared for it at the expense of nearly all else. If you wanted to find them, you could come to the farm. They'd feed you well and possibly put you to work, but they certainly weren't leaving their oasis. My grandparents are much the same, though it's hard for them to leave now, Grandpa with his blindness, Grandma with her feet.

I open the screen door, and Sasha barks from under the kitchen table. I shush her, willing her to be quiet. But Sasha is not easily put off and continues to bark as if volume will make up for any real effort. Neither of my grandparents is at their customary place in the kitchen. I tiptoe through the living room and find Grandpa sound asleep on the couch. Fox News is set many decibels above the aural needs of the average viewer. Sasha's barking fails to impact the overall din of breathless news coverage—Grandpa breathes softly and consistently through the cacophony—so I leave him be and look for Grandma.

I follow the noise of a second television in their bedroom, turned to CNN for variation, perhaps even for balance against political bias. Grandma sits in a baby blue easy chair manufactured in the '80s, loved ever since. She's slumped, her chin in her fist, elbow on the worn chair arm. Sasha follows me, still barking, but Grandma never even flinches. She must be exhausted.

I back away to the kitchen, where I contemplate how to spend the next thirty minutes until my grandparents return to consciousness.

One unique feature of an old family farm is the endlessness of its cubby holes and storage spaces. For example, Marjory and Raleigh's house from town was moved to the farm when they passed away. Demolished now, I remember playing in its upstairs as a small child. I discovered Marjory's china dishes in a cupboard, plain navy blue with gold trim. When I was to be married, I asked for those dishes. Now they lay in my china cabinet, as they once lay in hers.

There are other spots where I might find remnants of Marjory—another old house, now a storage shed. The big red barn rumoured to house rats. The log cabin in the garden.

The log cabin was built in the '50s to showcase family antiques, including things brought from Northern Ireland in the 1870s—a stove, several curio cupboards, and a beautiful Victorian settee, a gramophone, a stuffed baby alligator, a stereoscope with photographs of places long since lost to time, pots, pans, sleds, skates, pipes and paperwork. I pull the key from its customary hiding place and head across the garden.

The log cabin sinks on its foundation. Built of chinked logs and roofed in cedar shakes, the cabin is covered in moss, camouflaged into nature from which it was hewn. I unlock the deadbolt then duck under the low threshold. Inside, the open rafters give plenty of headspace. Lace-covered windows let in a bit of light, and as my eyes adjust to the darkness, I see the log cabin is mostly empty. The heavy woodstove will remain forever and rusted cast-iron pots rest upon it as if waiting for time to reverse so they might be usable again.

Beside the stove lies an old, wooden trunk, dragged into the middle of the room, as if someone meant to deal with it but ran out of time and energy. Its wood has weathered to a dull gray. Its mechanisms—straps and hinges—are stiff and cracked. I sit on the concrete floor and open its lid, leaning it against the stove for support lest its weight pulls the hinges loose.

A black garbage bag filled with newspapers lies at the top of the trunk. I slide the papers out gently, hoping for an announcement of the end of World War II or even the local newspaper celebrating Marjory's retirement. But instead, I find a Winnipeg Free Press from July 30, 1981. Charles and Diana kiss from a balcony. A second paper, the Winnipeg Sun, features the same story, howbeit with a different picture—the happy couple marching out of St. Paul's.

I sigh. Of all things to save, the newspaper coverage of Charles and Diana's wedding has to be the most unnecessary. It was probably the most documented event from the last century, just behind D-Day. There's no end of memorabilia from that ill-fated union, filling the shelves of used book stores worldwide.

Under the newspapers lie more interesting items—old school textbooks, monochromatic volumes, slim and easy to fit in one hand. I open the cover of "The Teaching of Mathematics" by J. W. A. Young and am rewarded with "Marjory Thompson" written prettily on the flyleaf. There are notebooks. A slim volume titled "Marjory Thompson, Spring Session, 1917 Normal School Winnipeg. Sewing Models" has little slips of fabric, hand-sewn with mostly even stitches. A photograph of a school teacher, nine pupils and a one-room schoolhouse is tucked into a cupboard folio. The photo was overexposed, so the faces are lost, but it's most likely an image of Marjory, kept as it was with her books.

A large book lies at the bottom of the trunk. A bouquet of irises grows over its front cover, embossed and foiled. Each page has tiny slits cut for holding postcards, vertically or horizontally, according to the card. The postcard designs are unique—sketches of flowers, early photographs of towns and scenes across Canada, cartoons, or even cartoons. Organized by date, the postcards are each addressed to Marjory.

Norah jauntily wrote in 1909, "How are you, Kid? Are your students any good at all?"

In 1911, a Miss Carter wrote, "The new teacher is coming a week from today. Her name is Jeannie Doffin. I do not know if that is how to spell it. I must go and preserve some blueberries as Mother says I have spent long enough writing letters."

"Not much new. Dreadfully cold. We miss you greatly," wrote Marjory's mother in 1915.

One after another, postcards give up secrets while others beg questions. Who was the John who signed his cards "with fondness?" Why did Norah thank Marjory for money but said she wasn't telling their mother about it? Why were the parents headed to town, the fateful day Harry froze his toe while driving the horses and had to be hospitalized for an amputation?

I'm mesmerized by the postcards, lost in Marjory's world of the early 1900s. Their language is mostly the same as ours, perhaps a little more formal, a little less familiar, but their concerns are the same. Weather. Money. Work. Communication. Someone anxious to hear from someone else. Others too busy to write. These people were the same as us. They just lived a hundred years ago. That is all.

"Amy!"

I jump at Grandma's voice. I have no idea how long I've sat on the log cabin floor, reading postcards. But I gather up my finds and stomp my feet until feeling returns in my legs. Locking the log cabin, I return to the house, marvelling at what can be forgotten in an old trunk.

—

"I wasn't asleep!" Grandma says, leaning on the screen door's knob as I return to the house.

"No?" I query, amused.

"Even if I was, the dog would have woken me if you had come into the house."

"The dog did bark for quite some time," I counter as I slip past Grandma into the kitchen, still carrying my load of treasures.

Grandma scowls at me. "You couldn't have come in. Sasha wouldn't have let you."

I jerk my chin at the kitchen table. "There's my purse. I stuck my head in the bedroom and said hello, but you were out cold, watching CNN."

Grandma rolls her eyes. "Must have dozed off for a minute. I'm in awful pain this afternoon. My pills make me drowsy."

"What's bothering you?" I ask. "Hip, back, leg?"

"It's this stupid stenosis or sciatica. I can't even keep it straight." She waves a hand as if her pain is too annoying to be granted an audience in our conversation. Who wants to hear about pain? What could be more boring?—she seems to say with her gestures. She's dismissive of her suffering, perhaps even to her detriment.

"What have you got there?" she asks.

I set the postcard album and the school books onto the table, shoving my purse to one side. "Went treasure hunting in the log cabin," I say.

Grandma lowers herself slowly onto a kitchen chair. "What are these?"

"I found these things in a trunk, middle of the room. They're a bit damp but otherwise remarkably well-kept."

Grandma lights a cigarette then sorts through the textbooks. "Old," she says then purses her lips. She opens their covers and spies Marjory's name. "There might be a few things of Marjory's in a trunk, now that I stop to think about it."

"I made it through to the bottom. Found this." I slide the postcard album over to her.

Grandma nods, still puffing on her cigarette. "It was a thing, back then, postcard writing. People would write little bits of nothing, just for fun."

"Like a text message."

"Yes, but with fewer abbreviations." Grandma gestures to her smartphone lying on the kitchen table, a few crumbs from breakfast scattered on its screen. "I can't get that thing to work at all."

"What do you mean?" I say.

Grandma Barb, at eighty-five, is a trooper for even trying a smartphone, but the complexities of technology were never her forte. She once famously took a picture of her own right eye in an attempt to photograph Grandpa for his gun owner's license application. We never let her live that one down. She is firmly in the analog age, even though she occasionally attempts a task from the digital age. Trimming the gargantuan thumbnail on her right hand might make texting easier, but she refuses. The thumbnail is useful for all sorts of things apparently.

"Nothing comes in. Nothing goes out," Grandma cryptically explains.

I hit the phone's on-button and immediately spot the problem. "It's set to airplane mode," I say, flicking the menu to turn the setting off.

"Now, who would have done that?" Grandma demands. "I certainly didn't!"

"Things happen. Settings get bumped," I say, thinking of her meandering thumbnail.

"It's a stupid phone," Grandma says, butting out her cigarette, grabbing a bottle of Tylenol off the cupboard. She swallows a few pills with a swish of lukewarm water left in a tumbler from lunchtime. I can't imagine how many pills she downs in a day.

Grandpa appears now from the living room, his short grey hair standing upright at the back of his head. He looks confused by my presence.

"Amy's here, George," Grandma says. "She's going to go on the deck with you and have a ginger ale."

This is news to me. I don't even like ginger ale, but Grandma must want to be alone, a sign of her pain. Grandpa heads to the fridge and retrieves two ginger ales cans. He fetches glasses and nods at me. It's my cue. I've been dismissed. I leave Grandma with her Tylenol and follow Grandpa outside. We'll have a confused, meandering conversation. But that's okay. It's where he's at now. Besides, Grandma looks like she needs the break.

Betty's Story
December 13, 1968
Pilot Mound, Manitoba
Betty is nine years old.

"I don't like school," I mumble, my mouth full of a ham sandwich.

"Don't you, Betty?" Grandma Marjory asks, nudging a little dish of dill pickles in my direction. I like pickles—sweet, crisp, zippy baby dills—but these thinly sliced pickles are limp and grey. I'll try to remember to ask Mom if I can bring a jar of our good pickles from the farm.

"No, thanks," I say cheerily. "Pickles aren't my favourite food."

"What is your favourite food?" Grandma asks.

"Lots of things," I say, taking another bite out of my sandwich. Pudding. Chocolate cake. Shortbread. French fries that my mom makes on Saturday nights. Lots of things. Food makes life enjoyable, that and summer, but food is a year-round treat. Speculating what might be for supper or guessing what my other grandma might have baked are daydreams that get me through school.

"And why don't you like school?" Grandma asks, brushing a tiny piece of fine white hair back into her hair bun. My other grandma keeps her hair short and curled like Betty White on television, but Grandma Marjory keeps a schoolmarm look even though she's retired.

"I dunno," I say, reaching for another sandwich. "I guess the boys are annoying."

Grandpa Raleigh smirks at that. He hasn't said much from his side of the table. Instead, he brushes crumbs with a chubby, red hand and burps softly, his ugly brown pants pulled up high over his tummy. His hair doesn't look combed, and his red eyes squint and water over bags of bulging fat. Coarse stubble sprouts erratically over his cheeks, and he chews more loudly than my mom would have permitted.

"What do they do to annoy you, Betty?' Grandma asks, reaching a shaky hand to serve herself a grey, limp pickle.

"They're loud and stupid. Unbelievably stupid," I answer.

Grandma nods sagely. "Boys at your age are often rambunctious. Their energy must be turned to productive ends lest they resort to mischief."

"They're not very bright either," I say, swallowing down a gulp of milk. It tastes a little off, but I don't say anything. I don't want to insult her, and she probably only buys it for me.

"Developmentally, boys mature later than girls, which is why their intelligence does not seem on par with the girls you know. It's a false equivalency, though," Grandma says, her voice trailing off as if she suddenly remembered she isn't lecturing newly certified teachers, but rather is sitting in her meagre kitchen with her husband and granddaughter.

I nod encouragingly, in case she wants to say more, but she doesn't. She just picks up her sandwich and bites a small half-moon shape, scarcely bigger than half the emerald green marble my brother John cherishes.

Grandpa Raleigh clears his throat. He rarely speaks when I visit, but he does now in a low, muffled slur. "Your grandmother kept the boys in her classes going straight. She spared no punishment on those poor chappies."

Grandma stares at him evenly, perhaps determining if he teases or taunts her. She purses her lips and doesn't answer.

"Gee, these sandwiches are tasty," I say, mostly to diffuse the situation lest harsh words are spoken. My grandparents never actually fight on my visits; in fact, they rarely talk to each other. They just tolerate the other's presence like I tolerate my brothers, knowing I can't get rid of them and might as well make the best of it.

Grandma continues to stare, but I realize she's not staring at Grandpa Raleigh at all, rather at a spot somewhere over his shoulder. "What was that boy's name?" she asks, biting her lip.

"What boy?" Grandpa says.

"You know the one," Grandma says, still staring. "The one to whom you made me apologize."

Grandpa wheezes as his belly shakes. Then his wheeze turns into an outright laugh. "Ivor Benson!" he shouts as if the name was gurgling in his stomach along with a chewed-up ham sandwich, waiting to explode out his mouth.

"Yes. Ivor Benson," Grandma repeats softly. "You're right. That was his name, wasn't it? Poor Ivor."

"Why poor Ivor?" I say, suddenly curious. "Did he not have much money or something?"

"No, no. It wasn't that." Grandma shakes her head slowly. She looks at the pickles for a moment, then breathes in sharply through her nose as if she's been called back to the present. "What time do you have to be back at school, dear?"

"Same as always." I shrug.

"And when is that?" she says with a furrowed brow.

"I go back for 1:00," I say and Grandma whispers "1:00" as if she might forget it if she doesn't remind herself.

Mom says Grandma's memory is not what it used to be. I noticed Grandma forgot to put napkins on the table. She's usually so organized, nothing out of place or haphazard, but she seems especially frail today. Her hands are more white than usual. It's December so everyone lost their summer suntans ages ago, but even so, Grandma is pale by comparison.

"I told that boy off in my class off today," I offer by way of explanation for my earlier statement that boys are annoying.

"Whatever for?" Grandma is suddenly interested.

"He called me fat and I called him stupid," I say matter-of-factly.

"He was ignorant, it's true," Grandma says, looking beside her plate for her napkin. "But you might have had a sharper retort if you had considered your words more carefully."

I hop off my little stool and go to the cupboard where the napkins are kept. I fetch three ivory ones and divvy them out.

"Like what, Grandma?" I ask curiously. "What should I have said?"

"Oh, I'm sure I don't know," Grandma laughs, embarrassed. "How about, 'I might not always be stout, but you might always be inconsiderate.'"

I contemplate this for a moment, then hop back up on my stool. "I don't think he'd know what inconsiderate is, Grandma. Or stout."

Grandpa Raleigh wipes his hands on the napkin I gave him. "A sharp retort has always been your forte. Hasn't it, Marjory?"

Grandma changes the subject. "Would you ask your father to come to see us? There are some little jobs I'd like done."

Grandpa Raleigh is suddenly alert. "What jobs?" he snaps.

"Just little things that are hard for us. The kitchen sink is leaking. The back step isn't level and I'm worried I'll slip."

Grandpa scowls at her. "We don't need George," he says, looking cross.

Bringing my dad into things is a sore point between them. I know that. My dad doesn't have anything to do with Grandpa Raleigh because he is ashamed of Grandpa. Mom told me that, but she wouldn't say it in front of Dad. Nor do I say anything in front of my grandparents. It's all a big circle of no one saying anything to anyone's face, but the point gets across regardless. We don't celebrate Christmas with these grandparents. We don't eat Sunday lunch with them. Dad picks up Grandma Marjory for a day on the farm, but Grandpa Raleigh is never included. When friends and family come to see Grandma Marjory, they always stay with us. "It's better that way," my mom says.

Grandma doesn't say anything. She just offers me a shortbread which is the official end of the meal. I take one, thank her for it, then go to the front door to put on my coat while she shuffles behind. On a whim, I give her a big hug, the kind I always give to my mom and my other grandma but rarely ever to her.

"I love you, Grandma!" I say.

She pats my head, murmuring, "What a nice little girl."

I pull on my coat, mitts and boots and cheerily say, "I'll see you next week!" But even before the door is closed, I hear Grandpa Raleigh shouting, "Marjory! You fool! Why would you bring George into it?"

I stand frozen on the front doorstep, but once the door is closed, I can't hear Grandpa's words, just his yelling. It makes me cry, all that shouting, and for nothing. Grandma didn't do anything terrible. She only asked for help. No one ever shouts at my house. Well, my mom yells occasionally, but no one pays any mind. My dad never yells. Not at me, nor my brothers, and certainly never at my mom.

Tears flow down my cheeks as I run over the frozen soccer field towards school, away from that sad little house. As I shove open the heavy school door, I spy my mom striding down the hall. She's smoking a cigarette and peering at her watch, which is never good.

"You're a bit late, Betty," she says, her cigarette dangling from the corner of her mouth. I have no idea what she's using for an ashtray. "How were they?" she asks, helping me shrug off my winter coat.

"Okay." I am unwilling to get into any detail.

"Did you get enough to eat?" she asks, and I nod, busying myself with my boots. "What's wrong then?" she asks, her sharp eyes spotting my tears.

I feel myself crying again, but other kids are clamouring through the doorway, coming down the hall. I don't want to be a crybaby.

"She seemed old today," I whisper, which is true, even if that's not why I'm crying.

Mom nods. "It will happen to all of us, Bet. Hurry to class."

Marjory's Story
March 15, 1929
La Riviere, Manitoba
Marjory is thirty-six years old.

How could this have happened? How could my temper have gotten away from me? Aren't I old enough to know better?

My face flushes red. Sweat drips down my back despite the winter wind whipping up the schoolyard, blowing my heavy wool skirt, biting through my stockings. I lock the school doors with the heavy key I keep on a string around my neck, then drop the key down the inside of my dress. I hurry, anxious not to encounter the other teachers—Annie Pollock and Marjory Jeffrey. They've probably heard though. News travels fast through a school with only three teachers. We live together at the boarding house too, so it will all come out eventually. But I don't want to discuss this with them yet. I need time to calm down and get my story straight.

I scan the street for some quiet place to sit. The little town of La Riviere lies in the Pembina River valley, a wooded gouge in otherwise flat farmland. Its few streets crowd the riverbanks and are threatened by flooding nearly every spring. La Riviere's only park is on the other side of town, in a grove of elms that flourish in a riverbend. Unfortunately, the park is impassable with snow at this time of year, so there's no point walking there. The only parkland on this side of town is the cemetery, and I have no desire to linger there either.

So I trudge away from town, up a small gravel road that leads out of the valley, towards a pile of logs left behind from some land clearing efforts last summer. The logs will be an impromptu bench for me to overlook the schoolyard and consider my sins.

Nature encroaches on all sides of La Riviere. The bush is hard to clear though farmers manage to carve out a few more acres every year. Deer run rampant through the town, eating gardens, nibbling flowers. The river floods. Winter winds are harsh. Despite all this, I like La Riviere. I don't know why exactly. Perhaps because I'm the school principal and I feel satisfaction at my efficiency. I certainly enjoy working in a school large enough to employ a caretaker for the coal shovelling and water hauling. No more early mornings at school, trying to get a fire started. Maybe even residing in a boarding house rather than in someone's spare bedroom gives me a sense of accomplishment. My wages are also the highest I've ever earned, and now that Joss and Norah are through college, I can spend a little money on myself.

I feel defeated today though as I sit on a frozen log. Maybe it's because I feel old at thirty-six years, that home is 150 miles away, or that Mother is dead in her grave. Or maybe I still can't believe what I did to that boy. He had it coming. He did. But that's no excuse for the way I behaved.

Tears spring to my eyes and I brush them away with the back of my hand. It's silly to cry at my age, but still, I dig for a handkerchief in my school bag. Head down, fully occupied, I don't hear the man approach until he is nearly upon me.

"Hullo!" he calls cheerfully.

Dressed in overalls with a thick wool turtle neck, the man wears a cap pulled low over his eyes and smokes a pipe as he saunters towards the village.

"Oh, hello," I say quickly, embarrassed to be caught crying at the side of the road.

He stops and I see he is young, in his twenties perhaps. I don't recognize him, which is strange. Between school and church, I know everyone in the village, or at least all those that live close enough to travel on foot as he does.

"Raleigh Smith." He transfers his pipe from his right hand to his left so he can offer a handshake. I shake his hand without getting up.

"Forgive me," I say, "but I'm admiring the setting sun."

Mr. Smith looks past me towards the west. "Not much of a sunset tonight." He thrusts his chin towards the grim, grey sky.

"No, that's true. Marjory Thompson is my name."

"The school teacher?" he asks, eyebrows up.

"Yes. Principal."

"Principal?" Mr. Smith seems humoured by this, not impressed like most villagers. "Since when did they let a little slip of a gal like you be principal?"

I am typically offended by flippancy, but something about him makes me like him. His eyes are bright. There are some nice lines around his mouth. He's jolly and I need cheering.

"I seduced the school board trustees, one at a time," I quip, rather dangerously.

His face brightens but he doesn't miss a beat. "Aye. I thought so. That sort of thing happens a lot in the lascivious world of rural education."

We both laugh and much to my delight, he crosses the road and sits on the logs beside me. "I live up there." He points up to a tiny house tucked into the valley's edge. "Built it myself. That's what I do."

"You're a carpenter?"

"Aye."

"But I don't know of any Smiths in the valley. None in school at least."

"I'm not from here. I came on a harvest train a few years back. Worked all fall and then never went home."

"Harvest train workers? You're known to be a rowdy lot. Did you come from Ontario?"

"No, New Brunswick."

"We sailed past New Brunswick when we came from England as children," I say.

"Is that right? England. Whadda ya know? And why is Madame Thompson, principal of the realm, sittin' on a frozen log bawling her eyes out? Your fella end it with you?"

I giggle, surprising myself even. "Heavens, no. I've no fellow. And I'm not bawling my eyes out. I had a trying day at school. That's all."

"Tell me," Mr. Smith demands, leaning against a log to puff on his pipe with his arms crossed.

"It's embarrassing."

"Tell me," he demands again.

Something about this cheeky fellow makes me think I could tell him, and he wouldn't be scandalized. He'd think it was funny and might give me some perspective, some position or defence I might use when this comes back to haunt me.

"Well, it all started when Ivor Benson and Bink Moffat ignored—"

"Wait! There's a Bink in your school?"

"He couldn't get his tongue around his nickname Bill, short for William, so he designated himself 'Bink' at a young age. He's very bright. He has a trap line along the Mary Jane Creek where he catches weasels, mink and muskrat. It's extraordinary, but rumour has it his mother lets him tend to his skinning and pelting and what have you in the middle of the kitchen, every day after four."

"You must be joking." Mr. Smith laughs.

"Indeed, I'm not, but I am getting distracted. So, Ivor Benson and Bink Moffat ignored the school bell at the end of recess every day this week. They didn't delay very much, but just the rest of the class returned to their desks, the front doors banged and—tramp, tramp, tramp—in walked Ivor and Bink. Each day I spoke to them calmly and firmly. 'Ivor and Bink,' I said, 'this must stop. You must be in with the rest of the class.'"

"What were they doing?"

"Who knows? Perhaps they have a muskrat trap under the school steps to check. Those boys have energy and ideas to spare. They dug up most of the turf on the south lawn one day, looking for arrowheads. Bink has thousands, apparently, and is in a competition with a classmate for the largest collection."

"Thousands?" Mr. Smith's jaw drops. "What were the ancients up to? Dropping arrowheads like confetti at a wedding?"

"Maybe. Or maybe Bink has shovelled through all the topsoil in the valley. Anything is possible. Anyway, the same thing happened today. Everyone came in from recess except Bink and Ivor. This time though—" I break off, feeling a little teary again.

"Steady on," Mr. Smith encourages. "You've got to the good part now."

"Well… Ivor was the first through the door and I hit him with the school bell on the back of the head."

"You hit him with the school bell?" Mr. Smith's eyes light up with mirth. "What happened?"

"He dropped like a leaf."

"Oh my! Oh my!" Mr. Smith rocks back and forth on the log, laughing. "Did you kill him?"

"Heavens, no! He came to nicely. Bink got some snow for the lump on the back of his head. And then I made him finish the rest of the day."

"And what did you say?"

"Say?" I sputter. "I didn't say anything. I just went back into the classroom and finished teaching geometry."

"And now you feel awful."

"I do," I admit, the quiver back in my voice.

"He had it coming."

"I expect they both did, but can you imagine anything more startling than to be hit over the back of the head with the bell on your way into school?"

"It would have made me look sharp for at least a week," Mr. Smith jokes.

"Only a week?"

"Ten days, at the most."

I giggle again and blow my nose. "Your poor teachers."

"I was never much for school," Mr. Smith goes on. "Left to farm as soon as I could and then left the farm shortly after."

"What was wrong with the farm?"

"Rocks! And trees. And more rocks and trees! New Brunswick farms aren't like prairie farms with black soil and grass to clear. They're not easy to scrape a living from, and my folks were hard up. Lots of mouths to feed. Heading west seemed like a good idea."

"West." I shake my head. "That's the solution to every problem—Head west. My father believed that. He immigrated because he thought everything was going to be better here."

"And was it?"

"I don't know. Nothing was the same after the war, here or in England with all those men lost."

We sit quietly for a second, then Mr. Smith slaps my knee as he climbs off his perch. "There's only one thing for you: a stiff drink and an apology."

"I don't drink," I protest, shaking my head vehemently at the suggestion.

"Not even a sherry?"

"Possibly a sherry," I demur, surprising myself. "But where does one get a sherry? Isn't La Riviere a temperance town?"

"Yes, of course. La Riviere is a very dry town." Mr. Smith winks and taps the side of his nose.

"Well, then? The hotel doesn't have a beer parlour. So where does one drink?"

"The hotel has sources not known to our provincial regulators. This way," he says, offering his hand, then pulling me off the log. "You can use the telephone at the hotel to call the Bensons and I'll order you something tasty. I think we might have a bite of supper."

"My landlady will be making me a plate, and I certainly don't know you well enough to eat supper with you."

"I'm charming and the hotel is quite respectable. Your landlady can eat the plate herself. Come on!"

I protest again but make little headway. Instead, I find myself walking into town on the arm of a good-looking young man. I am in a much better frame of mind than I was a half-hour before. I feel excited, optimistic even. However, I have a niggling feeling Mother would not have approved.

———

"Put me through to Bensons, please," I shout into the telephone. A busy hotel lobby is no place to make this telephone call, but I'm doing it anyway; such is Mr. Smith's power of persuasion.

"Sven Benson speaking," comes the crackly voice down the line.

"Mr. Benson!" I shout. "Miss Thompson calling, from school."

"The school has a telephone?" Mr. Benson says slowly.

"No, no. Well, yes, it does, but I'm not calling from there. I am the principal there."

"I know you are the principal."

"Right. Well, I've called to apologize. Ivor disobeyed me at school today. And… well… I hit him!" I blurt. There's silence on the other end of the line, so I press on. "Ivor should have been punished, but not how I did it. I called to see if he's all right." I wait for a response, some indication he's not about to report me to the school board or perhaps even the police.

"Miss Thompson," Mr. Benson finally says. "You are very good to call, but it is Ivor who owes the apology. He should not have disobeyed. He did not mention any punishment when he came home from school today. He's tending to his chores without complaint, so I expect you did not injure anything beyond his pride which is always in need of correction. Shall we let the matter pass?"

"Thank you, Mr. Benson!" I gush. "Thank you kindly!"

I return the telephone handset to its cradle, hopeful no ears heard my conversation along the party line. I smile at my reflection in a small, cracked mirror that hangs slightly askew, just above the telephone. I look thirty-six—there's no question—but I'm glad my chums convinced me to bob my hair. Of course, I did it five years after the bright young things did, but I still look a little glamourous. Parted to one side, my hair sweeps my chin, giving my angular face some interest. My face is flushed red, both from the embarrassing phone call and excitement. I'm going to eat dinner with a strange young man! What a lark. Mother's face flashes into my mind, but I push it away. It's not my fault Mother didn't have any fun in the last twenty years of her life. She squashed frivolity in her children, so now we feel guilty when we enjoy ourselves, as if we have to sit on the farm and be sad for the rest of our lives.

I stride into the dining room with my chin high. Mr. Smith sits at a table for two with a large beer and a short sherry. I had no idea such things were possible. Surely the hotel is risking a visit from an inspector and a severe fine for serving alcohol. But no one seems concerned, so perhaps there's no danger.

"They do a nice slice of beef here," Mr. Smith says, coming around the table to pull out my chair.

"You're sitting in work overalls and I have a heap of correcting to get through! This is hardly the moment for leisurely dining in the hotel." I laugh.

"Yes, you're right. But no one cares, do they? It's nice to do something unorthodox, every now and again, don't you think?"

"I don't do unorthodox things. I'm a school teacher."

Mr. Smith laughs as if I've said the funniest thing in the world. "Apart from seducing the gruff old geezers that make up the school board."

"I was only joking." I wave my hand dismissively. "But Mr. Smith, I don't know anything about you and here I am, dining with you."

"We don't need introductions! We're modern," he says emphatically. "And call me Raleigh."

"I couldn't do that. Mother would roll in her grave."

"Ah! The rolling of mothers in graves. Don't think about that. I've already ordered beef for both of us anyway. You probably aren't eating much beef up at the boarding house, are you?"

"Heavens, no. Jeff—that's my colleague, Marjorie Jeffery—says she's never seen so little stretched so far. We have roast chicken on Sundays, pot pie with the leftovers on Mondays, and a soup of dubious origins on Tuesday. Jeff says the bones have been boiled down, but I try not to think about it."

Mr. Smith laughs. "You poor girls. You're worse off than bachelors. You have to eat what the landlady makes. I scramble eggs and call it quits. But tell me about yourself. What backwater farm do you herald from?"

"Backwater? I beg your pardon." I sniff.

"Come on. Don't hide the truth from me." Raleigh smooths a napkin over his lap as our beef arrives. I ignore the side glance the waiter, my landlady's brother-in-law, gives me. "Most of

Canada is a backwater, and if your family immigrated when you were a child, you're not one of the early settlers, the kind that used to live in shanties but have fancy gaslight, brick houses now."

"That's true. My father bought a run-down farm six miles out of Oak River, north of Brandon. We lived in a log cabin for twenty years before the house was built, and you're right, it's wooden. No bricks for us."

"Twenty years in a log cabin?" Raleigh squints. "You must be joking."

"I'm not. When my brother went to war, my sister, Norah and I returned to work on the farm. It was the worst time then, with all the uncertainty. But after the war, the farm prospered and my father built a house. Mother didn't live long enough to see it though. She died in that awful log cabin."

Raleigh cocks his head and squints. "You made good then, eh?" he says, almost as a statement. "You might not have been one of the early families, but you worked just as hard."

"My father imagined we'd build a fortune quickly. But it's been many years, and the odds of me making a fortune in the schoolroom are non-existent."

"Skip fortune then. Aim for something else," Raleigh says, joking again despite my seriousness.

I wave my hand at his silliness. "School teachers are pillars of dignity and respect in the community. Principals even more so."

"Madame Principal, life is good fun beyond the four walls of the school. I'd go so far as to say it's less dangerous too. I've never had my head whacked with a bell while sitting quietly in this dining room sipping a pint."

I laugh at this and continue to laugh the whole evening through. Maybe it's the sherry, but I find Raleigh funny. The stories he tells—the accents of New Brunswick fishermen, the shenanigans of the harvest train workers, the awkwardness of inquiring if a double or single seat outhouse is required—and the lightheartedness with which he tells them endears him to me. He doesn't bother with pretence or formality. He's the most natural person I've ever met.

I tell my stories too. Life at university. Failed attempts at college sports. My reputation for frugality. I even recite the caption under my university yearbook photo, class of 1927:

> M – *Money with which she's a wizard;*
> A – *Ardent in cutting up lizards;*
> R – *Roaming in rus and in urb;*
> J – *Jollity, Jam, and Geology;*
> O – *Oak River which she learned to treasure;*
> R – *The three "Rs" she's taught to the rustics;*
> Y – *Years of success, may they be idealistic.*

He laughs at the bit about cutting up lizards, though I explain it only happened once—after a rain one day in May, a salamander crossed my path on campus and old habits from the farm overtook me. I stabbed the poor beast with my umbrella, and my reputation was forever marred.

"There's a violent streak running through you, Miss Thompson!" Raleigh jokes, which feels like an uncomfortably astute assessment today, all days.

Even as Raleigh walks me back to the boarding house, he keeps me giggling. Nothing is sacred. Nothing is overthought. He brushes all my worries away with a careless, "Well, I wouldn't bother too much about that if I were you." Despite all the warning voices in my head, I have the delightful feeling Raleigh Smith might be what I need. He's just so funny.

—

"What the deuce were you thinking of?" Marjorie Jeffrey stands in the doorway to my room, hands on hips, eyes wide.

It is not easy for mutual friends to know which Marjory is which—Marjory Jeffery or Marjory Thompson—so we've been dubbed "Jeff" and "Tommy," cheeky little nicknames.

"I called to apologize for hitting him, Jeff," I protest, glancing up from the pile of correcting on my desk.

"You hit him?"

"Yes! With the school bell."

"At the hotel?" Jeff's brow furrows in confusion.

"What?" I exclaim.

"Our charming landlady said her brother-in-law, whatever-his-name-is, saw you and Raleigh Smith drinking together at the hotel. And now you say you hit him?"

I'm laughing. Jeff is so earnest. "Let me explain," I protest.

"Please do because you are the school principal, and no end of gossip will fly if you take up drinking with Raleigh Smith."

"I had a bad time of it at school. I punished Ivor Benson too severely. I hit him with the school bell."

Jeff winces.

"But then I met Raleigh Smith and he encouraged me to telephone the Bensons and apologize. After this, I had a sherry and supper in the dining room with Mr. Smith. We weren't drinking like fish."

"But you were drinking at the hotel with Mr. Smith?" Jeff insists.

"Well, strictly speaking, yes. But you make it sound so tawdry."

"Maybe it is tawdry. Illegal too, come to think of it." She taps her forehead dramatically.

"Really Jeff! Can't we have any fun at all?"

"Maybe I can, but you certainly can't. That's the deal you made when you took the post of principal." Jeff shuts the door and sits uninvited on my bed.

"I don't remember asking you in," I say primly.

"Tough beans, old girl. I'm here to remind you what's at stake."

"I know what's at stake."

"Really? Drinking in a public house is not exemplary behaviour for a school principal. You could be fired for this. Furthermore, Raleigh Smith likes to drink a little too much. Everyone knows that."

"I didn't know that."

"I'm sure you didn't because you probably didn't even know Raleigh before this afternoon. I can't imagine how you met—I'm sure there's a fascinating story there—but Raleigh will step out with any woman who will give him attention. Most won't, of course, because he isn't from here. And no one knows much about him other than he drinks, and we're not talking a sherry. The home-brew that gets traded up and down the valley can be as strong as a horse's kick. There's no consistency. No regulations. Just a distillery in a shed."

I'm silent.

"And you know what else?" Jeff goes on. "There are rumours about him."

"What kind of rumours?" I roll my eyes.

"Rumours about what he's like when he's drunk."

"For goodness' sake." I fold my arms and stare at the ceiling.

"No! Don't you 'goodness' sake' me. You were raised Methodist. You have no idea what men are like when they've been drinking."

"And you're the expert?" I snip, thinking of my father with one drink too many. There is singing and snoozing but nothing nastier than that.

"I've heard he's punched fellas for no good reason. How respectable does that sound to you?"

I sigh. "Thank you, Jeff, but I'm sure I'll never see Mr. Raleigh Smith socially again. It was a random event. Not to be repeated."

Jeff frowns and I think what a cute face she has, when she's not scowling, that is. Round cheeks and bright eyes. She has no trouble finding respectable boys with whom to socialize, Jim Mitchell more than anyone else. His family was one of the first to homestead in the district, back when all that marked the land was an occasional surveyor stake and a few sod shanties. Jim is terribly respectable but over-stretched financially, so Jeff doesn't expect a marriage proposal any time soon.

"You're bored, aren't you, Tommy?" Jeff asks softly.

"No! How can I be with all this work in front of me?"

"You've taught geometry a dozen times. You're bored with the whole thing. The lessons—always the same. The students and their endless stupidity. The shuffling up the street in snow boots.

You crave excitement. Why else would you have sat drinking in a bar?"

"Dining room."

She rolls her eyes again.

"Maybe I'm at an age where I'm owed a little independence," I whisper, a quiver in my voice. "I've taught for twenty years, always sending wages home—paying for this, paying for that. I worked my way through my degree and now I'm a principal. Why am I not happy? I've achieved everything I've set out to achieve."

"Questions of the universe." Jeff pats the bed beside her. "Come sit here and I'll tell you my plan."

I toss my pencil onto the desk and flop down beside her. "What plan?" I sulk.

"We're going on a cruise this summer."

"Is that your solution? Spend money on ourselves?"

"Yes. We are going on a month-long excursion through Detroit, Chicago, Cleveland, Niagara. The whole works!"

Jeff reveals a tourist pamphlet she's kept hidden behind her back. Glamourous steamships and sophisticated hotels are pictured between shots of Niagara Falls and the Ford Motor Company Factory. I flip through the pages with a careless air. I hate to let on, but this looks exactly how I'd like to spend my summer—not holed up in an overheated boarding house reading next year's textbooks or swatting mosquitoes on the farm at Oak River.

I caress the pictures with my fingers. "This looks wonderful."

"Doesn't it just? It will be something to look forward to. Something to get us through the misery of teaching the last few months of the school year."

"You should be saving money to get married," I suggest rather bossily, noting the prices in the margins.

"You might be right. But if I don't go with my own money, I'll never go with Mr. Jim Mitchell's."

"And I'll never be anybody's wife, so why not?" I grump.

"That's the spirit! And, Marjory, no more Raleigh Smith. Not any port in a storm will do."

Marjory's Story
July 15, 1929
La Riviere, Manitoba
The same year.

"Your friend, Mr. Smith, called while you were out, Miss Marjory," Mrs. Fargey announces to all assembled at the supper table. Our landlady is not known for her subtlety, and as she stands at the far end of the table surveying her borders with a scowl, she plants her fists firmly into the mounds of flesh covering her hip bones.

We glance up in surprise—Jeff, Annie Pollack, myself—to see a smirk on Mrs. Fargey's ample face. It's as if she's satisfied at catching out one of us schoolteachers in an impropriety. The thing brings her joy, delight at being the bearer of such a shocking report.

"He was wearing workman's clothes," she continues with a jab in her voice as if I'm incapable of arousing enough fervour in a man that he might consider putting on a nice suit when he comes calling. "They weren't clean working clothes either. Not a tidy tie around the neck. Just filthy overalls and a ragged shirt."

I freeze, staring across the table into Jeff's eyes. Something must be done, something to quash the implications of Mrs. Fargey's words, the suggestion I might receive a caller ten years younger than I, a man who is known to drink and never goes to church.

Jeff shakes her head and throws caution to the wind. "Mr. Smith called for Tommy today whilst wearing workman's clothes." She uses my nickname with an exasperated tone.

I suck in, holding my breath. What tale is she weaving?

"And did he have papers to deliver?" Jeff continues. "I certainly hope he did because the school has been waiting for figures for repair jobs."

Mrs. Fargey looks immediately suspicious. "I don't remember any papers." She squints at Jeff, unconvinced.

Annie Pollack, bless her, picks up on the charade and contributes her own bit. "Oh dear!" She giggles nervously. "It's all my fault."

Jeff and I whip around to face her. Annie is not known for creating trouble. She's averse to it. She's a chronic apologizer, the sort of person who pleads your forgiveness when you inadvertently step on her toe in a crowded cloakroom. "So sorry! I shouldn't have been so close that you could tread on me!"—she might say. Annie continues: "I ran into Mr. Smith on the street today and complained about the window in my classroom. So drafty! He said he'd add it to the list of repairs and would let Marjory know the total."

Jeff starts to look worried now. Annie's classroom doesn't have a window. We're getting in a little deep with lies.

But Annie is just warming to her theme. "He said he didn't have anything written down, but he'd do a bit of quick figuring in his head and deliver his answer this afternoon." Annie wears a smile, bright and victorious as if she'd just won a three-legged raise on Dominion Day.

Jeff moves swiftly to close the conversation before Annie can go any further. "There you are, Mrs. Fargey. Mr. Smith made a business call. Perhaps he should have stopped by the school, but school is out for the summer, so he's not likely to find any of us there. Did he leave his message?"

"Of course not." Mrs. Fargey draws herself up in a state of indignation. "I told him he was a cad for calling on Miss Thompson in such a state of filth and dishevelment and that a man like him had better not call at all on a respectable teacher like Marjory."

"And what did he say?" Jeff asks, suddenly enjoying the conversation. "I'm sure it was memorable!"

"I wouldn't like to say." Mrs. Fargey shakes her head and purses her lips.

"Go on. Annie will cover her ears."

Annie complies but still, Mrs. Fargey shakes her head. "It wouldn't be right to repeat it."

"Oh, well," I say carelessly. "You know what tradesmen can be like, Mrs. Fargey. I'm sorry you had such a trying time of it. I'll send a note before we leave tomorrow for our cruise."

This appeases her and she goes off to the kitchen, leaving us in various states of amusement and horror.

"I've never lied to anyone before," Annie whispers, repentant.

"Come now," Jeff cajoles. "If you associate with Tommy, you'll find lying a necessary skill. That's the cost of being a friend to someone leading a double life." She glares at me.

"I'm not leading a double life!" I lean across the table. "I've told him not to contact me, but he doesn't listen."

"I wonder why that would be." Jeff raises an eyebrow. "Is it the mixed messages you're sending, Tommy? A little push and a little pull?"

"You're the expert in men, aren't you?" I snap back. "You'd know how to manage it, I'm sure."

Jeff folds her arms at this. "I don't cavort with dodgy men. Men are far easier to handle when they're gentlemen."

"Don't squabble!" Annie protests. "It's not helpful. We need to concentrate. What will I do if Mr. Smith calls while you're gone on your trip?"

"He won't," I say, annoyed at them both. "I will write to him before we leave. That wasn't a lie. He won't come by if he knows I'm gone for the summer."

"Do we need to have the school board hire him for repairs now?" Jeff still scowls. "So Annie can sleep at night?"

"Possibly." I sigh. "Very possibly."

—

I go as early as is respectable but not so late that anyone is out and about. I've written a letter, but I won't mail it. I tell myself I want Raleigh to get it right away. But in truth, I want to see him one more time before we leave.

Ours has been an unusual courtship. We don't see each other publicly—I can't risk that after the dinner at the hotel. I had a school board member speak to me privately about it. The rumours flew fast and the school board wasn't impressed. I managed to tamp down the gossip, dismissing the meal as a coincidence. I said the hotel was short of tables that night. Mr. Smith was eating alone and so was I. It was polite for us to share a table. He's so much younger, I said. I didn't see our encounter in the same terms as the gossip mill saw it. My tone was lofty. Aggrieved. By the end of the conversation, the school board member apologized for his inference, and I was sick with guilt about my lies, especially since he was right. Spot on. I dined with Raleigh Smith because I was attracted to him. Plain and simple. He is exciting and nothing about my life is exciting. My life is dull and he makes me feel young again.

But lying has become easy. I regularly fib to cover the fact I see Raleigh late at school, early at school, sometimes on a trail in the hills, sometimes at his house. It isn't right, but it is fun. Something to spice up my life.

I knock on his door and wait.

Raleigh's house is not something by which you'd purposely drive visitors so they might marvel at its splendour. Raleigh eschews the carefully laid stones that lie between most front doors and gravel driveways, straight paths through lush green lawns. Instead, his front walk is a track of flattened grass, leading from rough ruts to a sinking, uneven door stoop.

The house is flat and squat, built on a foundation without a cellar. The result is that only the smallest step is required to climb into the house and I perch on it as I wait for Raleigh to answer the door. It had been a warm night, so the door was left open, with the screen door keeping out the flies and allowing a cool morning breeze to sweep into the kitchen.

"Raleigh?" I call, unwilling to be left standing on the doorstep for long.

I hear sounds—bedsprings, a scraping noise, a cupboard closing. There aren't many rooms—just a bedroom, a kitchen, and a sitting room—and they're all small. The house is simply furnished with second-hand goods found at the church rummage sales.

Raleigh opens the bedroom door and calls through the screen door. "Marjory? What are you doing?"

"I have a letter for you," I say.

Raleigh comes to the front door, his unbuttoned shirt hanging on his shoulders. Embarrassed, I look away. I can't remember the last time I saw a man without his shirt done up. Probably, it was harvest time ages ago when my brothers were filthy and changed their shirts before sitting down to supper. I don't remember caring at the time, but something about the curves and lines I see on Raleigh's chest makes me feel differently.

"Get off the front step. Who knows who will see you," he adds sarcastically.

"Do up your shirt." I sniff as I enter, shutting both the screen door and front door behind me.

Raleigh doesn't budge. He just crosses his arms over his chest. "It's early, Marj. I've got a bit of a headache. Who is the letter from?"

"Well, it's from me," I say, stammering.

"You are delivering a letter from yourself? What on earth for? Why don't you just tell me what you want to say?"

"Because you don't listen when I tell you!"

"I don't listen when you say you can't see me anymore because then you march up to my house at some ungodly hour so you can see me. Confusing, no?" He cocks his head. "You could have mailed your precious letter."

"It's silly." I shrug, suddenly feeling like a schoolgirl. This charade is like the nonsense played out in normal school and university. Hurt feelings and broken hearts. I'm no better than those stupid girls I loathe. I just want out of his house now, so I press my letter to his hand, but he doesn't take it.

"Tell me right now," he says, "what you so badly want me to know because I'm not reading a prissy letter written in your schoolmarm twaddle."

I purse my lips. Raleigh can be so infuriating. No one else talks to me like this.

"All right then!" I say, properly mad. "I can't see you again. No more. This is it. No more walks in the hills. No more popping by the school after everyone is gone. It has to end."

Raleigh looks squarely at me without saying a word. Then he comes close, not touching me but standing nearer than Mrs. Fargey would approve. "Have it your way," he levels. "Go on your cruise. Eat in your nice restaurants. Visit those parks and museums and who knows what else. Enjoy yourself and spend a lot of money. But you and I both know it won't last. You'll be back because you must come back. And when you do, you'll find teaching is tiresome as ever, nights are just as lonely, and you're as fed-up as you were before. Nothing will change that. And that's when you'll come looking for me. Because I am the most exciting thing about this hick town."

His face is inches from mine. I want him to kiss me but not as he does in the hills, in the twilight. A kiss now would be different, dangerous even. I find myself wishing for it, not to tolerate it as I do when he's been chummy and sweet, but to enjoy it.

Something daring overtakes me. I raise my hand and twirl his chest hair my little finger, the dark curls rough. I whisper, "Raleigh, don't be so cross."

Shocked, Raleigh steps back as if I struck him, then yanks the door open. "Get out," he snaps.

Marjory's Story
July 17, 1929
Train to Port Arthur, Thunder Bay District, Ontario
Two days later

"Trees," I murmur, half asleep.

"Lots of them." Jeff stares out the train window in the early morning light.

We've been on the train since late last night, travelling from Winnipeg through the Ontario bush to our ship anchored at Port Arthur. We were economical with this leg of the journey, not purchasing tickets for the sleeper car. We might regret it though. I have a pain in my neck that is not going away, no matter how many times I stretch—ear to shoulder, one side then the other.

Jeff's hat flops crookedly on her head. Like mine, her hat is a cloche, lightly coloured for summer, simple in design. Our headwear is a far cry from the elaborate hats of our mothers' generation with their looped ribbons and sashes, jewel accents, and soaring feathers. Ours were ordered from the Sears Roebuck catalogue along with our other new travelling things. We selected everything months ago, just after we sent away for tickets.

"A face that is very round and full at the lower half must wear a hat that gives prominence to the upper part," Jeff read aloud in her firmest schoolmarm voice while perched on a bed, swinging her legs and smoking a cigarette, much to the chagrin of Annie who opened the window to let the smoke out before Mrs. Fargey might smell it. "A little study will soon teach any woman what is best suited to herself, and the opinion of others is not to be despised."

"What on earth are you reading?" I asked.

"'The Complete Dressmaker,'" Jeff replied, waving the magazine to aid Annie's efforts.

"What rubbish! A round face must wear a tall hat? Shall I purchase a top hat then?"

"'The opinion of others is not to be despised!'" Jeff quoted in a loud voice. "I'll put us both down for a nice cloche."

But our cloches are becoming flattened from sleeping in the train, so I pull them off our heads and set them on the vacant seat beside me. We'll get up in a minute and freshen up in the tiny lavatory. But, for now, we're happy to gaze out the window at the trees sweeping by.

Our train ride reminds me of our journey to Manitoba when we immigrated as children, only in reverse. When Jeff and I went to sleep last night, the train chugged through flat farmland, but when we woke this morning, we were surprised by the trees, just as my siblings and I were astonished by the prairies.

Trying to get comfortable, I shift my weight and hear the crunch of paper beneath me. As we left La Riviere yesterday, a letter from Norah arrived. I put it in the pocket of my new spring coat and forgot about it in the confusion of our departure. But I open it now and hold the pages up to the early morning light flickering through the trees.

Dear Marjory, Norah writes in her pretty handwriting.
I hope this reaches you before you set off on your grand adventure. I envy you. Cleveland. Chicago. Detroit. Niagara. What a lark!

Summer presses on with little reprieve to the heat here in Brandon. My landlady, 90 if she's a day, has a mortal fear of drafts or burglars (I can't remember which), so she doesn't permit windows open at night. I am dying. Dying. I tell you. I might take the train out to Oak River this weekend, just to get out of Brandon.

If I go back to the farm though, I will have to work the entire weekend. You know what Father, Harry and Alec are like. I thought the new house might encourage housekeeping, but no. The kitchen floor is unspeakable and the towels repulsive. Mary goes over about once a month, gathers all the linen, and gives it a proper washing. Bravo for her, but I fear they've grown to expect it and make no effort on their own.

Every time I go, Father asks if I might like to return to keep house for them. Good heavens. He doesn't understand, does he? I thought his recent speaking tour of England would have reminded him there's a big world out there that his children might like to explore. Alas no. He came home filled with praise for rural Manitoba. Maybe he believes his own lecture material. I suppose the CPR wouldn't have sent him as their representative, prosperous farmer if he didn't believe what he was saying. Do you sometimes wonder how Father sold himself as a prosperous farmer to the CPR? It's a mystery. He got a trip to the old country out of it though, so good for him.

In other news, Joss has written he's working for a mining and smelting company in British Columbia as a chemical engineer. I have no idea what he does, but he seemed happy in his letter. Educated, married, employed, and far from Oak River. He got what he wanted. I hope he writes you a thank you and maybe a cheque.

I might have news soon. I interviewed for a secretary job with the Minister of Education in Winnipeg. I think the interview was a success. If not, I had a pleasant trip to Winnipeg. Nothing lost there.

Must be off. Don't forget to write with details of your excursion.

Your loving sister, Norah.

PS I'm wearing the shortest skirt now. It's jazz music. One gets very bold.

PPS I've bought stocks for the first time. Fortunes to be made!

I tuck the envelope into my purse, alongside the letter Raleigh wouldn't take and next year's employment contract, which I meant to mail on the way to the train station but forgot. Odd how the letters lie alongside each other, as if all parts of me can co-exist in one place. Norah is my past. The school is my present. And perhaps Raleigh is my future. But that can't happen. I know that. If I were to marry Raleigh, and that's a big if—he certainly hasn't asked, I wouldn't be able to continue as a school principal. I might be able to continue teaching as a married woman, but not if I had a baby. No one keeps teaching after babies.

I think about that for a moment and wonder if a baby would make me feel happier, more accomplished, not on the fringe of womanhood, wondering what it's like to be a mother. I used to think teaching would satisfy my mothering urge, and it did, to a degree. Certainly, getting the post of principal gave me a feeling of accomplishment. But that pride didn't last. My students leave, the good ones along with the bad, pressing on to new heights or forgetting everything to drive spikes on a railway somewhere. Perhaps having my own child would give me someone to care about, someone for whom to work. I used to teach for my siblings. Their education was my entire financial goal. If nothing else, I took care of them to show Mother how they should be supported, not held back on the farm.

But Mother is dead. I don't have her approval to seek. I can't show her up. Father is pleasantly fading into retirement, bottle in one hand, a good conversation with his neighbours his greatest joy. His influence is diminished, and my siblings no longer need my support. Harry and Alec manage the farm just fine, the milk cows gone, electricity installed. Their work isn't as intensive as it was when we were children. Their lives are simpler. Perhaps, they might like to be married, but that seems unlikely now. Years ago, it was rumoured they were both sweet on the same girl. Such is their brotherly bond that neither wanted to step on the other's toes, so neither made any overtures. Her identity was never known to me, never mind her thoughts on the matter. I often wonder who she preferred or if she was even aware of the Thompson bachelors and their closeted admiration for her. What good husbands Harry and Alec would have made. Their manners are impeccable, and Harry's wit makes all the neighbours smile.

The thought of husbands brings me back to Raleigh. He isn't husband material. That much I know. Yet, no one else is remotely interested in me. Some days I don't understand why Raleigh is either. I am angular, thirty-six years old, and plain-looking. I have a sharp tongue and a quick temper. I am, in every respect, a typical school teacher. I wish it weren't so, but it is. And it's hard to change once you've been something for twenty years. The passing of time solidifies one's character. But Raleigh is not an easy man either. He has a reputation. Young women, fresh out of high school, won't give him the time of day. At twenty-eight, he's excluded from the market of bright, young innocents. So that leaves women like me. Older. Bossy. Not prime marriage material. If there were a point system for marriageability, we'd both score low, howbeit for different reasons—right at the bottom, looking 'round at the other candidates, eyeing up the leftovers. The marriage market is not encouraging when you're a 36-year-old schoolteacher.

"You look sad," Jeff says, sitting up, rubbing the sleep out of her eyes.

"Not a bit." I slap a smile on my face. "We're going to have such a jolly time! Today's the beginning of the best month of our lives. Shall we hunt down some coffee and make a start?"

—

"This is all right, isn't it?" Jeff sinks into a wicker chair in the S. S. Noronic's lounge.

"We nearly missed the boat." I laugh, sitting beside her.

The deck chairs are filling rapidly with passengers anxious to watch the ship pull away from Port Arthur. The chairs by the windows, facing inward, are much less popular than our seats in the middle of the lounge that face outward. A bright red rug runs between the rows of chairs. At the far end, the bare floor doubles as a dance floor. Happy young couples twirl while the jazz band plays.

"What's the tune?" I ask Jeff.

"'You're the Cream in My Coffee.'" Jeff bobs her head.

Jeff has a beautiful Silvertone Gramophone with a solid oak cover, an eighteen-inch flower horn, and a well-used crank motor. Her collection of Victor and Columbia records is significant. She may have a recording of this tune though Mrs. Fargey knocks the kitchen ceiling with a broom handle if she hears a peep out of the gramophone.

Pretty girls in short, shimmery frocks catch the eyes of young lads. Acquaintances are made. Conversations begin. We older, more reserved guests rest in deck chairs, the rush from the train station over. Besides, the sun is bright, and we are wise enough to know there are not many days in life wholly devoted to the pursuit of pleasure. Not many days when work and worry can be set aside. When we can tell ourselves we've earned this luxury, paid for it in full, so we're jolly well going to enjoy it.

"Oh! Did you feel that, Tommy?" Jeff exclaims as the ship lurches forward. "I think we're off!"

Jeff's enthusiasm is contagious. I give up my seat and walk to the window to view the activity on the dock.

"They're tugging the anchor!" I report.

This journey feels different than the one we took as children. We were frightened then and perhaps rightly so. Then, we were crossing the Atlantic. But now we're only bobbing around the Great Lakes. We have plans for fun and sightseeing and I'm determined to enjoy myself.

"I should fetch my little Brownie camera," I call but Jeff doesn't answer me.

A well-dressed gentleman in a striped suit and shiny shoes hovers beside her. "Is anyone sitting here?" he asks, pointing to the seat I've deserted.

Much to my horror, Jeff answers, "Well, if they are, they're awfully tiny, aren't they?" She winks at me and I glare back.

The gentleman laughs like she's made the funniest joke in the world and plops down beside her. "I say," he says, crossing his legs and depositing his straw boating hat on one knee. "Have you ever seen anything as spiffy as this?"

"Not remotely," Jeff answers carelessly. "Bee's knees."

I roll my eyes. Bee's knees? Where does she pick this stuff up?

"Bob's the name. American," the man goes on, shaking Jeff's hand. "I sell insurance. Is that awfully dull, do you think?"

Jeff purses her lips and gazes at the chandelier as if she's contemplating the question. "Insurance." She taps her chin. "So dull. So breathtakingly dull. You must prove yourself to be fun-loving, Sir. Right here. Right now!" Jeff hops up and points to the dance floor.

The man laughs—"Why not?"—and offers her his arm. A second later, they're dancing the Charleston like they were the ones who thought it up in the first place.

I can't help myself laughing. Outright. So this is what it's going to be—Jeff having one last fling with fun before tying herself to respectability. She loves to lecture me about my behaviour. Well, now I've got ammunition for her. I sit down and wait for a fun gentleman to come my way, but no one appears, not even when I plaster a pleasant smile over my face. Instead, an older woman toddles down the aisle and stops at Jeff's empty seat. She contemplates for a second before she turns and gracelessly falls into the chair. She doesn't even ask if the seat was claimed. She just deposits herself without a second thought. I shift, trying to add as much space between us as possible, but she turns to me regardless.

"What a racket!" she yells. "I can't hear myself think with that noise!"

I frown at her, hoping she catches my disapproval at her disapproval. "They're enjoying themselves," I chide.

"Well, they're young, aren't they?" she concedes. "Young and foolish. Not like us. We know there's nothing to be gained from trotting up and down a dance floor, exhausting ourselves."

I stare at the woman, taking her in. How does a human so adverse to dancing wind up on a pleasure cruise of the Great Lakes? She wraps her overcoat around her neck and pulls her hat straight down on her head like a helmet. Her shoes are planted firmly on the floor, spread wide to accommodate her ample legs.

"There's no harm in dancing," I say sharply. "One should enjoy life when one gets the chance."

"I enjoy life," she counters, "in my own way, and it doesn't require me to flap my arms and legs."

"Really?" I say, suddenly fascinated. "How do you enjoy yourself?"

She begins to tell me something about raising geese for their down when Jeff rushes over, her face red. "Come, Tommy." She tugs my arm. "Let's freshen up before dinner."

Her insurance salesman has disappeared.

"What's the rush?" I ask, certain the dinner bell won't ring for another hour.

Jeff pulls my hand, leading me out of the lounge, towards the stairs to the staterooms. "You'll never believe what that man said to me," she hisses.

"Probably nothing you didn't encourage."

"Touché. But it's always a shame when a man takes flirting seriously. It ruins everything. Every single time."

"What did he say?" I gingerly maneuvering the stairs in my pretty high-heeled travelling shoes.

"I'm not going to tell you because you'll say I deserved it."

"Cross my heart, I won't," I promise.

"He said, 'Nice gams, toots,'" Jeff whispers in shocked tones, glancing up and down the corridor.

"What are gams?"

Jeff is silent.

"Seriously! I don't know what gams are." I fumble through my purse for our stateroom key. "I'm not being ignorant. You'll have to tell me. It is a bosom?" I add in a whisper.

"Maybe…" Jeff stops. "Maybe, I don't know what gams are either. But I didn't think the comment was proper."

"You're probably right." I laugh as I push the stateroom door open.

Jeff hits my arm with her handbag. "It's not funny!" she protests which makes me laugh even more.

Jeff is an odd ducky. She seems so careless, flirtatious even, but really she's a puritan. All talk. No action. She'd never step out with a risky man. She'd never lead a double life. Suddenly, I feel glamorous, like Mary Pickford. I'm not a prudish girl, just off the farm. I'm a mature woman, capable of entertaining a man without blushing.

"Who was that dreadful woman you were talking to?" Jeff asks, opening her suitcase to fish out an evening dress. The dress is creased from our journey, but undoubtedly, Jeff will dance the creases loose. It's a shorter dress than I'd wear, certainly ineligible for my mother's approval. But times have changed. Here we are, dashing about without male chaperones. Having fun. Pretending this glamour is our everyday life, not a one-time achievement.

"Your insurance salesman's wife," I say.

Jeff dissolves in giggles, which was what I intended.

—

"I hope we're not stuck with our earlier acquaintances." Jeff looks worried.

We sit at a table for four, waiting for our assigned table companions to arrive. Light from the chandeliers bounces off of cut glass decanters and polished silverware. White linen tablecloths—like Jeff's dress—could have used a hot iron but otherwise are clean and tidy. Pink carnations in spindly milk-white vases adorn the tabletops.

"I shouldn't worry," I say, twirling a little in the swivel dining room chair. "The odds are low."

"These chairs are amusing, aren't they?" Jeff spins round in her swivel chair. A waiter casts her a tolerant look as her toes nearly clip his shins.

"Be careful, Jeff!" I call, disappearing behind the menu card while she giggles like a schoolgirl.

"Celery and olives with the cocktails," I read out loud. "Cream of cauliflower soup. Steam lake fish pickle sauce. A compote of pears on a veal fricassee with green peas. Roast turkey with cranberry sauce plus a prime rib with gravy. Mashed potatoes or boiled, according to your preference. Asparagus and chicken salad. Gracious!" I say, returning the menu card to its upright position in front of my plate. "What a feast!"

"What's for dessert?" Jeff asks absentmindedly, scanning the crowd for interesting people.

I take the menu again. "Steamed fruit pudding in vanilla sauce. Apple or pineapple pie. Ice cream. Assorted cakes and Canadian cheeses."

"Can we have a sample of them all? I wonder." Jeff laughs. "I'll be as fat as Mrs. Fargey by the end of this."

"Not at all. We're going to do so much walking. They say Cleveland is a city of Parks—Euclid Beach, Roosevelt Park, Fine Arts Garden, Gordon."

"Ugh," Jeff moans. "I only packed these dancing shoes and you're going to make me exercise every day."

"Nonsense. We'll also take in a Cleveland Indian's baseball game and an Elinor Glyn talkie at the Palace. I read somewhere the building is refrigerated for the summer heat. Can you imagine?"

Jeff shrugs her shoulders. "Sure."

"And the terminal tower at Cleveland—that will be exciting. The Ohio Theatre. What do we see there? Do you remember? 'After Dark' or 'Women Go on Forever?'"

But Jeff isn't listening. She smiles at a man who weaves around tables, heading, it would seem, in our direction. Nearly fifty if he's a day, he wears plain brown pants with a white collared shirt and nondescript tie. His grey hair is parted to one side, combed to cover a receding hairline.

"Hello, ladies!" he says, arriving at our table. "Bill's the name."

He kisses our hands dramatically then sits in the chair beside me, though I don't take it as a compliment. He had, after all, approached from my side.

"I'm sorry to keep you waiting further, but my chum Art will be along shortly. He's a younger chap than me, but somehow I still move more quickly."

We laugh at this and Jeff says it's the same with the two of us but she doesn't elaborate which of us is old and fast and which is young and slow. Must keep a little mystery, I can hear her say.

Art arrives a minute later and confirms Bill's description. He is younger and Jeff seems delighted he sits on her side of the table. Art wears his brown hair combed straight back, which gives his long nose a prominent appearance, but he also dresses well and apologizes profusely for his tardiness.

"I was seeing about getting a tour of Cleveland," he explains. "Bill and I plan to take in the sights, but we didn't know our options."

Jeff is suddenly animated. Although I didn't think she was listening a minute ago, she rattles off all the attractions I mentioned with the energy of a showman—Step this way! Step this way! Lots to see here!

Bill and Art are quickly taken by her charms. That much is obvious. "Why don't we all go together?" Art asks. "If that suits you, ladies," Bill quickly adds.

"Why not?" Jeff giggles, looking at me for approval. But I'm more cautious than Jeff. It's as if she's entirely forgotten the episode with the insurance man this afternoon. I hedge our bets. "Let's wait and make plans in a couple of days," I say. "We have three days on the ship and I haven't seen a forecast for Cleveland. If it pours rain, we might as well hole up in a theatre and watch vaudeville."

The men graciously demur—"What a good idea. Very sensible."

"Marjory is very sensible," Jeff jokes. "We're school teachers," she unimaginatively adds, moving the conversation along.

Art and Bill laugh out loud. "So are we!" they say in unison, slapping the table in surprise.

"How funny!" Jeff gushes. "We planned this trip for our summer holidays."

"Same here," Bill says. "We've looked forward to this all year."

"Haven't we just?" adds Art, smiling warmly at Bill.

Suddenly, Jeff and I are in the middle of the best dinner party we've ever had. The men tell stories, hilarious tales of science experiments gone wrong, losing children on nature trips to the forest, trying to teach young ladies of wealthy families how to play baseball. We contribute stories of outfoxing our landlady, avoiding the Women's Institute activities, and attempting curling. By the end of the night, we've lined up three days of touring in Cleveland without any hesitations, and Jeff and I fall into bed in the best of spirits.

—

"Why so glum?" Jeff yells, leaning over the rails at Niagara Falls, the pounding of the water masking the sound of her voice.

"I'm not glum," I yell back, stretching out my arms to catch some of the spray in the warm afternoon sun. "Isn't it magnificent?"

Jeff jerks her chin towards a park bench in the shade, away from the tourists crowding the rails. We've been at Niagara Falls for a day, arriving on the S. S. City of Buffalo, a glorious ship with two decks, a tall smokestack, and a lovely menu. We've walked all around Niagara Falls—the American side, the Canadian side, the power plants, Goat Island, the bottom of the gorge. But now we're tired, so we settle under a large elm and contemplate the activity around us.

The crowd moves slowly as the afternoon heat bears down. Hands are raised to shade tired eyes. Men fan themselves with fedoras and boaters. Children madly lick ice cream cones as drips roll down their arms. Honeymooners stroll with linked arms. It's the end of the day and the end of a season too. Soon it will be autumn. The bandstand will empty and shortly after that the 1920s will be over. A new decade will be before us, and if the pace of change and prosperity continues, we may not recognize ourselves a decade from now.

"Do you know what I noticed on the boat?" I ask Jeff.

"The coffee was superb?"

"Well that, but the boat was filled with honeymooners."

Jeff is silent. She flicks away flies with the back of her hand.

"They looked so happy," I muse, squinting at the bright flickers of water, rushing over and over the rocks, crashing end-lessly to the bottom.

"They were on their honeymoons," Jeff says.

"They all looked so young."

"True, old girl. True."

"What did you think of Art and Bill?" I ask suddenly. "We had such a jolly time with them in Cleveland and Buffalo."

"Fine fellows. Why?"

"I got thinking about how I'd feel if I was honeymooning with one of them, Bill—let's say. He's the older one. "

"And how would you feel?" Jeff asks, amused by my ram-blings.

"I would feel bored." I surprise even myself with my honesty.

"Boring is a good attribute in a husband when the opposite is recklessness and drunkenness."

I look at her sideways with a scowl.

"I have to tell you," Jeff continues, "neither of those lads would have suited us."

I nod my head stupidly. "Yes, teachers don't often pair well together."

Jeff rolls her eyes. "No, silly. Not that."

"What then?"

Jeff looks bemused. "I knew you had a sheltered, backwater upbringing, but every so often, I'm amazed by how innocent you are."

"Do you think?" I whisper as the meaning of her words slowly dawns on me. "You don't mean that Art and Bill are…?"

Jeff turns to face the water again. She folds her arms. "It is my experience that by the time you get to our age, men are either taken, drunken, or unsuitable. The pickings aren't great these days; we lost too many men in the War. There are more of us than them."

"How depressing." I feel rotten now. "But what about your Jim?" I ask, willing her thesis to be wrong. "He isn't taken, drunken, or unsuitable."

"Oh, he's taken," she says sassily. "I've staked a claim on that old boy though we're going to be crotchety by the time we marry."

"Vulgar money," I mutter.

"Yes, Tommy." Jeff nods. "Vulgar, vulgar money."

We watch the falls without talking. Water rushes from an endless supply, dropping over the edge and carrying on. Over and over, it flows like time and I've never seen anything so depressing. But then, I've always been vaguely depressed by beauty. Perhaps it's because I have so little beauty myself that a handsome woman fills me with envy, a vibrant sunset with loneliness or, in the case of Niagara Falls, the urge to throw myself over the rails. It's the tragedy of the whole thing—some are chosen for a life of glamour and ease and others are not. What did Elizabeth Bowes Lyon have to do with her birth? She was born into privilege, married the Duke of York, and was honoured with an entire edition of *Vogue*. But what did she do to deserve any of that? Nothing. Absolutely nothing. And what will any of us achieve in this world? Not the glamour of royalty or even the ease of the wealthy. Some of us can't even accomplish the simplest thing—to love and be loved by someone respectable. No matter how often I finger the frame of my university degree and congratulate myself for the hardships weathered, I can't help but feel I've failed somehow. That none of my efforts are sufficient. That I should have chucked it all in and married John McPhaden when I had the chance.

Jeff suddenly slaps her knees, then jumps to her feet. "There's plenty to see and no sense in sulking. I can hear a jazz band playing somewhere. We're going to find it and dance!"

"Jeff," I sigh. "My feet are so tired. Must we dance?"

"We must. We must dance like we will never dance again. You understand, don't you, Tommy? Life won't be the same when you're married and forty."

"We don't know I'll be married."

"But we do know you'll be forty."

I let Jeff lead me to the bandstand across the park. Couples have already broken into the Lindy Hop though it's scarcely five o'clock. Fringed hems and drop waists, strings of pearls and floral fabrics—the women blur together as gentlemen circle them. Toes cross. Fingers snap. Arms sway in the music.

"Is it Guy Lombardo and His Royal Canadians?" I ask a passerby.

The answer disappoints—"They skedaddled for Cleveland in '24, Sweetheart. This is just the band that plays Saturday nights in the drugstore"—but I tap my toe regardless.

"This is pretty much our last night, isn't it?" I call to Jeff, but she doesn't hear me. She's chatting with a young man who seems inclined towards dancing but doesn't have a partner. He offers a hand and she smiles enchantingly.

Suddenly, something inside me snaps and I realize I will not be left on a deck chair, stuck on the sidelines forever. I will not be an old maid complaining about young people. I will not. I am going to marry Raleigh Smith and the consequences can be hanged. What difference will it make to anyone anyway?

Marjory's Story
April 27, 1930
La Riviere, Manitoba
One year later. Marjory is thirty-seven years old.

"Listen to this," I say, my reading glasses perched on the end of my nose. "'On Thursday, April 17th, at 7 p.m., at the Manse, La Riviere, Marjory Thompson, daughter of Peter W. Thompson, of Oak River, Manitoba, became the wife of Raleigh Ranford Smith, of La Riviere, Rev. W. T. Hamilton officiating. After a brief honeymoon,'—yes, it was frightfully brief wasn't it?—'the happy couple took up their residence on the groom's farm adjoining the town. The bride has for some years'—some years! That's one way of putting it—'been the highly respected, efficient and successful principal of the town school. The community, though taken unawares, has recovered sufficiently to unanimously wish them abundant happiness and prosperity.' Recovered sufficiently?" I scoff. "What sort of wedding announcement is this?"

It's mid-morning on a Sunday and we're still in bed, though at least I'm sitting up, propped up on pillows. Raleigh languishes beside me, a faded coverlet still pulled over his shoulder. He snickers but it's a muffled gesture, tucked into the linens as he is.

"I can't say I've noticed unanimous wishes for abundant happiness and prosperity either," I complain.

Raleigh flops onto his back, laughing. "Mrs. Fargey was sorry to see you go," he offers as a consolation.

"'Miss Thompson! I'll miss your determination with the upstairs stove,'" I mimic in a priggish voice. "I bet she will. I was dashed good with that stove. She could never get it to burn, but it's all in the chimney dampers. Regulation of airflow."

"You taught in a country school for too many years." Raleigh yawns.

"True," I sigh. "Some of those stoves were beasts. Ice cold classrooms in the morning. Stifling hot in the afternoon. A constant battle. I was smart though."

"Undoubtedly. Stoves stood no chance against you."

"No!" I swat his leg. "I meant about my contract from the school."

"What exactly did you tell them?"

"That I was considering other options. Of course, they thought that meant a position somewhere like Brandon or Winnipeg, something with better pay or even access to a teacherage. They never imagined marriage as an option for me," I say, a note of bitterness in my voice.

"But you got a raise out of it too, old girl!"

I giggle at that. "Twas a double-cross, it was. You'll see. They'll fire me next year for sure."

"How so? There isn't anything in your contract about not being married."

"Just wait," I say sagely, flinging off the covers. "They won't like being made fools of and there's never been a married woman teacher, especially not a married woman as a principal."

"Well, we need your wages. And the world is changing. Married women have all sorts of jobs now. The war saw to that and you're 'persons' now, thanks to McClung and all those other rabid suffragettes."

I climb out of bed and wrap myself in a dressing gown. "The world might be changing, but I'm not sure it's for the better. The papers are filled with dire predictions for unemployment. If men have a hard time finding work, then women will get sent back to the kitchens."

"Where you belong!" Raleigh slaps the covers mockingly.

I roll my eyes. "Nothing's been the same since the stock market crash last fall."

"Thank goodness we've no money in the stock market then." Raleigh reaches out a hand to pull me back to bed.

I ignore his hand. "But others have money, or had, I should say. They won't be building new houses anytime soon. You might feel the pinch and I might be fired. And what will we do then? Hmm?"

"Since all is lost then, my jolly girl, why don't you hop back into bed with me?"

"Raleigh!" I shake my head. "It's ten in the morning. Aren't you hungry?"

"Famished, so hop in quickly."

I laugh at him, then walk through our barely furnished house to the kitchen. I stoke the fire and consider what to make for breakfast. Perhaps I'll fry eggs and brown some toast for breakfast.

Brushing away the flimsy curtain at the kitchen window, I survey the valley below. Early buds break out on the Manitoba maples. Shoots of grass protrude through the clumps of dried thatch leftover from last year. A thin layer of frost coats Raleigh's Ford truck. The truck box is filled with his tools plus a trunk of mine we haven't unloaded yet.

We've been married a week but I've been so busy I haven't had time to properly unpack or arrange the house more elegantly. It's been a blur of rushing to and from school, managing the shopping and the cooking, tidying up after Raleigh, lesson planning, marking and tutoring some extra lessons for the high school students who prepare for exams. It's no wonder most school teachers quit after getting married. Especially farm wives. I hate to admit it, but I miss Mrs. Fargey. Oh, for the convenience of arriving home at 5:00 to be told not to dawdle because supper is very nearly on the table! I used to think she was demanding. Now I long to sink into a chair and have someone feed me, look after me. To have one's laundry cleaned and folded, as if by magic, at no extra charge—"Just part of the rent"—ah! The luxury!

As the stove heats, I fill the coffee percolator at the kitchen sink. The plumbing in the house is simple—one pipe to the kitchen, another to the bathroom sink and a third to the toilet. Raleigh didn't have any plumbing installed, relying instead on a bucket of water, but I paid for the upgrade before we were married. I wasn't about to live like we did on the farm, trotting down to the well with a bucket in hand, morning, noon and night.

Father has built a proper house now, with plumbing though no electricity. La Riviere has had power since '27 but there's none to be had in Oak River, never mind the farms. I can't imagine him wanting to pay for it either. Lanterns and candles work well enough. The expense and unsightly poles dotting the landscape would discourage him against electricity.

I cringe. I haven't written to my father about my marriage and it can't be put off. Any more delay will only compound the insult. It's bad enough I didn't invite him to the wedding and he was never consulted, never asked for his permission or his blessing. He will be offended by that. I've never even mentioned Raleigh's name to him, never mind introduced him, not even by letter. I feel ashamed as if I've been sneaking around, which if the newspaper notice is any indication I have.

I retrieve two eggs from the icebox. One each will suffice. The price of groceries horrifies me. I had no idea how much it cost Mrs. Fargey to run the boarding house, how carefully she minded her expenses. I have greater respect for roast chicken on Sundays, pot pie on Mondays and dubious soup on Tuesdays. She was stretching her pennies as far as they would go, and I'll have to do likewise if we're going to survive on my wages.

Raleigh looks for work, but the farmers build their own barns and houses between caring for crops. Not many immigrants arrive now, so new houses aren't needed. The boom on the prairies might be over; it's not like twenty years ago. All the work left for carpenters is repairing porch steps or building new outhouses or fences between neighbours. No one is hiring. No one is building. Everyone is hunkering down and waiting for better times.

And Raleigh drinks. I know that. Too much. But it's the boredom, the waiting for work that drives him to it. I try to point him towards productive uses for his time, but gardening doesn't interest him. Reading has never appealed.

I crack eggs into the frying pan and listen to them sizzle. I remember Mother frying eggs on Saturday mornings while we were still in bed. She'd make us breakfast when we were little and she was still able to care for us. What a shame it is she died before the new house was finished. How she would have loved the running water, the sitting room, the elegance of painted walls and sunshine filtering through the windows. Oh, Mother. How sad it all was for you.

I slice the last bit of bread and make a mental note to buy more at the General Store tomorrow after school. I need to start making bread to save money, but I'm not sure how I'd go about that during the week. Could I start it first thing, run home at noon to form it into loaf pans and then cook it when I get home? I usually mark assignments at lunch. I'd be rushed if I ran home. I'll just have to make bread on Saturdays. I'll be the only woman in the village to do that, but it doesn't matter. I might be the only woman who works away from her home.

I have to admit I didn't think everything through when Raleigh asked me to marry him. We had talked about marriage for a while, off and on all winter. Sometimes I wonder if he only pressed the point because his finances were dwindling but as no happiness comes from that thinking I suppress the thought.

"Two minutes until breakfast!" I call and am rewarded by the sound of Raleigh stirring.

"Have you seen my blue collared shirt?" he yells.

"Still in the laundry basket. Sorry, I haven't had a chance."

Raleigh mutters something I can't hear through the wall. I bite my tongue to remind him that somehow he managed his laundry before we were married. I am his wife though; it's my duty to care for him.

I make a mental plan for the rest of the day—start hot water on the stove for laundry. Mark the grade 10 mathematics assignments as the water heats. Improvise a clothesline in the kitchen. I can't use the clothesline in the backyard to dry the laundry. I don't want the villagers to know I launder on a Sunday. There's a heap of it too, including the dress I wore last Thursday, our wedding day.

We deliberately chose the Thursday night before Easter for our wedding day. A four-day weekend beckoned, and all the Anglicans were busy at Maundy Thursday. As we hurried past the United Church on the way to the manse, evening light glowed against the church's lancet windows. A memory flashed of the grand windows of St. Peter's in Huddersfield but it quickly disappeared. The tiny churches built from Manitoba wood don't compare with a splendid cathedral hewn from Yorkshire stone. The structures are not similar despite their shared purpose.

In the diminutive La Riviere United Church manse, I vowed my troth and became Mrs. Smith, a name as understated as the surroundings at its conception. Reverend Hamilton, a kindly man, seemed preoccupied with the upcoming Good Friday services and talked us through our vows without noticing his purple pulpit stole dangling lopsidedly to the floor. He showed us where to sign the register and his wife chatted pleasantly to Jeff who stood up for me. The deed was done quickly— the signing of a marriage certificate, a quick peck, a few handshakes, and out again on the street. Jeff pleaded a prior engagement, so we set off alone to the hotel where we ate some dinner and spent the night. And that was it. There's hardly anything to write about to Father, but I must do it anyway.

"Breakfast is on the table!" I call.

Raleigh emerges from the bedroom, settles into a creaky kitchen chair and surveys the eggs and toast. "Capital job," he says.

"I'm not without domestic talents," I sniff. "I sat on the farm all through the war, waiting for a teaching position, milking cows and churning butter."

Raleigh laughs, stuffing fried eggs in his mouth. I suddenly realize I don't know how he spent the war, how he occupied himself while the empire sat on pins and needles.

"What did you do during the War?" I ask.

He looks surprised. "You forget you're a decade older than me. I was twelve when the war broke out. Father made sure I stayed in school, but he was so short of farm labour there was no choice by the end. I had to leave school."

"And hone your hatred of farming?"

"Something like that."

Raleigh doesn't say more. He doesn't relish discussions of the past or of his family. He prefers to keep the conversation in the present, without references to the time predating his trek west on the harvest trains. From what I've gathered, his family was respectable, just hard up. Raleigh says they were strict, but then Raleigh is one for pushing the rules. I'd probably side with his parents if it came to it.

"I'm going to drive out to Jim Mitchell's," Raleigh says, "and see about the granaries he plans to build. Maybe put a flea in his ear about hiring me to help."

I smile. It's an excellent time to go. Jeff will be in church, so Jim will be on the farm alone, pretending to be busy to avoid the trek to town.

"Take some change in case Jim offers you eggs!" I call as Raleigh pulls on his winter coat and wraps a wool scarf around his neck. Spring may be arriving but the mornings are still cold.

"Definitely not. I wouldn't want to lie when I say I don't have any change but will gratefully accept some eggs!"

I shake my head then clear the table. I've got a letter to write.

—

Dear Father—

I stop. My fountain pen lies heavily in my hand. The pen was a gift from the children when I returned to La Riviere as principal. I had just graduated from the University of Manitoba, possibly the first Bachelor of Arts ever to live in La Riviere. On the first day back, the children presented me with the pen after singing "O Canada." One of them made a speech—I can't remember who—something about me inspiring them to new heights. I opened the small red box tied with ribbon, the words "Swan Self-filling Pen" emblazoned on the top, and lifted the gold-plated pen to inspect it in the sunshine. It was beautiful. But their faces shone even more brightly than the gold-plating. "What a marvellous gift!" I gushed. "I will use it always!"

I use it now, but it doesn't flow across the page nearly as well as when I'm writing, "Although you showed correct methodology by adding the known angles then subtracting from 360 degrees to find the unknown angle, your addition skills failed you, hence the question has been marked incorrect." But I take a deep breath and make a start. This letter must be written.

> *I apologize for my delay in writing. I could blame many things—preparations for final examinations, assisting with the lower grades' Easter Egg hunt, leading the children in spring clean-up of the schoolyard—but you know that with Easter comes several days of holidays. So I have no excuse for not writing other than the distance that comes from repeatedly neglecting one's duty. Perhaps that's the wrong word—duty. I'd far rather be sitting in your kitchen, with its sparkling linoleum flooring and bright new paint, and tell you all that has happened lately. In truth, I don't know how to write in a way that doesn't make me seem secretive, furtive even. I best come to the point.*
>
> *I'm married, Father, to a man named Raleigh Smith. His carefree sense of humour is a perfect antidote to my seriousness. We saw each other on and off, even before I toured the Great Lakes last summer. He's a carpenter and builds houses and outhouses according to demand.*
>
> *We've kept things quiet because I didn't want to jeopardize my teaching contract—you know the prejudice against married teachers. On that note, I hope you're leading the way as a trustee of Marland to eliminate such outdated thinking.*
>
> *We were married on Maundy Thursday and spent the weekend settling me into his house. I hope we will all be together in summer, perhaps with Norah, though I fear a reunion with Joss will be beyond our conjuring powers. We shall aim to avoid the haying season though Allan seems to be at it every fair day in July if Mary's letters are anything on which to form an opinion.*

Must sign off. I will write several letters today and catch up on lesson preparation. Much love and best wishes for your health. Please share my news with Harry and Alec.

Your affectionate daughter,

Marjory

P.S. Raleigh's stock were loyalists. That should count for something.

I set my pen down and blow over the pages to dry the ink. I feel like a fraud even as I attempt a candid yet penitent tone. Nothing I wrote was untruthful, but I didn't write the whole truth either. What would I have written if I were completely honest?

"Father! Forgive me!" I might write. "I haven't told you about my husband because I'm ashamed of my weakness, my fear of being alone. I've married someone shockingly unsuitable because no one else will have me or take him and I want to be married. I want the respect that comes from having a husband, a home, children… a Ford truck, for goodness' sake! I don't want to live in a boarding house for the rest of my life. Oh. And Raleigh drinks. And he's a pig when he does."

Would I say that, even if I was speaking plainly? Of course not. Father drinks. He wouldn't necessarily judge. But Father is different than Raleigh. He never gets argumentative when he drinks. He just giggles at silly things and sings, "Down by the Sally Gardens." Father would be alarmed to hear that Raleigh's drinking makes him unsociable. Father's drinking makes him jollier, easy to entertain. He's not a danger to himself or anyone else when he drinks.

I push away these thoughts. No good comes of any of this. I'm a new bride in my own home. I'm going to make the best of it, and maybe Raleigh will see the error of his ways. Perhaps we can get him down to one drink every day before bed, no binges off to the pub, just a little sip to take the urge away.

The kettle boils. The water is ready for laundry, a task neither suitable for Sunday nor mentioned in my letter to Father.

—

"Where in Heaven's name have you been?" I sputter.

It's Monday morning and I'm dressed for school—coat, toque, gloves. My schoolbag is flung over one shoulder. I'm ready to walk out the door, but Raleigh stands on the stoop, leaning against the door frame.

"Ah! Marjory! Don't shout," he mutters with closed eyes.

Raleigh wears the same clothes he wore yesterday when he set off to see Jim Mitchell about a granary, but he's been sick on his shoes. Something's been spilt on his pants. His gloves are missing.

I look around quickly but don't see anyone on the road. How did he drive in such a state? Did someone drop him off?

"Get inside!" I hiss, tugging his arm. "I've been worried sick about you!"

He scowls at me. "Don't you try to mother me!" He flings my arm away, then falls into a kitchen chair.

"I'm not mothering you! You've been gone all night! How was I to know where you were? You could have been in the river."

He giggles at this, more like a cackle. "The river!" he snorts. "The river? How would I have landed in the river?" He drops his head into his arms and mutters something I can't hear.

He smells. Atrociously. His hair is matted. Grass litters the back of his jacket. I have a sinking feeling he spent the night on the side of the road, behind the hotel, somewhere wholly shameful. I'm mortified. What will the village think when this gets around? A week of marriage and he's out on a bender. Well done, Miss Thompson. You've sure made a match in heaven.

I try to touch Raleigh, pat him, give him some gesture of support to show I'm on his side, that we'll fight his cravings together. But he swats me away.

"Raleigh," I say in the tone of voice I use when vexed by a farm boy who is too big to thrash. "We will not live like this."

I wait for a response, but I only hear snores, low drags of air muffled between his arms. Defeated for the moment, I back away, pulling on my boots which I lace as quietly as I can.

Slipping out of the house, I start down the hill to school, walking quickly to make up for lost time. I have a horrible feeling in the pit of my stomach. Fear. Regret. Anxiety. What have I done? What in heaven's name have I done? Is he going to continue like this? Drinking and carrying on? We can't have children, not if this is how he's going to behave. And how will I ever maintain my teaching position like this?

John McPhaden's face comes to mind and I dismiss it angrily. It isn't helpful to think of the past, what might have been. I still achieved my degree. I still have my position as principal. No one at home knows what Raleigh can be like. All is not lost.

It's only when I cross the schoolyard, smiling and thanking students who wish "Mrs. Smith" congratulations, that I realize I left my lunch pail and will have nothing to eat today. But I'm not going back for it; that much I know.

—

Raleigh isn't in when I get home, but that's all right. It gives me time to think, to rehearse the speech I will deliver. It has to be convincing. Should I be firm or panicked? He dislikes my school teacher persona so perhaps I'll try panic. Something has to reach him.

I try to think about the next task to accomplish. Supper. I need to cook supper and then mark assignments. It doesn't matter where Raleigh is. I still need to do what needs doing. Someone has to be consistent. Stable.

Supper will be basic. I haven't made it to the grocery store. I tell myself it's because I'm short of time, but really it's because I can't bear walking into shops not knowing who saw what. Does the whole town know Raleigh was on a bender?

I stand at the sink peeling potatoes when the screen door bangs, but I don't turn around. I don't want to look at Raleigh, not right now. Instead, I grab a carrot and start peeling it.

Raleigh takes off his boots and hangs up his coat. "Marjory," he says softly.

I ignore him.

"Marjory, look at me."

I turn to face him. He's washed and tidy, and he holds a basket of groceries.

"I saw we were out of a few things." He sets the groceries on the table.

I don't say anything but it's evident by my face I've been crying. I can't remember the last time I've cried, not when Father left for Canada or when we left Huddersfield. Mother was sobbing and Baby Joss was wailing then. But someone had to be tough. Mary never let a tear fall, and I determined to be as tough as her. But Mother isn't here, going into hysterics, and Mary doesn't know how much I need her. Even if she were here, I wouldn't tell her my problems. I'd pretend, chin up, that everything was fine. Besides, I brought this on myself. Everyone warned me—Jeff, Annie, even Mrs. Fargey. Everyone knew what a terrible idea marrying Raleigh was.

Raleigh folds his arms and looks at the floor. "You know I have a problem. I can't help it. One drink turns into another and another."

"Raleigh," I whisper, tears flowing down my cheeks. "I received a reprimand today," I fabricate.

Raleigh's head jerks up. "You were sacked?"

I shake my head, wishing this charade wasn't necessary. "No. But very nearly. You were seen, you see." I emphasize the word "seen" as if it were the worst thing that could happen to anyone.

Raleigh buries his head in his hands. "Oh, Marjory."

I say nothing, letting panic stew in him for a moment, and then go on. "Raleigh, I don't pretend you can stop drinking cold turkey. That isn't possible. But you must never set foot in that hotel again. Not alone. Not with any of your cronies. You will have one drink every night before bed. And you will hang onto that thought all day. One drink. That's it. I will pour it for you and then I will hide the bottle. And tomorrow morning, I will explain, should any of the school board trustees come by again for a conversation. I will say what happened was exceptional. You are committed to better behaviour. You will never let it happen again."

I let my words sink in. Eventually, Raleigh nods. "Yes, Marjory. You're very right. This is what we must do."

"Can you imagine what this is like for me?"

Raleigh purses his lips and looks at the ceiling.

"Can you imagine how embarrassing it was to go to school this morning with the children congratulating me on my marriage, knowing my husband spent the night on the lawn behind the hotel?"

"I made it a little further home than that!"

I raise my eyebrows. "Is that relevant?"

Raleigh wheezes out a little laugh, but I'm not laughing. "There will be no joy in this household when I lose my job, Raleigh. Think about that. Look at the newspaper. Did you see all the charity expenses the town council paid? People's names are written in the newspaper, in the council minutes. If you are destitute, there's help, but the whole world will know you are a beggar. That would be quite a fall for the school principal to be a charity case."

Raleigh mutters something I can't quite catch, but I choose to take as agreement.

"I don't suppose this relevant either," Raleigh suddenly says, straightening himself up, "but I was drinking to celebrate. Jim's going to have me build not one granary but three!"

"That's good, Raleigh," I encourage as I do with children who show small steps in improving poor track records. In truth, as long as Raleigh has work, he'll stay off booze. He respects himself when he has work. Of course, there will be the celebration at the end of the project and then the melancholy of not having more work, but we'll deal with that later. I wonder if Jeff persuaded Jim to give Raleigh the work. There are other carpenters, carpenters more reliable than Raleigh. Often farmers build outbuildings themselves, so Jeff must have pressured Jim. I'm grateful to her, but I'm not joyous like Raleigh. The last twenty-four hours have been too awful for that.

"Why is this taking so long?" I moan. My bedroom is nearly dark, just as it was when these wretched pains began hours ago. Jeff stands beside my bed.

"Don't cry, Tommy," she says. "It will be over soon. I've sent for the doctor ages ago."

"It wasn't this awful with George," I murmur.

"Every birth is supposed to be different, isn't it?" She wipes my forehead with a cloth. "Think of George. He'll have a playmate."

Jeff is with me today but under protest. I should be having this baby in a hospital, in Pilot Mound or Manitou, or even in the larger hospital in Morden. I know not going to a hospital could be dangerous, but we don't have the money and everything was fine when I had George two years ago. Of course, that was in the Misericordia Hospital in Winnipeg. I was well-cared for by the Sisters. But it was easy then to stay with Norah until labour began. It's not easy now. I can't leave George and we don't have the $1.75 daily hospital fee. I can easily convalesce at home. Women always used to have babies at home. There's nothing to it.

I clutch Jeff's hand as another pain begins, my back arching as I cry out. She pushes my shoulder down. "Be brave, Tommy," she says. "Doctor will be here soon and all will be well."

I pant as the pain subsides and rise a little on my elbows as Jeff cautiously flips back the sheet that covers my legs.

"Am I nearly there?" I ask, then cry out again as another pain begins.

Tommy drops the sheet in place and takes my hand. "I don't have the slightest idea, and I'm desperately angry at you for not going to the hospital. But I expect everything will be all right."

She smiles widely, but something about her mannerism has suddenly changed. She's been cheerful all day, encouraging, but now she bustles around the room almost in a panic. She tidies things that don't need to be tidied. She folds towels already folded. She wipes her forehead and a sweat patch forms in the middle of her back. At the first sound of the doctor's car, she rushes from my room and I can hear a muffled conversation.

The doctor bursts in a moment later, asking questions as he takes off his overcoat and rolls up his sleeves. "When did the pains begin? How close are they?" Then, without hesitation or embarrassment, he flips back the sheet and nods his head. "We'll have you pushing shortly, Mrs. Smith," he says, reaching into his black bag and pulling out a stethoscope. Pressing the bell to my lower abdomen, he inserts the earpieces into his ear and waits with a furrowed brow. He moves the bell up and down, left and right, forward and back, but still, he frowns.

"Did you listen for a heartbeat?" he asks poor Jeff. She shakes her head with a quick jerk and bites her lip. The doctor scowls at her then turns to me. "Mrs. Smith—"

Pain has taken me in its grasp, so he doesn't continue. Instead, he stands silently while the agony passes. He listens for a heartbeat again, but nothing changes the look on his face. He glances at Jeff over the bed and I'm no fool. "There's something wrong, isn't there?" I ask.

"Perhaps," the doctor says. "But we can't know more until the baby is delivered. So we're going to have you push and will see what can be done."

Jeff helps me sit up against the headboard. She takes my arms in hers and holds me tightly even as I cry out in agony against her. The doctor counts and calls, "Now, Mrs. Smith. Let's try another good one," time and time again until I've barely the strength to hold up my head. But finally, fifteen, maybe twenty minutes later, the wee one is born.

"It's a girl," the doctor says, but I can she isn't breathing. The umbilical cord, dangling and wet, is knotted right in the middle. The doctor cuts it quickly and swats the baby's bottom, trying to shock her into breathing. But her colour is wrong. She's been starved of oxygen for a long time, not just in the last few minutes. She's small too.

The doctor tries a few more times, then turns to me. "Mrs. Smith, I'm sorry. But she passed a while ago."

I choke and jolt slightly, but I don't cry out. I haven't the energy. I just lie back while tears flow down my face. Jeff holds me, letting me cry. The doctor doesn't say anything more. He just pulls the soiled sheet down on top of me. He gathers the baby in a towel and carries her to the kitchen, presumably to wash her.

I sob now that the doctor is out of earshot. Sobs of sorrow and exhaustion. Broken dreams. Broken heart. I took this entire year off from teaching. We've no money left. And now this—it was all for nought. I shouldn't have been so tight with money. I should have gone to the hospital, but I'm not sure it would have made any difference. And that poor baby—that poor little girl will never play in the sunshine. I'll never do her hair, nor dress her prettily. She never even saw the light of day.

I can't bear the agony. It's too much. It's too great. I choke back my tears as the doctor returns the baby to me. She's swaddled in a clean white towel, and I hold her against my chest, trying to memorize her face. Her eyes are closed, probably never opened, and her face is peaceful.

The doctor stands at the foot of the bed. He doesn't say anything. He doesn't make judgements. He just surveys a scene that is probably familiar to him.

"What happens next?" I whisper after a moment. I'm sure the doctor wishes this business to be concluded as quickly as possible for all our sakes.

"Do you have a family plot?" the doctor asks.

"Not here. My parents are both buried in Oak River, north of Brandon. My husband's family are down east."

"Would you like to purchase a plot, do you think?" he kindly asks.

I choke over my words, tears rolling down my face again. "We're a little tight for cash at present, but I suppose we must. Would the grave be marked?"

"Of course. If you want a name on a plaque, that would be fine. Otherwise, it will be marked as 'Baby.'"

I know I should consult Raleigh, but I'm almost afraid to ask after his whereabouts. I take a deep breath. "Have you seen Raleigh?" I timidly ask Jeff.

"I believe he's celebrating down at the hotel," Jeff says slowly. "But don't worry about that. I'll send Jim down to break the news. We'll have him sleep off for a bit and I'll clean him up before I send him home."

"That might take days," I murmur, realizing I don't have time to consult, not with my husband, not with anyone. I need to make decisions and then get rested. George will need me.

Jeff reads my thoughts. "George can stay on at my house for a while," she says.

"I can't thank you enough, Jeff," I say, defeated by the pain, the disappointment, the blackness which colours the future. I close my eyes and clutch the baby.

"If you don't object, Mrs. Smith," the doctor kindly says, "I'll take the baby. But only once you're ready. I'll deal with the undertaker and will let you know where she is buried. When you're up and about, you can arrange a stone."

I nod. It all seems organized. Even amid my pain, the doctor has a plan. He's done this before—stillborn babies, afterbirth, bloody sheets. The mess must be cleaned up, like the kitchen the day you preserve tomatoes for winter. When you're halfway through and exhausted, you must keep going, if for no other reason than to clean up the mess.

I release my poor baby to the doctor and let Jeff find me a fresh nightgown. I've never felt so depleted.

Norah arrives the next day, walking up the hill from the train station with a small satchel on her arm. I am still in bed, staring at the wall when she lets herself in.

"Dear Marjory! What a terror you've been through." She rushes over to embrace me and I cry again. I don't have the energy to protest her dramatic descriptor. Terror seems about right. "When I got the call, I was frantic to get here. The train seemed slower than usual, but we arrived on time, rolling into the valley with screeching brakes. I practically ran up the hill—I was so anxious to see you."

"Thank you for coming," I manage. "Was it a problem to get away from work?"

"Bother work!" She pats my hip and straightens up. She wears a two-piece tweed suit with a wide black belt and a jaunty hat with a velvet bow. Her hair is rolled and pinned like a movie star's and I surprise myself by caring. I thought I was beyond the reach of fashion.

"We've got to get you out of bed," Norah says matter-of-factly. "You remind me far too much of Mother, lying there pitifully. The couch in the sitting room is bathed in sunshine. That's where you ought to be."

"I'm not sure I can sit," I say.

Norah cocks her head. "Why ever not?"

I almost smirk at this. "I had a bit of a bad time of it. A 'terror' was the word you used if I remember."

Despite being forty years old, Norah is easily shocked. She looks at me with eyes wide open. "Are you serious?" she whispers, eying up the region of my lower parts, despite being completely covered in a thick quilt. "Can you walk?"

"To the bathroom and back but only if necessary."

Norah shakes her head at this. "It wasn't an easy delivery then?"

"No," I say sadly. "The poor little thing couldn't help at all. She wasn't moving,." Tears come to my eyes again, and Norah quickly reaches into her bag for a handkerchief.

"You poor girl," she murmurs. "What a wretched thing has happened to you."

I choke back the tears. I don't mean to be emotional but I can't stop crying. I expect it's my body's reaction to everything that happened yesterday. I think of Mother again. She cried on and off for years. Was that her body's reaction to the shock of immigration, or was she genuinely that unhappy?

"Where is everybody?" Norah asks, retrieving yet another fresh handkerchief from her bag. She seems to have an endless supply. "Raleigh? George?"

"My friend, Jeff, is taking care of them both."

"Both of them?" Norah sputters. "Why in heaven's name isn't Raleigh here taking care of you?"

I wave my hand vaguely. "You know. Raleigh thought it would be a happy occasion, so he celebrated early. He's probably napping and wouldn't be any use anyway. He's quite childlike in stressful situations."

Norah looks increasingly deflated. She gives up her line of inquiry and sits on a chair, brought in from the kitchen early yesterday by Jeff when she had time between labour pains to crotchet.

"Marjory, you've got to get Raleigh in hand," Norah says.

"He's much better," I fib. "Just the thought of a new baby set him off a little. Also, I haven't been teaching this year—I haven't been pulling my weight, you see—so money's a bit tight."

"Pulling your weight?" Norah sputters. "Since when is resting through confinement not pulling your weight? And you're over forty. Not the best time in a woman's life for having babies."

"You're thinking of Mother, aren't you?"

"Actually"—Norah laughs a sad laugh—"I was thinking of myself."

"You would make a wonderful mother."

"But here I am. Forty years old without a gentleman caller in sight. I don't think motherhood is in my future."

"But you have a career: Secretary to the Minister of Education!" I protest. "And you sing so beautifully. Father used to send me clips from the Winnipeg papers about your concerts. Solos with the orchestra. Performances for charities."

"Did he really send them to you?" Norah chuckles, wistfully looking out the window. "Bless his memory. He knew I had you to thank more than anyone else. Poor Father. Strange to think of him in the cemetery beside Mother. We have become the older generation far too early, Marjory. But then, it's not like the old-timers had an easy time of it either. No wonder they died young."

"Father was proud of us both," I say.

"Yes, he was. Especially proud of you for taking your degree. 'Marjory is a smart one,' he always used to say. But on my first day of work at the Department, he sent me a telegram: 'That's my girl. Stop.' At least, I assume it was him that sent it! As frugal as he was, there wasn't a name on it."

"How are things at the Department?"

I am always interested in what changes might come from the provincial government. The quality of our rural schools seems more and more dependent on the support of the Department of Education. I almost long for the old days when a teacher could make an appeal for funds directly to the school board and have it make a difference. Now, it's all just requests sent up a flagpole, lost in a sea of bureaucracy.

"You ought to be resting, Marjory," Norah says emphatically. "Not talking shop with me."

"It's a good distraction," I say, not tired at the moment, just sore and desperately sad.

"If you insist." Norah folds her arms over her pretty suit jacket. "Things are dreadful, to be honest. Absolutely dreadful. The bottom is falling out of wages right across the province though things are worse in Saskatchewan and Alberta. Teachers are teaching for their room and board there, and the farmers boarding them get credit on their over-due tax bills as compensation. The worst of it is, when one poor teacher bails on the school because they are really and truly starving, hundreds apply to fill the vacant position."

"Gracious!" I say. "Men and women both?"

"Aye." Norah uses an old expression of our father's. "And you know how it is—even in Manitoba, where the situation isn't quite so bad, women are paid much less than men regardless of their marital status. They complain to the Department—long letters of rage and frustration—but the Minister won't interfere."

"How maddening. Men's work is always more valued than women's. Of course, the Department never says it outright, but the pay talks."

"Women lack advocates. That's the main problem. Never mind that eighty percent of school teachers and half of the students are female, women are not allowed as school board trustees, and the vast majority of positions of principals and superintendents are all male. No wonder female equity is but a distant hope."

Norah opens the curtain to look out into the valley. I can hear birdsong and picture a flock of starlings perched in the trees behind the house.

"You were fortunate, Marjory," she says. "You got that principal job, and then you weren't sacked when you married or even when you had George. You must be a dashed good school teacher."

"I am," I say proudly.

"Your case is truly exceptional. Especially with Raleigh's predisposition. I can't imagine why your school board hasn't sacked you."

"You're not encouraging, Norah."

"I see things in the department though, teachers who lacked advocates. You've been very lucky."

"Sometimes, I think the school board feels sorry for us," I say.

Norah laughs at that. "But we've got to do something about you, Marjory. You can't go on like this."

"On like what?" I ask, my pride offended.

"Impoverished. Poorly treated. Exhausted."

"I'm fine, Norah. I've had a bad time of it this year. Things will get better as soon as I get my strength back. This fall, I will teach the grade twelve class from home again, like I did when George was born. It will bring a steady income, and Raleigh is always better when we have a steady income. George will be in school in a few years, and I'll be back at work. Maybe even as a principal again, somewhere. I'm not afraid of moving. Might do Raleigh some good to get away from his drinking pals."

Norah sits back down again. "Drinking pals are ubiquitous."

I choose not to take her seriously. "What a big word, Norah."

Norah ignores my quip and leans forward. "Marjory, would you ever think of leaving him?"

I'm shocked at this. "And deprive George of his father? What a suggestion!"

"You could come and live with me. We'd make it work."

I shake my head. "No, Norah. I made this bed and I will lie in it. Raleigh is often quite decent to us. He plays with George; takes him fishing. When George is older, he'll take him hunting. It's good for a boy to have a father about."

Norah stares at me sadly. She looks so much like Mother, disapproval and concern mixed into a particular scowling expression. A wave of nostalgia sweeps over me and long-repressed memories tumble together, flashing in quick succession: Mother drinking tea at a makeshift table out on the lawn, swatting mosquitoes, trying to maintain the pastimes and gestures of an English lady; Mother weakly hugging me at the train station when I left for Normal School the first time; Mother lying on her side in bed as I am, slowly giving up on the people around her.

"I might try getting up," I say suddenly, "if you'll give me a hand, Norah. It will do me good."

———

Raleigh appears by supper, George at his side. I'm up, or at least I'm in day clothes, resting on the settee just off the kitchen. I open my arms to George and he toddles to me. "Mama!" he calls, as delighted to see me as I am to see him.

George is a handsome little boy, named after my grandfather George Beaumont. George has a thick head of blonde hair which I comb until it shines in the sunshine. His eyes are a bright blue, and he has an adorable smile. I pull him up on the settee beside me, and he breathlessly tells me something about a dog though I can't quite catch his words.

Raleigh translates. "The Fargey's collie had her pups," he says. "We stopped on the way home to see them."

"Ah!" I say. "The paternity was a mystery, last I heard from one of the children. Has the lineage been established?"

"Strong suspicions on a lab, though there's a husky, German Shepherd cross around town too." Raleigh still stands at the door as if he's afraid to wander close to Norah.

"Dark colouring then?" A plan is hatching in my mind. A dog might be the very thing for little George. Something to play with.

"The litter is a real mix," Raleigh says. "Each one is a little different."

Norah curtly greets Raleigh then opens her arms to George. He burrows deeper into me, suddenly shy. "He missed you, Marjory," Norah says, getting down on her knees beside the settee. "I brought animal crackers with me!" she coaxes, and George squirms around to look at her with one eye. "A nice tin of animal crackers."

"Bar-num-nums?" George asks, his head up now.

"Yes!" Norah exclaims. "A wonderful red tin of Barnum's animal crackers!"

George stretches out his arms, and Norah carries him to the bedroom to find her satchel. His shrieks of delight can be heard as she retrieves his present. I wonder how she had time to purchase animal crackers in her haste to catch the train.

Raleigh hangs up his cap on a peg by the door. "A bad time of it, Old Girl?" he finally asks.

"Perfectly dreadful," I whisper.

He nods and goes to wash his hands for supper. And that is the end of it. Those are the last words we speak of a child who will never see the light of day, who was loved but lost. And there's no point in discussing matters further. Our relationship has broken down to the point that Raleigh and I hardly speak. Feelings. Disappointments. Hopes or dreams. We don't discuss any of these things. Instead, we talk about what we must—money, work, bills due. We avoid the biggest sources of conflict, namely his inability to quit drinking and my inability to keep a steady teaching contract this past year. It wasn't my fault, of course. I couldn't work while expecting a baby. But he also doesn't think drinking is his fault. He can't control the urge. It's as simple as that. And so, we eat our meals in silence. George chatters but then quiets down, realizing his parents are lost in sadness.

Suddenly, I realize we haven't named the baby, the poor little one who passed through our lives so quickly that a proper christening was never considered.

"Raleigh!" I call. "What should we name her?" But he doesn't hear me running over the taps, so I let it pass. What would be the point? I decide to name her myself.

"Mary Ann" comes to mind after my mother, and I cherish the thought that my little one sleeps in her grandmother's arms. May she rest in peace, for there's no peace on earth. Not here, at least.

Marjory's Story
July 5, 1943
Oak River, Manitoba
Nine years later. Marjory is fifty years old.

"Why are you doing this?" Mary stares me down with her hands on her hips.

Mary has aged remarkably in the past twenty years. She's only fifty-three, but she looks like a little old woman, her white hair pinned in tight waves against her head, a dowdy kitchen dress hanging off her shoulders. She's not young anymore. Her children are grown. Her Allan is practically an old man. That's what years of hard work do to you. Breaking land with an axe and a plough, hauling lumber from the mill in the bush, cleaning grain, cutting wood, volunteering on the school board and the grain elevator cooperative association—Allan never stops moving. They have the boys, of course. Married, Frank farms and waits for Allan to retire to town. And Jack helped until he enlisted.

Dear Jack. Mary can't stop worrying about him.

"I don't believe you, Marjory," Mary goes on. "Here you are, uprooting from La Riviere to teach close to us, and now uprooting yourself for the summer so you can be with Raleigh at some God-forsaken work camp! These changes can't be good for your boys."

On cue, eleven-year-old George and six-year-old Jack burst into the kitchen. It's confusing that Mary and I both have sons named John, nicknamed Jack, but it shows Uncle John's influence in our lives. We remember him putting us on the ship, visiting us on the prairies, and giving us money all those years ago. At least I said it was Uncle John I remembered. Perhaps it was John McPhaden I thought of too.

"Mother!" George cries, clearly excited about something. "Uncle Allan is going to let us ride the horses!"

Jack jumps up and down with delight, clapping his hands and chanting, "Hors-es! Hors-es!"

"And where will you ride to?" I ask, amused at their enthusiasm.

"Over to see Uncle Harry and Uncle Alec!"

"Say hello and tell them I'll pop over this evening for a visit."

"Bring them these," Mary says, swiping two butter tarts cooling on the counter into a brown paper bag.

"I thought they knew how to cook," I say.

Mary shakes her head. "Bread, maybe."

The boys run out of the house again, banging the screen door. I hear them shrieking all the way to the barn, "We've got a treat for the uncles!"

I chuckle and sit at the kitchen table where my coffee cools. It's the same table the McPhadens were gathered round the night I rushed over when Mother was in labour. It's strange that it's Mary's kitchen table now and that her in-laws, Hugh and Emily, are in their eighties, living to see the end of this war as if the last war wasn't enough. They're both out in the yard now on hard kitchen chairs, watching the farm activity with their arms folded, their busy days behind them.

"Why are Hugh and Emily here and not with John?" I ask. John McPhaden has farmed the neighbouring place since he returned from the Great War. He's taken care of his parents in their golden years, to his credit.

"They are here because John is doing what he often does when you come home."

"What is that?"

"He goes away, you twit. Haven't you noticed?"

I drink my coffee in silence as Mary sinks a chair at the end of the table. She looks at me with sad eyes, and I squirm under her scrutiny.

"I know I'm not young to keep starting over," I begin, but Mary interrupts.

"You certainly are not. You are fifty and your hair is white."

"It's not white!" I protest, to which Mary rolls her eyes. "There's some grey in it but it's not white."

We frown at each other for a second, then start to laugh. What does it matter how white our hair is or isn't? It doesn't change anything. We are middle-aged women looking at old-age as the next reality. Perhaps Mary feels it more than I do. She has grandchildren whereas my children are still young.

"As I was saying," I begin again, rather loftily. "I know I'm not young to keep starting over, but I have to, you see. I've only had temporary teaching contracts in La Riviere since I had Jack. And he's six now. If things were going to improve, they would have improved by now."

"What's the problem, do you think?"

"The '30s." I shrug my shoulders. "What a desperate decade. People moved away from La Riviere. There are fewer children in school, so there was no need or money to hire teachers."

"Things were bad here too. That's why Allan started grain cleaning and woodcutting. We had to do something to feed five children."

"And they're such lovely children." I smile.

"They are." Mary nods. "I feel I can say that. But my Jack worries me."

"What's the latest?"

"I'd let you read his letter, but you'd just take a red pencil and correct his spelling."

"I would not!" I protest, but Mary chuckles.

"You would in your head."

"Possibly. Go on," I urge.

"He's been stationed all over England and Scotland, and he's earned the rank of Flight Lieutenant. They're hunting U-boats over the Bay of Biscay mostly."

"Between France and Spain?" I ask, not entirely sure. Geography isn't a course I teach.

"Yes. I had to look it up in the atlas. We've had the atlas out many a night, studying what we've heard on the CBC."

"And has he looked up the Beaumonts? Aunt Bertha is still alive, isn't she?"

"Of course! She wrote at Christmas. The mill is doing tremendously well with a government contract for khaki. Her sons, George and John, are making a great go of it. Anyway, Jack intends to look them up, but there's a certain young lady, also in the Air Force, who claims much of his spare time." Mary smiles.

"How nice! We might get another English woman in the neighbourhood. Some fresh blood of refinement!"

"That may be a hasty wish. Early days, you know. Also, things aren't looking good on the Western Front."

I look down at my coffee. "And the RAF is so important."

"Allan has read some things, things I wouldn't like Jack to be part of. It seems Churchill is shifting the bombing. They are not just targeting U-boats but are bombing civilian targets—factories and so on. Their nighttime navigation is getting better too. Who knows? If the war drags on, might they start bombing cities?"

"Hitler is certainly bombing London."

Mary nods, pouring us more coffee. "But that's Hitler for you. I hope we don't bomb civilians. I'm glad Jack is with Squadron 502. The 502 targets U-boats and those dashed U-boats don't care what they sink."

My head whips up. "Mary! Did you just swear? 'Dashed' is a euphemism, you know."

"Sorry. It's this war. It brings out the worst in me."

"Well now, I don't know if you are the proper person with whom to leave my children," I tease.

"I can assure you that taking them to a work camp out west will not be any better for them, linguistically, I mean."

"And from what I hear about the food, they are far better off here, nutritionally." I wave a hand at the freshly picked salad greens draining in the kitchen sink.

Mary folds her arms and leans back in her chair. "But a work camp is no place for a woman either," she says. "Marjory, you know Raleigh is drinking on his off days. It will be awful for you there."

I look down at the well-worn table which has seen so many plates of food dealt out to young, hungry mouths. The wood is nicked and scratched in a hundred places. The legs are scuffed. The leaves are permanently extended. The table is everything a kitchen table in a farmhouse should be. Well-used. Surrounded by family.

I finally speak: "Mary, I married Raleigh for better or worse. That's what I promised. And if I don't go and see him, he'll deteriorate. He'll collapse, mentally. His will is not strong, just his body, you see. He can work in a lumber camp, though, and make money for us. Money to feed and clothe my children. He's doing his part and I need to do mine."

"And what is your part?"

"Being strong. Bolstering his morale. Keeping him off of drink. Keeping him company."

Mary shakes her head. "My dear Marjory. It's a fool's errand."

—

I walk over to the Thompson farm after supper. Alec kindly sent an invitation back with the boys for the supper meal, but I telephoned that Mary had already planned for us. It wasn't quite true as Mary makes large vats of food every night and a few mouths, either way, make little difference. But I wasn't about to sample my brothers' cooking if I could help it.

It is a beautiful evening for a walk. The wheat is growing well; a lush green crop waves together in the prairie wind. The sun is still high even despite the late hour. That's the beauty of our northern country—long days in summer. But we pay for it in winter, when darkness stretches into the morning hours and comes just after school ends.

Harry and Alec are out in the yard when I arrive. Middle-aged now, they are resigned to bachelor life. But they have each other and don't seem to mind. Their garden is well-maintained though the house is not, Mary tells me. It's a pity, she says, because it was such a triumph for Father to build the new house, and Harry and Alec scarcely know what a washrag is.

The house, a simple storey-and-half structure, was built further from the barn than the log cabin was, a sensible adjustment to the layout. Times have changed since the farm was homesteaded, and most of the animals are gone now anyway. A McCormick-Deering tractor sits in front of the barn, its red paint shining in the evening light. The lean-to no longer houses the farm wagon but a Chevy truck with a hoist that doubles as a grain wagon and a ride into town. A recently installed powerline brings electricity to the barn and the house. I hear the hum of a kitchen fan, though Harry and Alec seem happy to sit out in the yard on folding chairs.

"The boys have sure grown, Marjory," Harry offers as a conversation starter, his thin face and twinkly eyes pressed into a smile.

"Hmmm," I say absentmindedly, looking over the yard which has changed so much since my childhood. "Have you got a washing machine?" I ask, suddenly curious.

"Aye," says Harry, folding his arms. "Its name is Alec."

Much guffawing ensues. Once recovered, Alec adds, "Harry won't let me buy an electric washing machine on account of electricity costs."

"But the farm is doing well?" I press. "You're not worried about money?"

"We're fine," Harry says again. "The farm is better, but we had a bad time these past ten years."

Alec chimes in. "Drought. Grasshoppers. Dashed Russian Thistle. We learned to modify our farming techniques. Not so much tilling, you know. Father would always work the soil completely under. We leave a little stubble. We also started fertilizing."

"Fertilizing!" I say. "But you haven't any animals."

"Artificial fertilizer," Harry explains. "Joss sends us samples from his factory. We try things out. We're working with him to develop some sort of applicator device which can spread fertilizer evenly."

"How extraordinary!" I say. "I thought his company— what's it called?"

"Consolidated Mining and Smelting Company," the brothers say in unison.

"Yes, that. I thought they were doing more hush-hush work for weapons."

Harry and Alec exchange a panicked look. "How do you know that?" Harry asks.

"I'm pretty sure it's common knowledge," I say.

"Anyway," Harry goes on, "Joss's research is focused on fertilizer for domestic agriculture, and I have to say the fertilizer pays for itself immediately. It keeps the soil consistently productive. Unfortunately, the war is creating other problems though. Demand for some resources is high—lumber, mining for ships and bombs. However, for grain, it's a different story. There's a ban on shipping grain to Europe—don't want to give those dashed Huns any help—so prices haven't been good."

"I was thinking about you and the Great War, Harry," I say. "How horrid that the next generation also fights."

"It's terrible," Harry agrees. "Did you see Churchill was in Washington to address Congress?"

"Yes, and the Americans bombed Naples." I read the news whenever I can lay my hand on a newspaper.

"It's that bombing that bothers me," Alec murmurs. "Can you imagine waking in the night to the air raid warning, rushing down to the shelters, only to come back and find your house is gone? What a dreadful thing." He shakes his head and we all sit quietly for a while.

"Mary tells me Jack is doing well bombing U-boats," I offer as a way to cheer the conversation.

"Aye," Harry says, "and we've heard he's met a girl."

"Mother would have been pleased," Alec adds, "the girl being English."

We chuckle at that.

"Poor Mother and Father," Alec murmur.

We listen to the crickets. Then Harry shifts in his seat and Alec clears his throat. I get the feeling they're working up to something.

"Lovely boys," Alec says, and I'm not sure to whom he's referring—Jack and his comrades bombing U-boats or my sons.

"Who do you mean?" I ask.

"Your boys, Marjory. Absolutely lovely. So polite."

I nod. "They are polite. Well-mannered as a rule. Though Jack can be a little boisterous."

"Like Mary's Jack," they say together, then smile.

"Let's hope there are no wars for my Jack," I say.

More silence. More crickets. Eventually, Harry clears his throat one last time and launches in: "So about you travelling west, Marjory…"

"Yes?" I snip as if I've been interrupted for the fourteenth time in a calculus lesson by a completely mystified student.

Harry looks at Alec for support. But Alec purses his lips and says nothing.

"Well…" Harry begins again. "We just wonder if it's for the best. These work camps can be rough places."

I look from one brother to the next, calculating my response. "Have you looked at me lately?" I demand.

"What do you mean, Marjory?" Alec asks.

"I'm a fifty-year-old woman with white hair—so Mary tells me—with no looks whatsoever and a sharp tongue. What are the odds I'll be preyed upon by the unruly?"

"I'd say none," Harry says, rather uncharitably in my mind.

"But that's not what we're worried about," Alec rejoins.

"What are you worried about then?" I ask, daring them to come out with it.

Harry and Alec look at each other again, willing the other one to speak. "It's a matter of drink," Harry eventually says. "Alec and I rarely touch the stuff, on account of Father."

"Father wasn't a mean drunk," I counter.

"No, he wasn't. He was always rather good-natured, as far as alcoholics go. But there was that incident at the hotel back in '13."

I roll my eyes. "Yes, Yes. You're worried about Raleigh's drinking, is that it?" I hope to bring them to their point which they circle like crows flying 'round the barnyard.

Harry nods. "But more to the point, we're worried about you."

"Where do you get your information? I certainly never write about Raleigh's challenges. Is it Norah?"

My brothers look down at their work boots, caked in mud. "Norah is concerned about you, Marjory," Alec says slowly as if calming a bird with a broken wing. Perhaps if he speaks slowly enough the flapping and the fussing will stop.

I stare them both down. "Norah shouldn't meddle. She wants me to leave Raleigh. Can you imagine? Mother would roll in her grave. Father too. I wouldn't take the opinions of anyone who advocates divorce."

"You wouldn't have to divorce, Marjory," Harry says, "just remove yourselves and the boys from harm's way."

"Harm's way?" I sputter.

Alec leans forward. "Norah worries Raleigh might, well, you know…"

I raise my eyebrows.

"Raise a hand," he adds, nearly at a whisper.

"Norah told you this?" I ask, shocked.

"Fellows who drink sometimes do."

"Norah shouldn't jump to conclusions!" I cry. "Norah shouldn't speculate! Why on earth would she suggest that Raleigh might hit us?"

Harry and Alec cast more worried glances at each other.

"Raleigh drinks. I won't deny it, and he's not very nice when he does," I snap. "But that isn't to say that he's a roaring alcoholic. And he never lifts a hand, not to me nor the boys. And he's a good father. I don't know what Norah thought she was accomplishing by gabbing away nonsense."

"We didn't mean to upset you," Harry says, reaching out a hand to pat my knee.

But I'm in no mood to be mollified. I jump up and fold my chair. "I'm going to go back to Mary's. I don't want to discuss my personal affairs any longer. I'm dreadfully upset at Norah."

"Marjory, sit down," Harry pleads. "Norah was worried, you see. We've all got to look out for each other. You looked out for Norah, sending her money so she could stay in school. I looked out for Alec when Father was on his benders. Mary looks out for us now, fresh linen and the like." He chuckles, trying to break the tension in the air. "We're just trying to help each other, just as we always did. The Thompson children!"

"But we're not children!" I snap. "We're adults who can look out for ourselves. I knew what I was doing when I married Raleigh. Norah can't stand the thought that the benefits of marriage outweigh the benefits of spinsterhood, even if the marriage isn't perfect. It's a slap on her face. A rebuttal, if you will. She wants me to become a *divorcée,* like Wallis Simpson. What a glamorous sister I'd be then!" I wave my hand in the air mockingly, hoping they'll see how ridiculous Norah is.

But my brothers just look sadly at the green grass growing under their work boots. "No..." Alec says slowly. "Norah was just worried about you. That's all."

Harry squints into the last rays of daylight, fading into the west. "Divorce isn't the worst idea, Marjory. It really isn't. Not for the sake of your boys, you know?"

Without even a goodbye, I turn and stalk down the lane of the Thompson farm into the twilight.

—

The birds wake me before my alarm clock. Chirping and cheeping, the birds delight to see the sun rise through a low fog. This July has proven warm, and as the sun rises, the land gives off the moisture it collected overnight, puffs of mist, soon to burn off.

My sons sleep on floor mats at my feet, undisturbed by the birdsong. I press my toes carefully between their limbs—arms and legs splayed across hardwood—and walk to the window. Sweeping back the curtain, I see Mary's son Frank going in and out of the barn, carrying milk pails, moving cows from the milking station back to pasture. McPhadens still milk cows, a ritual my brothers have given up. Instead, Harry and Alec buy their dairy items from Mary, claiming it gives her a bit of pocket money, though I think the early morning milking in the dead of winter lost its appeal years ago.

Allan's father, Hugh, totters across the yard. All but blind, he still manages to feed the chickens on Mary and Allan's farm, a task he seems to enjoy. The chickens provide him with a wealth of conversation material, evidenced at dinner last night. "Little Lottie isn't laying as well," Hugh mourned while we ate.

"Is that so?" Mary asked absentmindedly. "Could you speculate why?"

No further encouragement was necessary and Hugh launched into a monologue of the life span and productivity of the laying hen, stopping along the way to expound upon the quality of feed, the security of the coop, and the need for regular inspection. Once he finished, he lapsed into silence, a silence he maintained to the end of the meal when he declared himself done in and asked Allan to see to evening milking. Allan smiled and said he'd take it in hand.

But now, in the warm morning light, Hugh crosses the yard with a chicken feed pail in hand. He's met by Allan, who has just arrived back from town in the farm truck. Allan's morning started much earlier than mine, but he's hauling last year's oats to the elevator. I suppose the granaries must be emptied before this year's harvest begins. Hugh stands back, seemingly surprised to see the Chevy farm truck roll into the yard. Mary told me Hugh resents the new equipment, claiming the horses were more reliable, a lot quieter, and better for the soul. He may be right, but I remember how long it took my father to haul grain to the elevator. The wagon would be filled with grain bags, and the tired horses would pull load after load into town. It's obvious using the grain truck is more efficient than hauling grain the old way. But Hugh stares in awe at the Chevy farm truck as it lumbers past him towards the grain auger emerging from a granary. His memory isn't very good. Perhaps he forgot the truck existed, that the hour-long procession of horse and wagon to town has changed to a fifteen-minute run in a vehicle.

"George! Jack!" I say, shaking the boys' shoulders. "Breakfast time."

George's eyes open slowly, but Jack sits up quickly. "Can we ride in the grain truck?" he asks, remembering a promise Uncle Allan made the night before.

"Possibly," I say, "but you must brush your teeth, get dressed and eat breakfast first."

Jack is off like a shot, but George is more circumspect. "Is this the day you leave, Mother?" he asks, slowly rubbing his eyes.

"It is." I run my fingers through his golden hair that glows in the morning light. He nods without any real show of emotion. He's a tough kid, my George. "But I'll be back at the end of the summer, and we'll go back to our house near my school. We still have the lease. So it will be the same as last year, no different."

He nods again and my heart breaks, just a little. We have to be tough though. This war. The instability. Everyone has to make adjustments.

"And when will Father come home?" George asks.

"I don't know. Not for a while."

Seemingly satisfied with the uncertain answers I give, George flings back his blankets and pads down the hall to the washroom. I can hear Jack gargle noisily, spit out his toothpaste and giggle. Spitting is a favourite activity for young Jack.

"Don't spot the mirror!" I call down the hall.

"Too late!" George calls back, and I make a mental note to clean the bathroom before leaving.

From the kitchen, Mary calls that breakfast is on the table. Jack runs to the top of the stairs to yell, "I'm coming, Auntie Mary, only I haven't got any pants on!"

I smile at this. Jack is irrepressible, a jolly little character. Not as serious as George, but not so wild as to irritate, Jack brings humour to every room, enthusiasm where energy has been sapped. He tugs on his clothes then dashes down the stairs, chattering about a ride in the grain truck.

—

The letter sits at my place at the breakfast table. Addressed, "Marjory Thompson Smith, Oak River, Manitoba," the letter found its way to me with a magical simplicity. I recognize Jeff's handwriting. She may be Mrs. Jim Mitchell, but I'll always think of her as Jeff. She knew I was spending two weeks at the end of term with my family. Not knowing a specific address, she cleverly included my maiden name. Small town memories are long, and post office workers tend to have an intricate knowledge of the goings-on of everyone in the district.

"If you're still determined to leave today, I'll take you to the train station in the grain truck," Allan offers.

"Oh," I say, surprised at the suggested conveyance.

"If that's all right with you, Marjory." Mary pours fresh, hot coffee for me.

A pitcher of cream from yesterday's milking is offered by Mrs. McPhaden who breakfasts beside me. Emily McPhaden is a shadow of her former self, often ill, stone deaf, and quite forgetful now. She smiles at me though, and perhaps she remembers me, for she asks me how my mother is.

"She's resting peacefully, Mrs. McPhaden," I say, accepting the cream. "And thank you, Allan. The grain truck will be quite sufficient. Do you propose this next load or the one after?"

"The one after will give you plenty of time to catch your train. It will also be my last trip."

"Then that had better be the one I take," I say.

"Aye," says Allan, finishing off his coffee with short sips. "I'll take the boys on this load."

"Thank you. They've been looking forward to it."

Jack nods frantically at this, his mouth full of bread, still warm from the oven.

I don't know how Mary keeps up with the work—so much cooking, a vast garden, in-laws to care for. But she's always been ruthlessly efficient, our Mary. It's just a pity that all those years of effort have worn her so low. She's pale and thin.

Mrs. McPhaden suddenly puts her hand on my arm. "Does your mother always use beautiful china, or is it just for me?"

I glance at Mary and she smiles. Mrs. McPhaden's mind is in the past.

"I believe she did it just for you!" I say.

"How very nice of her. She seems very tired, your mother."

"Farm work is hard," I say, by way of explanation.

"And you girls don't stay home to help either, do you? You, Norah too. As quick as two bunnies, you scamper off."

I draw breath, shocked at Mrs. McPhaden's words. Is that what she thinks, that we all dashed away from mother as quickly as possible?

"We tried our best," I say helplessly.

"No, you don't!" Mrs. McPhaden is indignant now. "You off to Brandon and parts unknown, teachers college and the like. And Norah! No one ever knew where Norah was. Some said town. Others said Brandon. I heard she might be as far as Winnipeg."

"She is in Winnipeg," I say, "working for the Department of Education and doing very well."

"The Department of Education!" Mrs. McPhaden sputters. "Government? My, my. She is very grand then. No butter churning for Norah now. Nor manure forking. Nor any of those endless tasks your sister Mary does, without complaint. I've told my Allan he picked the best from the litter, the hard-working one. And my John! He was fond of you, all those years pining after Miss Marjory. But I told him it was pointless. Farm work is beneath you, isn't it?"

There's silence now. Allan and Mary look embarrassed but don't say anything. I suppose there isn't any point in correcting old Mrs. McPhaden. She's confused, not kind like she was forty years ago. She doesn't understand what she's saying.

Mary breaks the awkward silence: "Marjory has a letter to read. She'd better hurry."

"Leave me the dishes," I say, getting up from the table, my coffee cup in hand.

Mary ignores me, turning her back to scrub bacon splatters off the stove. She'll be at the dishes in five minutes if I don't hurry. She has no patience, which I suppose is her gift when it comes to household management.

Mrs. McPhaden calls to my retreating back, "Sure nice to have you visit. Say hello to your mother for me."

I run up the stairs and slam the bedroom door behind me. Jeff's letter is thin, so it won't take long to read.

Dearest Tommy, Jeff writes.

I hope the fresh air of rural life has revived you. Teaching is such a bore by the end of the year, not that I would know anymore. Little Carol will start school in the fall—can you believe it?—though I can't imagine the teaching quality is nearly as good as when you were principal! We ran a tight ship, didn't we? Jeff, Tommy and Annie. Anyway, little Carol's beside herself with joy, and I look forward to having my mornings to work in peace and quiet. I don't know how the farm wives coped before electricity. As it is, I still fall into bed each night exhausted.

I write with good and bad news. Let's start with the bad:

Do you remember Ivor Benson? The poor chap you whacked with the school bell? It was fifteen years ago, at least. Well, anyway, Ivor's character was not marred, nor was his daring dampened by your correction. He served with the Air Force, and by now, you must note my use of the past tense. He was out on a mission, but he never returned. Presumed dead. I suppose there's a slight chance he might be in a POW camp, but it doesn't seem likely. His poor wife and family are devastated, but it doesn't stop his mother from volunteering for the Red Cross Society. She's feverish in her efforts. Quite touching if it wasn't so sad.

Our own Mrs. Fargey started the Red Cross Society, by the way. Commendable, I have to say. And her boys—now this is funny—were featured on the front page of the paper. They were photographed inside a wine vat in Italy with a tin can nailed to the side for their mail. I am glad to see some humour still exists. It balances out the dreadful newspapers we see. Last year, there was a special feature paper called, "IF Manitoba Were Occupied." It was terrible. Each article applied what's happened in Europe to our society: "All Jews sent to a ghetto in Winnipeg" or "Lower Fort Gary Turned into Concentration Camp" or, the real heartbreak for Carol, "Girl Guides to be absorbed into 'Children of the State.'" Of course, every article followed up with "Buy War Bonds." Jim said not to worry too much about it, but he bought more war bonds all the same.

And now to my brighter news: there's talk the current principal of Pilot Mound will finish out the war and then retire. Once the war ends, there will be a flush of servicemen returning to the prairies, needing jobs. I'd write the school board directly and get your foot in the door if I were you. I don't need to tell you that Pilot Mound is just up the road from La Riviere. We'd see each other often, and your boys could return to a community with which they're familiar. Do think about it, Marjory. This horrid war can't last forever, at least not at the rate Jim buys war bonds.

    Your loving friend,

Jeff

    P. S. On a bright note, the unsightly heap of scrap metal outside of town has been requisitioned! Three cheers for the war effort!

Good old Jeff, keeping her ear to the ground for me. I'll write a letter to the Pilot Mound school board trustees before leaving. As Jeff wrote, a principal post would be ideal, just like the old days. We did run a tight ship, back before all those gallant boys were taken from us. Ivor Benson, flying away never to return. It's hard to believe. I'm still staring into space when Mary calls up the stairs, "Harry and Alec have come to say goodbye."

Funny enough, I find myself ready to make peace with my brothers now there's the prospect of a good job. It's a ridiculous reaction as Jeff's information may be false, or I may not get the job. But the knowledge that the opportunity exists rallies me. It's as if I can say to my brothers, "I might not have the most reliable husband in the world, but I can create my own stability. I can provide for the boys. So you needn't fret and bother about us."

But I say none of those things. None of us apologizes. We just carry on as before. That's our family's way. Don't talk too much about disagreements. Just go on.

"We're sorry we've nothing to bring you from the garden," Alec says. "It's too early though fresh carrots might have been nice to eat on the train.

"It's all right," I say as I press my cheek to his. Alec will always be my baby brother, whether or not he's a grown man. I love him as much as I did when he was a child, scouting out baby kittens, running errands to the garden for Norah cooking in the kitchen. He's as sweet and companionable as he was then.

Harry seems rushed. He says he has arrangements to make for a Children's Aid Society fundraiser and doesn't have much time to spare. Like our father, Harry is interested in the community and the war provides endless opportunities for charitable activity. "Take care of yourself, Old Girl," he says, hurriedly kissing me. His smooth, thin face is still damp from shaving. "If you need anything, a place to stay, somewhere to leave the boys, the farm is much yours as it is Alec and I's."

"I couldn't ask for better brothers than you two," I say, noticing Mary wipe a tear out of the corner of her eye. "I miss you all desperately when I'm away. We're so scattered. Joss in British Columbia. Norah in Winnipeg. It makes me nostalgic for the old days, I must say."

"Think of milking cows in January, Marjory," Alec quips. "That cures my worst cases of nostalgia."

We laugh, just a little.

"It's been a journey, hasn't it?" I say.

They smile at that, chuckle even. But perhaps they don't feel as lost as I do, rooted in their farms and crops. When I'm with my siblings in Oak River, I remember the past—the uncertainty of the last war, the deep fear I'd never get off the farm, the sorrow of watching Mother die. It all comes rushing back. But Mary, Harry and Alec never left. Perhaps they've made peace with the past in ways I have never have. And here we are— grown-ups! Capable of creating our own fates. We should be joyful. Liberated in our stability, the wisdom of our experiences. But somehow, it seems we're all just tired, lacking the energy to capitalize on our success and experience. Funny how deflating adult life can be, even in its happiest moments.

Part IV

When older still I daily grew,
Time flew.

"**D**o you think I ought to retire from Pilot Mound?" I ask.

Norah looks at me sharply, then turns back again to the wheel. We're driving to Edmonton to see my son Jack. It's a long way for the two of us, fifteen hours at least. We spent one night in Saskatoon and now we're cresting the rise of Edmonton, the banks of the North Saskatchewan river beside us. We're not especially young for such a long trip, but Norah was determined. "Oh, let's go!" she said. "It will be a nice trip. You need something to look forward to."

But now, she drives with a furrowed brow. "Why? Do you want to retire?"

"Not especially," I say. "But I'm not principal anymore and when you're no longer the boss, you feel like you're on a downward decline. Maybe you're being pushed out."

"You're a good teacher. I'm sure you're still appreciated even if the administration work has been taken from you."

I purse my lips. It wasn't easy to give up the principal's job. But I'm getting older. Someone new needed to take on the responsibilities. I hate to admit it, but I can't see well. Macular degeneration is taking hold of both eyes. A few more years and I might not see at all. I've been lucky to be in Pilot Mound though. Since 1944, I was the principal and Raleigh built us a house across the street. George and Jack attended high school, and now George is married to a local girl, Barbara, who expects a baby in October. Both boys are both well-educated and settled. But it hasn't been easy, all these years, but the boys have been the joy of my life.

"Can you afford to retire?" Norah asks, concentrating hard on the road in front of her. She's been a marvellous driver, but it's been a long trip.

"Not really," I say. "I'm just getting tired."

"I feel that way myself. I'd like to lie on a lawn chair on the farm some days and not get up until supper time."

"The mosquitoes would feed on you," I sensibly counter.

"True, but I can dream, can't I?" Norah looks confused now. "Would you check the map? Where do we get off of Highway 16?"

I take the map, but I'm not good with the fine print and pale grey lines.

"You've got it upside down, Marjory," Norah snips.

"No, I haven't."

"Yes, you do." Norah reaches over to turn the map. "Here!" she says, pointing. "That's where we are."

I look up to check for street signs, only to see a stop sign whiz past my window.

"Norah! Stop!" I yell. But it's too late. The last thing I see is a blue Mack truck barrelling towards us. I think I scream. But maybe I don't. There isn't much time.

—

The people hovering above me are strangers. They're dressed in white, surrounded by a glowing light. I blink, trying to focus. Who are these people? They wear peaked caps and cloths over their mouths. I don't recognize them. One of them says, "She's awake. That's a good sign." Another comes close, which is better. I can focus my eyes on her. "Mar-jor-y," she overenunciates as if I'm deaf. "Marjory, can you hear me?"

Of course, I can hear her, but it's hard to speak. I can't make the words come out. Something seems a little off with my mouth, as if it doesn't remember how to form words. I try nodding instead, but I can't move my head either. I feel as if I'm in a dream where you need to run or scream, but you're stuck.

"Marjory," the woman says again, "I want you to blink twice if you can hear me."

I blink twice, though I'm surprised how much effort it takes. It's just blinking, for goodness' sake. What's wrong with me?

"Marjory," the woman goes on, exasperatingly using my name to start every sentence as if she's afraid I've forgotten it. "You've been in an accident. You're doing good."

I mentally correct her English. Well. I'm doing well. I'm not doing good like a charity worker spreading good deeds. I'm doing well, apparently, because I can blink twice.

The woman pats my hand and I close my eyes. I'm too exhausted to open them any longer.

—

I recognize George's voice even before I open my eyes. He's talking about me, maybe with one of the people dressed in white. "Will she recover, do you think?" he asks quietly.

"We can't speculate. It's too early at this stage. She broke both legs, and until she wakes up completely and starts to speak coherently, we can't determine if she has brain damage. Yesterday, she seemed unable to move her arms, but that may have been the medication. We kept her sedated through surgery, so we don't know her mental state."

"How is my aunt Norah?" George asks.

"Remarkably well. Shaken mostly. Your mother's side of the car got the greatest impact. Thankfully, the truck driver said he saw them before they entered the intersection, so he reduced his speed."

"Is that what happened?" George asks. "They were hit by a truck?"

"Yes. Your aunt says she was distracted and pulled into an intersection without stopping. She was hit by a red Mack truck."

"Blue," I say, opening my eyes.

The nurse and George whip around to look at me.

"What did you say, Mother?" George asks, coming close to take my hand.

"It was a blue truck, Darling, not a red one. Norah gets her facts confused sometimes."

George laughs at this, a shaky laugh, the kind that comes after you've thought you've left a stack of unmarked exams behind on a train only to discover they are in your bag after all.

"Mother!" he says. "We've been so worried."

"Why on earth have you come?" I ask, realizing with a flash of insight that I must be in the hospital in Edmonton. I wouldn't have been moved to Manitoba, not with two broken legs.

"Oh, dear Mother. They thought you weren't going to make it," George says. He's crying now, and I see the stumble on his face, his bloodshot eyes, and matted hair.

"Darling, you look dreadful!"

"I know, but I drove through the night to get here. I wanted to be with you."

"Dear George. I just need to rest and then I'll be up and about.

George pulls up a chair and sits beside me. "You broke your legs, Mother. You'll have to stay here in Edmonton until you heal."

"I'm all right," I say, far more confidently than I feel. "You shouldn't have bothered with such a fuss. It's a long drive. And with Barb expecting too."

"That's a bit of a concern right now," George says, his eyes filling with tears again.

The nurse stretches her hand across my bed. "Maybe it's better not to worry your mother," she says.

I dislike the nurse intensely at this moment. How dare she decide what will or will not worry me. I've got broken legs. But that doesn't make me unable to comprehend the news of the day.

George pats my hand with a forced smile. "Best rest," he says cheerfully, moving like he will get up and leave. I'm not having it though. I've lived too long and have faced too many tragedies to be put off that easily.

"Tell me," I say, grabbing his hand with as tight a grip as I can manage, "or I will have no peace."

George looks apologetically at the nurse who shrugs her shoulders. He clears his throat and strokes my hand. His hands are rough from his work as an aircraft mechanic. He has a nice-look-ing face, probably the best thing Raleigh could have given him. He's not like his father in any other way. He never touches liquor except to be sociable at Christmas. He's a kind son and a good husband. And soon he'll be a father.

"It's about Barb, you see," he finally says. "We don't know why exactly, but she went into labour yesterday."

"Too soon," I murmur.

George nods. "Two months too soon. But she had the baby last night, late. A little girl. Two pounds."

"Oh!" I cry, remembering my lost baby. Losing her was one of the worst things that ever happened to me. It took a great deal of bravery to go on after that.

The nurse casts George a warning look and he soothes me. "It's all right, Mother. The baby survived the night. Just like you! You both survived and neither of you was supposed to. So per-haps it's a good omen. As you survive, so will she."

He's crying again, poor boy. Somehow, I will my hand into motion and stroke his hair as I did when he was a little boy. "Shhh, George," I whisper. "We'll get through this. No matter what happens. We'll get through this. I'm going to be fine! I have a granddaughter I'm desperate to see. I've got to get better so I can go home."

George drops his head onto his arms while I continue to stroke his head. He must be exhausted. His wife had a premature baby the same day his mother was in an accident. And then he drove fifteen hours through the night to be with me. What a good son he is. I couldn't possibly love him more.

"What is the baby named?" I whisper, fading back into sleep.

"Betty," he whispers back, and it's the last thing I hear for a long while.

Betty's Story
January 10, 1969
Pilot Mound, Manitoba
Betty is nine years old.

I have to take the street to Grandma's house. A recent storm left big drifts over the soccer field, and I don't want to trudge through snow. It's bad enough the wind stings my face. Snow down my boot won't help anything. I bury my face under my collar and wish I had put on my scarf as Mom suggested. I was in a big hurry so I didn't bother. Now I'm sorry.

This week was our first back to school after the Christmas holidays. I thought Friday was never going to come. Going back to school after Christmas is so gloomy. Two weeks of sleeping in, good food, and presents are over. Monday morning hit everyone hard, even my mom who smoked and yelled a lot. "Betty! John! Jim! Move it. We're going to be late if you don't hurry up!"

Mom can't be late. She's a teacher, and nothing would embarrass her more than being late. My history teacher wasn't so fussed. He sauntered into class three minutes late, looking completely exhausted.

"Okey-dokey," he said. "Who can tell me one world news event from over the Christmas holidays?"

We all looked at him like he was stupid. We're nine years old! Does he think we sat up over the Christmas holidays to watch the ten o'clock news? Who does that?

One of the Nelson boys perked up. He would. He's a nerd. "On Christmas Eve," he chirped, "the manned U.S. spacecraft Apollo 8 entered the orbit around the Moon. Astronauts Frank Borman, Jim Lovell and William Anders will be the first humans to see the far side of the Moon!"

Bored silence followed that announcement. Our teacher wasn't really listening, but he said that was wonderful and asked for any other world events from over the holidays. We looked at each other, our hands, the ceiling. Finally, our teacher gave up and asked what had happened to us over the holidays. That was much easier. We all had presents to talk about and relatives visiting.

We had a big Christmas dinner on the 25th. We started with Santa's presents at breakfast at our house, then moved to my other grandma's house for lunch. Dad drove into town and picked up Grandma Marjory, but Grandpa Raleigh didn't come. I'm not sure if he didn't want to or wasn't invited. Grandma Marjory said he wasn't feeling well, but I don't believe grown-ups when they say things like that. It's usually a cover for something else.

I went into town to pick up Grandma Marjory with Dad. I think Dad had me do it so he wouldn't have to go up to the door to fetch Grandma. That's how little he wanted to run into his dad on Christmas day. I heard him tell Mom they never celebrated Christmas when he was a kid. It just would have given his father an excuse to drink more, and there wasn't money for a celebration anyway. So, Dad just stood at the car door and opened it for Grandma Marjory as she shuffled down the steps, holding my arm lest she fall on the ice and breaks a hip.

"A jolly Christmas to you, George!" she said as she reached the car.

But it's January now. And the jolliness of Christmas has been shelved away with the twinkling lights, vanishing into thin air like a plate of gingerbread cookies placed in front of my brothers.

It's a dismal day, even at noon, with an overcast sky. Most people have their kitchen lights on as they eat their lunches, but I notice Grandma's house is dark. She's probably trying to save electricity; it is high noon, after all. But high noon in the middle of the winter is different than in summer. Manitoba summer days go on and on forever. It will be ten o'clock at night and Mom will still be trying to herd us into bed. Winter are dark, even at midday, especially with an overcast sky.

I knock on Grandma's front door, but she doesn't answer. I wait a few seconds and then try again, but still there's silence. "Grandma!" I call but there's no point. If she can't hear me knock, why would she hear me call?

I tramp over the snow-covered lawn, across the yard to the kitchen window at the back of the house. I get snow in my boot but I don't even feel it. That's how cold I am. I'll feel it at two o'clock when my socks are still wet. Standing on my tip-toes, I press my nose against the kitchen window, using my mitted hands to shield my eyes from a bit of glare. I see the table, but it isn't set for lunch. A plate with toast crumbs and an empty glass lies on Grandpa Raleigh's side, but that's it.

I don't understand. Grandma never forgets our lunch appointment, and even if she did, she would still make lunch for the two of them. I trudge back to the front of the house and sit down on the frozen steps. I can feel the cold concrete through my Fortrel slacks, and I wish I had taken the time to put on my snow pants. Mom told me to do that too.

It just doesn't make sense. My grandparents' Chevy coupe is parked in the driveway, and they wouldn't have gone anywhere on foot. I scan the street for someone who might know where Grandpa and Grandma went. But there's no one. Noon in Pilot Mound on a cold January day—not a great time for foot traffic.

Just as I decide to give up and go back to school to see if Mom still has some lunch she can share with me, I hear a shuffling, thumping noise inside the house. It sounds like Grandpa Raleigh coming down the steep stairs that run up the middle of the house.

I bang on the front door again. "Grandpa! Grandpa!" I call. "It's me! Betty!"

Grandpa opens the door slowly, the hinges creaking, a floor mat rolling up at his feet. His hair is as unruly as ever. "The door's unlocked, Betty, but good luck getting lunch," he mutters, squinting at me or the glare of daylight on snow. It's hard to tell.

I push through the doorway and into their living room, tracking snow across the floor. The air is stale and heavy. A bit of grease. A bit of beer.

Grandpa gestures to the couch. "She's there," he says.

I see Grandma lying on the short, threadbare couch, one leg off, one leg weirdly bent. Her hands are white and her head lies oddly on a pillow as if she is turning her face away sharply from the room, from Grandpa.

"Grandma!" I call, rushing over to her.

Her eyelids flutter and her lips move slightly, but I can't hear what she's saying, if she's saying anything. She tries to raise a hand but her wrist falls limply back to her side.

"She's been like that all morning," Grandpa Raleigh says. "I had to make breakfast and now it's past noon and still she's like that."

I whirl around to look at him. Grandpa has always been a slightly scary figure. Someone to avoid. A big man. But now I realize he's a child trapped inside an old, drunk man's body. "She's sick!" I snap at Grandpa.

He shrugs, rolls his eyes and sinks into his chair in the corner. "I called your dad but no one answered."

"No one answered because we're at school or work! Grandma needs to go to the hospital!"

"Pah!" Grandpa waves his chubby hand. "What would they do for her there? She's an old woman. Needs to rest."

I kneel beside Grandma and take her hand. "Can you hear me?"

Her lips move so I lean my ear to her mouth. Her words are barely audible, just a whisper, but what I hear launches me into action. I cover her up with the afghan draped over the back of the couch, then set off at a run out of the house, banging the front door behind me. I dash towards school, cutting across the soccer field, stomping through snowdrifts. By the time I reach the school door, my lungs hurt and I can't feel my cheeks or ears.

We're not supposed to run down the hall with our snow boots on—the snow melts and forms dangerous puddles—but I do it anyway. I run through our low, flat school building, past the early grades' homerooms, past the gym, around the corner, down the hall. Kids step out of my way. Teachers call—"Betty!

Stop running!"—but I don't stop until I reach the teacher's lounge.

Pushing the door open, I'm choked by a haze of cigarette smoke. I cough, then look around for my mom. She's on a couch in the corner, listening to one of the other teachers tell a joke. He's a new one, young with shaggy hair and bellbottoms. He finishes the punchline to uproarious laughter as I burst in.

"Mom!" I call, pushing between shift dresses and bell-bottom slacks. "Mom! Come quickly!"

Mom butts out her cigarette in an ashtray. "Betty—what's happened?"

"It's Grandma Marjory! Come!" I realize I'm crying. Salty tears flow over my red cheeks.

Mom pulls me through the room of stunned teachers into the hall. It's always remarkable how fast my mother can move in high heels when she wants to. "What's happened?" she asks again, bending down to look me in the eye.

"Grandma's on the couch. She hasn't got up all day Grandpa says, and she's talking funny."

"Like how funny?"

"Whispers, but slurred. Her eyes don't open and she isn't moving."

"Shoot," Mom says under her breath as she straightens up. She pulls me back into the teachers' lounge and dials the olive-green telephone that hangs on the wall. "Gloria!" she calls, immediately recognizing the hospital receptionist's voice. "Will you send an ambulance to Marjory Smith's? Yes, across the street from the school. Betty was just there and it sounds like Marjory's had a stroke. I'll meet the ambulance there."

Mom hangs up the phone as the other teachers gather in a semi-circle around us. Many of them would remember Grandma Marjory. She was their colleague until her accident nine years ago. My homeroom teacher bites her lip and pats my head. The funny, young teacher looks sympathetic and pats Mom's shoulder—"I'll combine classes, Barb. Not much is planned for this afternoon anyway. Don't worry." A few others murmur best wishes as we hurry down the hall towards the coat racks.

"Did Grandma say anything to you?" Mom asks over her shoulder as she weaves around kids pulling things out of their lockers.

I struggle to keep up with her. "She said something about mother, so I think she wanted me to get you."

Mom kicks off her shoes under a coat rack and pulls on her snow boots. "Think hard, Betty." Mom yanks her heavy winter coat off a hanger. "What exactly did she say?"

I shut my eyes, trying to remember. "I think she said, 'Mother, did I do all right?'"

Mom stops moving mid gesture, one arm in her coat, the other still hanging. "That's not good."

"Why?" I ask. "Why is that not good? Is she confused?"

Mom pulls on her coat completely, then bends low again. Her eyes are filled with tears, something I've never seen before. "Betty, when older people start talking about their parents as if they're in the room, that's usually a sign their minds are in a different place. She's leaving us. Maybe not today, or even tomorrow, but she's not going to be the same again. Do you understand?" she whispers.

I nod, not crying anymore, but being a big girl.

"Good. Now stay here. I'm sorry you didn't get lunch. Go find John and tell him I told you to take his apple."

"Oh! Mom!" I call after her. "That was the other thing. She said something about John. Something about being sorry."

Mom shrugs, even as I hear the ambulance siren on the street. "Typical of a stroke. She's just confused. Grandma loves you so much," she says. "Just remember that." And with that, Mom is gone. Gone across the soccer field to save Grandma Marjory, though that might be too hard a job, even for my mom.

Amy's Story
Saturday, January 11, 2020
Ottawa, Ontario
Amy is thirty-four years old.

"He's close to the end," my mom, Betty whispers. I press the phone to my ear to hear her more clearly. She speaks softly even though Grandpa George is unresponsive. A hearty yell probably wouldn't rouse him at this stage.

"What's happening?" I ask.

"He's not eating or speaking, just sleeping. His blood pressure is very low."

"What are the nurses saying?"

"All this is to be expected," Mom says.

"How's Grandma Barb?"

"Tired. She was here for part of the day. She's gone home now to rest. I'm still here with him."

Silence sits heavy on the line. I don't know what to say, what words to offer. I wonder if Mom will be slightly relieved when this is all over. Her Christmas holidays were decidedly non-festive this year. She ferried Grandma Barb back and forth as Grandpa George was hospitalized and then moved to a long-term care facility; its very name is ironic. Long-term. Nothing is long-term when you're nearly ninety with advanced cancer, no longer treatable. Nothing will improve. No recovery is possible. The end is coming instead. One must just lie quietly and wait for it.

"You know I'd come if I could," I say, indirectly referencing my health, my inability to travel freely.

"Your pregnancy is the most important thing," my mother interrupts. "Grandma doesn't expect you to come home. No one does. You just need to rest."

"I just thought I'd be home one more time, but there's little point. He didn't know me in summer so he wouldn't know me now? Does he know you?"

"Called me Betty one day this week."

"That's good."

"That was his last good day. He's not responding now. Just sleeping."

"I wonder who or what he's thinking about," I muse, mostly to myself.

"I'm not sure what happens when the body starts to leave, and the brain shuts down. I don't know what fog he's in. It's just a gradual slide away from the body. I will stay for a few more hours to hold his hand. Read him Scripture. Remind him how loved he is."

"Give Grandma a hug for me when you see her."

"Tomorrow probably."

"I'll let you go. I love you, Mom."

"I love you too."

—

"Did you know about the box in Grandpa's underwear drawer?" Mom asks, again over the telephone.

It's been a week since Grandpa George's funeral and the tidying up has begun. Underwear drawers. Old runners on the shoe rack. Sweat-stained ball caps piled in teetering stacks. Everything is being sorted. The trappings surrounding the human body must be disposed of now that they're no longer needed. Surplus to requirements—that's what possessions become the moment someone leaves this world. "Surely these things can be used by someone," survivors longingly say. And perhaps some things can be reused, donated to the charities that sell the stockpiles of the dead. But no one wants the things closest to the body, the things that lay against the skin—the socks, toothbrushes, hair-filled brushes. These things must go into the trash. They can't be put back into the world, recirculated for another lifetime.

And then there are the other possessions, the things with names on them—bank accounts, life insurance policies, investments. These must be cashed out or transferred, for they have no meaning without an owner, someone who claims them or manages their existence. Sorting these belongings consumes endless hours. Appointments must be set. Certificates must be requested. One task cannot be completed without another. Undertakers. Lawyers. Bankers. Investors. They blend into a single sympathetic smile, a well-pressed suit. And so, a life is cashed out, tidied up. Put to rest in every sense.

"A box in the underwear drawer?" I ask.

"We found letters. Marjory's letters."

I suddenly perk up. "This is news. Who are they from?"

"I haven't read through the box completely. The ink is faded and the handwriting is hard to decipher," Mom says, "but I see many from a John McPhaden during World War I. There's a dashing picture of him too. It looks like it was taken in France. Some letters from Harry, but John often writes, sometimes without even writing his family, he says. He asks permission to look up her relatives in England."

I'm silent, flipping madly through my binder of research. John McPhaden. John McPhaden. Who is John McPhaden?

"Did you know a John McPhaden who wrote to Marjory?" Mom asks.

"No, I don't know him," I say, thumbing through printouts of old family pictures, the pages curling up from the wetness of dark, monochrome print jobs. Unfortunately, my research binder isn't very well-organized either. Census records, newspaper clippings, screenshots of websites from Beaumonts, Thompsons, McPhadens, and Smiths all lie together, in no particular chronology.

"Wait!" I say. "I've found him."

John McPhaden stares from a family portrait, a hundred years ago or more. His family—brothers, sisters, father, mother—peer as if to say, "Who are you to dig us out of history? What accident of proximity to your ancestors makes us interesting to you?"

"Is he Allan's brother?" Mom asks.

"Yes. Spitting image." John could be Allan's twin. Though Allan is seated in the middle of the family portrait, John stands tall with thick hair combed over his head. He wears a dark suit and vest, a white shirt and tie. He rests his hand on the back of his mother's chair.

I flip through binder pages again to a printout of the Oak River community history book. In the "M" section, I locate "McPhaden" then run my finger down the columns. Long paragraphs recall the lives of Hugh, then Allan, then Allan's sons Frank and Jack. Finally, a sidebar, almost an afterthought, references John.

"Here's something!" I say triumphantly. "He returned from World War I and then farmed with his youngest brother, Cedric, next door to Allan and Mary. He lived until he was 94 and never married. That's all it says."

"Never married," Mom whispers to herself.

"Hang on a second," I say, turning to my laptop. "Canada has all its World War I records online."

I quickly type in a search, the letters "J-O-H-N M-C-P-H-A-D-E-N" falling from under my fingertips for the first time. The results flash on the page. There's a John McPhadens from Manitoba whose father is listed as Hugh and brother as Barclay. Occupation farmer.

"I found his war record."

"And what does it say?" Mom presses. "He wasn't killed in the war, not if he lived to ninety-four."

I scroll through pages and pages of scanned documents, handwritten and yellow from age. Like most old documents, they are hard to read. Scanned with wrinkles and tears, they lie angled and mangled on the screen. The handwriting, illegible to begin with, faded before the scanning rendered it immortal.

"Shoot," I mumble, my eyes settling on John McPhaden's medical record.

"What is it?"

"G. S. W. behind right ear. Passchendaele."

"What's G. S. W.?"

"Gunshot/shrapnel wound. After being wounded, he was moved from one field hospital to another until he was brought back to England, hospitalized, and discharged. He was gassed three times."

"Three times," Mom says under her breath. "Poor man."

"Yeah," I murmur, quickly reading through the document. "There's not much more here other than his pay, which seems minimal, was directed to his brother Barclay. Also, he enlisted. Wasn't drafted."

"He writes what a shock England is," Mom says. "'Very green,' he says several times. The stone and brick houses impress him. I guess he was used to sod and wood from Manitoba. Not so many letters from France though, just from England, waiting to go over."

"They probably had time on their hands in England."

Mom sniffs as if she's come to the end of the stack. "And nothing indicates John and Marjory were sweethearts. Perhaps they were just friends."

"But then why did he ask permission to look up her relatives?" I counter. "And why did she keep these letters her whole life?"

"It's curious," Mom agrees.

"And how did Grandma not know about the letters? I've been asking for things for a year now."

"Grandma said she scarcely knew what was in the box. She only opened it because she was getting rid of Grandpa's things. Grandpa would have never thought about it. Not with dementia."

"So, it's because Grandpa died that we found these letters."

"I suppose." Mom sounds sad. "But what if we hadn't found them? What if the box was junked without being opened?"

"It's how history disappears. In a forgotten shoebox. Pitched when someone dies or buried with a thousand other letters in an archive, anonymous by that point."

"But we did find them," Mom says. "And it's not for nothing these letters were saved, one decade after another. They found their way to us. To you."

"It's as if Marjory got the last word," I chuckle. "The last thing we find is the hint she may have had a sweetheart. She could have junked the letters, but they were important to her. Perhaps she wanted her descendants to know something about her."

"She was quite a gal, our Marjory."

Soon I shall find, in passing on,
Time gone.

From "Time's Paces"
by Henry Twill
Hymns and Other Stray Verses

My great grandmother, Marjory Thompson Smith, was born at the end of an era. Her family was part of the last wave of English immigrants who homesteaded the prairies. Their courage was laudable; their work ethic, commendable.

Marjory's early years were grounded in tradition. Women's career options were extremely limited in the early 1900s and school teaching was a popular choice for young women. However, despite the conventionality of her career, Marjory achieved a great deal. She started teaching when she was sixteen years old and went on to fund her own and her younger siblings' university studies. She moved throughout the prairies for teaching posts and was a high school principal in an era when women were generally not considered for those positions. And then she married Raleigh.

Our family doesn't understand the marriage. We have theories—perhaps Raleigh wasn't an alcoholic until later in their marriage. All my grandfather, George Smith, remembered was that his father drank. But how old would he have to have been to remember that? Six? Seven? Could there have been tranquil years? Did Marjory misjudge how problematic Raleigh's alcoholism would be to their relationship and family life? Or was she just desperate for children and tolerated any behaviour from Raleigh to have them? Any or none of these theories may be true. There's no way to know, now.

By the time I started researching this book, Grandpa George was already suffering from Macular Degeneration and dementia. His stories ran together—generations overlapping, one side of the family mixed with the other side. I turned to family members for memories he might have shared with them, but he hadn't talked much about his childhood, so there wasn't much family folklore.

What I did learn was telling: Marjory and Raleigh didn't celebrate Christmases or birthdays. George lost a girlfriend because he was the son of the town drunk. There was no love lost between him and his father.

Sometimes, Grandpa George would remember stories—the telegram from Marjory's mother that was never delivered to her father, or the many hatboxes brought across the ocean, or even that Marjory's mother was desperately unhappy and died at a relatively young age—and from these stories, I got a picture. But the picture was foggy, and there was no evidence, no paper trail.

So I dug into census records, ship manifests, letters, immigration papers, a book of Marjory's postcards left forgotten in a trunk, community history books, newspaper articles, yearbooks, a birthday book, war records, and several picture albums. I spoke to former neighbours and distant relatives. I visited the Thompson farm, the Bankburn, Marland and Pilot Mound school sites, and the towns of Oak River and La Riviere. I hunted down the addresses of boarding houses in Winnipeg and Brandon on Google Maps and tried to imagine the street from the early 1900s. I looked at notes tucked into jewellery boxes and I was helped enormously by the volunteers who found Marjory's daily schedule and attendance records from Pinkerton School in an archive. Even Manitoba's Department of Education found some records despite the gaps in their historical files.

The picture cleared and then, between the cold hard facts, I imagined the details. For example, I knew from ship manifests, border crossing records, and a local newspaper announcement that John and Bertha Beaumont visited from England, but I imagined their shock at seeing Oak River for the first time. They sailed on the Virginian's return trip from attempting to rescue Titanic passengers. I tried to envision their anxiety at sailing after the historic sinking.

Harry's war record was available online, and it listed the three times he was gassed. Each time his heart and respiration were checked, and he was deemed fit to return to the front. What were his letters like?

I found Marjory's photo album from her Great Lakes tour taken with her dear friend, Marjory Jeffrey Mitchell (Jeff). They wrote in the margins what a jolly time they were having, all while linking arms with Art and Bill, two gentlemen acquaintances they picked up along the way. I tried to place that journey in a larger context. The Great Depression began within months. Marjory married Raleigh a year later. How did the two women remember their journey in later years? Did it cement their friendship? Then, while wandering through the old La Riviere cemetery, I found Mrs. Jim Mitchell buried a matter of feet from Marjory. At that moment, Jeff and Tommy felt truly inseparable.

After a year of writing this story, Grandpa George passed away and Grandma Barb discovered the box of letters in his dresser drawer. Cherished yet forgotten in the fog of dementia, the letters hinted that John McPhaden was not just Marjory's neighbour but a writing companion and possibly a sweetheart. His wartime letters are glimpses into the boredom, suffering and horror that World War I was for many Canadian infantrymen. He wrote often and with fondness. The true nature of their relationship is not known, but John never married and Marjory kept the box of letters her entire life. Another mystery.

I never met Marjory, never knew her. She passed away before I was born so I have no memories, no impressions of her. Furthermore, as I talked to people, I realized she had many sides. She was a highly intelligent, complicated woman, but different people remembered her differently. Even Grandpa George looked confused when Grandma Barb described how scared she was of her mother-in-law and how terrified she was of her wit. Grandpa didn't remember her that way. He said she was clever, yes, but also kind.

And so, Marjory remains elusive; her personality and temperament, a vague impression. All I know is that a woman who, really and truly, hit a student with a school bell was eulogized with these words:

She is not dead: She lives in the hearts of scores of former pupils. She was born to teach and she gave of herself until she could no longer carry on. Even in her retirement, she helped stumbling students over rough places with her kind and patient advice. She gave of herself unstintingly. In the days when she taught three full grades in high school in La Riviere—the days before electricity had reached the school, she stayed on in the classroom preparing the following day's lessons until dusk closed in on her. Later in an improvised classroom in her own home on the side of the hill overlooking the tiny village, she taught her first Grade Twelve class. Although her son George was scarcely a month old when the fall term commenced, she gave us, her six pupils, her undivided attention, her personal instruction and always her encouragement—something which would have been sadly lacking in a larger establishment. She gave her best; she asked of us the same and we could give nothing less. She followed the career of each of her students with interest and expectancy.

The word for Mrs. Smith was gallant. She went through life tall and erect, full of enthusiasm and vitality. When she became severely injured in a car accident several years ago, she was told she would never walk again. But by sheer grit and determination, she did walk, first with the aid of crutches and later, alone. Even in blindness, her keen mind remained alert...

...She lies at rest in the beautiful valley where she laboured long and where she is held in such high esteem as a teacher and in such deep affection as a friend.

Pilot Mound Sentinel Courier

HISTORICAL NOTES

Although the characters and locations are historically accurate, some changes were made for the flow of the story:

The precise chronology of Marjory's early teaching placements and sessions at Normal School has been slightly adjusted. Community history books occasionally conflict with the address on a letter or the details of a census, so it is difficult to determine exactly where she taught or studied and for how long. As best I can tell, Marjory's early education and career path is as follows:

1909, completed Third Class Teaching Certificate.

November 1909 to July 1911, taught at Pinkerton School, Treherne, Manitoba.

Fall 1911 to December 1911, taught at Marland School, Oak River, Manitoba.

January 1912 to Fall 1912, unknown.

Fall 1912 to December 1912, returned to teach at Pinkerton School.

January 1913 to July 1913, attended Normal School at Brandon Collegiate. Achieved Second Class Teaching Certificate.

July 1913 to December 1914, taught at Norquay, Saskatchewan.

January 1915 to July 1915, attended Normal School. Achieved First Class Teaching Certificate.

Fall 1916 to December 1917, possible return to Pinkerton, or at least Treherne.

January 1917 to July 1917, attended a course in Winnipeg for the teaching of Physical Education.

October 1917, attended a four-week course at the Manitoba Agricultural College.

Duration of 1917, unknown.

1918, taught at Miniota, Manitoba.

1919 to June 1920, unknown, perhaps at home, working on the farm.
July 1920, summer school in Physics and Chemistry.
Fall 1920 to Summer 1921, taught at Isabella, Manitoba.
Fall 1921, possible start of teaching tenure at La Riviere, certainly by 1923 and until 1925.
Fall 1925 to Summer 1927, attended the University of Manitoba. Graduated with a Bachelor of Arts.
Fall 1927, returned to La Riviere, Manitoba as principal.

Mary and Allan McPhaden's baby, Roy, passed away at five months in 1914, not 1917.

The school bell incident occurred not in the late-1920s but in the 1940s in Pilot Mound. Although Marjory's actions are shocking to modern sensibilities (and quite possibly the sensibilities of the time), the Education Act of 1891 permitted teachers to act in place of parents in meting out discipline. The story was placed in the 1920s to focus on the year before Marjory's marriage to Raleigh. Ivor Benson was, however, taught by Marjory in La Riviere, and he was lost over Norway during World War II.

Norah was used as Marjory's travel companion in the car accident in 1959 to minimize the number of characters in the story. However, Lottie Smith, Raleigh's sister, travelled with Marjory to Edmonton. Lottie and Marjory were close friends though Lottie was dismayed over Raleigh's alcoholism and stayed with George and Barbara whenever visiting.

Also, Betty did not find Marjory after her stroke. Raleigh found her and called the hospital. She died shortly after.

Another fictional story is Marjory's interaction with the McLachlans at Pinkerton. Mary and Gordon McLachlan are listed on Marjory's attendance record at the Pinkerton School, though the Treherne community history book does not refer to them. Marjory did replace the schoolteacher in the middle of the term, but the reason for this is unknown. Certainly, ill health or some other circumstance could have contributed to the departure, but rules regarding teacher conduct were stringent at that time. Ironically, according to one source, male teachers could spend an evening a week courting, but "Women teachers who marry or engage in other unseemly conduct will be dismissed."[1] Women teachers, prior to the mid-19th century, were generally unmarried.[2] This rule could have contributed to the departure of the Pinkerton teacher in the middle of the term, but also sheds light on Marjory's employment in the 1930s, after she was married.

The 1931 Census found only four percent of women teachers in Manitoba were married.[3] Yet, during the economically depressed 1930s, all married women on staff in the Winnipeg school division had to provide concrete evidence to their School Boards as to why they should keep their jobs.[4] During the depression years, "Only a few married women could show just cause for seeking employment by successfully proving their family conditions failed to meet normal expectations and they should remain employed as teachers."[5]

Did Marjory have to argue for her employment or did the La Riviere school board understand she needed the work? No evidence remains, but perhaps Marjory was a dedicated professional whom the La Riviere School Board couldn't bear to dismiss, even after her secret marriage (the sensational marriage announcement really was published in the Western Canadian newspaper, April 27, 1930), the birth of her children, and the fierce competition for teaching jobs during the Great Depression. The reason for her unlikely employment isn't known.

Aside from these deviations, every effort was made to portray the facts unearthed in research accurately.

---

[1] J.W. Chafe, Chalk, Sweat and Cheers a history of The Manitoba Teachers' Society commemorating its fiftieth anniversary 1919 – 1969 (Winnipeg: The Hunter Rose Company, 1969), 11.

[2] Ashby, Suzanne. "The History of Women Educators in Manitoba Between the Years 1880 and 1940." Athabasca University, History 363, 2009, pp. 9–12.

[3] Kinnear, Mary. In Subordination: Professional Women 1870 – 1970, p. 139.

[4] "Should Married women be permitted to hold Job? Yes!", Winnipeg Tribune, Jan 24, 1947.

[5] Mary Kinnear, In Subordination: Professional Women 1870 – 1970, 124.

Acknowledgments

I thank Kay Haggarty whose help was so enlightening. What started as inquiries from a stranger turned into many conversations, introductions to other sources, and a tour of the original Thompson farm. Also, I am grateful for all family and friends who offered a careful eye to the manuscript—Barbara Smith, Don and Betty Esler, Mavis Sullivant, Allison Smith, Julia Schroeder, and Jeff Larose—to name a few. I am very grateful to Susan Peterson and Nancy Holman who edited the manuscript and shared references from the Sentinel Courier archives. Thank you, Josh for feedback and patience. And finally, thank you, Chris Needham of Now Or Never Publishing for taking on this project. I owe a debt of gratitude for your confidence in Marjory's story.

Seeds

by Marissa Kirkman

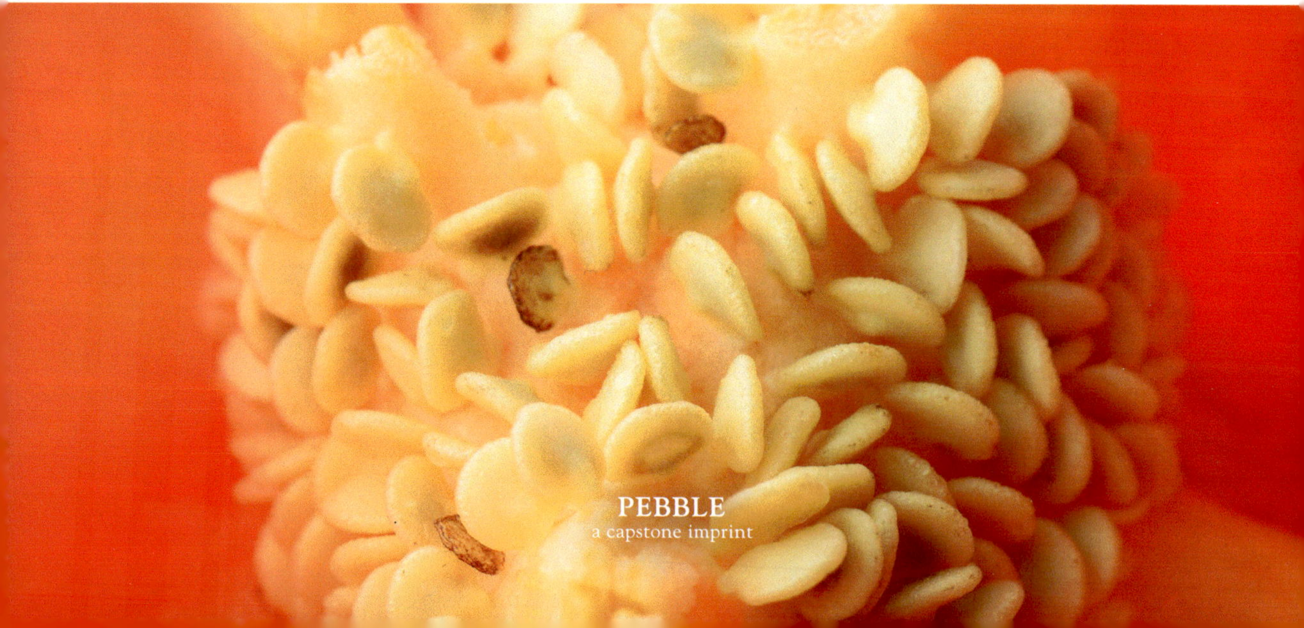

PEBBLE
a capstone imprint

Little Pebble is published by Pebble
1710 Roe Crest Drive
North Mankato, Minnesota 56003
www.mycapstone.com

Library of Congress Cataloging-in-Publication Data
Names: Kirkman, Marissa, author.
Title: Seeds / by Marissa Kirkman.
Description: North Mankato, Minnesota : an imprint of Pebble, [2020]
| Series: Little pebble. Plant parts | Audience: Age 6–8. | Audience: K to Grade 3. |
Includes bibliographical references and index.
Identifiers: LCCN 2018054138| ISBN 9781977109262 (hardcover) |
ISBN 9781977110244 (paperback) | ISBN 9781977109323 (ebook pdf)
Subjects: LCSH: Seeds—Juvenile literature.
Classification: LCC QK661 .K567 2020 | DDC 581.4/67—dc23
LC record available at https://lccn.loc.gov/2018054138

Editorial Credits
Erika L. Shores, editor; Charmaine Whitman, designer;
Svetlana Zhurkin, media researcher; Laura Manthe, production specialist

Image Credits
Capstone Studio: Karon Dubke, 5; Shutterstock: Alta Oosthuizen, 12, Anastasiia
Malinich, 9, Drakuliren, 15, Ekaterina Kondratova, 6, Hayati Kayhan, 11, Imagine
Room, 1 (top), isak55, cover, Leonid S. Shtandel, 8, Maryia Kazakova, 4, NataliaVo,
17, niteenrk, 1 (bottom), oksana2010, 19, Protasov AN, 13, Thanan Kongdoung, 21,
Tharnapoom Voranavin, 7, theoldman, 16

Printed in the United States   5666

Table of Contents

What Is a Seed?

Here is a seed.

It is little. Put it in the ground. It will grow into a plant.

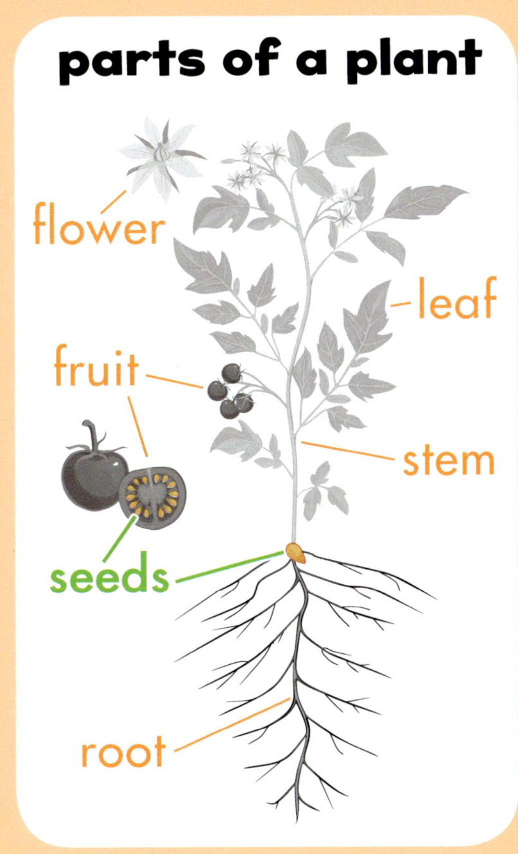

seed

Plants make seeds.

Seeds are inside of flowers.

Others are inside of fruit.

Seeds can be
different shapes.

Some seeds are smooth.

Some are bumpy.

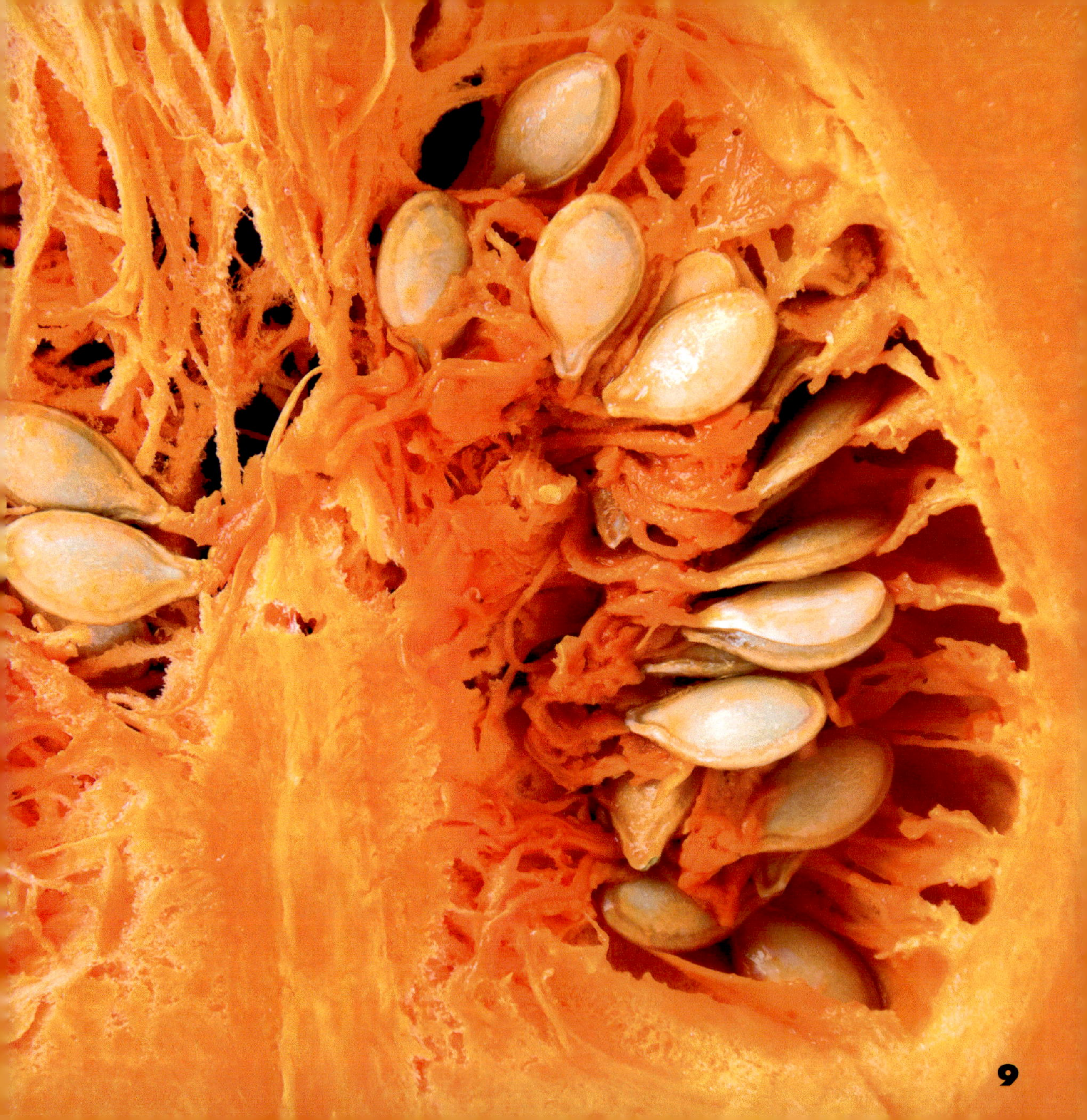

What Do Seeds Do?

Seeds grow into new plants.

Seeds need soil and water.

Seeds travel.

The wind carries some seeds.

Water carries seeds too.

Animals carry seeds.

They drop the seeds.

The seeds fall to the ground.

New plants will grow.

All Kinds of Seeds

A strawberry has many seeds. They are on the outside.

A watermelon has many seeds too. They are inside.

We eat seeds.

Peas are seeds.

They grow in pods.

Pods keep the seeds safe.

Rice is a seed.

Yum!

Glossary

flower—the colorful part of a plant that makes fruit and seeds

fruit—the fleshy, juicy part of a plant that contains seeds and usually can be eaten

pod—a long case that holds the seeds of certain plants, such as peas

seed—the part of a plant that will grow into a new plant

soil—the top layer of ground where plants grow

Read More

Hansen, Grace. *Seeds.* Plant Anatomy. Minneapolis: Abdo Kids, 2016.

McMullen, Gemma. *Seeds.* Parts of a Plant. New York: Smartbook Media Inc., 2018.

Page, Robin. *Seeds Move!* New York: Beach Lane Books, 2019.

Internet Sites

PBS Learning Media: From Seed to Fruit
https://illinois.pbslearningmedia.org/resource/evscps.sci.
life.seedint/from-seed-to-fruit-interactive/

Seed Survivor: Planting Games for Kids
http://seedsurvivor.com/just-for-kids/games/

Science Kids: Plants for Kids
www.sciencekids.co.nz/plants.html

Check out projects, games, and lots more at
www.capstonekids.com

Critical Thinking Questions

1. What does a seed look like?

2. How does a seed move from the plant to the ground?

3. What seeds do you like to eat?

Index